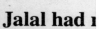

Jalal had r

Maybe it was tl   ,
or the pulse ge   e
fear of discovery in her eyes.

Or it was all of that and a thousand other instantaneous, involuntary signs that coalesced and painted a picture worth a thousand confessions.

It all added up to one thing. One thing that lodged
in his mind with the force of an ax. Something
devastating.

The truth.

Lujayn's child was his.

Dear Reader,

Jalal Aal Shalaan, the hero of *The Sheikh's Claim*, was an enigma to me as I started writing his story. He's already appeared in most of his brothers' stories, but he's been the one who wouldn't show me more than what he showed the world—the devil-may-care façade of a prince with the world at his feet. Then, in *The Sheikh's Redemption*, his twin Haidar's book, we finally got hints that not all was as it seemed with this knight of the desert. He was the "wolf" to Haidar's "lion," and their radical differences had torn them apart. By the end of that book, it seemed their lifelong rivalry and conflict were resolved, and they were finding their way back to their childhood closeness.

But the twins are still competing for the throne of Azmahar. And Jalal wants it with a burning passion. He believes he has nothing else to look forward to. His siblings and father have found their soul mates and are happy with their families, and he feels left out, aimless and alone. He believes he'll always be that way, for the only woman he could ever want is lost to him.

Is it any wonder, when she reappears in Azmahar, that his pursuit of Lujayn is relentless, even when her rejection is as single-minded? And that was before he discovers a secret that will make it even more unquestionable that he *will* claim her as his own, for life.

I loved writing Jalal and Lujayn's story as they came from totally opposite life situations—a prince and a pauper in love-story format—and not only met halfway but became one. I hope you enjoy reading their story as much as I enjoyed writing it!

I love to hear from readers, so please email me at oliviagates @gmail.com and connect with me on Facebook at my fan page Olivia Gates Author, on Goodreads and on Twitter @OliviaGates.

Thanks for reading!

Olivia

THE SHEIKH'S CLAIM

BY
OLIVIA GATES

Published in Great Britain 2013
by Mills & Boon, an imprint of Harlequin (UK) Limited,
Eton House, 18-24 Paradise Road, Richmond, Surrey TW9 1SR

© Olivia Gates 2012

ISBN: 978 0 263 90445 1
ebook ISBN: 978 1 472 00039 2

51-0113

Harlequin (UK) policy is to use papers that are natural, renewable and recyclable products and made from wood grown in sustainable forests. The logging and manufacturing processes conform to the legal environmental regulations of the country of origin.

Printed and bound in Spain
by Blackprint CPI, Barcelona

Olivia Gates has always pursued creative passions such as singing and handicrafts. She still does, but only one of her passions grew gratifying enough, consuming enough, to become an ongoing career—writing.

She is most fulfilled when she is creating worlds and conflicts for her characters, then exploring and untangling them bit by bit, sharing her protagonists' every heart-wrenching heartache and hope, their every heart-pounding doubt and trial, until she leads them to an indisputably earned and gloriously satisfying happy ending.

When she's not writing, she is a doctor, a wife to her own alpha male and a mother to one brilliant girl and one demanding Angora cat. Visit Olivia at www.oliviagates.com.

To my endlessly patient and supportive husband.
Thank you for being there for me always.
Love you, always.

One

Twenty-seven months ago

"So you managed to get away with murder this time."

Jalal Aal Shalaan frowned at the words he'd spoken aloud.

He was standing at the door of an opulent sitting room in one of the most breathtaking manors in the Hamptons, where he'd been received for years as an esteemed guest. He'd thought he'd never set foot in here again because of the woman who stood with her back to him. The woman who was now lady of the manor.

Lujayn Morgan. His ex-lover.

She'd been picking up letters from an antique marble table when his words had hit her. After a start, she'd frozen midmotion.

His own body was tense all over, too. His fists and jaw were clenched, his every muscle bunched, buzzing.

B'haggej' jaheem——by hell, why had he said that?

He hadn't intended to show her any hostility. Or any emotions at all—he'd thought he'd had none left. He'd come here for one reason. To see her without the lust that had blinded him for the four-year duration of their affair. He was here for closure, something she'd robbed him of when she'd stormed out of his life, giving him no chance to defend himself, to negotiate, leaving him wrestling with shock then rage and groping for explanations.

But he'd thought the resolution he was seeking was strictly intellectual. He'd thought he'd properly recovered during the two years since she'd walked out on him, working through his feelings until nothing remained but cold curiosity and mental aversion.

So he'd been deluding himself. What he'd felt for her, though it had reversed in nature, had remained as fierce.

He'd always presented the world with a devil-may-care facade. It was partly his nature and partly defensive. Having Sondoss, the notorious queen of Zohayd for a mother, and Haidar, the enigma who'd tormented him since childhood for a twin, made defenses necessary. They were the only ones who had ever managed to crack his control. Then had come Lujayn.

He was still vulnerable to the mere sight of her. And she hadn't even faced him yet.

Then she did.

Air deserted his lungs, heartbeats started to thunder.

Her beauty had always been mesmerizing. Her Middle Eastern and Irish genes conspired to create the personification of the best of both worlds. By the time she'd left him, brand names were starting to compete to have her willowy grace showcase their products, and makeup lines wanted that unforgettable face with those one-of-a-kind eyes to smolder at consumers out of their glossy ads.

But throughout their affair, she'd shed weight continuously. It had alarmed then angered him that her obsession with getting ahead in her career had blinded her to how she was harming herself to achieve a perfection she already possessed.

But the gaunt woman she'd been at the end of their affair had disappeared. In her place was the epitome of health and femininity with swells and dips that not even her severe black suit could tame, and had everything male in him roaring to life.

Marriage had been *very* good to her. Marriage to a man he'd once considered a good friend. A man who'd died less than two years after the wedding. A man whom he'd just more or less accused her of killing.

She inclined her head as she straightened, the movement emphasizing the elegance of her swan neck, the perfection of her raven chignon-wrapped head.

Her cool tranquility was a superb act, but her shock registered in something beyond her acting abilities. The pupils of uncanny irises, as silvery as the meaning of her name did that thing that had enthralled him when she was agitated or aroused, expanding and shrinking, giving the illusion that her eyes where emitting bursts of light.

The need to look closer into those eyes propelled him forward. Then words he hadn't known he'd been thinking, taunts that segued from his opening salvo, spilled from his lips.

"Not that I'm surprised. You've managed to fool the most suspicious and shrewd people I know, including myself. It shouldn't come as any surprise that not even New York's Finest were a match for your cunning."

"What are you doing here?"

Her voice jolted through him. Once a caress of crimson passion, it had filled with dark echoes, deepening its effect.

She shook her head as if exasperated with the inanity of her own question. "Scratch that. How did you get in here?"

He stopped two feet away, though every cell was screaming for him to keep going until he'd pressed his every inch to hers. Like when they'd been lovers. When she'd always met him more than halfway, impetuous, tempestuous...

Cursing inwardly, he shoved his hands in his pockets in feigned nonchalance. "Your housekeeper let me in."

She shook her head again, as if finding his answer ridiculous. Then her eyes widened with harsh accusation. "You intimidated her!"

Something twisted in his gut. In the past, she'd made him believe she thought he walked on water. Now the first thing that occurred to her was that he'd done something reprehensible. Worse, criminal.

But why would that upset him? He'd long accepted that her early adoration had been an act. One she hadn't been able to maintain once she'd suspected it wouldn't fulfill her purpose. Though he should marvel that it had taken over two years before she'd begun to slip, for instances of discord to accumulate.

He'd still refused to see that for what it was, pure manipulation. Instead, had assigned it all to the stress of her competitive job and the provocation of the dominant personality he became with her. He'd thought friction had only fueled their already incendiary relationship, had reveled in it to the point of instigating it on occasion. He'd misguided himself so thoroughly, that final explosive confrontation had utterly shocked him.

But after two years of dissecting the past, he now saw it clearly. He'd dismissed all evidence of the truth to maintain the illusion because he couldn't live without her passion. Or so he'd thought. He had. Hadn't he?

She now pulled herself to her full statuesque height, six

feet in her two-inch heels, her pose confrontational. "You might have scared Zahyah, but you must have forgotten all about me if you thought your arm-twisting tactics would work. You can walk out as you walked in, under your own power, or I'm calling security. Or better still, the police."

He flicked away her threat, his blood heating with the challenge and ardor she'd always ignited in him with a glance, a word. "What would you tell them? That your housekeeper let me in without consulting you and left you alone with me in an empty mansion?" Any other time he would have recommended the housekeeper be sternly chastised for such a breach of protocol and security. For now he was only glad she'd acted as she had. "On questioning, she'd swear there'd been no intimidation of any sort. As one of your mother's former colleagues, it was only natural for Zahyah to let me in."

"You mean because as my mother's former colleague, Zahyah was one of *your* mother's servants, too?"

He stiffened at the mention of his mother. The knowledge of her conspiracy to depose his father, King Atef, and remove his half brothers from succession to the throne of Zohayd was a skewer constantly turning inside him.

But Lujayn knew nothing of the conspiracy. No one but he and his siblings and father did. They'd been keeping it a secret at all costs until they resolved it. And resolution would come only when they discovered where his mother had hidden the Pride of Zohayd jewels. It was a backward and infuriating situation, one dictated by legend and now enforced by law—possession of the jewels conferred the right to rule Zohayd. Instead of calling for whoever had stolen them to be punished, Zohayd's people would decree that his father and his heirs, who had "lost" them, were unworthy of the throne. The belief that the jewels "sought" to be possessed by whoever deserved to rule the kingdom was unshakable.

But even when threatened with life imprisonment, his mother wouldn't confess to their location. All she'd told him and Haidar was that she would continue to destroy their father and brothers from her prison, that when the throne became Haidar's, with him as his crown prince, they would thank her.

He shook away the gnawing of ongoing frustration, leveling his gaze at the current cause of it. "I mean that Zahyah, as an Azmaharian who spent years in the royal palace of Zohayd—"

"As a virtual slave to your mother—as was mine."

The knot in his gut grew tighter as yet another of his mother's crimes sank its shame into him.

Ever since the exposure of Sondoss's conspiracy, they'd been realizing the full extent of her transgressions. *Slave* might be an exaggeration, but from recent findings, it had become evident she'd mistreated her servants. Lujayn's mother, as her "lady-in-waiting," seemed to have borne the brunt of her ruthless caprice. But Badreyah had left his mother's service as soon as Lujayn had left him. Seemed she could afford to when Lujayn had married Patrick McDermott.

That was probably one reason Lujayn had married him. Not that it made him any less bitter about it. She should have told him if she'd known Badreyah had been suffering at his mother's hands. He should have been the one she'd gone to for help.

He answered her cold fury with his own. "Whatever views Zahyah holds of my mother, she evidently still considers me her prince. She welcomed me in accordingly."

"Don't tell me you think people really buy this Prince of Two Kingdoms crap."

Her sneer had blood surging to his head. As half-Azmaharian half-Zohaydan princes, he and Haidar had been dubbed that. He couldn't speak for Haidar, but *he'd* always felt like a prince of neither kingdom. In Zohayd he was cut off from succession for being of impure stock. In Azmahar... well, he could count the reasons that no one there should consider him their prince.

The grandiose slogan that had been plastered over them from birth had always felt—as she'd pithily put it—like crap.

But then their mother decided to make it a reality. She was out to mangle and reform the region in order to do so.

He exhaled. "Whatever I am or am not, Zahyah welcomed me, and so did your guards before her. I've been welcomed here enough times that they didn't think twice of continuing the practice."

"You conned them using a defunct relationship with Patrick—"

"Who's no longer with us, thanks to you." He cut her off, the bile of pent-up anger welling again. "But you didn't prepare for developments as I thought you would. You didn't make allowance for my reappearance, didn't revoke my standing invitation."

"Like I would a vampire's, huh? Though one would be preferable to you since you're a *soul* sucker. And you're harder to banish. But I'll rectify that oversight right now."

He caught her arm as she strode past, felt awareness fork in his body. He gritted his teeth against the response, kept his breathing shallow so her scent—that of jasmine-scented twilights and pleasure-drenched nights—didn't trigger full-blown arousal.

"Don't bother. This delightful visit won't be repeated."

She jerked her arm free of his loose grasp. "It won't even start. You have some nerve coming here, after what you've done."

She was referring to his business clashes with Patrick,

which had resulted in major losses to them both. More damage *she'd* caused.

He misunderstood her on purpose. "I'm not the one who dumped you and married one of your best friends, only to turn her against you."

"You give Patrick too little credit if you think I influenced his decision to cut all business ties with you."

"You'd influence the devil himself. And we both know Patrick had too much angel in him. He was the perfect prey for the black widow you turned out to be."

Her eyes swept him from head to toe in disdain. "Listen, Jalal, cut the cloak-and-dagger melodrama. If you traveled across the world just to accuse me of overdosing my husband, you accomplished that with your opening statement. Don't be redundant as well as unfeeling and overbearing. You can now go back to your sand-infested, backward region to wallow in your unearned power."

Heat splashed in his chest. Not because her views insulted him, but because she had them at all. Disappointment only intensified his reaction to her, sent blood roaring to his loins.

His lips twisted with grim humor. "You were always a spitfire, yet you never spoke this brazenly to me."

"You just never bothered to listen. Not that that was a privilege you reserved for me. Your Exalted Highness didn't consider anyone worth listening to. But you're partially right. I was once guilty of embellishing my attitude and opinion of you. I'm not the person I was anymore."

"You're *exactly* the person you always were. But now that you're an heiress to an empire worth billions, you believe you have the luxury of showing me your true face and the clout to take me on."

Her eyes grew ridiculing. "That's not why I don't have to suppress my abhorrence of you and all you stand for anymore. But since I'm not inclined to explain my reasons, thanks for coming."

Thanks?

"I've been seething for two years that I didn't let it all out when I last saw you. Thanks for giving me the chance to get it off my chest. Now, since you've done what you've come to do, and indulged your evidently long-repressed desire to call me names—"

"But that's not what I've come to do." Before she could lob back something caustic, and without willing himself to, he dragged her to him, slamming her against his now burning body. "And that's certainly not the desire I've long repressed."

A hot sound of protest escaped her. He bent, caught it in his lips. He snatched in air laden with her breath, let it storm through him, uprooting the restraints he'd long placed on his senses. He let the feel of her invade his control, tear it away. Her taste eddied in his system, hurtling him back to their nights of delirium.

"No matter what you hate about me, you always loved this." He poured the words into her open-from-shock mouth, his lips gliding over her plump ones, pushing them farther apart, unable to wait to plunge inside her warmth and welcome. "You craved it. My touch, my hunger, my pleasures. Whatever else was pretense, this was real. Still is."

"It isn't..." Her words caught in her throat as soon as her lips moved against his. They trembled before they clung to his flesh.

It had always been like this. One touch had been all it took to ignite them, to start the chain reaction to the mindlessness and ecstasy of their overriding need for each other.

"Yes, Lujayn. It still is. This all-consuming need that ignites between us and only the other can satisfy."

Her breath hitched as it mingled with his, tumbled from

her on a ragged moan of arousal, as his tongue sought her concession. She gave it in a blatant seeking of her own, delighting him in her taste, her response. But at the first rub of slick flesh on flesh, a jolt of pleasure electrified both their bodies, made her start, try to escape the deepening intimacy. The move only had her teeth grazing his lips, tearing a groan from his depths, igniting her response again, her body involuntarily arching into his, their lips fusing again, sending his senses roaring for more.

He walked her back to the nearest wall, pressed against her lushness, imprinted her silent demand with his. "Tell me you have lain at night like I have, burning to have me again, take your fill of me. Tell me you have been going insane like I have. Tell me that you remembered all that we shared the moment I showed up, that even as your lips antagonized me, all you really wanted was for me to fill you, ride you, assuage the ache that maddens you."

He raised his head, looked down at her to get her confirmation. He got it.

She still wanted him. She'd never stopped.

It showed in the burning desire and dismay in her eyes. Whatever she'd been telling herself since she'd left him, her explosive response to him had forced her to face facts.

Holding her eyes, still seeking her affirmation, he scooped her into his arms. She clung to him, gave him more proof of her consent.

His heart almost uprooted itself in his chest with relief and urgency as he almost ran with her filling his arms, her eagerness tugging him deeper into mindlessness. It was only when he lowered her onto a king-size bed that he realized that his feet had propelled him to the master suite.

He came down half on top of her, stopped her roaming hands, stretched her arms above her head, capturing her wrists in one hand. The other slid down her face, her neck, skimmed over her breasts. Then, holding her gaze clouded with feverish desire, he leaned in, capturing her lips at the same moment he snapped open her jacket.

She gasped and turned her head as if suddenly shy, making his kisses trail over the hot velvet of her cheek. At the first suckle of his lips on her earlobe, she arched up, bringing her luxurious breasts rubbing against his chest, shuddering hard at the electrifying contact, intensifying it.

He rose to let her expression guide him to his next action. She stared up at him, her eyes emitting those hypnotic bursts, her breath choppy, her nipples pushing through her bra and blouse.

Satisfaction spread at the explicitness of her response, heightened as a gasp of disappointment escaped her when he sat up. His smile placated her as he shrugged away his jacket. Then, analyzing every iota of expression in her eyes' eloquent depths, he slowly, so slowly, unbuttoned his shirt.

His deliberateness gave her time and opportunity to take action if she didn't want this to go further. Gave him the luxury of studying her as she watched him expose his body to her. The body she'd worshipped for four years, laid her indelible brand over every inch. He reveled in each of her nuances as hunger and memories flooded her eyes, igniting them, swelling her lips, staining her cheeks.

"Isn't this what you've been burning for?" Her nod was drugged, her eyes glazing over as silent confession strummed her voluptuous body, shook her lips. He brought her hands pressing against his flesh, one over his thundering heart, the other over his abdomen, which quivered with need. When her volition took over, he invited her to go lower, groaned long and deep as she shaped him, cupped him, in trembling greed.

He hissed his torment, encouraging her, his mind unraveling with the sheer power and pleasure of her longed-for touch, and that of her desire. "Feel me, Lujayn. Take what you've always wanted. Enjoy me, revel in me. Devour me with your hunger like you used to, *ya'yooni'l feddeyah*."

A jolt racked her at hearing him call her one of his favorite endearments for her, *my silver eyes*. Their intoxicated cast deepened until they were the color of twilight in Zohayd. Snatched breaths escaped her lips as she explored him with intensifying boldness, each ending on a fractured moan. His intention to draw this out until she begged for him dwindled with each siren sound. But it was when she squeezed her eyes shut and agonized enjoyment gripped her face as she roamed him, that it vanished.

On a growled oath, he removed her hands from his rock-hard flesh. Before he moved over her, she jerked, as if coming out of a trance and scrambled up. "Jalal, we have to stop...."

He went still. "Tell me why."

She squeezed her eyes again. "Patrick..."

He caught her head in both hands, made her open her eyes. "Is dead. And you and I are not. But we're not alive, either. Tell me you've been able to truly *live*...without this...." He took her lips again as he moved his hard length over her until her tension dissolved, into seeking surrender, her body straining against his. He tore away his lips from hers to rise above her on extended arms. "Tell me you have known any real pleasure or satisfaction since me. Say you don't crave me as much as I crave you and I will go."

The truth blared in her eyes, but she still said, "Craving is not everything...."

"It's enough." He dug his fingers into her prim chignon, setting her raven silk free, burying his face in its luxury. "It's what we have, what we need, what we can't fight."

She pulled up his head by his hair. "It won't change a thing."

She held his focus. She was setting terms for this encounter. That it would only be physical? Or that it would be a one-off?

He refused to concede. "It will. It will stop this need from gnawing us hollow. Now admit it. You've been dying to have me again as I've been dying to have you. You'll give me everything as you always did, let me give you everything you've always begged for, everything we've always had together."

After a long moment, she nodded. Then with sooty lashes lowered to hide her expression, she dragged his mouth back to hers.

He growled his relief inside her as her tongue tangled with his, dueling, demanding, allowing him all the licenses he needed, taking her pleasure from him as she always did, her fervor and boldness intensifying his, her hunger and warmth and taste flowing in his lifeblood.

One hand harnessed her by her hair's tether as one of hers did him by his as he undid her blouse and skirt, swept them off her velvet flesh. Her other hand trembled at his zipper as he snapped open her bra, spilling her breasts. He swallowed her cry of relief, of spiking arousal, as he settled his aching flesh on top of hers, rubbing against her until she begged.

"Do everything to me, Jalal. Fill me, ride me now, *now*."

He rose to tear her panties off her hips, probe her satiny folds. His fingers slid in her flowing need, until she undulated against him in a frenzy. When he couldn't stand one more heartbeat outside her heat and yearning, she clamped her thighs around his back, writhing in the grips of the same fever to merge. Then he plunged inside her.

She screamed with the shock of his invasion. She was as impossibly tight as ever, their fit still almost unmanageable, their pleasure excruciating. She arched, smashing herself against him with the mindless need for his domination.

Overwhelmed with feeling, his girth gripped inside the molten pleasure that was her essence, he groaned her name and withdrew, only to plunge again, then again, forging deeper with every penetration. His escalations rocked her beneath him, wringing sharper cries from her depths. She met his thrusts, strengthening them, her demands for him to give it all to her tearing away any restraint he'd still clung to.

Their coupling was primal, savage. They groped and bit and thrust in ever-roughening abandon, nothing existing but the need to soothe the pangs that had long maddened them, to burn in a conflagration of release.

The first clench of her orgasm hit him like a sledgehammer. Her core clamped around his shaft with such force, he tore his lips from hers to roar at the unendurable spike in pleasure. Then she heaved beneath him, her intimate flesh tightening around his erection, singeing him with the rush of her satisfaction, wrenching his own from the depth of his loins. His body felt as if it was detonating with the force of his own climax as he released inside her, feeling he was pouring his life force into her.

Ecstasy finally relinquished its merciless grip and her strangled cries died into whimpers as aftershocks sparked and lurched through both of them.

He sank on top of her, oblivious to anything but her body cushioning him, her chaotic heartbeats echoing his as their systems struggled to recover from the exertion of their explosive lovemaking.

He might have slept. Or passed out. For a minute. Or an hour. All he knew was that he was coming back with a start into a body that was leaden with an excess of fulfillment. Then a move beneath him had him jerking up. *Lujayn.* He must have crushed her.

He groaned, then louder with the ache of separation, as he uncoupled from her with great regret. He bent to kiss her, but she scooted away from his touch. His heart clenched as she swayed up and sat at the edge of the bed, long hair tumbled, her body still and stiff.

He was reaching a caressing hand to her again when she turned her face and the look in her eyes halted the gesture of tenderness in midmotion. And that was before she spoke.

"I hate you, Jalal. When I've never hated anyone. So consider this the validation or the goodbye or whatever sex you think I owed you. It's never happening again."

She got up like an automaton. In seconds she disappeared inside the bathroom.

He stared at the closed door, heart booming, mind churning.

One thing that had been erased had been resurrected. His confidence in his ownership of her body. If he went after her now, he'd have her begging for him again. But her antipathy seemed to be real. He had no idea what he had done to earn it. But whatever *she* thought he had done might change everything. It might explain why she'd left him.

It was almost an hour before she exited the bathroom glowing, remote and dressed. He'd also dressed. He knew their mindless interlude should not be repeated. Not until he knew what was going on.

He stood there as she stopped before him, eyes devoid of expression. "I'm sorry I said I hate you. It's not true."

His heart unfurled from the tight knot it had become, the broken pieces mending. Something warm fluttered inside it as he moved closer.

Her next words froze it solid, shot it down like a bullet would a bird in flight.

"It's worse than that. I hate *myself* when I'm with you. I hate what I do, what I think, what I feel. What I *am*. Patrick taught me that I'm better than that—that I don't have to ever feel this way again. I was certain I'd never do this. But you're like an incurable disease. One exposure, and I relapse. There's only one way I'll stop being reinfected. I won't let you come near me again. If you try, I'll make you regret it."

The lash of her antipathy sliced open the dam of his accumulated, if briefly forgotten, bitterness.

He moved away from her, as if to escape the searing disappointment, heard himself taunting, "You mean more than I already regret coming here and exposing myself to *your* virulence again? Not possible. So save your threats and theatrics, Lujayn. It will be a snowy day in my 'backward region' before I come near you again."

He didn't only regret coming after her—he despised his stupidity for being unable to hate her, even now, for succumbing to his weakness, taking her right in her marital bed, then not being the one who came to his senses first, or at all.

At the door he turned, and the look on her face had his heartache boiling over. It wasn't just over, she didn't only hate him now—she always had.

It had been an illusion, a sham.

More harshness spilled from his lips, the only shield he found so the icy shards of her rejection wouldn't hack his heart to pieces all over again. "Thanks, by the way. You gave me exactly what I came for. The certainty that you're not worth another thought. *Now* I can delete you from my memory."

He walked away then, the relief that this retaliation had provided already evaporating, despondence seeping in its place, settling into his recesses. For it was another lie. No matter that he now knew nothing they'd shared had been real, he knew the memory of her would never relinquish its hold over him....

Two

The present

"...the memory of this day will burn bright for the rest of my days, with the blessing and wonder of your love and belief, your very existence. I, Haidar Aal Shalaan, pledge my life to you, Roxanne, owner of my heart..."

Jalal hit Pause, his chest tight as he watched the power of love radiating from the two faces frozen on the screen.

He'd never believed in miracles. But there was no denying he'd watched one unfold in real time. Had been replaying it on video over and over again. His twin's wedding ceremony. He'd watched that specific part, when they'd made their un-rehearsed vows, for the umpteenth time. Today.

Each time had only ratcheted up his reaction to the sight of Haidar staring with such profound adoration into the eyes of his weeping bride, of hearing him, then her, commit to a lifetime of unity and allegiance, body and soul.

He *was* fiercely happy for both of them. The twin who felt like an extension of his own life force, and the woman who felt of his own flesh and blood, too. But seeing them, *feeling* them, bound together in abiding love forever, inflicted something besides joy. It made him feel even more acutely that gaping emptiness in his core. One he knew would never be filled.

He'd once thought he'd had a chance of having something approaching what Haidar and Roxanne had. With Lujayn, the one woman he'd wanted with all he had. But even when they'd been lost to passion in each other's arms, he'd felt something missing. Now he knew what it was. *That.* That connection. That alliance. That totality of acceptance, agreement and appreciation.

The extent of the deficiency had been driven home to him during the past years as his brothers had found their soul mates. But it had taken Haidar and Roxanne to solidify the realization. He'd now seen and felt what completeness was like.

He hadn't had anything like it with Lujayn. But then how could he have? It took two to progress to that level of intimacy. She'd been unwilling to move beyond a certain threshold. She hadn't wanted intimacy, she'd wanted wealth and status.

He saw that now. At the time he'd thought any issues had been due to the intermittent nature of their relationship, dictated by their hectic schedules and living on different sides of the world. But the truth had been that, beyond sex, she hadn't really wanted *him*. She'd only wanted him to propose.

He'd bet she would have kept trying if another opportunity, almost as big a catch, hadn't presented itself.

He hit Stop. The screen went black—as black as his thoughts.

He wouldn't see it again. There was no point in replay-

ing the living, breathing example of what he'd never have.
He'd have a lifetime of experiencing it in real life.

He rose and threw down the remote. It took him seconds
to get his bearings, to remember where this sitting room
opened onto the veranda. He'd rented so many houses in
the past two years that he regularly woke up not knowing
immediately where he was, or even in which country.

Ever since his mother's conspiracy had been exposed
and the scandal had rocked the region, he'd been roaming
the globe. His father and half brothers, Amjad, Harres and
Shaheen, insisted that no one associated Haidar and him to
her crimes. But he felt tainted by them anyway. He'd felt
worse when he'd clashed with Haidar over that mess, and
ended up placing the lion's share of the blame on him. He'd
driven Haidar to say he felt he no longer had a twin.

That breach *had* been resolved, thankfully, and he no
longer felt sundered forever from his other half. But though
he felt whole now that their relationship was regaining the
closeness they'd once shared as children, that wholeness
was still…hollow.

He walked across the marble-spread veranda and stopped
at the cut-stone balustrade, looking out at the desert to a horizon that seemed farther away than ever.

What was he doing here?

Why was he trying to claim the throne of this land?

So it was up for grabs after the now former king of Azmahar, his maternal uncle, had abdicated after a public outcry
and all his heirs had met with the same rejection. Just as his
mother had almost destroyed Zohayd, her family had taken
Azmahar to the edge of destruction, too. He'd thought he'd
be lumped in with his maternal family as the last people
Azmahar would want near the throne again. So he'd been
shocked when those representing a third of the kingdom's
population had demanded he be their candidate. They'd in-

sisted he wasn't tainted by his family's history and had the power and experience to save Azmahar. Even his Aal Munsoori blood was an asset, since people still considered the bloodline their rightful monarchs. But he had the potent advantage of mixing it with the Aal Shalaan blood, which would win them back their vital ally, Zohayd.

Still, why was *he* running for the throne? So he knew he was qualified for the position. But he also knew that he could swim among sharks, literally. He'd done it before. But that didn't mean he should—and running for the position of king in such a chaotic land was worse than braving shark-infested waters. Not to mention the minefield of being pitted against his twin *and* his former-best-friend-turned-nemesis, Rashid.

He could find one real reason. Because if he didn't do this, what else was there to do?

He'd exiled himself from Zohayd, had been performing from afar the royal duties his brothers hadn't taken over in his absence. He'd installed such an efficient system to run his business empire, it took him only a few hours a day to orchestrate its almost self-perpetuating success. And he had no personal life. Apart from a few good-but-not-close friends, he had no one.

Sure, his family insisted he had them, and he supposed he did, in the big-picture sense, but on a daily basis? His family back in Zohayd he seldom saw. And he now had his twin back, but only in an emotional sense. As a newlywed and another candidate for the throne, Haidar had no real time for him.

No wonder he felt empty. As vacant as this desert, with as nonexistent a possibility for change.

An insistent noise broke the stillness of his surroundings. He frowned down at its origin. His cell phone.

It took him seconds to recognize the ring, one he'd assigned to a specific person. Fadi Aal Munsoori. A distant cousin, and the head of his security and his campaign for the throne.

Though Fadi came from the one branch of Jalal's family on his mother's side that he considered "family," Fadi himself had never considered he had any relation to the former royal family of Azmahar. Fadi's father had maintained marginal relations with them, but Fadi had renounced the relationship completely, not to mention publicly and viciously. The moment they'd been deposed, he'd pounced on the tribes he had influence over, had been the one who'd orchestrated their nomination of Jalal for king.

But even as the one he trusted with his life, his business, his campaign and even his secrets, Fadi had never accepted Jalal's efforts to form a more personal relationship. Jalal insisted he was foremost a friend, but Fadi behaved like a knight of old with Jalal as his liege. He only ever called him when there was something urgent to convey or to discuss.

He almost wished Fadi would hit him with something huge to deal with, to get him out of this vacuum.

"Fadi, so good to hear from you."

Not one to indulge in niceties, Fadi got to the point, his deep voice pouring its usual solemn gravity into Jalal's ear.

"Considering you have not renewed my orders concerning this matter, or asked about any developments in the past two years, you may not be interested in what I have to tell you. But I decided to let you know in case you still are."

Jalal's gut tightened. This didn't sound like something that concerned his business, his personal safety or his campaign. There was only one other thing Fadi had ever taken care of for him. One person he'd entrusted him with keeping tabs on. Lujayn.

It seemed he hadn't groaned her name mentally but out loud, for Fadi said, "Yes, this is about Lujayn Morgan."

The desert wind suddenly stirred, as if in response to the questions and temptations that stormed through him.

He'd been holding himself back with all he had so that he wouldn't "renew Fadi's orders" or "ask about any developments." And he'd succeeded. At least he'd managed not to seek her out, or learn news of her, thereby renewing his exposure and losing any hard-won closure.

The sane thing to do now was to leave Fadi certain that his orders concerning her were at an end. That he was not to even report any information that came his way by accident.

At his prolonged silence, Fadi exhaled. "I apologize for presuming you would be interested."

And he did the one insane thing. Heartbeat spiraling out of control, he growled, "*B'haggej' jaheem, ya rejjal,* just *tell* me."

His bark silenced Fadi instead. Fadi, like everyone else, believed Jalal was the epitome of sangfroid. While this was mostly true, control and Lujayn had always been mutually exclusive.

He could almost hear Fadi's miss-nothing mind clicking on the new conclusion before he finally said, "She is back in Azmahar."

"Did you think I wouldn't find out you were in Azmahar?"

Lujayn pulled away the cell phone to groan at hearing a voice she'd come back here hoping to avoid.

Aliyah's.

She and Aliyah had once thought they were cousins, with both their fathers belonging to the Irish-American Morgan clan. But Aliyah's mother, Princess Bahiyah Aal Shalaan, had turned out to be her flesh and blood aunt, with Aliyah actually the daughter of now-ex-King Atef Aal Shalaan of

Zohayd from his American lover, and now new wife, Anna Beaumont.

It had been years since Aliyah had been declared an Aal Shalaan and become the wife of King Kamal Aal Masood and the queen of Judar. Quite a change from the minor royalty she'd been when Lujayn had known her.

But while their false family relationship had introduced them to each other, they had become true friends when Lujayn had followed Aliyah's footsteps in modeling. Aliyah had offered her unfailing guidance and priceless support, steered her from many a mess and hooked her up with the few people it was safe to know in that turbulent world.

Aliyah had also been the reason she'd met Jalal, back when they'd thought she was a cousin to them both. Now that they knew Aliyah was his half sister, there was an even bigger chance she might pull Lujayn into Jalal's orbit once more. That was why she'd been avoiding her. That and the fathomless joy Aliyah radiated ever since she'd gotten married.

"So what is an appropriate punishment for you, now that I've caught you in Azmahar unannounced?" Aliyah's vibrant voice teased.

Lujayn wasn't about to confess to the woman who'd shown her unforgettable kindness when she'd most needed it that she'd been avoiding her because she inadvertently made her feel bad about her life and because she didn't want to risk seeing Jalal.

So she told her what she felt, free of pettiness and anxieties. "I missed you, too, Aliyah."

Aliyah let out a laugh as clear and tinkling as crystal. "And here she is. The woman who knows just how to thwart me and still leave me with a smile on my face. You're more slippery than an eel, you know that? I hear it's an Azmaharian trait."

A smile pried Lujayn's stiff lips apart. It had been an endless source of fun among them to compare notes on their "hybrid" nature. "Since I'm only half-Azmaharian, the trait must be diluted, so I can't be that slippery."

Aliyah hooted. "My dear, you're talking to a bona fide halfling. Being half-and-half only augments any traits we inherit from each side. Just ask Kamal."

And there it was. The woman was unable to form five consecutive sentences without leading back to her husband and love of her life.

She knew she was being pathetic, but it wasn't just hearing the wealth of love in Aliyah's voice. She'd seen them together, alone and with their two children. Seeing and feeling that lion of a man's fierce love and devotion to Aliyah had been amazing, but it was also evidence that such passion existed—and that she would never have anything like it.

"So how long are you in Azmahar?" Aliyah interrupted her darkening thoughts. "Last time you were here was more than four years ago and you stayed less than four days."

"I don't know, Aliyah. It depends on my aunt's health."

"Suffeyah?" All levity left Aliyah's voice, alarm replacing it. "What's wrong with her?"

"She's been diagnosed with breast cancer."

"Oh, Lujayn, I'm so sorry. Bring her over to Judar. We have one of the best medical systems in the world, thanks to Kamal. I'll see to it that she has the best health care the kingdom can offer."

"I can't thank you enough for the offer, Aliyah, but I have to decline it. I tried to make her come to the States, but she refuses to leave her daughters behind for the months the treatments might take. One is a senior in high school and the other just had twins."

"I understand all too well putting your kids before yourself. But Azmahar isn't in good shape and I understand one of the sectors suffering most is health care."

Lujayn's heart constricted at Aliyah's words. "I know. But Aunt insists she'll take her chances with the medical care here like any other Azmaharian would. All I could do was arrange for a consult with some of the best doctors in the States. I'm flying them over in a couple days. We'll take it from there."

"That's great. And if what they recommend can't be carried out in Azmahar, I'll provide you with medicine, equipment and personnel. If she won't come to us, we'll bring the best of Judar to her."

"Oh, Aliyah, that is beyond anything I could have hoped for."

"But you didn't hope for anything, did you? You have this infuriating thing against a helping hand from a friend."

Lujayn exhaled. Aliyah was right. Being the daughter of a servant in the palace Aliyah had grown up in had been enough. She hadn't wanted to tip the balance of their situations more by accepting favors she'd be unable to repay. She'd only accepted Aliyah's help when Aliyah had insisted it was the fruit of her experience, nothing to do with her royal status.

Even now she had nothing of equal value to ever offer Aliyah. That made it impossible for her to be the recipient of favors that had everything to do with Aliyah's status.

"I can hear your mind churning, Lu," Aliyah said. "But since it's not you on the receiving end this time, it should ameliorate your allergic reaction. Now promise you won't say no, and you'll let me do what I can when needed."

She chuckled even as tears rushed to her eyes. "I forgot how well you know me, Aliyah. And about this pesky total recall of yours. *And* just how incredible you are." She sighed, swallowing the lump of emotion. "Thank you, and I promise."

"Good girl!" She could just see Aliyah's unbridled smile. "Now when will I see you?"

Ugh. Now she had to make another promise.

But why not? She knew it would be beyond either of them to keep this one. She doubted the queen of Judar would find it feasible to continue a friendship with someone of her background.

She exhaled. "As soon as we know more about the plans for Aunt, I'll call you to set up a girls' day out."

Aliyah whooped. "And I'm holding you to that."

After more chatting, Lujayn started to regain the fluency they'd once shared, until Aliyah had to rush to extract her daughter from a literally sticky mess and laughingly bade her adieu.

Lujayn collapsed on the nearest seat. If she was already coming apart, what would the next weeks or months here be like?

It was just her terrible luck to come back to Azmahar now, with Jalal on Azmaharian soil for the first time in years. She hated being in the same airspace as him. And Aliyah's call had made her feel as if his shadow was closer and darker than ever.

Which was moronic. Not only had he said he'd delete her from his memory, he had a throne to think of. Even if he hadn't, she'd be the last thing to cross his mind. She'd been the last thing he'd thought about or considered when she'd been his sex partner. She'd been one of many, after all.

He'd arranged their rendezvouses when it had been convenient for him, sometimes weeks apart, and no way had he suppressed his overriding libido that long. She'd spent the times apart alternating between a hell of doubt, and telling herself it was only her insecurities talking. But she'd seen and heard too much proof that instead of "storing his hunger to be expended on her luscious self" as he'd once claimed, he'd had a different body in his bed every night.

To her shame, that hadn't been what had finally made her walk away.

After all, he'd promised her nothing to justify her feeling bad, let alone betrayed.

Cursing herself for regurgitating those sordid memories, her eyes darted around the hotel suite. She'd reserved it for the coming weeks as it was within walking distance of the hospital so she'd be constantly available for her aunt.

She'd just come back from starting arrangements at the hospital. Just thinking of what lay ahead filled her with dread. No wonder Aliyah's call had shaken her. She was already in turmoil. And it had nothing to do with any other Aal Shalaan.

She rose and headed to the kitchenette to make a cup of herbal tea. She needed to be calm for the drive back to her aunt's at the outskirts of Durrat al Sahel. Traffic in the capital had gotten far worse than she remembered.

With the first sip from her hibiscus brew, a loud, melodious noise shattered the suite's silence. She gulped the hot liquid, scalded her tongue and choked.

She was coughing her lungs out when the noise went off again. A doorbell. She hadn't even realized the suite had one!

It must be housekeeping. And she hadn't thought of hanging a Do Not Disturb sign—she'd planned to stay only an hour.

She stalked to the door, flung it open, intending to let them in and herself out...and froze. Her heart did, too.

Filling the door, dwarfing her and causing the world to shrink, stood Jalal. The reason behind every tumult in her life since she'd laid eyes on him.

But he wasn't only that man. He was…more.

She'd once thought nothing could surpass him in beauty and magnificence. And nothing had. And during their affair, he'd proved only he could best his own standards. That six-foot-six broad-shouldered, divinely proportioned body she'd thought the epitome of manhood *had* kept maturing to godlike levels, as she'd had hands-on proof. Every day they'd had together had hewn his face further with the chisel of maturity and virility, manifesting his intelligence and sensuality and dominance in its every slash and angle and expression.

But something had happened to him since she'd last seen him two years ago. As if the darkness and danger she'd long suspected he'd hidden beneath the facade of graciousness and gorgeousness had manifested in his looks, emanated from his every nuance. It turned his beauty, his impact, from breathtaking to heartbreaking.

He was staring down at her as if he, too, was shocked to see her. When he was the one who'd almost given her a heart attack just by showing up.

After what felt like an hour of suspended thought and escalating distress, his whiskey-colored eyes narrowed, singeing her. Then his voice poured over her, feeling like a dip in lava.

"I said I'd delete you from my memory, but it appears there is no forgetting you without erasing it altogether. So I've decided to stop trying, to go all the way in the opposite direction. I now think my only cure is to revive every memory, to reenact every single intimacy we ever shared."

Three

Lujayn stood paralyzed as Jalal pushed past her. The door clicked closed, sounded like a gun going off at close range.

She still couldn't move. Speak. Breathe. Reactions deluged her as she watched him walk farther into the suite, memories and sensations and compulsions tangling, trapping her volition in their maze. It had always taken him just a look to neutralize her will, her sense of self-preservation.

And that he still retained the same influence over her, after all she'd suffered and lost and continued to struggle with because of him, made her spitting, foaming mad.

The moment he turned to face her, his eyes sweeping her in tranquil appreciation and intent, she seethed, "What the hell do you think you're doing? Get out."

"I will. At some point." His shoulders moved in a languid shrug. "But since it won't be now, how about saving your obligatory apoplectic tirade and getting on with discussing the particulars of my proposition?"

"How about I revive our first memory? Reenact the first 'intimacy' I shared with you?"

His wolf's eyes flared with remembrance as he walked back to her. "When I first saw you hiding behind Aliyah and watching me like a wary, hungry kitten? Or is it when I walked up to you and took your hand in mine—" his hands clenched and unclenched, as if reliving the sensations "—and it shook from the power of your response, with the promise of what it would later do to me?"

A ragged scoff escaped her. "Way to go rewriting history. I was at a loss at how to react to a stranger's forwardness."

"I was never a stranger to you. You've known who I was probably since you were old enough to know anyone."

"I knew *of* you. And what I knew accounted for the wary part of my reaction."

"What about the hungry part?" His eyes turned goading. "And I never asked—didn't Aliyah sing my praises? How... un-cousinly of her at the time, if she didn't."

"If she'd sung anything about you, I bet it wouldn't have been praises. And since you went to great lengths to divert her from your intentions concerning me, she never did the cousinly thing for *me,* and warn me to keep you at world's length."

"I diverted her in the interest of preserving the eyes you said you adored."

And those eyes, damn him, were as magnificent as ever, emitting the golden lust that put common sense on the fritz whenever he trained them on her.

"From the mother cat routine she had going with you, she would have scratched them out had she known my 'intentions.'" A frown gathered the spectacular slashes of his eyebrows. "So which first intimacy were you talking about?" Suddenly his eyes blazed with sensual challenge. "You mean when you sucker punched me?"

"I did no such thing. I gave you plenty of warning."

"*Aih,* to let you go or else. When I wasn't holding you against your will. I wasn't even touching you."

"You were backing me into a corner."

"I was walking toward you. You were the one who kept retreating, cornering yourself."

"Because you had me alone in your hotel suite."

"Where you came under your own power and of your own free will."

"I came to attend a party, with Aliyah."

"My party, in my suite. And I wasn't the one who made Aliyah leave you there to bail out one of her other lost souls."

"I was never a lost soul of hers. And I only stayed because she said she'd be back in thirty minutes."

"You still didn't leave when she was much later than that."

"I was new in New York and I thought I was safer in your suite than I would be on the streets alone at night."

"And you were."

"It didn't look like that when everyone left me alone with you. A man twice my size, twenty times as strong, not to mention a prince with diplomatic immunity and god-level entitlement."

"And you thought I sent them away to have you to myself."

"I was right."

"Not about the sinister intentions that earned me that one-two combo."

"Don't exaggerate. That follow-up punch didn't even connect."

"Only because the first one almost felled me." His hand wrapped around his throat as if feeling it again. "Not to mention the shock of the angel I couldn't wait to have turning into a harpy. *Ya Ullah,* if I wanted you one karat before that, I wanted you twenty-four then."

She'd been horrified at what she'd done, had tried to run out. He'd stopped her. Without touching her still. Just by calling to her. It had been the first time he'd called her his "silver eyes."

And just like that, her fears of who he was, of the kind of power he wielded and the unbridgeable gap that existed between them, had disappeared. He'd stopped being the son of a woman she'd grown up hating and become something far more dangerous. The personification of every forbidden desire she'd never thought she harbored. He'd been warm and accessible, witty and eloquent in ways she'd never encountered, admiring her beauty, her spunk, then teasing her about her attack, leaving her in no doubt he knew what had fueled it. Frightening attraction, which he shared in full.

He hadn't taken her to bed that night, but they both knew he could have. He'd waited two months, driving her out of her mind with wanting him in the interim. After that first time in his bed, serviced and pleasured, devoured and dominated, she'd become addicted, had wanted him with an intensity and an obsession that had sent her in a tailspin. For the next four years.

Their intimacies had been wild, greedy, explosive. But the escalating physical gratification had only plunged her deeper into emotional and psychological deprivation…

"Not that you ever need to punch me again," he said. "You knock me out just by looking at me with those spellbinding eyes, by wanting me as much as I want you." She opened her mouth to contradict him and a caressing hand below her chin closed it for her. "Don't bother. This is the one incontrovertible fact we share. So are you sure this is the intimacy you want to reenact, with so many to choose from? Like the first time we made love…."

Her assertion that they'd never "made love" went un-scoffed as he again placed a finger on her lips and the heat of his flesh almost fused them shut.

She staggered back and he sighed, dropping his hand, his eyes growing hotter as minute details of that first time replayed in their depths. "I remember every glide of skin on skin, every press of flesh into flesh, every sensation as you opened yourself to me, surrendered your every response, begged for my possession and pleasuring, as if it were encoded in my every cell. I remember each and every time after that."

She stared at him, shock and fury giving way to languor. It was as if his nearness produced chemicals inside her body that were more potent than any mind-altering drug.

No. She wasn't ever going to fall under his influence again. He'd cost her too much. And not only her...

Anxiety started to bubble and seethe inside her. She had to make sure he walked away forever this time and would avoid thinking of her for the rest of his life. But she'd been going about this all wrong.

The best way to do that was to *not* give him a challenge. Wounding his massive pride might have driven him away, had kept him there for a while, but the need to satisfy it had driven him back. She had to learn from her mistakes, if only this once.

"Memories are nice, I'm sure," she said. "But you're focusing on inconsequential memories and forgetting relevant ones. Like why you intended to delete me from your memory in the first place."

Ice suddenly extinguished the embers of sensual fire in his eyes. "I forget nothing. It's a curse Aal Shalaans suffer from. It's also why I failed to perform that deletion I intended. The moment I knew you were back here, I admitted that I never would."

She'd known about Aliyah's amazing eidetic memory but this was the first time he'd mentioned possessing something similar. But then, what had he ever *told* her? He'd *talked,* a lot, but it had all been about passion, both sexual and contentious. Besides that...nothing.

She shrugged. "This infallible memory must also mean you haven't forgotten the bad parts. And those were ugly enough to douse anything you imagine was so wonderful."

"You mean the parts where you got close to one of my best friends and conned him into marrying you, only to dispatch him in record time? Though maybe I shouldn't call 'almost two years' record time. As always, I salute your tenacity. You must have wanted to get rid of him sooner."

"So you *ass*ume."

At the reigniting challenge and enjoyment in his eyes, she almost smacked herself. *Focus. Just be a neutral bore and defuse his confrontational circuits.*

"So why don't you fix my *ass*umptions?"

She wanted to tell him to go fix himself.

Instead, she decided to deflate the misapprehension that clearly fueled his perverse interest in her.

She released her breath in a resigned exhalation. "I wasn't at liberty to disclose the matter when we...last met. I'm still not comfortable talking about it, but I guess there's no reason to keep it a secret anymore, at least from you."

"Is that your oblique way of warning me to keep this a secret? Because I'm known to be such a blabbermouth?"

"You mean you won't run to the media with my disclosures, or rush to tweet about them?" She tamped down another wave of bitterness, lips twisting with it. "But you're right. The way you keep secrets, I bet anything I tell you would be even safer than it would with a corpse. But I wasn't thinking about your ironclad discretion when you showed up two months after Patrick's death. With the turmoil I was in and the dangers I was facing, not to mention your added aggravation, sharing the truth with you was pretty low on my list of considerations."

"Are you going to share said truth now? About how he 'really' died? If it's what you told the police, don't bother."

"I don't know how the police work in this region, O Prince of Two Kingdoms, but in New York they don't care what you 'tell' them. They only listen to solid evidence. *Especially* when someone so rich and young dies of un-natural causes."

"But they found no evidence of foul play, hence my ac-cusation a couple of years ago."

"About getting away with murder?" She cocked her head at him, hating the way her heart sputtered as his eyes fol-lowed the movement of her hair when he was more or less accusing her of being a murderess. "So you think I'm ca-pable of it?"

"I know you're capable of driving a man to take his own life."

"Based on what? My infamous former career as a woman who used my body to make a living? Or as the woman who dared to end things with you?"

She stopped, cursing herself silently, viciously. She was sliding into inciting recriminations again.

"How about as the woman who 'used her body' to trap herself a billionaire when I didn't make the bid you were after?"

It was no use. This man could goad a rock into hurtling itself at him. "You're saying I was after a proposal? As in marriage? Did it seem to you like I thought fairy-tale mov-ies were based on true stories? Last time I looked, those and rom-coms were the only realms where the prince married the servant's daughter."

"When you said you wanted a man who 'wouldn't hide

you like a dirty secret,' who'd 'walk with you in the sun,' you meant you wanted a proposal. You let me know I was useless to you if I didn't cough up one only when you had a suitable substitute secured."

"*Suitable substitute secured?* I bet you can't say that five times in a row." She coughed a furious laugh. "It never crossed my mind that our...liaison would be more than what it was—trivial, sporadic, not to mention base. And that's why I decided to end it. Sex was no longer enough to put up with the degradation."

"Degradation?" he hissed. "I went to every effort to make sure our...liaison, as you put it, remained only between us so you wouldn't be exposed to anything of the sort."

Bile rose again. "And I knew it couldn't have been different between us. But that doesn't mean it was okay or even sane. I was trapped in a vicious circle, wanting to end it then letting you walk back into my life anytime you pleased, to lure me back into that...toxic compulsion. *That's* why I ended it. The inequality, the unbridgeable gap, the pointlessness, on every level, was corroding my self-esteem and psychological health."

"And the only cure for both was a besotted billionaire husband."

She snorted. "That's your favorite assumption, isn't it? You have to find a mercenary, borderline criminal rationalization to explain that a woman would choose to deprive herself of you, don't you?"

"When I'm left with no explanation, apart from an ambiguous rant, I had to fill in the blanks, before and after the event."

"And you couldn't find a rationalization where you were in any way to blame, right?"

"If I were, you should have aired specific grievances and given me the chance to undo them. Instead, you chose to become hysterical before storming out. And you promptly ended any chance for me to approach you with reconciliation efforts. What could I do but adopt the harshest explanations?"

"Wow, your Cambridge English major is sure coming out to play, isn't it?"

His smile turned lethal. "So you're telling me that blowup wasn't a pretext to get me out of the picture while you grabbed the opportunity to land a far more malleable man with almost as much money?"

"Patrick was far more of a man, period, and a human being than you can ever dream of being." And she was pathetic, because knowing that had never extinguished the hunger that consumed her alive. Not that she'd let it steer her now that she had far more than herself to safeguard, to defend. "And I certainly didn't marry him for his money and assets. In fact, he married me for them."

After that first punch, Jalal had managed to anticipate Lujayn for the next two years. Her pattern had changed in the following two, but after some readjustment, he'd still charted it.

Then had come that day two years ago. Nothing had happened according to his expectations then or ever since. It was as if he'd lost his insight where she was concerned.

She kept throwing curves he remained unprepared for. She'd just insulted his manhood, his humanity. But that wasn't what he'd taken issue with. It was that riddle she'd hurled at him.

Suddenly, every frustration of the past four years blew away his intention to play this cool and seductive. The suaveness he'd maintained till now became a seething mass of urgency.

"You prefaced all this with your intention to tell me the

truth. So *b'haggej'jaheem,* skip the cryptic teasers. What in *hell* do you mean he married you for *his* money and assets?"

Those unique eyes of hers echoed his ire and passion. "Nothing cryptic to it. He wanted to make sure his wealth and projects didn't go to his so-called family after he died."

He'd demanded she give it to him straight. But he hadn't expected she would, or that much. It was so straight that his mind stalled with implications he'd never considered.

"If you were any kind of friend to Patrick, let alone one of his best friends as you like to claim, you must know his relationship with his family was...pathological, to say the least."

He nodded slowly. After Patrick's mother died, his father had married a woman who turned out to be a wicked stepmother straight out of a fairy tale. Her evil became even more evident when she had children. She did everything she could to destroy Patrick's relationship with his father to make him cut Patrick off from his inheritance. To her fury, Owen McDermott did the opposite. Unlike a typical, oblivious fictional father, he was aware of his new wife's flaws and that their children shared her hatred of Patrick. His will cut *them* off from the bulk of his fortune, leaving it to the honorable Patrick to give them what he saw fit.

And Patrick *had* given. But nothing had ever been enough.

She continued, "Patrick told me his life story the first night we met."

How he remembered that night. It had been one of the handful of times he'd gone out with her, meeting in a secluded restaurant. They'd stumbled upon Patrick who'd been out drinking alone. Jalal had been called away to handle a business emergency, and Lujayn had driven the intoxicated Patrick home. He'd thought nothing of it in his certainty of their exclusive interest in each other.

His heart clenched at the expression that came over her, as if she were looking into the past with longing and regret.

"We became friends from that night. He started coming with me on my vacations to Ireland, the homeland he hadn't returned to since his mother died. He found a new family there."

"Yours."

He didn't need her nod of corroboration. All the time they'd been together, she'd been taking another man home.

"He and my father grew very close, and along the way, Dad gave him advice that multiplied his inheritance a dozen times. His so-called family came swarming back, demanding their 'share.'"

"And he didn't want to give them any more." Her poignancy chafed him so badly he wanted to shake her out of this melancholy over another man. He clenched his fists on the urge. "So you're saying he married you to give it to you instead."

"Me and my family. We were the ones he trusted."

"Why should he have wanted to trust anyone with his fortune?"

"It wasn't simply money. He had many projects, companies and charities. He knew if his stepmother and half brother and half sisters got their hands on those, they would liquidate everything and go somewhere tropical and live like retired despots. He wanted to make sure they didn't have legal claim to any of it."

"Thanks for the elucidation, but that wasn't what I asked. Why would he prepare alternative heirs when he was so young? It's as if he knew he was going to die. Did he have psychiatric problems? Was he suicidal?"

"He certainly was not!"

Her denial barreled into him. It felt real. Too real. As if an emotional charge was building inside her as she talked about Patrick, remembered him. The mere mention of something

she considered insulting to Patrick had her on the verge of
another attack.

The blackness that had been roiling inside him ever since
she'd left him and married Patrick spread. She'd once been
passionate about her displeasure with him, but now she
treated him with cold contempt. Patrick commanded her
respect and allegiance, even in death. Had he been so wrong
about what he'd thought they'd shared? About her relationship with Patrick?

Scowling at him as if she'd like to give him another one-
two combo, she said, "Patrick was the most psychologically
healthy person I've ever known. He was also the most be-
nevolent. He would never have done anything to harm himself, not only because he was stable as a rock, but because
so many people depended on him."

That he knew to be true. He'd admired Patrick from the
day they'd met, over fifteen years ago, for his boundless
energy and enthusiasm, his progressive views, but mostly
for his unswerving humanitarianism. It had been bitterness
over Lujayn that had driven him to sever all ties with him,
business and otherwise. That was what he'd regretted most
when Patrick had died. That he had died with them at odds.

"Patrick had inoperable testicular cancer, having already
spread to his major organs."

His breath clogged in his throat. He didn't know what
shook him more—this revelation, or her reaction to remembering it.

Anguish seemed to crash over her, shaking her features,
her voice. "I was with him the day he was diagnosed. He was
told he had a year at most, with treatments, far less without.
But he wouldn't spend what time he had left suffering from
side effects when there was no chance of a cure. He wanted
instead to live what remained of his life as a full member of
the extended family who loved him as their own."

Something inside him withered.

He hadn't known. Hadn't even suspected. He'd been so blinded by jealousy, by his wounded pride and thwarted passion, he hadn't bothered to investigate beyond the obvious. He'd chosen to think the worst, of Patrick, and of her.

But this only exonerated Patrick. *She* might have still used his approaching mortality to entrap him.

Yet what mattered was that instead of being there for Patrick at the end of his life, he'd become his enemy.

Could she be inventing all this to exonerate herself?

He glared at her, praying he'd read something in her eyes that would tell him he hadn't been so oblivious. "You know I can unearth his medical records if I want to."

Distaste bloomed in her eyes. "That's why you have to believe me even if you hate doing so. The evil bitch you're painting me to be couldn't be stupid enough to lie about something you can so easily check."

He staggered back as more realizations pummeled him. "*Ya Ullah*...so it's true. And he hid his diagnosis so that his businesses wouldn't collapse, taking thousands of jobs with them. That's why I never heard about it."

She nodded, turned away, discreetly dabbing at her cheeks.

She didn't want him to witness her tears. He never had. He'd never driven her to them, in pleasure or pain. More proof that where he was concerned, her emotions had never been involved.

She sat down, looked at him, tears sparkling in precarious ripples. "But his doctors' predictions didn't come true. He had twenty months with us before he began to deteriorate. It was the best time of our lives. All the while he coached me and my family in what we should do once he was gone. When his decline began, it was...painful...." Tears arrowed down her cheeks. "He chose not to prolong his suffering and ours, chose to end it on his own terms."

He was breathing like he'd just escaped a runaway car by the time she fell silent. *Ya Ullah...Patrick!*

Frustration and futility crowded in his head until he felt it might burst. "How could you not tell me?"

She raised her gaze at his growl, anguish turning to incredulity. "I never gauged your ego correctly, did I? Even gods can't have that much entitlement. You see this only in terms of feeling slighted for being excluded? Why would I have told you anything, pray tell? You were no longer his friend."

"Because I didn't have a full picture. Because I didn't know what had driven him to do what he did."

"If you think his condition drove him to slam the door in your face, think again. He remained clear and calm till the hour he died. He did what he thought was right, like I did, severing a toxic relationship he realized he should have ended long ago."

"But none of his grievances against me, real or imagined, mattered. Not *then*. *B'Ellahi,* he was dying, and I should have known. *I should have been there for him.*"

She gaped at him as if he'd grown a third eye.

Figured. It was the first time she'd seen him agitated.

Then, as if trying not to rouse a beast she'd just discovered was dangerous, she said, "I would have encouraged him to tell you if I'd thought you'd feel this way. But it didn't occur to either of us that it would matter to you, beyond a passing regret for someone you used to be friendly with."

If her words hadn't paralyzed him, he would have swayed where he stood. "Is that what you both thought of me? That I am some sort of psychopath? Only one would feel nothing but 'passing regret' for such a tragedy. And I wasn't 'friendly with' Patrick. He was one of only three real friends I ever had in my life."

"I didn't know that. From observations I—" She stopped, color creeping into her blanched cheeks. "I didn't have enough observations to build an opinion on. So I filled in the blanks, like you did, with what made the most sense to me. And what most supported my analysis was that you weren't that close."

"When could I have demonstrated that closeness? I never saw him again while you were with me, as we kept our relationship a secret. But I must have let you know what he meant to me?"

Censure surged back into her gaze. "You don't remember if you did? Whatever happened to your unfailing memory? Let me boost it, then. You never did. And when he helped me make the decision to end our liaison, I assumed he knew from experience that anyone was better off not being close to you."

"Why, thanks. To both of you. It's so heartening to know you two had such high opinions of me...."

He stopped. He'd heard those words before. Or something to their effect. Haidar had communicated a similar hurt to him and Roxanne, for condemning him based on circumstantial evidence, without giving him the benefit of the doubt.

He'd lived his life thinking he and Haidar were opposites. It was becoming clearer by the day that they were truly twins. But Haidar had resolved the mess of misunderstanding with both him and Roxanne. A similar resolution wasn't in the cards for *him*.

But... "None of that explains why you kept all this a secret after Patrick died."

She gave a cheerless huff. "I had to because his family sued to annul his will. With his overdose, they were claiming what you assumed—that he wasn't of sound mind when he drew up that will. Contrary to you, who can find out anything with a phone call, police investigations and medical reports were confidential, so they couldn't know that he'd been terminally ill—which would have only strengthened their case. We had to keep it a secret until we won."

This explained so much.

The only thing it didn't explain was the way she'd walked out on him. So she'd wanted to be there for a man she'd clearly cared about, even if other factors had been involved, like his billions. There'd been no need to end things with *him* so...dramatically.

She claimed she'd suffered the "degradation," the "inequality and the pointlessness" of their relationship. Even if that had once been true, everything had changed. His situation, hers. The gap between them had almost been obliterated.

He moved, and every step closer brought her beauty into sharper focus. If he'd thought she'd filled out two years ago, now she'd ripened. And he couldn't wait to sink his teeth and...everything else into all that fire and lushness.

He held her gaze as he came to stand before her. "You should have told me, both of you. You deprived me of the chance to do what I could, what I would have wanted to do with all my heart—even if you don't think I possess one. But it's too late. The only thing I can do now is see that Patrick's legacy remains intact, that his vision for his enterprises is maintained and evolved. Will you promise to leave our... problems out of this and let me help?"

Those incredible eyes flashed again as she looked up at him, making him dizzy with desire. Then she nodded.

He exhaled, nodding, too, then sat down beside her.

"Now we need to agree on something else." Her nod was wary this time. "You have the secret code to my libido." Haidar had always said he was a wolf. And damn it, he'd turned out to be right. His body had declared her his mate, had refused substitutes. "And I have yours. When it comes to passion and pleasure, to finding absolute satisfaction in another's body, we're each other's lot."

She exhaled in resigned agreement. He held her focus, demanding she translate her consent into action. And she did. With her eyes filled with turbulent thoughts and desires, she moved into his arms as he pulled her to him, met him halfway in a kiss that made no attempt to temper its ferociousness and carnality.

Melding with Jalal's hunger and the hot vise of ecstasy that was his lips, desire swelled, flooded all considerations and obliterated every moment since she'd been in his arms like that.

She spiraled down the abyss of need as his breath mingled with hers, his hands unraveled her, his lust stoked hers, opened her recesses to his possession.

Her clothes gave way to his expert urgency, her flesh burgeoned for his dominance, her mind hazing, short-circuiting...

"From the moment you put that supple hand in mine," he groaned against her lips, "everything about you became everything I craved. Whatever happened or will happen, nothing will change that. I must have you again, and you must have me. Say yes, Lujayn. Give yourself to me again. End our starvation."

His coaxing demand went off like a warning shot in her head. The overwhelming need to obey it felt like staring into an abyss. One she wouldn't be able to crawl out of this time. Horror tore her out of her surrender to the conflagration of their mutual need.

"No."

She wrenched herself away from his body, from the desire to merge with him. She struggled up, panting. The brooding hunger that always tampered with her sanity simmered in his wolf eyes, and her heart stampeded with her internal war not to just give in, straddle him, lose her mind all over him again.

She turned, felt the world teeter with every step away from his insupportable temptation, her hands shaking uncontrollably as she rearranged her clothes.

She forced herself to turn to him at the door. "Walking away from you was the best thing I've ever done for myself and I'm not falling into your...addiction again. This isn't a challenge so you'd try harder. This is final, Jalal. I'm just putting my life back together and I won't let you destroy everything all over again. If you have any honor, stay away from me. Please."

Four

Jalal stared at the screen of his laptop.

Something wasn't right....

Frowning, he reread the document he'd just finished writing.

He was wrong. *Something* wasn't wrong. *Everything* was.

It was as if someone bent on sabotage had written the page in front of him.

But that someone was him, unable to stop obsessing over a certain ebony-haired, silver-eyed spitfire and perpetually in a state of crippling, mind-scrambling frustration.

In other words, he should be wearing a sign saying "Keep away from all rational decisions."

He closed his laptop, backed his chair from it as if it were a bomb. He *had* been about to cause an explosive mistake.

Rising to his feet, unrest fueled his strides to the veranda.

Exhaling forcefully, his eyes roamed the tranquil vastness of the desert, Lujayn's voice echoing in his head.

Stay away from me. Please.

And he had stayed away. For four weeks now.

No wonder his mind was disintegrating.

But it hadn't been honor that had made him stay away.

It had been that "please."

Had she walked out of that suite without uttering it, he would have kept going after her until she succumbed.

But—*ya Ullah*. That *please*. And that desperate look that had accompanied it. It had been their combo of pleading and dread that had depowered him, defused his intentions.

It was as if she did believe that giving in to her desires in the past had almost destroyed her life, would certainly do so now.

He couldn't see how it had, how it could. And this "degradation" thing. She'd more or less accused him of doing to her what he'd thought Haidar had done to Roxanne, manipulating and taking advantage of her.

But *their* relationship hadn't started because of a bet, as he'd thought Haidar and Roxanne's had. Haidar hadn't had an as-valid reason to hide his relationship with Roxanne, the daughter of a prominent diplomat. And Roxanne had been living in Azmahar where Haidar had almost relocated. Jalal had had to travel halfway across the world every time he'd wanted to see Lujayn.

Another major difference had been that Roxanne had told Haidar she'd loved him. Haidar hadn't reciprocated the confession, but continued their intimacies, making it appear as if he'd been taking advantage of her. There'd been no mention of anything beyond passion between him and Lujayn.

They'd been young and preoccupied with establishing their careers and *that* had enforced the sporadic nature of their relationship. The secrecy, considering what his mother would have done to Lujayn and her whole family had she suspected a thing, had been a no-brainer. What could he have done differently?

If she'd had grievances about their arrangement, she should have spoken up. She'd never done so. So he could be excused if he didn't take her unrelated temper flares at the time as evidence of past discontent. Or if he didn't accept this alleged degradation he'd exposed her to. Or her other stated reasons for walking out.

Why wouldn't she just admit she'd wanted a clean break to be with Patrick? Why was she persisting on that twisted version of history? It didn't make sense that she'd play the wronged female. It didn't sit right with her character. And she claimed she wanted one thing from him. That he stay away. Yet blame was a lure not a repellent. If she wanted him to stay away, she shouldn't have accused him and gotten him even more engaged.

Yet, he couldn't deny the authenticity of that *please*.

That left only one answer. There was more to all this than she was letting on. And to make her confess it all, he had to do one thing. Alter reality. At least, her perception of it.

He now had the means to do that. Late last night, Fadi had provided him with a windfall of a discovery. The plan to use it to fulfill all his goals had come to him fully formed.

Now before he caused actual damage—to his business, not to mention his sanity—he had to put it in motion.

He produced his cell phone. In seconds, the familiar voice rumbled in his ear like faraway thunder. *"Somow'wak?"*

He gritted his teeth at hearing Fadi calling him Your Highness. It wasn't just a title to Fadi. He meant everything it stood for. Everything Jalal felt he had no claim to.

He exhaled. "I have new orders concerning Lujayn Morgan."

A long silence stretched after he'd specified his orders. He frowned. "Fadi? Are you still there?"

"Ella, Somow'wak."

"Did you hear everything I said?"

Another long silence. A rare show of opinion from the stoic Fadi. "Are you sure about this, *Somow'wak?* These... intentions might interfere with your campaign. They might even damage it."

Of course that would be what Fadi would worry about. And if he'd voiced his concerns, he must think the consequences of Jalal's tactics could be catastrophic.

If only. If they were, it would also mean they had worked.

"You have your orders, Fadi."

This time Fadi didn't take time to answer, the matter grave enough it made him go against his unquestioning fealty. "Have you given possible ramifications enough thought? If you allow me, I can come up with an alternative scenario that would right this wrong, but keep you away from any hint of further scandal."

His lips spread as he visualized the success of *this* scenario. With Lujayn back in his bed. In his life.

"This is what I *need* to do, Fadi. And yes, I'm sure. I've never been more sure about anything in my life."

Lujayn gaped up at the dark colossus looking solemnly down at her.

Rationally, she knew he wasn't bigger than Jalal. But while Jalal made her acutely aware of her femininity, made her feel soft and pliant in comparison to his chiseled power, this guy made her feel...dwarfed, vulnerable.

Other than that, Fadi Aal Munsoori shared much with Jalal, had that force-of-nature-embodiment thing going. And like one, he'd walked into her family home and made them all feel as if they were there at *his* discretion.

Knowing everything and everyone relevant in Azmahar from her family, and everything about Jalal from her own obsessive research, she'd recognized Fadi on sight. Everyone had. He'd still introduced himself, *after* he'd walked in. It hadn't been her imagination that he'd stressed his positions as Jalal's head of security and campaign director for her benefit. And that menace had spiked when he'd specified the latter.

He hadn't been with Jalal during her time. But one look into his eyes told her he knew of their defunct relationship. And disapproved something fierce. *And* was warning her off. Had they been alone, she would have told him where he could put his precious prince and his probable future throne.

But that was before Fadi had made his offer. Something so ridiculous that her mind shrieked to a halt.

"You—you can't possibly— Prince Jalal can't possibly mean…"

The faltering words jogged her back to the fact that her mother was right beside her. Her gaze dazedly moved to her, found her looking more flabbergasted than she felt.

"*Somow'woh* says and offers only what he means," Fadi said. "I brought this information to his knowledge only last night and eight hours later he insisted I conveyed to you his gracious offer. I can understand your reluctance…"

"I-it's not reluctance!" her mother blurted out, cutting him off, to his obvious displeasure. "It's shock. I—I never thought this would ever be brought to light again."

Fadi grimly nodded. "It would have been forever buried if Prince Jalal hadn't directed me to unearth the evidence. Still, your justifiable reservations may be averted if…"

"Is it true?"

The haunted voice dragged Lujayn's gaze to her uncle. It was the first time he'd talked since he'd welcomed Fadi in. She'd totally forgotten he was there.

Her uncle had once been almost as gorgeous as Jalal, if in a very different way. His striking good looks had long been dulled, like the magnificence of a gleaming sword would be by rust.

Now something trembled below the layers of resignation, of...defeat. It was as if his soul was being reignited.

Her uncle suddenly moved, almost stumbled as he grabbed hold of Fadi's arm with a shaking hand. "Is it? Prince Jalal is in possession of proof?"

Fadi gazed at her uncle's stooped form. "He is, *ya sayyed* Bassel. At his orders, I unearthed deeply buried but incontrovertible proof. He will see to it that your family members are reinstated into *gabayel el ashraaf*."

Lujayn knew Arabic perfectly, especially the Azmaharian colloquial dialect. She'd learned it, at her mother's insistence that language was power. So far, it had been one, in Jalal's hands. He'd used her comprehension of his verbal passion as another element of her enthrallment.

So she understood what Fadi had just said. But that couldn't be what he'd meant. When had the Al Ghamdis ever been considered among the "tribes of nobility" around here? They were from the class who emptied their ashtrays and fetched their slippers!

"Okay, time out!" Lujayn made the gesture, stepping between her mother and uncle, who vibrated with emotion, and that monolith who'd come at his master's command to spout impossibilities and spread more heartache. "What the hell are you all talking about?"

Fadi's eyes shot her a bolt of disapproval. Didn't approve of ladies swearing, eh? Tough luck. Right now, she'd do far more than swear at any further provocation.

Her uncle turned to her, that aching mixture of disbelief and hope fluctuating in suddenly expressive eyes, turning their turbid hazel into pools of agitated flame. "Our family is related to the royal family..."

"*Ex*-royal family," Fadi corrected.

The growled qualification zinged through her. Though her mind was spinning from her uncle's revelation, Fadi's vehemence still had her curious antennae standing on end. Though he was related to said family, too, those core royals seemed to have left no one with an ounce of goodwill toward them.

Which wasn't important now. She urged her uncle on with a gesture, and with her other hand she warned Fadi to just shut up and let the man explain before her head burst.

"The Al Ghamdis were once Aal Ghamdi," her uncle said, his face working as if he'd weep any moment now.

Lujayn stared at her uncle. That difference in *tashkeel*—the diacritic that changed pronunciation—transformed everything she'd ever known about her mother's *ailah*—family. It changed them from a family who took their name from a *gabeelah*—a tribe they served, to that *gabeelah* itself. It was one known for its warriors who "sheathe their swords in their enemies' chests" in the service of their kings, and second only to them.

"We are first maternal cousins to the Aal Refa'ee."

That was Jalal's mother, Sondoss's, maternal family, the other half of the royal lineage of Azmahar. The serpents named after a snake master. One quarter of Jalal's heritage.

Her gaze traveled from her uncle to her mother to Fadi. Then she burst out laughing.

At her mom's and uncle's gasps, and Fadi's deepening scowl, she spluttered, "C'mon, guys, you gotta admit...this *is* hilarious."

What could be more ridiculous than finding out that her family was related to Sondoss's? That her mother was related to her former enslaver?

That she was related to Jalal.

Another bubble of incredulity rose from her depths, burst on her lips in unrestrained cackles.

She heard her uncle's choked apologies. "I beg your pardon, Sheikh Fadi. We've never told our children, so this is a surprise to Lujayn."

"Surprise?" And she howled with laughter again, tears of hilarity beginning to pour down her cheeks, her sides starting to hurt. She leaned forward, pressing her hands to the ache clamping her midriff, barely catching enough breath to cough out words. "A surprise is when you pop up on my doorstep in New York, Uncle. This? Try identity-pulverizing cataclysm!"

Fadi pursed his lips, the timbre of his displeasure abrading. "The issue is in no way primarily your own, but your uncle's and mother's. They were the ones who lived through their family's disgrace and dispossession firsthand. And they were the ones who lived with the knowledge and injury. While you might think this rewrites *your* history and identity, it's them that this reinstatement will vindicate."

She shook her head as she straightened, his sternness suppressing the advancing hysteria. That and the sinking realization of what this meant, for the future, and for the past.

This explained so much about her mother's and uncle's characters. She'd thought they were like this as a result of their hard lives in an unforgiving land. But that thread of melancholy, of mourning, in both of them had been the result of injustice and oppression of an even worse sort than she'd imagined.

"So what happened?" She turned to her mom and uncle. "How did you get demoted from relatives to servants?"

"It's...it's a long story," her mother mumbled, looking anywhere but at her.

"Nothing can be long enough to explain this. I'm going nowhere until you tell me everything."

Before either her mom or uncle could react, Fadi raised a hand, silencing them. She was beginning to hate this guy.

"I will thank you all if you postpone your familial disclosures until I'm gone," Fadi said.

She turned on him. "You came to make your prince's offer. Now you did. So what are you waiting for?"

One dense, imperious eyebrow rose at her unveiled attempt to kick him out. Then with his voice lowering, deepening, becoming even more hair-raising for it, he only said, "An answer."

"You expect my uncle to give you an answer about something so…out of the blue, just like that?"

"What I expect him to do is talk for himself."

She'd never presumed to have a say in her family members' opportunities or decisions. But when one would involve her uncle with Jalal, she'd damn well have one. A resounding *no way!*

There was only one reason Jalal was making this offer. Her. And she'd be damned if she let him use her uncle as a bridge to reinvade her life.

She turned to her uncle, her eyes pleading with him not to commit to any answer now. His feverish eyes didn't even see her. His gaze was turned inwardly, flitting from the ordeals of his lost youth to the dream of a dignified future.

Then he turned his gaze to Fadi, his focus barely on him, either. "Please, convey my deepest gratitude to Prince Jalal for his generous offer and this unrepeatable opportunity. It would be my honor and privilege to join his campaign for the throne."

A groan bled from her as she turned her eyes to Fadi. And again his expression distracted her from her distress. Her uncle's delighted acceptance had been the last thing he'd wanted.

Sure enough, after a terse nod of acknowledgment, and a moment's thought, he said, "I was honor- and duty-bound to convey *Somow'woh*'s offer as is. But I will take the liberty of adjusting that offer, to ease the steps of your reinstatement, and to make sure no...ill-considered—" his eyes left her in no doubt this was meant for her, too "—decisions on *Somow'woh*'s part upset the delicate balance of his campaign."

If his adjustment offered her uncle anything *else* that didn't involve Jalal, she might forgive the guy. She might even kiss him for averting this catastrophe-in-the-making.

Her uncle nodded, all the animation that had been creeping into his stance and demeanor draining. "Yes, yes, of course, the first priority is to safeguard Prince Jalal's efforts."

God! What was it about Jalal that made people ready to throw themselves under a train to please him?

She knew exactly what it was. Hated him more daily for it.

"I'm offering a place on *my* team," Fadi said. "You'd still be ultimately part of *Somow'woh*'s team, as valuable to his campaign, but it would alleviate any friction that would arise from his passing over many high-ranking hopefuls for the position in your favor."

That went right over her uncle's head, lodged right into hers. Fadi thought Jalal's decision to associate with her family would be a terrible faux pas. He was trying to protect him from taking an "ill-considered" step. Not that her uncle was unqualified for the position. If anything, her uncle, who'd obtained Ph.D.s in political sciences and local and Sharia law and master's degrees in accounting and business management, was qualified to *run* the campaign. But Fadi only considered the possible damages of unfavorable public perception in a society that sequestered people into rigid classes. That "reinstatement," and the reason behind it, if it were suspected, could harm the popularity of his master and candidate. In short, Fadi was being a political weasel and privileged snob.

She still wanted to kiss him for it. His reluctance to let them contaminate his precious prince's environment gave her a way out of this new corner Jalal was backing her into.

Her uncle finally nodded. "Whatever you see fit, Sheikh Fadi. I'll be happy to offer my skills and services to Prince Jalal in whatever position I'm best suited for."

Fadi nodded, looking relieved. "I will be in touch with you shortly with further information."

He bowed respectfully to her mother, gave Lujayn a far less steep bow, clearly as deep as he thought her worthy of, then turned on his heels.

She followed him, her words for his ears only. "You think Jalal would agree to this 'adjustment' of yours?"

He slanted her a glance that seemed to measure her. No doubt wondering how his princely master had suffered being around such an unladylike creature. And was still coming back for more. "It's nothing you should concern yourself with."

"That's where you're wrong, pal. We're both on the same page on this. You don't want him near us, and I would rather he lived on another planet. So do whatever you can to 're-instate' my uncle and make use of his considerable abilities, but let's keep it all as far away from Jalal as possible. For everyone's sake."

His eyes grew incredulous. She'd managed to stun him. He probably couldn't understand how a woman wouldn't want his prince's attention. But it seemed her fervor got to him. He looked like he believed her.

For now, anyway, his gaze seemed to say. He gave her another of those military nods and strode ahead, his footsteps on the stone floor of her uncle's modest dwelling those of the soldier he'd been, and still clearly was.

He was at the door when a commotion erupted from the inner part of the house.

Lujayn froze as squeals and calls preceded running feet that came closer, intermingling with more shrieks and giggles.

Fadi stopped. Lujayn's heart almost burst.

He looked into the distance, listening, then he lowered his gaze to her. Her nerves snapped one by one in a countdown to shoving him out the door.

A split second before she gave in to the urge, he walked out.

She almost slammed the door behind him, then sagged against it, forehead first, shaking all over, scolding herself for the panic attack that had almost engulfed her reason.

Why had she been so terrified? Nothing would have happened even if he'd seen them. In a worst-case scenario if he suspected something, he would have kept it under wraps so he wouldn't sabotage his own purpose.

Not that she could grow complacent. Look what had happened when she had. Jalal had sent her a missile that was about to explode her family to smithereens.

But then...maybe the only way to dislodge said missile was with revelations of her own. She'd bet those would have Jalal taking his offer and his pursuit and running the other way.

No. Even if this was an assured outcome, she wouldn't want him to know. Not for any reason.

Exhaling heavily, she walked back to where her mom and uncle were deep in overwrought emotions, deciding she had two purposes. To shield her family from Jalal's manipulations. And to make sure that he left her and her secrets intact.

Five

Fadi's adjustments had failed in record time.

He'd called within an hour to say that Jalal's original offer wouldn't be "adjusted." Lujayn had the feeling that Jalal hadn't even let him state his suggestion.

Figured. Jalal made his decisions then made everyone bow to them. She would have wished this one would bite him in the ass, as Fadi feared it would, if it didn't involve collateral damage to more relevant parts of her family, namely their hearts and souls.

But she had a feeling Fadi had other concerns. She'd been about to probe when her uncle had swooped down on her and snatched away the phone.

She now stood watching him as he listened to Fadi. It was amazing. It was as if the man she'd known had only been animated enough to simulate the appearance of life. Now he was coming into existence for the first time under her eyes.

If she didn't hear this "long story" soon she'd bust something vital. But both her mom and uncle had so far avoided telling her anything more.

Her uncle ended the call and turned to her with a blinding and blinded expression, his voice ragged with elation. "Prince Jalal isn't only adamant about my becoming a personal adviser, but also a member of his future cabinet."

Sarcasm rose through ratcheting dismay, twisting her lips. "He's so sure he'll become king, isn't he?"

Her uncle, oblivious to her mood, gave an earnest nod. "If Azmaharians know what's best for them, they'll choose him."

"And we all know people usually steer away from what's best for them." Which to her meant they *would* go for Jalal.

Again missing her derision, her uncle said, "I believe the people will make the right choice in this instance. Prince Jalal gathers both Azmaharian and Zohaydan royal blood and the personal traits of a true leader. In short, everything Azmahar needs."

"The same could be said about his twin."

Her uncle shook his head emphatically. "Prince Haidar has stepped down from the race."

"And his new wife convinced him to step right back up."

Too engrossed in his need to prove his point, he didn't ask how she knew that. "But Prince Haidar didn't exactly rescind his decision, just qualified it by saying he'd take the throne if the majority still chose him."

"If this is a real decision and not a political maneuver, it proves he is not power hungry, yet capable of taking its mantle if it falls to him. Add that to his not spouting promises of reform if he becomes king, but being out there already deeply involved in seeing it through, and you might just have the combo that no other candidate can beat."

Her uncle's eyes took on the shrewdness of the diversely knowledgeable man he was. It never failed to stun her that, until he'd joined her in sorting through Patrick's legacy, he'd never maintained one job worthy of his skills and experience.

"Prince Haidar's efforts would have been a definite advantage," he said, "if the two other candidates weren't as involved in reforms as vital as the ones he's implementing. In fact, it's said they're all involved in the first political campaign of its kind in history."

"Sure they are. They're the first trio who're campaigning for a throne, not a presidency. I wonder why the people of Azmahar want the monarchy system to continue."

"Because before our last king, it worked too well to want to change it. Now if we pick the next, preferably Jalal in my opinion, as a king he will do far more than he'll be able to do as a president. Also you can't change the basic constitution of a people or their culture without paying a huge price, as evidenced by how badly the democracies in the region are faring. But that's not why this throne campaign is unique. It's the candidates' approach that makes it so. Instead of trying to convince people they're the better candidate by tearing the others apart, and spending untold millions to sway opinions, they're all out there showing their desire and ability to work for Azmahar's best by solving its problems now, not later. But what's really remarkable is that they're doing it together if need be. It's how they cornered the oil-spill catastrophe."

That she hadn't known. And now that she did, it stunned her.

She only knew Haidar was Jalal's twin and the male edition of their supernaturally beautiful yet soul-free mother. Evidently he wasn't as devoid of humanity as she was, since all evidence showed that he was head over heels in love with his new wife. From the grandly romantic proposal to the equally heart-fluttering wedding vows to his adoring expression in every photo with her, he actually seemed to be the reverse. She knew even less about the third candidate, Rashid, who from all reports was an unknowable quantity.

But those two men weren't only doing what all power seekers never did, putting their promises into practice first, they were curbing their egos and lust for power to do what should be done even if it meant putting their hands in their rivals'. What flabbergasted her was that Jalal was doing the same. She hadn't known he was capable of reining in either ego or lust.

"I think you've just proved that both Haidar and Rashid are as worthy, not to mention as equipped, to be king. So where do you get your conviction that Jalal is the best choice?"

"My conviction isn't built on wishful thinking as you're implying," her uncle said. "While Sheikh Rashid is a pure-blooded Azmaharian, a decorated war hero and a formidable power in the world of business, he doesn't have any ties to Zohayd. And since it's a fact Azmahar needs Zohayd to survive, let alone prosper, that's his fatal deficit. He doesn't have a chance against someone who has all of his assets plus Zohayd's king for a brother."

"That still puts Jalal in an equal position with Haidar. So unless he quits the race, Jalal's chances are only fifty-fifty."

Her uncle shook his head again. "You're assuming Prince Haidar is equal in assets, but that is far from true. He too has a fatal flaw. He bears his mother's face. You might think it shouldn't be a factor against him, but it definitely is. You of all people know how abhorred she was here."

Yeah, *that* she knew. And she'd experienced some choice abhorrent behavior firsthand.

Her uncle went on. "But Jalal doesn't suffer from this stigma. To us he's more of a Zohaydan, when Zohayd has nothing but respect, even love, for most of our population.

And he bears the likeness of his father, our biggest ally for the past decades and the one thing that had stopped Azmaharians from overthrowing our ex-king long before now. Prince Jalal is also very much like his oldest brother, King Amjad, and he'd be the one most likely to convince him to resume the vital alliance he'd severed because of the foolish transgressions of our former royalty. Added to that strong Zohaydan ingredient and influence, he has the necessary Azmaharian royal blood, making him the best of all worlds."

She gaped at her uncle, her head spinning at that unbeatable sales pitch. "Seems he did exactly the right thing in picking you for his campaign. You'd sell him to his worst enemies."

"I always believed he was the best of the candidates, always admired how he never forgot the other part of his heritage, how he'd started and supported so many worthy causes here in Azmahar long before there was any possibility of his becoming king. But now, after what he's done..." His voice thickened as he drove his hands through his silvered mane, his every facial muscle trembling with emotion. "*Ya Ullah, ya* Lujayn, you can never grasp the...the *enormity* of what he's done, the weight he's removed from my chest, what's been suffocating me all my life. If I respected and admired him before, now that I owe him my and my family's honor, now that he's renewed my will to live, I am forever in his debt."

And *that* must be exactly what that gargantuan rat was after. What better way to insinuate himself into her life than to inspire something of this intensity and permanence in her closest kin?

But she didn't believe that he'd found out about her family's secret only yesterday. As a master of manipulation, he knew how to pull people's strings as instinctively as he breathed. He must have long uncovered the secret, must have been keeping it to use when it most suited his purposes. And so he had. She'd bet her uncle, and probably her mom, too, would walk off a cliff for him now.

He'd gotten what he wanted. Just like he always did. She'd pushed him away, so he'd swerved, reentered her life from a gaping hole she hadn't known existed. She had no doubt he'd entrench himself there for as long as he saw fit.

All she could do in the meantime was thwart his intentions and steer away from him until she could flee.

Then nothing would ever bring her back.

Meanwhile, she wouldn't voice her blasphemous opinions of her uncle's newfound deity. While she believed this would end in heartache, as everything involving Jalal always did, she didn't have the guts to extinguish her uncle's rekindled appetite for life. She'd keep her apprehensions to herself. For now.

This was something her uncle and mom needed, something they hadn't let themselves dare to dream of. If they were to wake up one day to an ugly reality, she wouldn't be the one to shock them awake now. She could only speculate what Jalal's endgame would be…

"…tonight."

Her uncle's last words crashed into her train of thoughts, piling them up. He—he couldn't have said…

But, looking about to sprout wings and take flight, her uncle said it again. "You heard right. Prince Jalal has invited us all to his residence tonight to celebrate my addition to his team."

"Marhabah ya bent el amm."

The voice that had echoed in her being for most of her adult life reverberated in the still, warm night. As smooth as the steel of a burnished sword, as calm as the desert. And it had said…

Welcome, cousin.

Fury surged like a geyser. She swept around with the momentum of her frustration at being cornered again, with the blade of her family's fragile expectations held to her throat.

And she snarled, "Oh, no you don't."

In answer to her vehemence, a chuckle rumbled as if out of nowhere and everywhere, echoing on the deceptively placid breeze.

Her hairs stood on end as Jalal seemed to materialize out of the darkness, forged of its magic, imbued with its menace and magnificence. His face emerged from the velvet gloom in a masterpiece of hewn grandeur, stamped with an ancient birthright as merciless as the desert that had spawned him. His eyes reflected the flames of the brass torches flanking the cobblestone path she'd just traveled as if to the hangman's noose.

"Don't what, Lujayn? Call you what you really are to me?"

"I'm *nothing* to you."

"You were always many things to me." A smile twinkled gold in the cognac depth of his eyes, played seduction on the sculpted lips that had taught her what passion was, reminding her of every second when he'd plumbed her body and soul for ecstasies that had branded her for life. "And we discovered you're more to me than we ever thought."

"Finding out that we share a couple of stray blood cells and gene strands makes us as related as humans and apes."

"Hmm, I assume I'm the one on the lower rung of the evolutionary scale here." Merry demons licked their lips at her as he obliterated the distance between them.

"Don't." She didn't know what her "Don't" meant now. Or she did. Don't mess with her. With her will. Her need to stay angry.

"Don't what? Come closer? Like this?" She gasped as

his arm slid around her waist, and again as her body surged into his without her volition. "But you're right about my evolutionary status. Where you're concerned, at least. You devolve me to my essential beast. One who only wants to possess, plunder—" he gave a slight tug, had her melting against him from breast to thigh "—pleasure."

His feel demolished her balance and his scent deluged her lungs as her gaze flitted around frantically.

The only signs of life were the sounds of conversation and laughter emanating from the two-level sprawling villa at his back. She'd seen guards at the gates when she'd been driven into the estate's extensive grounds, but none since arriving. Maybe they were so ingeniously hidden that she couldn't even feel them.

No. He wouldn't be doing this if any eyes were around to witness it. Her driver had driven away in haste, probably following Jalal's orders for everyone to disappear once she arrived.

He'd set up his trap and lay in wait, like a panther on the hunt, now playing with her like one would torment its prey.

"Take your hands off me, or your guests will know exactly what happened to you from the way you'll limp back inside."

His grin widened, his large, talented hands securing her without force, spreading over her back in gentle caresses.

"So you'll knee me this time?" His fingers accessed the pleasure points that hadn't been activated before or since him. "I'd risk way worse to feel you like this again."

She glared up at him as every word, every gust of breath, every rub against that virility, hit her bloodstream like an aphrodisiac, spasming her core, swelling her breasts.

"And then, it's not like you don't want to feel me every bit as much." To prove his point, he took his hands away. Her traitorous body remained pressed against his.

No matter what her mind was screaming, her every inch was begging for his feel, for everything. And it made her furious. Far more with herself than with him. For he was only making her admit and succumb to her weakness. She was the one responsible for it.

Yet when she spoke, she seethed, "So you had your fun forcing me to come here and to endure your pawing without being able to retaliate. Can I go now?"

The teasing in his eyes intensified. And that pout. She didn't know how she kept from grabbing him by that mane that brushed his collar and yanking down his head so she could bite him. "First, you're here of your own free will, as usual, as my esteemed guest and newfound if admittedly distant cousin. Second, you can retaliate in any way you choose. I'll wear the marks of your passion with pride. Third…" He gathered her closer again when she didn't step away, let her feel his daunting hardness throb into her belly. "I haven't had my fun yet, not by a long shot."

She barely held back from grinding into him. "You should have one of your concubines take care of this…big problem."

Another chuckle revved in his expansive chest. "It's you who made it that big when you didn't show up with your family."

Her uncle and mom had been puzzled and dismayed when she'd excused herself from going. But she hadn't been able to come up with a good enough reason why. She'd thought even the *real* reason wouldn't have been good enough for them.

So she'd pretended to cooperate but when the escort team Jalal sent had arrived, she'd said she'd gotten distracted, wasn't ready and they'd had to go without her.

She'd thought she was saved, for that night, at least. Then the call had come. Her mom was distraught, thought her absence had offended Jalal. Why else would he so closely inquire why she hadn't come? Knowing she had to capitulate,

Lujayn had promised to be ready this time when he sent a limo for her. And here she was.

"Excuse me for not prioritizing your whims," she gritted out, careful not to breathe deep or be flooded with his intoxication. "It wasn't high on my list to drop everything to 'celebrate' my uncle being roped into your servitude for life."

His smile was all forbearance. "Had you been here the past three hours, you would have heard your uncle and mother expressing how happy they are to finally claim our relation and how excited about our forthcoming collaboration."

"That's what you're calling this artificial situation you've manufactured?"

"I didn't create this gem of a 'situation.' I'm only making the best use of it after uncovering it."

"Uncovering any tie between us, no matter how insignificant and distant isn't a gem, it's a…a…*semm*."

And there it was. That pout, again. "Poison? Aren't you getting this backward? It was the dishonor your family unjustly suffered that's been poisoning their lives. And it is that grudge you're nursing against me that's been poisoning yours."

"And you're the benefactor who wants to administer the antidote out of the goodness of your nonexistent heart? My family is free to be eternally grateful for your crumbs of benevolence, and I'm free to prefer my poison, which is at least gulped down with no strings attached."

"Take a deep breath, Lujayn." He smiled down at her as he bent, had his lips tracing her every feature with feather-soft torment from her forehead to her lips to her pulse point. "Go to your happy place for a moment."

Electricity forked from his lips to shriek down her nerves. The blow of arousal finally had her lurching out of his loose hold, had her glaring her resentment up at him. "Can't do that. You've left me none."

Lightness deserted his eyes and stance by degrees, until he stood brooding down at her. "I won't even touch that exaggeration, Lujayn. But whatever our problems in the past were, this is me taking the steps to eliminate them."

"What—what do you mean by that?"

He shoved his hands into his pockets, his eyes growing serious. "In our last confrontation, you mentioned the 'unbridgeable gap' between us. It made me realize that while I never thought there was any real gap between us, you did. This gap, whether real or imagined, is no more."

She gaped at him. Did he mean...?

Then she snorted. "If you mean it was all in my mind, please! Anyone with half a brain lobe would say the gap was actually a gulf. And that it will always remain unbridgeable."

"Not true. While it never meant a thing to me, that socalled gulf that existed between us on a social level, with the new discoveries of your true lineage, it no longer exists."

"Wow, really? You're saying some second-grade royal blood equals being from a line of purebred kings and queens and the son of one of the most venerated kings in the region, the *world*?"

His shoulders rose and fell in a dismissing move. "I also come from the line of an ousted king and I am also the son of the most infamous ex-queen in that same world. You fare better in any comparison coming from a lineage of hardworking, honest people on one side and another unanimously known for valor and honor."

"You mean that side of my lineage that was stripped of honor and reduced to serving their so-called relatives?"

He exhaled. "That's in the past now. Your line will be

restored. When everything's out in the open, they will be looked upon with greater sympathy and respect than ever."

"And this will happen only according to your whim."

"According to the proof Fadi uncovered."

"I meant you used this proof because you saw fit to. It could have remained buried for all you cared if it wasn't to your advantage to make it public now."

"The timing is fortunate, I can't deny that." That smile, fueling his irresistibility, was back radiating from his eyes, filling his lips. "Are you suggesting I shouldn't have brought it out in the open because I stand to gain from doing so?"

He had an answer for everything, could twist anything to make himself come out looking right, logical, honorable even.

"You're unbelievable, you know that? You're in the middle of campaigning for a throne, and you waste time going to all this effort to get into my pants? You're taking asserting your will and winning this imaginary challenge too far, aren't you?"

He shrugged again, that movement laden with lazy poise. "Apart from the fact that I *would* do anything to 'get into your pants,' I would have done this for anyone."

"Yeah, sure, you go around investigating people to see what wrongs were dealt them in generations past so you can right them."

His nod was infuriatingly calm. "I do what I can when it comes to my notice, yes."

"Well, you might as well take back anything you've done for my uncle and family now and not later."

His eyebrows rose in feigned questioning. "You think I'll do that after I have my way with you…again?"

"After you make sure you're not having it, ever again."

His tut-tut was indulgence itself as he gently pulled her against his will-sapping gorgeousness. "Is this a way to talk to a newly discovered distant relation?" Her neck arched for him as he nuzzled it, her body plastering to his as his hands dipped below her blouse to spread against the burning skin of her back. He suddenly groaned against her flesh, which vibrated with need. "Sooner or later, you won't be able to resist me, won't find a reason to. I've already given up trying. This…affinity we share is unstoppable, *ya jameelati'l feddeyah.*"

That sick jolt of longing lurched inside her heart. He'd always been too generous with his verbal passion. Hearing him call her his silver beauty brought a wave of moisture to her eyes that intensified the illumination of the full moon. She turned her face away from its glare and his lips trailed a path of fiery temptation down her cheek, her jaw.

A shudder shook her when he reached her ear, his croon pouring into her brain, liquefying it. "We're going to be together in many ways from now on. Through my involvement in Patrick's legacy, through your family's involvement with me. This—" he crushed her against him, giving her aching breasts the contact they needed with his hardness and heat "—is inescapable."

Wariness, logic, hostility were disintegrating, everything else inside her yearning to expose his flesh, to sink her teeth in his power. Everything else was receding, leaving only the need to drag him on top of her on the lush lawn, open her body to his invasion, writhe beneath him as he thrust her to ecstasy.…

"You might as well stop fighting the inevitable now."

Suddenly, she snapped out of spiraling down the abyss of lust and pushed against him, arms feeling like a rag doll's.

He let her push him, showing her he'd only been holding her with her own desire.

Her palm spread against the vital wall of his chest. "So

what's this inevitable thing? Another affair? While I'm here?"

He took the hand splayed against his chest to his lips, singed its clammy flesh with nibbles. His eyes blazed with the passion that had once made her feel craved to her last cell. "It's another affair for as long as we both want. If you leave, I'll forever come to you, like I always used to."

"And this social-status upgrade and cleansing you gave my family, and therefore me, is so we wouldn't sully your image if our liaison is discovered?"

"Of course not."

In spite of herself, his earnestness thrilled her. Could it be he didn't care about her status, now or before…?

He aborted all foolish conjectures. "You have my word our relationship would not be discovered. My efforts were for your family, and for you, so you would no longer feel any inequality in our situation."

So. No matter who or what she was or became, he'd always think her only good enough for an illicit liaison.

He'd polished her family name, not because he cared, or even intended to ever let her name be linked to his, but to placate her. To give her a false sense of worth. To make her feel good enough about herself so she'd walk back into his bed without the insecurities that had plagued her in the past.

Something she'd sworn she'd never feel again, corrosive oppression and shame, spread to eat through her vitals.

No. She wouldn't let him do this to her again. She'd promised Patrick she wouldn't.

She tugged her hand away from his. His arms fell to his sides, didn't try to pull her back.

He still attempted to with words. "Don't push me away, Lujayn. The past is done, and I don't want to bring it up again. We're here and now, and everything is different."

She smoothed trembling fingers over her hair and clothes

that the tiny taste of his passion had messed, stepped farther away.

"That's where you're wrong, *Somow'wak*. Nothing's changed. Or if it has, it's for the worse. Sex without emotions or the most basic commonalities would only end up in something catastrophic this time."

He balled his fists as if against the urge to grab her. "Who says there aren't emotions? And we do have commonalities. Starting with how much we crave the hell out of each other and ending with our common interest in upholding Patrick's legacy and seeing to your family's reinstatement."

"And we can each take care of all cravings and interests without the other's participation. It's even advisable, just ask your campaign manager. So why don't you go pour all that drive into becoming king? You have my uncle chomping at the bit to help you sit on that throne. Contrary to me, he believes in you. Me, I'm here only until Aunt is well enough and she's almost..."

He frowned. "Your aunt?"

"Your investigations didn't bother to uncover more about me and my family than what would have us in your debt, right?"

"What's wrong with Suffeyah?"

She blinked, surprised by his apparent concern, that he not only knew but remembered her aunt's name.

He made an impatient, prompting gesture. Warily, hesitantly, she told him, watching him closely, trying to analyze the solemn intensity in his eyes as he listened.

"...the specialists agreed she only needed a simple mastectomy, which she had two weeks ago. We're now waiting to see if they'll forgo chemo and radiation and have her just on antihormonal treatments. Test results so far support that, so we're looking at a few weeks at most before everything is concluded. By that time you'll probably be the new king of a country where I never intend to return for the rest of my life."

He said nothing after she stopped talking, just brooded down at her. Might as well take advantage of the temporary interruption in his temptation campaign.

She moved away on unsteady legs, adding over her shoulder, "I'll attend what's left of your 'celebration,' for my family's sake. If you don't intend to reconsider your intentions about that 'reinstatement' and Uncle's position now that you know mine, you'll be civil and impersonal with me for the rest of this infernal night. Then I'll leave and you won't come after me again."

He folded his arms over his chest. "I thought you had a reason for pushing me away. Now I'm certain you do. There's something more behind your refusal to be with me again. And I *will* keep coming after you until you tell me what it is. I will…"

"Somow'wak."

The quietness of the word sundered the still night. *Fadi.*

As much as she hated thinking that Fadi had witnessed Jalal's near-seduction of her, his appearance had shattered Jalal's focus. Cursing something under his breath, Jalal turned to him.

Using his distraction, she strode to the marble steps that glowed with the moon's silvery light. They led to a vast veranda where open French doors emanated golden light, mellow music and relaxed merriment.

As she crossed the portico, she looked back at Jalal and Fadi. The two juggernauts were watching her, each with a different brand of intensity that invaded her taxed nervous system with a fresh bout of tremors.

Suppressing her agitation, and taking one last bracing breath, she stepped over the threshold of a superbly decorated sitting room drenched in soothing illumination and spread in warm earth colors, feeling she was stepping onto a stage.

She forced a smile as everyone rose to welcome her, and started playing the part that Jalal had cornered her into again.

Jalal watched Lujayn disappear inside the villa, heard voices rise in welcome. Gritting his teeth, he turned his eyes to Fadi.

Before he could pour some of his frustration and displeasure over him, Fadi preempted him.

"I might regret telling you this, but you need to know."

This was about Lujayn. He just knew it was.

If it was something that might drive her further away, he didn't want to know it.

But Fadi was already talking. Already telling him. And it was too late. Too incomprehensible. Too...impossible.

Long after Fadi had delivered his report, Jalal stared at him, nothing left in his mind, in the world, but five of the words Fadi had said.

"Lujayn Morgan has a child."

Six

Jalal walked into the room he'd left half an hour ago to intercept Lujayn. He'd thought he'd walk back in alongside her, with at least a preliminary agreement to resume their intimacies.

He returned alone now to find her looking relaxed and at home with her family, the center of his guests' attention. At his entry, as the others showed their pleasure and enthusiasm to have him back, she regarded him as if she'd never seen him before.

He looked at her in the same way. He did feel as if he was looking at a stranger. A breathtaking stranger with crystal cool eyes who lived inside the body of the woman who'd ruled his thoughts and desires for too long. The woman he'd thought he'd known to the last reaches of intimacy but whom he was finding out that he'd never known. The woman who hadn't even hinted at the life-changing fact of being a mother.

This had to be the answer he'd been looking for—why she'd been adamant about pushing him away. Because her life and priorities had changed, *she* had changed, when she'd had a child.

The knowledge rocked through him all over again as he watched everyone returning to their seats, all looking at him expectantly, waiting for him to direct what remained of this gathering.

He looked from Bassel and Faizah, Lujayn's uncle and his wife—people he'd met for the first time—to Badreyah, her mother. He'd decided getting close to Lujayn would be through those who constituted the major part of her life. He'd been determined that, even if he found nothing about them to like, he'd put up with them. He would have endured anything to have her again.

To his surprise and delight, they'd stopped being a means to an end within minutes of meeting them. Everything about and from them had felt genuine, heartfelt. It had restored his jaded senses to be shown esteem without fawning, gratitude without groveling. They were good-natured, highly educated, well-spoken. They were dignified, refined. The hours he'd spent in their company had been a pleasure he'd looked forward to repeating on a regular basis.

Until Fadi had detonated that revelation.

Not that he would renege on restoring their name and honor. Or the position he'd offered her uncle, for which he was more than qualified. But any further personal interaction depended on what he found out about Lujayn's child.

He hadn't even asked Fadi if her child was a girl or a boy.

He hadn't asked how old it was. *Whose* it was.

Even if Fadi knew the answers, Jalal hadn't wanted to know them. Not from him. Lujayn had to be the one who answered his questions.

And he wanted those answers now. *Now.*

His head and heart felt they'd rupture with the frustration of not knowing. But no matter how terrible the need to know was, he had to proclaim his commitment to the Al Ghamdis first.

Forcing a smile on his spastic lips, he looked over to Labeeb, his *waseef,* his gentleman's gentleman. Taking his role as seriously as Fadi did his, Labeeb was already enacting the agreed-on sequence, distributing coffee, the stage where Jalal would deliver the evening's summation and declare his intentions.

After everyone had filled crystal cups in hand, and the aroma of freshly brewed Arabian coffee and cardamom filled the air, Jalal moved to face the gathering. Apart from the quartet of Lujayn's family, there were fourteen other people: four men and three women—the supporting players in his campaign—plus their spouses.

He enveloped them in a glance, avoiding looking at Lujayn. If he looked at her now, he'd forget everything.

He raised his glass in a toast, waited until everyone did the same, then said, "Thank you for coming to my humble rented abode, and for making this evening far better than anything I could have anticipated. You know what we're celebrating tonight, but let me make it official." He turned his eyes to Bassel, found him flushed, eyes sparkling with barely repressed emotion. "It's my privilege and pleasure to welcome Sheikh Bassel Aal Ghamdi to our campaign. Sheikh Bassel has honored me by accepting the position of my personal liaison within our campaign. He'll be coordinating your efforts and reporting directly to me or to Fadi."

Murmurs of approval buzzed throughout the room as everyone turned to Bassel shaking his hand, patting him on the back and congratulating his family. Bassel and his wife and sister looked too moved to articulate, could only answer with tearful smiles. Jalal ventured a look at Lujayn, found her accepting collateral congratulations. He bet it was only he who could see that her smile was brittle and her eyes were cold with fury. He walked closer, until she raised grudging eyes to his.

His heart thudded at their inevitable effect as he insisted her family remained seated as he shook their hands again, sealing the deal. "And though Sheikh Bassel was reluctant to flaunt the scope of his expertise, no matter how much I prodded him throughout dinner, trust me when I say we've added an invaluable asset to our team today. I'm only thankful for the circumstances that brought his abilities to my attention."

Ire sparked in Lujayn's eyes. She clearly didn't appreciate those "circumstances."

He swerved his focus to the others. "Now with Sheikh Bassel's contribution, if I don't get that throne, you'll know you've just bet on the wrong horse."

Laughter rose. He had to conclude this before the general good mood snapped the tenuous control he had over his increasingly agitated one. He hated to bring up the touchy subject, but he needed his aides to be absolutely clear about it.

His gesture indicated he had more to say. Instant silence fell as every eye turned to him again.

"But I didn't only gain an instrumental supporter and adviser today but a valued relative, one who's totally on my side. *Ullah beye'ruff*—God knows I don't have many of those right now, and I need all I can get." Chuckles were leashed this time, realizing this was no laughing matter even if he made light of it. His lips twisted in concession. "Which brings me to the most important issue at hand. You all now know how Sheikh Bassel and his family have been unjustly stripped of their name and status...."

"Actually, we don't *all* know. *I* sure don't."

Lujayn. Leave it to her to break her silence only to say

something contentious. From the gasps that issued from her family, it appeared her forwardness had distressed them. They evidently thought she might offend him. If only they knew how hard she'd tried and failed to do so.

He turned his eyes to her, turmoil seething with challenge. "You mean no one shared the details with you?"

Her eyes raised his annoyance. "Apart from 'long story'? No."

"And this is not the time to recount it." Bassel put a hand on his niece's, a gesture imploring her to leave it.

She didn't. "When is a better time than now, with all relevant parties present, so this new beginning would be built on a solid ground of full disclosure?"

At this moment he wanted to roar for everyone to get out, leave him alone with her so he'd have that full disclosure. Whether it led to a new beginning or a final end, he had no idea.

"Prince Jalal, please excuse Lujayn," Badreyah said, a tremor traversing her soft voice. "This has been quite a shock for her, to find out we've hidden something of this nature all her life…."

He raised his hand, unable to bear having this gentle lady apologize to him when he would never be able to offer enough amends. "No need to explain, *ya* Sheikha Badreyah."

The woman lurched, those near-tears filling her eyes again.

Jalel could see that she'd accepted her brother would have his sheikh title once again, but hadn't expected to hear the title applied to herself. But that was what she was, and that was what he'd always call her.

"Wow, does this make *me* a sheikha, too?"

Lujayn again. Lujayn *always*.

"If it does, I'm giving you all license to *never* call me that."

No longer pretending that anyone else had his attention, he approached her. "So what will you answer to?"

Those silver eyes narrowed, their ebony lashes that he'd once told her were thick enough for him to lie down on intensifying the light they seemed to emit. "My name has been known to work just fine."

He almost touched her legs as she sat on the couch, could see himself going down between them, dragging them over his shoulders, bearing down on her to crush those rose-petal lips and swallow those contentious words. He could feel everyone's eyes clinging to them, no doubt sensing the field of tension they generated between them now that they were no longer harnessing their emotions.

"So...*Lujayn*." He stressed each syllable as if tasting it, felt a rev of satisfaction as her pupils fluctuated, that sure sign of response. "In the name of full disclosure, let me tell you the whole story. This mess happened in the time of your grandfather. And my grandmother."

Her eyes widened. "You mean your grandmother was involved?"

"Involved?" He gave a bitter huff. "You could say that. She was the one who accused your grandfather of a very potent mixture of theft and treason. But never fear. She was merciful in her righteousness and when he was convicted, she asked for a compassionate demotion in lieu of banishment or imprisonment. When your uncle was fifteen and your mother was twelve, their family lost a tiny bit of their name, becoming Al—instead of Aal—Ghamdi, and stumbled from a high branch of nobility into dishonor. Your grandfather had been my grandfather's *kabeer'l yaweraan*—head of the royal guard, but after his conviction, neither he nor any of his family could find a position in the kingdom. Again, only my grandmother was humane enough to employ them, as her servants. Also as per her clemency, your grandfather's transgression along with his family history was to never be talked of again. At the threat of some very creative penalties. It was, of course, so your family wouldn't relive the disgrace, being reminded of what they lost. Needless to say, no one, starting with your family, brought it up again ever since, and the whole debacle has been suppressed or forgotten."

Silence rang in the wake of his searingly blunt account.

Lujayn gaped up at him, the shock reverberating inside her buffeting him in waves of furious incredulity.

Suddenly, she heaved up, almost sliding against his body on her way to her feet, sending awareness roaring inside him in spite of everything.

She glared at him, antipathy crackling silver bolts in her eyes. "I should have known your family had something to do with this. But they had *everything* to do with it. Your mother fell right off *her* mother's tree, didn't she?"

"Lujayn! Stop it!"

Her mother's mortification barely registered on Jalal's inflamed senses. All he felt was this mass of incendiary passion seething at him. He was a hairbreadth from forgetting everyone surrounding him, and the questions eating at him.

"Your grandmother framed my grandfather, didn't she? Over something personal, right? And with the only evidence being her word? You discovered his innocence easily enough, after all, when you bothered to scratch the loose dirt she buried my family under, right?"

His jaw muscles bunched. "That just about sums it up."

She snorted. Gasps rang from around the room this time.

"So why didn't the truth come out after she was dead? Because your mother picked up the torch after her? And why not when *she* was exiled? Then when your uncle and cousins were ousted? Why did everyone remain silent including my martyred family? Why did it take your so-called accidental digging for some other irrelevant purpose to un-cover this piece of gratuitously evil art?"

"*B'Ellahi,* Lujayn, what's gotten into you?"

Lujayn tossed her distraught uncle a glare before swing-ing her gaze back to Jalal, slamming him with the force of her outrage. "Do you think I'm crossing a line here, Your Highness? You think I shouldn't be angry for a few minutes for the decades of my family's disgrace and oppression at the hands of yours?"

Bassel surged, caught her arm, agitation blasting off him. "Lujayn, you *are* way over the line here."

Badreyah placed a trembling hand on Lujayn's other arm. "Whatever happened between our family members in the past has nothing to do with Prince Jalal or his mother."

Lujayn rounded on her, her scowl spectacular, her voice a magnificent snarl, one worthy of a lioness. "Really? You mean she had to show you her compassion and employ you, of all people, as her head slave and punching bag? She had to deprive you of continuing your education at only fourteen so you can fetch her slippers and be the lab rat on which she perfected her cruelties? Excuse me as I *don't think so.*"

Jalal's heart twisted with the force of shame. He felt sul-lied by yet another permanent taint inflicted by his fam-ily and his mother. By guilt for never bothering to find out Lujayn's real history, or the extent of the abuse of her mother by his.

"It's in the past," Badreyah insisted. "And the moment Prince Jalal found out the truth, he not only took the nec-essary steps to reinstate our family, he offered your uncle a prestigious position he offers only to those he considers most trustworthy."

"So we're supposed to bend backward and yodel his praises?" Lujayn growled. "Then prostrate ourselves forehead-first in thanks? Or do we even need to go further and…"

"Lujayn!"

Her uncle's soft admonishment finally brought her tirade to a halt, though she still vibrated with affront and anger.

Any other time, an hour ago, before he'd found out about her child, he would have reveled in the sheer magnificence of her fury and antagonism. He would have only invited her to hit him with more, vent all the justified ferociousness of her rage.

But he'd expended the last vestiges of his restraint. He had to end this, *now.*

He moved away from her, stood facing the others who looked like they'd rather the ground split and swallowed them.

Unable to agree more with the sentiment, he drew in a deep inhalation, unlocked his jaw. "Thanks everyone for coming and helping me celebrate Sheikh Bassel joining our team. We'll have another meeting soon to discuss our future structure and strategies in depth. But I think we're all ready to end this evening now."

He thought he heard Lujayn mutter, "Boy, am I," could almost hear the collective sigh of relief that issued from the group, venting their rising tension.

His lips twisted wryly. "Yes, everyone, if you're waiting for me to spell it out, you *can* go."

Lujayn was the first one to move, not sparing anyone another look, as if it would be too soon if she never saw anyone present again, maybe even including her family.

Everyone else gave him uneasy smiles and handshakes, relieved to escape the embarrassing situation. Her family seemed mortified and sounded like they'd never regretted anything as much as insisting that she come.

He stopped their attempted apologies, assuring them that ending the evening was for their sake not his. Looking marginally reassured and even more grateful, they followed Lujayn.

As everyone cleared the doors, he called out after them, "I said everyone can go. But 'everyone' does not include Lujayn."

Lujayn shook under wave after wave of outrage.

She would have marched out and handed Jalal his head if he'd tried to stop her. Too bad it had been her family who had, with nothing but the force of their mortification. Even as fury disabled her brakes, her innate desire to please them had won. *Jalal* had won. He'd known exactly what buttons to push to get what he wanted from her.

Now he closed the doors after the last departing guest.

"What's this? Detention?" she seethed as he turned to her. "For talking back to the headmaster? You did have us sitting there like kids who had to placate you or risk failing. Worse, like hostages forced to put up with the theatrics of our captor in fear of our lives."

He stopped steps away, his eyes like turbid honey, something unsettled and unsettling buzzing. "I didn't see you placating me or putting up with anything."

A frisson of danger skewered through her.

Which was ridiculous because she'd never feared him. But his inexplicable intensity had her heart quivering. And it made her even angrier. If he thought he could intimidate her into cowering or simpering like he did all the others, as someone who didn't give two figs about his rank, wealth and power, she was obliged to adjust his inflated view of his importance.

"You got enough of that from the others to turn the strongest stomach," she hissed. "Not to mention the truckloads of adulation you got from my family. I always knew your family screwed mine over in so many ways, but to find out the real depth of their abuse, their...*crimes,* and to have the sordid details accompanied by my family's gratitude and martyrdom was just too much. So if you detained me to chastise me for daring to voice my disgust in front of the thralls you call your campaign managers, let me tell you I'm only sorry that I didn't get to say more before my family's grossly misplaced sense of decorum and their impending collective stroke silenced me."

The ferocity in his gaze rose with her every word. It made her barrel on. "Here, let me tell you what I would have said. I would have moved from condemning your family to condemning you directly. Your family members were straightforward in their subjugation of mine, showed them the kindness of open cruelty, leaving them the dignity of knowing their enemy and the relief of being able to hate them in their hearts. But your pretense of compassion and generosity is far worse since it makes them unaware of your abuse, and tricks them into being your slaves by choice."

His stare remained unwavering, as if he were trying to read her mind, to decipher her last thought and impulse. But why, when she was whacking him over the head with it all?

Maybe she needed to be even more explicit. "You must think you've succeeded in using them to have me where you want me, since they almost pleaded for me to stay when you ordered me to. So enjoy this triumph because it'll never be repeated. From now on, they know to leave me out of any feet-kissing rituals. And if you're thinking of new ways to pressure me, let me tell you now nothing else will work. This Prince of Two Kingdoms thing clearly works on Azmaharians programmed to bow down to their royalty. But even if I wasn't now a businesswoman who's long left behind any tendencies to be bowled over by you, I'm an American and we generally have allergic reactions to royal entitlement."

"Is that all you are, Lujayn?"

She blinked. His voice. She'd never heard it like that. Like the roll of approaching thunder. And what did he mean...?

"A businesswoman, an American. Aren't you leaving something vital out?"

She frowned at that searing spike of emotion in his eyes, her heart starting to thud with confusion and wariness. "If you're talking about my Azmaharian side, think I might have royalty-worshipping tendencies to unearth, save it. My only local ingredients are some genes and a passport that I never use."

Suddenly he was closer, and not because he'd moved. It felt as if he'd expanded, as if everything inside him had reached out to engulf her. She felt him all over her, inside her head.

Then in that heart-snatching tone, he said, "I'm talking about your maternal side. I'm talking about the ingredients that make you a mother."

Jalal had no idea what it was.

Maybe it was the stiffness that invaded her body, or the pulse going haywire in her throat, or the blast of horror in her eyes. Or it was all of that and myriad other instantaneous, involuntary signs that coalesced and painted a picture worth a thousand confessions.

It all added up to one thing. One thing that lodged in his mind with the force of an ax. Something devastating. The truth.

Lujayn's child was his.

Seven

The knowledge mushroomed in Jalal's skull.

Lujayn had had his child.

He had a child.

"Jalal…"

Numb to his recesses, paralyzed in soul before body, he stared at her stricken eyes, his ears ringing with the softness of the dread in her voice. His heart, his mind, everything he was made of, swelled with the enormity of the belief, unraveled with the scope of its implications.

Moments ago he'd been just himself, the man he'd been struggling to formulate a peace treaty with all his life. And she'd just been herself. The one woman he wanted, and with whom peace seemed an ever-receding mirage.

Now he no longer knew who either of them were.

They were no longer the once-lovers who sparred and parried with nothing but consuming passion at stake between them. They were two people who shared far more than their unquenchable, if according to her, better-off-suppressed needs.

They shared a *life*. They had since she'd conceived his child. But by hiding the fact, she'd stopped it from becoming a reality to him. It had only become one the moment he'd known of it.

The instant freeze that had struck him, buried him under layers of icy shock, started to crack under the heat of her dismay. Then she relinquished his gaze, swung around. The curtain of raven gloss cascading down her back arced with the force of the motion, lashed his cheek. Then she was receding like a wobbly image from a dream.

He found himself launching after her, his need to stop her, to demand...everything, propelling him.

He caught her at the door, his fingers digging in her flesh through her long-sleeved jacket, felt like they'd sunk into lava. She twisted in his hold and he brought both arms crossing beneath her heavy breasts, felt as if he'd enfolded a live wire as he subdued her against his vibrating body.

"No more fighting me off, Lujayn." Was that his voice? That wounded beast's? "I'm never going to let you walk away from me again." He turned her around, not knowing if it was his hands that were shaking or the shoulders he held her by, or both. "This is no longer a game."

She tried to shake off his hands, her eyes escaping his. "Thanks for admitting it was a game all along. But you're right. It's not, because I'm not playing. Game over, Jalal."

He almost ground his teeth to powder as the last vestiges of shock melted in the blast of rising rage. "It was you who've played me all along. *You never told me you had my child.*"

Her gaze met his at his shout, attempted derision, but the dread she'd managed to leash blossomed again, betraying her. "Don't be ridiculous...."

"No, you don't." He gave her back her earlier fury. "Don't you *dare* try to misdirect me again. It won't work. Not only did you have my child and didn't tell me, you were *never* going to tell me."

The acknowledgment in her eyes incinerated any wisps of uncertainty into nothingness.

And he realized. That he'd hoped. For some indication that she'd hesitated in that decision. That it had weighed on her. That she'd afforded him a trace of consideration before ruling him out.

She hadn't.

He let go of her shoulders, stumbled back under the cruelty of realization, his eyes burning as they searched hers. "*Ya Ullah, ya Lujayn...b'Ellahi...laish?* Why?"

Her eyes wavered. The vulnerability of consternation gave way to the toughness of control again.

"You're kidding, right?" she scoffed. "The question is, why should I have told you?"

She truly didn't see why. How could this be? "You didn't think I should know I've fathered a child?"

Her stiff shoulders jerked. "You've probably fathered a dozen children you don't know or care about. What's one more?"

His hand rose to his chest, almost convinced he'd encounter something sharp sticking out of it. "Is this what you think? That I'm not only indiscriminately promiscuous, but that I go around having unsafe sex?"

"Seeing as how safe sex wasn't one of your considerations with me, why should I think other women warranted any better?"

He'd only ever had "unsafe" sex with her. She'd been a virgin and he'd unfailingly observed safety before her. He'd only protected her from pregnancy at first then she'd done so later. He'd thought employing contraceptive measures herself had meant she'd wanted to enjoy full intimacy, something he'd never considered doing before her. What he'd gotten addicted to with her.

And she'd thought he was… "…so callous I care nothing about the consequences, to the women I bed, and to children I must occasionally sire?"

"So you 'care'? And engage in that delightful practice you royalty types favor in this region, giving your illicit spawn the coveted title of *mansoob?* So generous of you to 'occasionally,' 'sort of' proclaim responsibility for your offspring from unsuitable wombs. The children of your servants or anyone inferior to you must be so grateful to be declared illegitimate but 'associated' with you. So isn't it just lucky for me that I don't need your 'association'? And neither does Adam."

Adam. His child was a boy. And he was nineteen months old.

The extent of what he'd missed in that time felt like a noose tightening against his windpipe, suffocating him. And for the first time in his life he knew what it meant to be helpless.

This chunk of his child's life was gone, and he could never get it back, for either of them.

It must have showed on his face, the anguish and defeat. It twisted her stony expression into a grimace.

"Let's not pretend this was something you considered at all, let alone with me. You didn't even acknowledge me, but you would have my baby? But it wasn't your fault I got pregnant. You probably thought I was protected. I wasn't. I let contraception go when I married Patrick."

So if it had been her choice, her child would have been her husband's. She'd had his only by mistake.

"Then he died, and sex was the last thing on my mind, so when you popped up out of nowhere and we ended up in bed, repercussions didn't even occur to me except when my period was a month late. So it's really none of your business that I got pregnant. Adam is none of your business, just like I never was."

Bitterness choked him. "You were never my business? I was unable to have a moment, waking or sleeping, for eight years without thinking of you, craving you...*obsessing* about you."

"Lighten up on the exaggerations, please," she sneered. "I was there, remember? At least through the years we had together. I know for a fact that during those, you spent weeks, sometimes months, without doing any of that."

"I never stayed away by choice, and all the time we were apart, I did *all* that. Then you left me, and the moment I thought it possible to come to you again, I did."

Her eyes flared silver fire. "And you came to have closure or sex or both, not father a child."

"I told myself I came for the first. But what I really wanted was to clear away the bitterness, at least come to terms with it so I can...reconnect with you, claim you again."

"You never connected with me or claimed me to start with."

"That's your version. Or maybe it was the truth, for you. My truth was that I did. As much as you claimed me. I was yours."

She looked as if he'd punched her in the gut.

When she spoke, her voice was as strangled as if he had. "Are you implying that during our time together you had no one but me?"

"That's not an implication. That's a fact."

She gaped at him as if she'd never heard anything so preposterous.

Heart aching with affront and frustration he hissed,

"What could have possibly raised any doubts about my faithfulness to you?"

That shattered the stasis of incredulity, hardening her eyes and voice again. "Oh, I don't know. Probably the dozens of nubile, and let's not forget to mention 'suitably ranked,' bodies hanging on your arm in every public appearance. While I was safely tucked a world away to be brought out to play with, in secret."

"Those 'bodies' sought me out, because of who I am, not for myself. I didn't want anyone, starting with my mother, to speculate if I rebuffed their public advances. I *told* you that." Disappointment seared through him as he saw it in her eyes. She hadn't considered believing him, then or now. "So you believed I was sleeping around, yet took me back into your arms, welcomed me into your body when I came back to you?"

"Pathetic, isn't it? What's more sickening is that I would have indefinitely put up with being one of your steady stream of exchangeable bodies if I wasn't the only one you wouldn't stoop to associating with in public. Now you know that my anger and disgust weren't all directed toward you."

His lips twisted. "You gifted me with more than enough of it. You started by leaving me, then turned Patrick against me...."

Her eyes turned to steel at Patrick's mention. "It was your unethical business practices that cultivated his enmity, not me."

Everything inside him went still, to ward off yet another unexpected and unearned blow. "He told you that?"

Her gaze wavered. No. Patrick hadn't told her that. She would have said yes if she could. But she couldn't lie—for Patrick. She wouldn't mind saying anything to hurt *him*.

Was all this hatred for him? Or was he paying the collective price for his family?

Her shoulders jerked. "Patrick only made me face facts I'd been avoiding for years—about how you manipulated me for your conveniences, made me consent to being one of your...entertainments. I applied your methods with me to your dealings with Patrick and extrapolated his reasons for ending your partnerships. Why else would he have endured all those losses if it wasn't to stop you from manipulating him anymore?"

"How about that he was so jealous of me, he was making sure I was out of your life, even after he was gone?" Bile filled him up to his eyes. "And I thought him a good friend and a man of honor. All the time he'd been plotting to take you away from me. And he did."

"I had to be *with* you in the first place for him to take me away from you. I never was."

"*B'Ellahi,* that's a lie. You were closer to me than any other person in my life."

"*That* is a testimony to how superficial it all was. You're light-years distant from everyone in your life. You have formed no closeness with anyone starting with your twin. As for what we shared, it was nothing resembling a relationship."

"What did you think I was doing with you for four years, if that wasn't a relationship?"

"Anyone hearing you saying *four years* over and over would think we lived together or something. Do you know how many days out of those four years we had together?"

His heart compressed at yet another proof of how differently they'd perceived the past, how much she held against him that he'd been unaware of. "You counted?"

"Not at the time, but I went back and looked over my schedule, and all the last-minute cancellations I had to make when you had an opening and could grace me with your presence. You acted with the conviction that my life and commitments were of no consequence, and the only one who should be accommodated at the drop of a hat was you."

"You never told me you had to cancel plans to be with me."

She gave a furious laugh. "So you didn't listen when I did. Or you did and it only fed your ego, that I'd drop everything, at whatever cost to me, to jump back in bed with you."

Had they both lived through the same past? Or was she talking about some parallel earth to his?

"I believed you only rescheduled. You never made it sound important, so I assumed your plans were flexible, unlike mine."

"*And* he says that with a straight face. Wow. You're really something. You assumed that I, a struggling model trying to build a name for myself in a sea of women with better qualifications and looks, had the luxury of canceling shoots or even rescheduling them? While you, the prince whom everyone would sacrifice their firstborn for a handshake from, couldn't change your plans at your whim? If you gave it a moment's thought you would have seen the truth, but you didn't bother. You had everything compartmentalized for your convenience. Your business and power games, your sports tournaments, your political and promotional schmoozing, and when you needed to unwind in a sex marathon, you called me, expected me to be there where and when you dictated. And self-degrading fool that I was, I was there. Every single time."

A kaleidoscope of agony spun inside him at her every slashing word. "So you thought I didn't care about you one way or another, thought I'd feel the same about the child you bore me. So why didn't you tell me anyway? Just to make sure? Why were you so anxious to divert me from the truth?"

Sarcasm emptied from her eyes, discomfort replacing

it. "Because this way Adam remained mine alone and your reaction to his existence wouldn't…taint him. I thought if you knew and rejected him, he'd somehow feel it. *I* didn't want to make that rejection real, and it would only be real if you knew…."

Her words petered out, her cream complexion blotching with crimson agitation.

"So *this* was how you rationalized it all. You painted me as exploitative, cheating scum so you could walk out on me with a clear conscience. Then you condemned me as an unfeeling monster so you could justify depriving me of my *child*."

Silence crashed after his last butchered growl.

Nothing fractured its suffocation but the sounds of his thundering heartbeats and her labored breathing.

Then she croaked, "You—you're really upset?"

"Upset?" A mirthless laugh shredded out of him. *"Upset?"*

His laugh died. He pressed his fist against his chest where it felt it had been ripped open.

She stared up at him, horror settling into her eyes by degrees. "I—I really…really believed it would be the last thing you'd want, to know you had a baby, from me. Y-you did walk out that day saying you'd delete me from your memory."

"You'd just told me that you hated me, hated yourself when you were with me. You said that after I told you how I couldn't forget you, after we almost died of pleasure in each other's arms. What did you expect me to say? If you'd given me any hope, I would have never given up. And if you'd told me when you found out you were pregnant with Adam…" A lump pushed its way up his throat.

"Wh-what would you have done if I'd told you?"

"*Ya Ullah,* what *wouldn't* I have done? Had I been the

second one to know that you carried my child, as I should have been, I would have been there with you, *for* you, for *him,* every moment of the past twenty-eight months. And you deprived me of all that."

The silver of her eyes dimmed until it was eclipsed in a wave of reddened realization and blackening contrition.

Suddenly she staggered around and collapsed on the couch.

"I didn't realize, never believed…" She dropped her face into her palms on a hiccuped gasp.

He looked down at her, witnessing the distress shaking her frame, chopping her breathing for the first time. His own was wildfire that razed through his every nerve.

He walked to her slowly, feeling if he went any faster, he'd keel over. He went down on his knees before her.

She gasped as he took her clammy, trembling hands in his. Tears streaked a pale track down the velvet of her flushed cheeks as she raised her face level with his. Her lips contorted to form words, her voice a thick, tear-clogged tremolo. "Oh, God, I'm so sorry, Jalal…."

One hand pressed against her lips, silencing the flow of her regret. He couldn't bear her apologies. He didn't think he deserved them. Didn't want them even if he did.

He needed only one thing. "I want to see my son, Lujayn. Take me to him. Now."

Eight

Lujayn snatched her hand from his, heaved up to her feet and wiped away the tears that had abruptly stopped. "I can't do that."

He rose to stand, feeling as unsteady as she seemed. His lips and heart compressed on the anger condensing inside him. "Even now, you still persist in trying to deprive me of my son? *Zain, kaif ma tebbi*—as you wish. I only asked you as a courtesy. I don't need your permission or your co-operation to see my son. I'll go to your uncle's to see him, right now."

She lunged at him, caught his arm in a frantic grasp, her face urgent. "You can't. They have no idea you're his father."

A suspicion skewered him in the chest. "You told them he was Patrick's?"

Her color rose into the danger zone. "N-no, they knew he couldn't have been Adam's father. I—I told them it was someone else, but it wasn't important who he was."

Would everything she said keep hurting more? "And they just accepted that?"

She winced. "My father's side of the family did. My mother's, being conservative Azmaharians, were mortified. They rationalized my 'lapse' by my grief, and placated themselves that I'd make it…lawful. When I told them there was no hope of that and I'd decided to keep the baby and would disappear from their lives forever if they couldn't deal with it, they eventually succumbed."

"Decided to keep the baby?" He caught her by the shoulders, each heartbeat a wrecking ball inside his chest. "You considered…terminating your pregnancy?"

"No." Her eyes filled again. "It was a shock to find myself pregnant, under the circumstances, but no matter how difficult I knew it would be, how it would change my life forever, I wanted Adam more than I wanted to live."

A mixture of overwhelming sweetness and bitterness, of longing and regret, expanded inside his chest. He wanted to crush her into him, assuage the alienation, wanted to push her away feeling her nearness would cause him permanent injury.

He did neither, kept holding her at arm's length.

Then he rasped, "Do you have photos?"

"O-of Adam?" Her eyes widened, brightened as if he'd handed her a lifeline. She stumbled out of his hold and to her purse, produced her phone, her hands trembling as she accessed her photos. "I should have thought of this."

She thought he'd be satisfied with seeing his son in photos.

His hand covered the phone's screen as she extended it to him. This wouldn't be how he'd first lay eyes on his son.

"Photos of yourself. When you were pregnant."

The relief on her face drained as hard as her arm fell to

her side. "I wasn't in any condition to think of posing for photos. I'd decided to have Adam, but I wasn't exactly..."

"Happy?"

She shook her head, her eyes filling with the days of anxiety and anguish she'd lived, a woman becoming a single mother.

Suddenly it was vital for him to find something out. "Did you stay in the Hamptons during your pregnancy?"

He'd known from Fadi's reports that she'd put the mansion up for sale around the time she must have given birth. He'd had Fadi acquire it for him, through a third party so she wouldn't refuse to sell. Now, imagining her there, pregnant with his child in Patrick's house, was another turn of the lance embedded in his gut.

"Leaving the mansion and leaving the States was the first thing I did after I discovered my pregnancy. I was too high profile there, and I didn't want anyone finding out."

"By anyone, you mean me."

Her exhalation was laden with resignation. "Actually, you weren't my main concern. Your mother was."

His mother's mention, when he least expected it, was another blow out of blue sky. "Why would you have worried about her?"

"Because she would have realized it's your baby."

"Why would she have?" Confusion screeched inside his head, picking up momentum, churning his thoughts to a sickening mess. "She had no more access to you after your mother left her service, probably never had any interest in you to start with. Why would she have followed your news? And if she had, you'd been married, and she couldn't have found out the exact stage of your pregnancy." He shook his head. "What am I saying? She wouldn't have suspected a thing even had she known the baby wasn't Patrick's. There'd been no reason for her to suspect me being the father. She knew nothing about us."

"She knew everything."

The quiet assertion went off in his head. Time slowed, filled with the debris of the history he'd thought he'd lived as each fragment flew in his face, crashed into him with the force of realization.

His mother had known.

But how? Did he want to know? He'd found out enough crimes his family had perpetrated against hers. Could he bear knowing more?

Aih. He owed it to her, to them, to his son, to know everything, set straight as much of it as he could.

Yet… "I find it impossible to believe she'd known about us and hadn't done something about it."

Her body and expression tensed defensively. "You can believe what you like."

"I am not disbelieving you, I'm…boggled that she knew and just…let us be. She was the main reason I kept us such a heavily guarded secret. She had a way of making anyone we ever came close to…disappear. Admittedly, it was worse with Haidar, *qorrat enha*—the apple of her eye, and she was downright vicious in what she'd done to Roxanne. But I am still her son, and I knew she'd do the same to anyone I came close to that she didn't approve of. And she approved of no one. But when it came to you…"

Her lush lips twisted. "Yeah, her servant's daughter."

"You were never that to *me*. But I knew you were that to her, warranting a whole new level of disapproval if she knew, and consequently an even more…creative intervention."

Her eyes cleared of the rawness of agitation, filled with the mist of contemplation. "You thought she'd harm my family?"

He let out his breath on a ragged exhalation. "I didn't even want to think what she might do if she knew."

Her shrug was dismissive, assertive. "She knew. She told me."

He should be getting used to the constant turmoil being with Lujayn created. If he hadn't till now, he never would.

"And she never did anything," he said. "All right, there goes another corner pillar of my belief system."

"She didn't think she had to do a thing. She thought you were taking care of not sullying your image or family name with such an abominable liaison well enough. She commended you for knowing what my kind was good for, and keeping me where I belonged, in the dark, unacknowledged and reviled."

His blood burned cell by cell as every vicious word that reeked of authenticity bludgeoned him.

He had no doubt those had been his mother's words. What remained to know was… "When did she tell you that?"

She attempted a shrug of nonchalance, failed miserably. "Oh, a bit over six years ago."

When she'd started being contentious and ill-tempered. Now he knew the reason, he thought it a miracle she hadn't walked out on him on that same day. That it had taken her two more years of what must have looked like proof of his mother's words.

So his mother had managed to spoil another vital thing to him. In an even more evil and damaging way than he'd feared.

"It wasn't true, what she said," he finally rasped. "I am now realizing my actions could have been interpreted in a way to validate everything she'd said, and I bet she was counting on that, too, but none of it was in any way true."

Her arms went around her body, as if hugging herself against sudden cold. "She was so proud of what you'd done

OLIVIA GATES   109

to me. She said you did what she'd promised me she'd do
one day, put me in my place."

"When did she say *that?*"

"Ten years before I met you."

This time it was he who staggered around to find the
nearest surface to collapse on.

Lujayn had been only eleven when his mother had threatened her.

After sitting down with the stiff care of someone who
had trouble coordinating her movements, she said, "On one
of her trips to the States, she called my mother. My mother
was in turmoil over answering her 'summons' but she buckled under her conditioning and went. She took me with her.
Without inviting us to sit, your mother demanded that she
leave her family and come back to her service.

"God, I've never seen Mom like that, couldn't imagine
that my vivacious, outspoken mother could stand before
anyone so shaken and unable to stand up for herself. She
stood there, head bent, taking your mother's cruelty as she
hacked at her, saying she'd deserted her in a pathetic attempt for independence that only landed her with a slob of
a husband who'd never be out of debt. That she'd gone from
a highly paid lady-in-waiting to a queen to the servant of a
bum and his children for free. I saw my mother shriveling
under her barrage, and I couldn't bear it."

He couldn't either. Was there no end to his mother's transgressions? Had he ever had a chance with Lujayn? He must
have always been inextricable in her mind from his mother,
and her feelings toward him had no doubt been tainted by
his mother's degradation of hers. Then she went on, and he
realized there was always worse than the worst he could
think of.

"I put myself in front of my mother, as if I'd protect her
from your mother's attack. My mother tried to stop me, but

I walked up to your mother and told her I never thought anyone could be as beautiful as her. Or as mean. I told her she was scary and ugly inside and that my mother left her because she made her miserable like she made others, and that everyone hated her. And I could see why. Then I told my mother that I wouldn't let her go back to work for this woman, that I'll give up everything, my ballet and piano lessons and get work to help her."

He could see her, a slip of a girl, standing up to his dragoness of a mother, to defend her family. His heart slowed to a painful thud as she went on.

"Your mother looked at me in contemplation all through my tirade. Then she said that as a princess from birth, then a queen by marriage, it was her duty to maintain order, restore balance. She took it upon herself to put people in their correct places. But to do so, it took time and patience, so she was not in any hurry. But she never forgot her purpose, refused to stop until she saw it through. And she would put me in my place, no matter how long it took, since I clearly had no idea what it was."

He wanted to shout, *enough!* But he knew it wasn't, not for her. She had to let this all out once and for all.

Gritting his teeth on the sharpening pain in his chest, he willed her to go on.

She did. "But I was too young and didn't believe anyone would be as vindictive and long-term as that. Mom begged Sondoss to please forgive us, me for my foolishness and her for not being able to leave her family. Sondoss only said my mother would change her mind, when life with us, her miserable family, became impossible.

"Mom was a wreck as we left, and remained one for the next year. Dad lost his latest job, and couldn't find another. Soon, what had been a barely manageable situation became impossible as per your mother's predictions. Mom had to go back to her service, while Dad had to go back to his family in Ireland. Mom took my younger sister and brother, while Dad took me, tearing apart our family. Dad asked Mom to take me, too, said I shouldn't be away from my mother and siblings. But it wasn't for him that Mom let me go. She knew if she took me with her, your mother would find ways to 'put me in my place.' I cried for days, begging her to take me with her, saying I would do anything to make your mother forgive me. But she knew. Your mother never forgot, or forgave. So your infallible memory comes from both sides of your heritage."

He'd already known his mother had orchestrated a conspiracy that could have only played out in endless bloodshed. Why would he consider this premeditated cruelty any more shocking?

But it was. Her conspiracy had been, to her, justified, to give her sons, those she considered the ones worthy of being kings, the thrones they deserved. What she'd done to Lujayn and her mother had been nothing but pure malice.

Lujayn angrily wiped at the fresh flow of tears. "But Mom promised it would only be for a couple years. Sondoss was a slave driver, but she paid her servants very well. Mom estimated she'd be able to put aside the capital Dad needed to start the business he'd always dreamed of. But as if knowing Mom's plan in advance, your mother offered a salary only large enough to support us and pay a portion of our debts."

His mother *had* known. She had a way of knowing everything. And using it to her advantage. To everybody else's loss.

The voice that had steadied began to shake again. "Dad kept losing every job he got, to his growing despair. He'd think he was doing so well then he'd be let go. He believed he was jinxed."

A jinx called Sondoss. This had his mother's claws all over it. No need to draw her attention to that conclusion if she hadn't reached it herself. Nothing to be gained from infecting her soul with even more rage and hatred.

"I did give up everything I was involved in, started to work when I was fourteen. But by the time I was eighteen, I knew the jobs I kept getting were hand-to-mouth solutions. There was no way I could afford college and even if I could, I couldn't wait for the well-paying jobs a degree would afford me. I needed something that didn't take long training, something that would pay well fast. I had nothing to use but 'my body' as you put it. I always had people complimenting my 'exotic' looks, saying I could be a model. But it wasn't as easy as that. It took me a whole year before I landed my first paying job. It paid enough to buy a new outfit to wear to auditions, and a bottle of cheap champagne to celebrate with Dad. Not that there was much to celebrate.

"I was exposed to some...scary situations. People started coming out of the woodwork, wanting to be my 'agent,' 'manager' or 'entourage.' I'd just decided to admit defeat and get the first shop-clerk job I could find, when I met Aliyah again and told her I saw why she'd left modeling. She offered to help financially first, but when I refused she decided to teach me to 'fish.' She took me under her wing, showed me the ropes, introduced me to the right people and I started working, making money, started paying our debts, and I thought my life was finally on the right track. Then I met you."

His eyes squeezed without volition. The way she'd said that. What he considered the best memory of his life, she considered the worst. Forcing his eyes open, so he'd see for himself how totally wrong he'd been about everything he'd ever shared with her, he watched her struggle to continue her account.

"I was horrified. You were the son of my mother's en-slaver, a part of the reason I didn't have my family in my life, and might never have them. To my mortification, I found you fascinating. I'd seen you so many times from afar before that...."

"You did?"

"I'd been in Azmahar many times to visit Mom, when your mother was too busy. Then after that first meeting, after every exposure, I found myself unable to think of any-thing else but you. I told myself I'd have some more time with you before the inevitable end, because the moment I told you who I was, you'd be the one to walk away."

"And you told me."

"Yeah. And instead of coming to your senses as I thought you would, you decided to have your cake and eat it, too. And it kept eating at me, how I wanted you, when I shouldn't.

"At first, it was because I couldn't let my family find out about you. I felt I was betraying them, not only by being with the son of the woman who'd torn us apart, but because I was acting like anything but the person they'd raised. I was ashamed of the way I breathlessly did anything you even hinted at, accommodated your whims at my expense. I cut myself off from them because I couldn't bear the shame of lying to them with every breath, since that was how fre-quently I thought of you.

"Then your mother validated all my suspicions and far more—and you kept proving her right. I despised myself, escalating those feelings every day because of the way I let you treat me, and I still couldn't quit you. Then I really started hating what I had become when I kept inventing quarrels with you, hoping to nudge you into addressing the issues that were poisoning me. I was too much of a coward to face you with them, out of fear that you'd just shrug and say, 'If this bothers you, tough,' and walk away. So I started to self-destruct. I couldn't eat, couldn't sleep, kept obsessing over every day you didn't call, every minute you stayed away. I lost weight and jobs. I was on the verge of losing my mind. And I didn't have any support system to fall back on, since I'd shut everyone out. I felt I had to choose between being with them or being with you.

"I chose you, and lost everything. The one person I had left, the only one I could talk to, was Patrick. And he stepped in and gave me the support I needed to save myself."

And she fell silent. He knew she had no more to say.

She'd said enough.

He threw back his head against the couch, closed his eyes, suppressing the chaos that threatened to tear him apart, soul and psyche.

Finally he opened his eyes, rose and walked to her, holding her raw, stormy gaze. Then he went down on his knees before her again.

He gently aborted her jerk to get away, taking her hands in his. "You should have told me everything long ago. What I have to say is not much, but it's all I have, for now.

"I can't begin to describe my shame and regret at what my mother stole of your childhood and family life, what she told you about me and the cost to both of us. But I was never party to her manipulations, was never tainted by her snobbery. I was *never* ashamed of you—I was the very opposite, and this had nothing to do with the secrecy I imposed on our relationship. I thought there would be only losses and trouble if the world knew what we had.

"I also thought we had the perfect arrangement, the best of all worlds. We were young, were building our careers and we had each other. I didn't think there was anything more than that to dream of. I was ignorant of the true history between our families, didn't realize you came to our relationship with baggage and insecurities and bitterness. But

I should have realized something was deeply wrong when you started flaring up, shouldn't have rationalized it because I was content with the way things were. At the time, I did think you appreciated the secrecy as much as I did for your family's conservative sensibilities, and so you wouldn't be dragged into the crosshairs of the paparazzi who hounded me. I welcomed having those women on my arm because they diverted attention from you, kept you safe. But I was yours alone, Lujayn...." Something still stopped him from admitting that he'd never stopped being hers, would never stop. "And I believed you were mine. That's why I went out of my mind when you left me for Patrick. Anything I did with him, anything I said to you, was fueled by my pain and jealousy. I was blind and I hurt you just the same as if I'd meant to. And for that, I will never forgive myself, will do anything so you can have the peace I robbed you of all these years."

Her features trembled and she pitched forward to bury her face in her hands, ended up pressing it into their entwined fingers. Her flesh, her tears, singed him, had him groaning, dragging her to his chest. She burrowed her face into him, rubbing against him like a cat desperate for her human's feel and affection, her lips over his heart.

His hands felt like they didn't belong to him as they fumbled his shirt buttons open, needing that touch like he needed his next heartbeat. Her moan against his flesh as those petal-soft lips crushed their lushness into him was a bolt of pure emotion and carnality, striking him dead center through his being.

His fingers tangled into her silken tresses, dug into her scalp, shaping her beloved head. Her moans grew longer, louder, confessing her equal upheaval as she opened her lips and the wet heat of her tongue scalded him. That simmering state of arousal she had him in by just existing, that had been hovering on the verge of igniting with her near-ness, exploded into a conflagration that consumed him body and soul.

He crushed her to him, the starved for feel of her sending his senses spiraling beyond retrieval. He took all he could of her worshipping, before a hand at her nape raised her to him, brought her roving, tormenting lips up to his, bit down into the lower one, almost breaking the inner flesh in his urgency. His teeth held there as he trembled all over like she did, with the effort of holding back. Her cry razed through him as she opened fully to him, her ripe breasts pressing into his chest, demanding his domination. He laved away his bite, thrust his tongue inside her, draining her sweet-ness and whimpers of pleasure. His kisses grew wrenching as he pushed away her jacket, dipped beneath her blouse to spread his hands over the scorching velvet of her back, arching her against him.

He poured his demand, his plea, his confession, into her depths. *"Wahashtini ya'yooni, bejnoon. Guleeli ya rohi, wahashtek? Tebghini kamma abghaki?"*

"Yes, Jalal, yes...I've been going insane with missing you, craving you, too. How I missed you—*how* I crave you...."

That was all he needed. The license to claim her, reclaim them both from the desert they'd existed in without the oth-er's passion and fulfillment.

In one movement, he was on his feet with his woman in his arms. But when he neared the room's door she gasped, wriggled. His lips buried into her neck. "We're alone."

His reassurance defused her tension, had her resume owning any inch of flesh he'd exposed to her.

In a minute he took her across the threshold of the expan-sive bedroom suite where he'd lain awake, burning in a hell of deprivation, for the past weeks. Her teeth were scraping his stubble as he placed her on the bed. He straddled her hips and started to rid her of those prim clothes that had been playing havoc with his imagination, had her naked in what felt like a torturous hour. Then he pulled back to look down at her.

Her breasts were a feast, her hips flared with fertility, making her waist look more nipped, her belly no longer flat, but a lush curve, her arms round and firm, her legs long and smooth and honey-hued, her mound plump and trimmed.

He followed all those treasures, in sweeps of wonder. "You robbed me of my sanity from the moment I saw you, when you were nothing like what you've become. Now— now I'm in danger of devouring you for real. *Ya Ullah, Lujayn*...what have you done to yourself? Nothing should be this beautiful."

"Don't exaggerate—I've put on too much weight...."

"There can't be too much of you for me. You were slim, then you became almost gaunt, not that it made me want you any less. But now..." He skimmed a coveting hand from the curve of her strong, square shoulder to her heavy breast, blood roaring in his ears, his loins, as its warmth and resilience overflowed in his large hand. "Now you're beyond glorious. My silver-eyed enchantress has become a goddess."

She thrust her breast into his hold, inviting a more aggressive possession. "You were always a god, now you've become something even more."

He bent to award himself with compulsive suckles of her peach-colored, erect nipples, groaning at her taste and feel, as she pushed her flesh deeper into his mouth, whimpering her greed for more as she treated his clothes as he'd treated hers.

Delight expanded through him as he surrendered to her impatience, wallowing in it as she exposed him to her hunger.

He came down on top of her, plundering her fragrant mouth in savage kisses, his hands seeking all her secrets, taking every license, owning every inch. His fingers sought her molten depths, delighted in feeling them clamp around him in demand, as she keened and undulated beneath him, accepting the pleasure, inviting him with movements and words to do whatever he wished to her. She was too ready, as she always was for him; he brought her to orgasm around his fingers with just a few thrusts.

As she shook with that warm-up pleasure, he slid down the bed, draped her legs over his shoulders. She wantonly arched her hips, opening herself wide for his devouring. Her taste and scent blanketed his sanity as he lost all sense of self, becoming a beast bent on drinking his mate dry. And he did, while he suckled and tongued her to two more climaxes, his growls inhuman as he drained her overflowing pleasure.

She lay melted beneath him, aftershocks discharging through her as he rose above her. Her hands shook as they delighted in shaping and feeling him. Though his mind was unraveling, he let her own him like he'd just owned her. But when her hands wrapped around his now-painful erection, and her tongue licked her lips, miming her intentions, he stopped her.

Her eyes flared and subsided with that hypnotic light, her flush intensifying it. "Not fair. You had your way with me...."

"You'll have your way with me, whenever and however you want. Just not now. This time I need to be inside you." Something penetrated the fog of lust wrapping his mind. "But if you're not..."

She shook her head against the light gray sheets that echoed her eyes and deepened the gloss of her raven hair, opening her thighs wide for him. "It's safe. Come inside me, Jalal, just fill me, with yourself, with your pleasure."

"Lujayn." He could swear he heard something snap, crumble. The last shred of restraint.

He snatched up her silken legs, hooking her ankles around his neck, the only position where he could plumb deepest inside her, where she almost accommodated him. He cupped her buttocks, mounted her, then holding her focus, groaning her name, he thrust inside her, felt as if he'd plunged into a vise of pure, molten pleasure.

Her scream echoed his roar as her hot flesh stretched for his invasion, her back arched, her whole body trembling like a strummed string with the shock of pain and pleasure. He withdrew, plunged again, seeking to breach her completely as he knew she needed him to, sensation slashing through him. Another sharp keen squeezed out of her depths as she smashed herself against him, seeking his full domination. He gave it to her, forging deeper with every thrust. She orgasmed over and over, shrieks shredding her voice, convulsions racking her whole body beneath his and her inner muscles around his girth.

He waited until pleasure was electrifying her in a continuous current, squeezing him beyond insanity, then erupted in his own release, his buttocks contracting into her cradle, his erection buried to the hilt inside her quivering flesh. He held himself at her womb as his seed seared through his length in jet after jet of excruciating pleasure.

Somewhere in his brain thoughts floated among the lethargy of satisfaction. The last time they'd had such profound fulfillment in each other, a life had been created, their son. And if it wasn't safe as she thought, this time another miracle might happen, another son, or better still a daughter....

He lurched back into the present, found himself spread beneath the warm, satiated embodiment of all his desires.

His heart contracted with remembrance. The last time this had happened, she'd broken away from him, her eyes cold and reviling. He couldn't survive it this time if she...

She purred something, a sound of total satisfaction, secured him in a more intimate embrace. Everything inside him fell apart in relief, in thankfulness, as he luxuriated in gliding his hands over her lushness, grinding his unabated arousal against that belly that had borne him his son. She turned her face up at him, opened for him as their mouths mated again and again.

As she dived back into his hold, his gaze fell on the wall clock. It was 1:00 a.m.

Uzeem. Great. By the time he had her in any shape that didn't say "savagely pleasured female," it might be dawn. He couldn't return her to her family looking like that, eyes barely open, mouth swollen, skin flushed with simmering lust.

He sighed, deciding this was too incredible to waste any of it worrying. He'd somehow iron this out with her family. For now, he'd savor each breath and nuance of this reunion. This revival.

He hugged her tighter, arms and legs. She sighed in bone-deep bliss, melted deeper into his full-body embrace.

He sighed again, brought up the only other thing he had on his mind anymore. "I want to see Adam tomorrow. Make that today."

She raised a wobbling head, her blissful expression receding, resurging tension clamping her every muscle. "I can't, Jalal."

He stiffened, didn't stop her when she struggled to sit up.

Her eyes pleaded as she looked at him. "I'm not contesting your right to see Adam. But I won't turn my family's life upside down while I'm here. It will be difficult enough to explain away tonight."

Unable to bear her agitation, wanting only to alleviate her worries, he brought her back to him in a searing kiss, whispered against her lips, "Then you bring him to me."

Nine

"Do you realize how huge this is?"

Lujayn winced at the nerve-fraying excitement in her younger sister's exclamation.

She ignored her as she tried to talk Adam out of wriggling down from her arms to run up the cut-stone path toward Jalal's villa on his own.

Dahab pounced on Adam, took him from her, distracting him with whooping tickles. Adam shrieked, delighted with his favorite playmate's antics. It made Lujayn realize again that while she was the one he reached for in almost everything, he never laughed with her as wholeheartedly. She hadn't been as playful with her son as she should have been. She'd let the circumstances of his birth dim her spirits, though she'd been determined not to. Seemed in spite of her best intentions and efforts, she had shortchanged him.

Now she was entering a new level of turmoil, with Jalal

invading her life on all frontiers…as he'd invaded *her* last night.…

God, what he'd done to her! She'd been in a state of molten agony ever since. She'd thought she'd remembered in distressing detail the pleasure he'd wrung from her, had even exaggerated it. Turned out she'd downplayed it. Had he always been this…?

"Huge! As in *humongous!*" Dahab exclaimed again, securing Adam on her hip. "You and Prince Overwhelming himself! Man, is this going to blow millions of hopeful females' dreams to smithereens when they know he's taken!"

Biting back a retort that he wasn't, so those millions could still hope, she kept her tone sweet for Adam's benefit. "Dahab—shut *up*. You're making me sorrier by the second that I told you."

Her impish sister stuck out her tongue at her. Adam followed suit, then burst into giggles again. Lujayn groaned. Dahab might be a fun companion for Adam, but she was no role model. Anyone would think she was twelve not twenty-two.

"First, you had to tell me. You needed me as a decoy because otherwise everyone would have wondered why you're taking Adam out when you've been leaving him with me for weeks. Second, you should be sorry indeed. How could you keep it from me—*me*—that Adam is Prince Jalal's?" Dahab swung up Adam. "No wonder you're the most gorgeous boy on earth. You take after your father."

Lujayn grimaced. Great. Even her own sister was infatuated with Jalal. But then, what female with a pulse wouldn't be?

But he'd taken her last night as if he'd been suffocating and she'd been air. Or maybe she'd reflected her feelings on him…

"I mean, I understand not telling Mom and the rest of

the Al—oops, *Aal* Ghamdi clan, what with their fourteenth-century brains. But *me?*" Dahab squinted at Adam. "Can you believe it, you edible tyke? She didn't tell *me!*"

"I'm still wondering how you lived your formative years here and didn't develop the basic persona. But you did develop the modern *me, me, me* one, didn't you?" Lujayn smirked as she slowed down more, loath to reach their destination.

She didn't know how she'd face Jalal again, what his reaction would be to Adam and Adam's to him. She'd brought Dahab to defuse the situation with her lighthearted vivaciousness.

"Actually, I'm all about you, *you*—" Dahab squeezed Adam "—and *him,* right now."

Lujayn gave her a warning/pleading look. "Speaking of *him,* you will attempt not to voice every thought and question that flits in your mind, right?"

Dahab feigned indignation. "Hey, I'm not *that* bad!" Then she wiggled her eyebrows. "But don't worry. I'm here to take a close-up look at the Prince of Many Gorgeousnesses and witness this historic meeting between father and son, but I won't stay. Got a hot date at two."

Great. So she'd get the disadvantage of her unpredictability without the advantage of her presence.

For the rest of the way, Lujayn looked around the grounds she'd barely noticed last night. Without Jalal's presence blinding her, she realized the place was like a mini-oasis. Teeming palm trees surrounded the periphery. Beyond that, the grounds were landscaped in mini-dunes and lawns with breathtaking beds of desert plants in the shadow of more palm trees of all shapes. A huge crescent-shaped *ein*—spring sparkled emerald and curved around the central two-level sprawling residence crouching on the most elevated dune and overlooking the desert that stretched into the horizon. The villa itself was a masterpiece in modern elegance and exotic design with an amalgam of Arab, Ottoman and Persian influences.

And as per Jalal's promise, the place was deserted, to assure their privacy. At some point up the winding path to the veranda where she'd entered the villa last night, Adam threw himself into her arms again in order to point things out, curious to know everything.

She was explaining about the *ein,* and debating with Dahab whether it was natural or artificial when suddenly nothing was left, in her mind, in the world.

Jalal was striding across the veranda eagerly. She was grateful for Dahab's presence when the sight of her slowed him down. But it was only seconds before they reached him where he stood at the top of the stairs, the intensity in his eyes almost evaporating her, even when it was, for once, not directed to her.

All his being was focused on Adam.

The next minutes, as father and son looked at each other in total stillness and silence, were the most tempestuously emotional of her life.

It felt as if all the months since the day Adam had been conceived were compacted, everything she'd felt and thought and suffered condensing in her heart, almost imploding it.

Holding in the tremors and tears with all she had, she watched the two people who possessed the lion's share of her heart and soul and destiny.

Adam, who was never still while awake, remained motionless, all his faculties trained at that larger-than-life entity who was looking at him as if nothing in the world existed but him. Having been born within an extended family, Adam was used to being around people, to accepting new ones. But he'd never reacted that way to someone new. To anyone. She could see it, sense it. He just knew Jalal was different from anyone else. And it wasn't because he was the largest man he'd ever seen, or who emitted the most power. She could swear she could feel, almost *taste* the bond that existed between them. It arced out of each, caught her in the cross fire before it sank into the other, transforming them all forever.

Suddenly, Jalal moved, fracturing the unbearably poignant moment, and almost her tenuous coordination and consciousness. Her sight blurred as Jalal reached a hand that visibly shook to feather a touch laden with awe down Adam's cheek.

"*Ya Ullah, ya* Lujayn—*ya Ullah!* Our son!"

The thick, ragged wonder in his voice, the agonized delight gripping his face, had her heart quivering, her nerves firing haphazardly, each jolt a tiny electrocution.

She'd never even let herself imagine this moment. She'd refused to paint scenarios of what he'd do, how he'd feel, if he saw Adam when he knew he was his. She'd strangled any thought before it came to life. Because any imagining would have been a shard embedded in her heart, an injury that would have constantly bled and drained her of life and will.

"*Ma ajmalak men subbi. Enta mo' jezah!*"

What a beautiful boy you are. You're a miracle.

"*Baba?*"

Adam's chirping voice articulated the word softly, carefully. It detonated in her head and heart, snapped her control. Tears poured, squeezed from her very essence.

Jalal's eyes, struck and reddened, tore from Adam to her, their question dazed but clear. She shook her head. She hadn't told Adam anything. But Adam knew other kids had their *babas.* He'd recognized Jalal as his.

A shudder shook through Jalal's great body, tears filled his wolf eyes as a smile she'd never thought to see trembled on his lips, one of heartbreaking tenderness. "*Aih, ya sugheeri, ana Baba."* One finger touched Adam over his heart. *"W'enta ebni."*

Yes, my little one, I'm your father. And you're my son.

Then he held out his arms to Adam.

A whimper escaped her as emotion spiked, twisting her insides. Adam always checked with her, asking her consent in a smile or a verbal encouragement, before he let a new person hold him. He asked for none now, pitched himself into Jalal's arms.

A groan of overwhelmed joy and relief rumbled from Jalal as he received Adam's robust body with care and reverence.

Adam pointed to himself, said his name, had Jalal repeating it after him before he proceeded to name his articles of clothing. Then examining Jalal with utmost concentration and interest, he pawed his face and triumphantly named his features. Satisfied with his preliminary exploration, he smiled at Jalal shyly, produced his precious pink elephant from his pocket.

As Jalal accepted it, looking more moved than she had thought possible, she heard Dahab's voice as if coming from another realm.

"You should consider yourself privileged beyond imagining. No one, and I mean *no* one is allowed to even touch Mimi."

Smiling with his whole body, Jalal turned to Dahab. "I assure you, I feel far more than that. I feel blessed for the first time in my life, when I in no way deserve to be." He reached out one of those immaculate hands to her. Adam squeaked out her name. Jalal chuckled. "Thanks for the introduction, *ya sugheeri.* I certainly see why your aunt was called that."

Dahab was Lujayn's very opposite in coloring, with hair of pure gold, hence her name, and dark chocolate eyes.

As Jalal shook Dahab's hand, his eyes warm and his smile warmer, a sick frisson went through Lujayn. In spite of her bravado, Dahab was fluttering under Jalal's influence, and she was also the most beautiful woman Lujayn had ever seen. What if...

Jalal swung his gaze back to Adam, looking down in awe at the upturned cherubic face that looked back at him with the same fascination. At length, he let out a ragged exhalation, looked at her for real for the first time today.

"*Ya Ullah, ya* Lujayn, what is this miraculous being we managed to have between us? This prodigy who recognized me on sight?" He grinned at Adam, squeezed and tickled him. "So who am I? Who am I, you most wonderful and intelligent tot? Let me hear it again."

Adam wriggled his excitement, shrieked his delight. *"Baba!"*

"That's right, you magnificent boy, you! I am *Baba* Jalal. Can you say that?"

"Baba Jalal!"

Jalal's eyelashes fluttered, as if blinking back tears. "*Ya Ullah,* I didn't even think you'd be able to talk at this age."

"Oh, he talks." Dahab chuckled. "*All* the time. A lot is still in his own language, like 'bandend' for balloon, and 'minkilonti' for macaroni, but he manages to make you get his drift."

"He says fifty-six words, in Arabic and English." Lujayn realized she'd spoken only when they all looked at her. "Uh...I write down everything he says. It's beyond his developmental age, which is fifty words at most, in one language...."

Her voice petered out at the flare of intensity in Jalal's eyes. Suddenly she found herself tucked into his body with Adam. Before she drew another breath, he took her lips in a scorching, devouring kiss that had blood whooshing in torrents in her head.

In the periphery of an awareness that overflowed with sensation, whoops and whistles echoed, until he unlocked the seal of their lips and raised his head to smile at their approving and encouraging audience.

Adam mashed their faces back together. "Kiss, kiss."

"Son, your wish is my command." Jalal chuckled, searing her with another kiss punctuated by the enthusiasm of their son and Dahab.

He released her seconds before she swooned, passion and mirth setting his eyes on golden fire. "You have to give me that list. And another of his own words." She nodded numbly as he looked down at Adam who nestled into him contentedly. Pride blazed in his eyes as he turned them back to her. "How can I ever thank you for the priceless treasure of our son, *ya'yooni'l feddeyah?*"

She almost said something as inane as "You have a fifty-percent share of his pricelessness, so we're even." Only her scrambled speech centers stopped her.

"Whoa, and he's verbal and poetic, too!" Dahab whistled again. "Anything you're not great at, Prince Jalal?"

"Do you want an alphabetized list? From what I've been finding out lately about my mess ups, it might be a good-sized volume." Jalal raised one formidable eyebrow at Dahab. "And just Jalal. If you don't want me to call you Sheikha Dahab."

Dahab shuddered. "Ugh. Reserve that for Mom and Aunt. I still don't know how I'll survive my friends finding out about this little gem of archaic pompousness."

Jalal chuckled. "Is being a sheikha such a terrible thing?"

Dahab quirked her lips at him. "You tell me. How's being a prince been for you so far?"

He sobered, exhaled. "*Aih.* The perks have certainly been

far outweighed by the aggravations, enmities and heart-aches."

"There you go. I'd rather remain plain old Dahab Morgan."

Jalal exhaled. "Seems I owe you an apology for outing your family for the nobility they are."

"Are you kidding? That's the best thing that has ever happened to them and I can't thank you enough on their behalf. Me, I'll just deal with it by being as un-sheikha-like as possible."

Jalal smiled down at Adam, smoothing his hand in wonder over his silken raven hair and his downy-soft face. Lujayn could swear Adam purred in pleasure. "Tell your aunt she'll never owe me any thanks. She needs only to ask anything and it's done. I'm at her command, just as I am at anyone's who loves you."

"Wow. Now I know what Aladdin felt like!"

As if understanding his aunt's quip, Adam burst out giggling, took Jalal's face in his chubby hands and kissed him soundly.

Jalal squeezed his eyes and groaned, looking as if he'd been punched in the gut with a battering ram of emotion.

Dahab chuckled at his distressed expression. "Excuse me, Jalal, but you're behaving as if you've never heard a baby laugh before. Or been kissed by one."

"I've never heard mine laugh or been kissed by him." Jalal hugged Adam closer to his heart, rubbed his face against his silky hair, kissed the top of his head. Realizing he was being worshipped by this huge man, Adam dived more securely into Jalal's embrace as if he'd always been there.

Jalal hugged him and Lujayn tighter, alternated his gaze between their upturned faces, his voice becoming a ragged rasp. "He has your eyes. He has your *everything*. But he somehow also has mine. He makes us look alike."

She gaped at him, then at Adam. Her mouth fell open. He was right. She'd never wanted to see Jalal in Adam, but he was there, in just about everything as he'd said. In the shape of the eyes, the dimples in the cheek, the cleft chin, the hairline, the hair itself. It wasn't hers as she'd always assumed, had the exact hue and shine and wave of Jalal's....

"Now that you've put your finger on it, oh yeah!" Dahab exclaimed. "You two suddenly do look alike, when just a second ago I saw nothing in common between you but that fabulous black hair, which on closer inspection isn't even the same color, after all!"

Right then, Adam decided they'd had enough introductions and exclamations, tapped Jalal's shoulder with a commanding "Down."

Laughing at Adam's nonnegotiable order, and still holding her to his side, Jalal bent and put Adam on the ground. Adam darted toward the open veranda doors.

At the threshold he turned. "Play."

Laughing again, Jalal took both her and Dahab by the shoulders. "The little prince has spoken."

At that humorous declaration, Lujayn's heart dropped a handful of beats. She almost stumbled as Jalal led them inside where he had a sumptuous lunch prepared. He insisted that Dahab postpone her date and have the meal with them.

All through the late lunch, he laughed with Dahab, doted on Lujayn and Adam, and answered Adam's incessant curiosities and demands for his attention with unending patience and unwavering enjoyment. Lujayn barely ate, or participated, upheaval intensifying as realizations piled up.

She hadn't even thought any of this possible. Jalal's response to Adam, the fluency of interaction between them, that instant bond and mutual appreciation and delight. And it left her in an untenable situation, both retroactively and going forward.

She *had* deprived Jalal—both—no, *all* of them of all that. And she couldn't see how she could stop doing it from now on.

The only way she could was if she agreed to Jalal's earlier proposition. After she left Azmahar, he'd come to them whenever he could, to continue their affair and be Adam's father. She had to admit, after what had happened between them last night, after today, there was nothing she wanted more from life.

But that would only be a finite solution. According to her uncle, the throne was almost in Jalal's bag. Once he became king, he'd need a queen and heirs. Legitimate heirs. Which meant their...arrangement would be temporary. And though their relationship would end when he married, his relationship with Adam wouldn't. But it would remain clandestine for his throne's and rightful heirs' sakes. That might be acceptable now, with Adam so young and unaware, but in a few years? She would never let Adam suffer being an unacknowledged, second-class son.

But how could she deprive him of his father now, after she'd seen them together, realized what a difference Jalal would make in Adam's life? While Jalal's duty to the throne would force him not to acknowledge Adam publicly, he would love him, would want to be his father in every other way that mattered.

But would that be enough? Could she make the decision for Adam, when whatever she chose would end up hurting him?

Feeling like she was about to tear down the middle, she barely interacted with the others until Adam napped and Dahab left. And she had nowhere to hide from Jalal's focus.

Before he could say anything to make any coherent thought impossible, she spoke up as soon as he returned from seeing Dahab off. "We have to talk."

His smile sizzled over her as he came closer. "First let me thank you for not telling your sister what a son of an ex-royal bitch I was with you. I bet if you'd told her half the things I did, instead of acceptance and laughter, she would have ripped my head off. And though I don't deserve it, you also didn't influence Adam in any way, either, but let him make up his own mind about me."

The lump that now perpetually occupied her throat expanded. "What happened between us remains between us. And I realize I've misinterpreted a good chunk of it, anyway."

"It still doesn't change the facts of what happened. So I'm deeply grateful that you didn't expose my...wrongdoings."

Her throat closed completely. "I'd never say anything to anyone, and I'd certainly never try to turn Adam against you."

He didn't stop until he had plastered himself against her. "Jalal, please, we need to talk...."

He pulled her fully against him, "And we will. But before anything, we have to do what all parents must always do." He hugged her off the ground, buried his face in her neck. "Make love, hard and fast, before our baby wakes up."

She stood paralyzed as his hands and lips roamed her, worshipping and accessing all her triggers. She drowned in his kiss, his hunger, her body blossoming under his appreciation and ministrations...then a thought detonated in her mind.

She pushed out of his arms. "God, how didn't I think of this?"

He tried to reach for her again, his hands gentle, his eyes concerned. "What is it?"

She stumbled away. "I know Dahab will keep our secret, but how didn't we think of Adam? He's not about to forget this visit."

"I certainly hope he won't!"

"But he'll tell everyone about *Baba* Jalal," she exclaimed.

His face relaxed in such a smile, indulgent and proud. "I certainly hope he would."

She shook her head, implications falling into place, each a new blow. "I'll have to leave Uncle's home and go live in that hotel until we leave Azmahar so he won't be exposed to anyone."

"There's no need for any of that. You can tell everyone now."

She gaped at him. "You know I can't do that. One scandal already consumed most of my family's lives. I won't cause them another. And it's out of the question for *you*, now of all times. With your campaign, the last thing you need is a scandal of the caliber of an illegitimate child."

He took her by the shoulders, his face gripped with fierce emotions. "Adam is not any such thing. He is my son and I'll proclaim him my heir in front of the whole world."

She had no answer to that. For what felt like eternity.

Then she could barely whisper, "Y-you can't do that."

"I can and I will. I have a son and I will be his father, in every way possible."

Suddenly a suspicion spread through her like wildfire. She pushed away his hands as if they burned her. "If you're thinking you can take him from me…"

He raised both hands as if to ward off a blow, his expression agonized. "Don't even complete that thought. *Ya Ullah*, you think I would even consider such a thing?"

She shook her head slowly, confusion rising. "It's just I don't see how else you'd do all…that."

"I will do it the one and only way. We will get married."

Ten

"We can't do that."

Lujayn's ready rejection hit a bull's-eye in Jalal's heart. It hadn't even been an exclamation, but a statement.

His gaze left hers, moved to that miracle that was their son sleeping so peacefully facedown over his thick, color-ful blanket on the floor. Adam felt already integrated into his being, as if he'd been a part of him since long before he'd been born. Like she was. Their presence had turned this place into a home. The intensity with which he wanted to claim them, have them with him, forming the most vital parts of his life, was frightening, exhilarating, transfiguring.

But he was just beginning to wrap his mind around what Lujayn had suffered, from childhood up till this day. He didn't have the right to feel bad that her first reaction was to reject the idea of marrying him out of hand, even after she'd made soul-searing love with him last night, and had already borne him Adam.

He had to put her needs as his first and only priority. From now on, everything would be about her. And Adam. About his family.

Emptying his face and voice of any emotion that might push her in the wrong direction, he asked, "Any reason why we can't?"

"How about every reason?"

"I can only see we have every reason to get married. Each other, Adam..."

"We don't have each other, we just slept together a couple times during the last two years."

"I would have been in your bed every night of those two years if you hadn't told me you hated me. It was why I walked away...."

"If you respected or valued me, nothing I said would have made you walk away," she cut him off, her eyes feverish. "But you despised and mistrusted me, when you had no reason to. You felt I betrayed you, but betrayal is when you give something of yourself, and someone takes it and screws you over. You gave me nothing, so what was there to betray? I exercised my right to self-preservation and you came after me, maligning and accusing. And you walked away because you always intended to, never looking back. Then I came here and you wanted to have more no-strings fun. Then you discover Adam and suddenly you want to marry me? I don't think so."

Every word gouged him deeper for being true. "I confess to all my crimes against you, Lujayn. You gave without taking, never gave me reason to mistrust you. You told me why you were leaving, but I couldn't accept it. All I could think of was my disappointment, my pain. The more I thought about it in your absence, the more I twisted everything to soothe my wounds. I am wired to think the worst of everyone first if it would explain their behavior. It comes from having Sondoss for a mother. But I'm never mistrusting you, and I'm never walking away, ever again."

Those ready tears filled her eyes, making them flash like diamonds. "For God's sake, don't even pretend this has anything to do with me. You only want to marry me for Adam."

"Legitimizing Adam is only a factor in the timing but—"

"Did you ever think of marrying me before?"

He wanted to say yes. But there'd never be anything but the whole truth between them from now on. "In the past, I never thought of getting married, no. I thought there was no reason to."

Her lips twisted. "There you go. And there's no reason still."

"I didn't mean it the way you're taking it. You know now I thought we had it all. I didn't think marriage was in either of our horizons. We were too busy, and I thought you were too young, and with your career, wouldn't afford the distraction of marriage let alone the responsibility of a family."

Her eyes narrowed to silver lasers. "Are you saying you did think of marriage and decided against it?"

"I'm saying I didn't think of it for all those reasons, not the ones you're implying. You were my woman, my lover, and I didn't think of changing the context of our relationship…and I lost you. Then we met again and till yesterday I was struggling to get you to *talk* to me. I didn't think beyond getting you back."

Sarcasm huffed out of her. "You already planned our future liaison, following the same noncommittal pattern of our past one."

"Because when it comes to you, I'm not the long-term businessman but a beggar who can't hope enough to plan ahead. I felt I'd be lucky if I even got you to agree to that much. All I knew was that if we got together again, I wanted to be together always. So yes, I would have wanted marriage. Adam just accelerated the process. He's not the reason I'm proposing, he only gave me the reason to do it now."

Disbelief still blared from her eyes.

"I *can* legitimize Adam without marrying you, Lujayn."

A wave of bristling hurt rose off her, buffeted him. "Then by all means, go ahead."

He wanted to whack himself upside the head. Would he ever learn to not stoke her insecurity and poke her scars? "I'm only trying to prove to you I want to marry you only for you."

Cagey as an aggravated tigress, she said, "How would you legitimize him without marrying me?"

"I would say we were briefly married when he was conceived, an *orphy* secret marriage, or even a regular one, that ended in divorce. It would only take your corroboration, a few retroactive documents and he'd be my lawful son and heir."

She nodded, slowly, watchfully. "I'll corroborate anything that will be best for him."

He gauged the moment when she'd let him approach again, then reached for her. "I only want you to grant me the blessing of becoming my wife."

He felt her internal struggle, unable to let belief take hold after so many years of letdowns. "Is it my family's discovered rank that makes it possible for you to consider me for a wife now?"

He almost doubled over with the pain. Hers. What *he'd* inflicted when he'd made her feel she'd meant nothing to him.

"Let me make this unequivocally clear," he said, barely curbing the tremor in his voice. "I am proposing to *you*. If your family were criminals or worse, I would still propose to you. The woman who's been responsible for my life's most intense happiness and heartache. The only woman I've always and will always love."

Tears gushed from her eyes as if under pressure, her whole face crumpling under the onslaught of emotions too brutal to bear. "Don't...don't say what you don't mean...."

He cupped her face, hands trembling to the same frequency of her anguish. "It's another crime, my biggest one, that I never told you how much I mean it. I love you so much I was yours from the first moment I laid eyes on you." She hiccuped, her eyes enormous, her body shaking. "Even when I thought I'd lost you forever, when I told myself I should hate you, I couldn't be with anyone else. There *is* no one else for me."

And he saw it, the moment her barriers crumbled and belief flooded in, deluging her in its healing rush.

She surged into him, coming apart, burrowing into him, mashing her face into his chest, his neck, singeing his flesh with her tears, his name a litany on her lips. "Jalal...Jalal... oh, Jalal..."

"*Baba* Lal!"

They swung their heads as one at hearing Adam's voice.

He was running toward them with a smile showing off all his pearly teeth, his silver eyes crinkled with glee.

He threw himself at their legs, demanding to be picked up. They both bent, took him between their trembling bodies.

In between deluging his family in kisses, Jalal said, "I asked your Mama to marry me, *ya sugheeri*."

"Mama Lu!" Adam squeaked triumphantly.

Jalal chuckled, his heart expanding at the unbelievable blessing of having his family filling his arms. "That's what you've reduced us to? Lu and Lal? Sounds good to me."

Joy shone over her beloved face. "At first he likes to say things correctly, then goes on to interpret them to his liking."

"He can call me anything he likes."

"Oh, no, you're not making up for your absence from his life by letting him walk all over you and spoiling him." She pinched his cheek playfully. "You've been warned."

"And I'm duly chastised." He took her lips in a clinging kiss. "Adam is a wonderfully sunny and adjusted child, and I'll never sabotage your discipline. You show me the ropes until I put in the necessary time and effort to earn my role as his father."

"Easy for you to say now the sleepless nights are over."

He squashed her to him, and Adam in between them, who thought it was a game, squealed his enthusiasm. "Losing those months with you will remain a scar in my being, *ya rohi*. But I promise I'm never losing any more. I'll always be there for both of you till my dying day."

"It wasn't your fault you weren't there from the start. I…"

His lips silenced her agitation. "You never need to take responsibility for anything we lost. I wasn't there, didn't go with you to prenatal visits, didn't hold your hand during labor, didn't shoulder my share and yours of every second since when you needed me to. So you'll let me carry this." She gave a difficult nod. He quirked his lips, desperate to lighten the moment. "And though I escaped the sleepless nights, I'll now attend the toilet-training drama from the start."

She burst out laughing, a desperate edge to the brittle mirth, sounding relieved to leave this behind. "And secreting the keys to locked apartments, playing hide-and-seek with turned-off cell phones and eating breakfast from our golden retriever's bowl."

He looked in mock sternness at Adam. "Is that right, *ya sugheeri?*" Adam smiled unrepentantly and he sighed dramatically. "Seems I have my work cut out for me." He met her eyes, delighting in seeing the openness of emotion there at last. "But you realize you only soaked my shirt but didn't actually say yes?"

She flung her arms around him, squeezed him with all her strength, Adam and all. "A million yeses! A trillion!"

He shuddered in her arms, his lips roaming in prayer and gratitude over her and Adam's faces. "One will do, *ya hayati*. An irreversible one, my life."

Since Lujayn was twelve, she'd lost all those she'd loved.

Her mother and siblings to years of separation, her father to the pursuit of jobs that never lasted, Jalal to the gulf that had never let her have him in the first place, and Patrick to the end she'd known would take him away from their first day together.

Even when she'd managed to rescue her mother and father, she hadn't really had them back. The years apart had taken their toll and they weren't the people she remembered. Her siblings had barely reentered her life, with her brother mainly gone from all of theirs. Then she'd discovered her pregnancy, had suffocated with fear that she'd lose her baby, too. Adam had been born perfect and she'd still suffered panic attacks daily.

She'd hidden her turmoil, for Adam's sake, for her fragile family's. But inside, she'd come apart, expended all her energy to look intact. Then Jalal had reentered her life.

Her ferocious resistance hadn't been fueled by anger, but by fear. Fear of succumbing only to find him a mirage again.

But if she could believe the past twenty-four hours, he wasn't only real, he was forever.

Surely nothing could be so perfect. She couldn't really have the completeness of Jalal and his love, the transcendent joy of their united family. Could she?

But he pledged she could have anything she dreamed of. He swore that she not only had him, but had always had him.

And here she was, in the middle of their family room, in the villa he'd bought by a phone call the moment she'd said she loved it, watching him and their son playing and talking and laughing as if they always had.

When Jalal anxiously had inquired about her silence, she'd said she was luxuriating in watching him and Adam together. From then on, he'd stopped worrying and let her indulge her every starving sense and unborn hope in the wonder and beauty of her man and her son forging a life-long bond.

Dahab came back at night and took a sleeping Adam with her to the hotel, where she told her family they'd all stay the night. She'd cooked up this plan when Jalal had announced his proposal and Lujayn's hard-won acceptance. After going ballistic, especially with the prospect of preparing a royal wedding, Dahab thought the newly engaged couple needed a night together, before wedding preparations drove them crazy and apart for the duration.

Though all Lujayn wanted the moment they reentered the villa was to tear Jalal out of his clothes and lose her mind all over him, he had other plans.

He wasn't gulping her down like he had last night, not even if she begged. And how she did. Tonight, he was wooing her, sealing their pact of forever with affection and harmony before moving on to abandon and ecstasy. In short, he drove her insane.

For the next hours till midnight, he and Labeeb—who now answered her every word with "my eyes to you"—collaborated in waiting on her, cooking for her, serving her and just all around spoiling her.

She'd endured it all, reliving every sensation of Jalal's possession. It all blossomed inside her mind and body, a memory replaying the glide of his flesh on and inside hers, the harshness of his desire biting into it, filling her body, his voice filling her ears, his breath filling her lungs, his taste her mouth. She'd sat there trying not to squirm with rising arousal and was immensely relieved when Labeeb finally disappeared.

Jalal, who'd watched her with knowing indulgence, his eyes promising her the satisfaction of her every hunger, now rose, came around to her. He took her to the middle of the floor, drew her into a gentle yet possessive embrace, danced with her to the thrilling beauty of a dreamy Azmaharian piece.

She laid her head on his chest, swaying to the tempo of his steady heart, her own stampeding, her lips and nipples stinging, every nerve discharging....

"Now to abandon and ecstasy."

His bass voice caressed her ear, had her core contracting, her toes curling. He'd almost driven her over the edge with just a declaration. Knowing how devastatingly he carried out his promises was enough to unleash the full force of her arousal.

She erupted in his arms, dragged him behind her to the bedroom suite. Theirs now.... She closed the double doors, leaned on them.

"I want you to do something for me."

His mirth evaporated at her husky words, his face settling into the stark lines of passion—fierce and resolute. "Anything. And everything. Always. Just ask."

"Let me have my way with you. *All* the way."

The flare of sensual savagery in his eyes seared through her already-inflamed flesh until she felt like one exposed nerve.

"Then have it. Any and every way you crave."

He started undressing as he talked. Her first reaction was to cry out for him to let her do it. But she held back, let him perform that mind-melting striptease for her, watching and burning, her muscles buzzing with the effort not to charge him. Soon, she placated herself. Now, she got to revel in the beauty she'd thought she'd live deprived of.

The night Adam had been conceived and last night had been too mindless and short-lived. She hadn't had the chance to savor his magnificence. And even this description was an understatement. Time had conspired to turn what she'd thought was virile perfection into something that defied description, even belief.

Burnished bronze skin overlay heavy yet lithe muscles, sculpted from power and symmetry. Broad shoulders flowed into defined chest and abdomen, narrow hips and taut buttocks, dominant thighs and muscled legs, every inch chiseled from maleness and stamina. She knew from experience that even his toes were beautiful. He was a work of divine art down to his pores.

Then he stepped out of his briefs.

Letting her get only a glimpse of what she'd soon, please soon, impale herself on, he turned, simmered an inviting look over his shoulder and sauntered like a smug feline to the bed.

In languorous movements, he propped his great body against the headboard, stretched out his long limbs, his erection hard and long, heavy and thick, ready for her to come ride it.

Feeling that nip of familiar intimidation, she tore things in her haste to get rid of her clothes. She didn't care. Any slower and she would incinerate them right off, anyway.

Then she bolted for him.

She crawled over him, worshipping him from legs to lips. By the time she straddled his hips, he'd given up any pretense at deliberateness and was panting as heavily as she was, his groans as pained as hers, his hands roaming her in a fever, his body matching her own shudders.

He still didn't hurry her, didn't drag her over him and thrust inside her to end their suffering, letting her set the pace. But she only wanted to hurtle through this first joining. So she did.

Digging her hands into his shoulders, crashing her lips down on his, drinking deep of his taste, she bore down, taking him all the way to her womb in one downward stroke.

Agony and ecstasy ripped her apart. The unforgettable, almost unbearable expansion his size forged inside her had her thrashing over him, withdrawing to escape the shredding pain, plunging back to gorge on the maddening pleasure. She was molten yet his girth almost didn't fit. And still it fit to such levels of perfection, the carnality, the reality of feeling him like that again, now when love had been declared, had her weeping. He licked her tears, growling her name, igniting her fire higher, driving her harder, until she burst into the flames of a devastating completion.

Shock waves expanded, collapsed, then again, milking his hard flesh of every pleasure, for her and for him. She shrieked his name as the detonations of each orgasm severed all her nerves, as his seed shot inside her in one scalding surge after another, bathing her intimate flesh, filling her womb, fulfilling her....

From the depths of boneless bliss, she felt his hands stroking awareness into her satiated body. She was sprawled over him, her flesh still fluttering with aftershocks around him as he remained buried inside her.

A lion's purr rumbled beneath her ear. "I need you to promise me you'll frequently override my Neanderthal tendencies to dominate you and just have your way with me like that."

Her lips spread lazily. "You got it. Very frequently."

His chuckle changed into a groan as her inner flesh spasmed over his intact hardness. "Forget what I just said.

The need to go all caveman over you is becoming unstop-pable."

She giggled as he heaved up, swung her beneath him and pressed her between the mattress and his hot, hard bulk.

A long time after he'd devastated her, he brought her over him again and sighed in contentment. "You feel...different."

Euphoria screeched to a halt. "Not as tight as before?"

"No." All bliss drained away as she wriggled, severing their union. He caught her, turned her on her back, rose above her. "I mean it's *not* that. Physically, you're the same, or it might be a bit less of a struggle to fit inside you. You just *feel* different."

Still unsure, still worried, she probed, "Because of Adam?"

"Because of *us. You're* different. *I* am. We've matured. We're certain we want each other, no substitutes. It makes us better at this." His lips quirked. "Though you must stop improving right here. Any better and I might expire."

Flooded with relief, hoping she'd soon stop having those attacks of uncertainty, she looked up at him adoringly. "Do you know you have the most beautiful eyes in existence? If we have a girl, I hope she'll have your eyes."

He stilled. "You want more children?"

Every uncertainty crashed down on her again. She swallowed. "I'm just saying, if one day you think we should..."

He interrupted her agitation. "I think we should have as many children as you're willing to have. I want anything you want, whenever you want it."

Wobbling with yo-yoing anxiety and relief, her hand trembled as she smoothed it down his stubbled cheek. "Then I want to binge on you without interruptions a bit longer before we embark on our next miracle."

"Then binge away." His grin was delight itself as he swept her up in his arms and took her to the bathroom.

* * *

The rest of the night, followed by next day, were spent in a blur of lovemaking.

By evening, they reluctantly considered the rest of the world, called her family back to the villa and announced their news.

They'd agreed on a story. They met after Patrick died, sought solace in each other, got married. But she thought she'd made a mistake, insisted on a divorce. He'd been trying to get her back ever since. He'd told her it wasn't far from the truth.

Her family's reaction was one of dazed delight. And they were even more stunned, along with Lujayn, when Jalal announced they'd get married a week from now. He'd assured them it would be enough time to prepare a wedding worthy of Lujayn.

Carried on the wave of collective happiness and enthusiasm, Lujayn spent the next day at the royal palace where Jalal had decided to have the wedding. He gave her and her family, foremost Dahab, free rein to set the place up for a legendary wedding. Lujayn didn't want any of that, but he insisted he wanted to give her this, and to please humor him.

Spiraling deeper than ever in love with him, she accepted this as another of his efforts to make up for the years they'd lost, and the unintentional pain and alienation he'd inflicted on her. Though she didn't need any tributes or any amends, she knew *he* needed to make them. She'd always give him everything he needed.

She'd just left her family and Adam in the *Qobba* hall, literally the Dome, the name coming from its residing under the palace's central, hundred-foot mosaic one. She had to find Jalal, get his opinion about the seating plan for his personal friends.

Entering the antechamber to the royal office on the first floor, she heard a voice that wasn't his.

If voices could have colors, that one would be pitch-black.

"...already behaving as if you own the place."

She heard Jalal exhale. "And it's great to see you again, too, Rashid."

That had to be Rashid Aal Munsoori, the third candidate for the throne. She knew he was a distant maternal relative of Jalal's, and a once-best friend. She had no idea how things stood between them now, especially with being rivals for the throne.

From what she'd heard so far, it didn't sound like they were on particularly friendly terms. At least, from Rashid's side. He was more or less accusing Jalal of usurping the palace as his own.

But Jalal wasn't abusing his power, had paid a major sum to the kingdom's treasury to use the palace for their wedding. She'd said they could have rented the Taj Mahal for a month for that amount. He'd countered they could have used the royal palace of Zohayd for free, which was better than both places. In fact, King Amjad, his oldest brother, had snarked his head off, telling him to skip along and have a rehearsal wedding in his motherland to please his in-laws, then come have an actual one in his *father*land, in a palace *really* worthy of his wife and heir.

But Jalal considered he was hitting two birds with one stone having their wedding here. Giving her a wedding in *her* motherland, reinforcing her family's status and pumping money into the kingdom without it looking like a charitable donation.

She chewed her lip as she debated if she should wait until Rashid left, or leave and return when he had.

Her intimate flesh quivered at contemplating the long walk to and from the *Qobba* hall. Though the soreness she'd begged Jalal to inflict on her was delicious, it did make walking straight quite a feat. She didn't want to give everyone *too* clear an indication how they'd spent the time since their reunion. Now that Azmahar would feature heavily in their future, she had to get used to observing the land's conservative tendencies.

Deciding to wait, she picked one of the Arabic books in the mini-library in the antechamber. Might as well brush up on her Arabic reading skills as she waited.

She started reading then everything inside her froze as something Rashid was saying made her listen.

"...after Haidar thwarted your plans to use Roxanne to gain the upper hand in the campaign, you think giving the fairy-tale-addicted Azmaharians a sob story about restored honor, estranged spouses and a secret male heir will sway them in your favor?"

Her heart choked on its beats waiting for Jalal's answer. He would hit Rashid's venom back with as much conviction.

But he didn't. He didn't answer at all.

She couldn't even fathom his reaction from the quality of his silence. How was he looking at Rashid? Ridiculing? Exasperated?

Rashid was talking again. "Go ahead, shackle yourself with a woman and a child you don't want in your desperate bid for the throne. It will be a fitting punishment for you to be literally left holding the baby with not as much as a cabinet seat to collapse in defeat on."

She was shaking from head to toe when Jalal finally talked.

"Haidar told me how you had changed. I thought he was exaggerating. Turns out he's been his usual reticent self and left out the juicy parts. What happened to you, Rashid?"

A long, nerve-racking silence followed.

Then in a voice as still as the grave, Rashid said, "Didn't you just say your distorted mirror image told you?"

"He only told me the end result, not the process. We know nothing about you beyond the time when you joined the army and kept drifting farther and farther away until you disappeared on us totally. And then—" she could almost see Jalal's frustrated gesture in the beat of silence "—*this* came back in your stead."

"*This* is the real me." Rashid's voice remained expressionless, and more hair-raising for it. "The only me you'll ever see again. So if either of you deficient hybrids thinks you have a prayer against me, spare yourself the indignity. You in particular are so pathetic I decided to show you the mercy of advising you not to sacrifice your freedom at the altar of the kingly ambitions that you are destined to never fulfill."

Lujayn stood rooted as Rashid's voice approached and as he opened the ajar office door. He saw her immediately, stopped.

He stared back at her, a force of darkness in male form.

And that scar...

She would have lurched if she wasn't frozen, inside and out.

Then he exhaled. "I'm sorry you had to hear that, Sheikha Lujayn. At least now you can make an informed decision."

He bowed deferentially as he passed her even as Jalal's shouted curse penetrated her numbness.

Jalal charged into the antechamber, aggravation blazing at Rashid's receding back, morphing into anxiety as his eyes fell on her.

Before he could say anything, she whispered, "Is this why you want us, Jalal?"

His face twisted as if she'd stabbed him. "You still think that badly of me, Lujayn? You mistrust me that deeply?"

She swallowed, shook her head. She trusted him, but...

He took her shoulders in trembling hands. "Rashid was just messing with me, like he's been messing with Haidar since he's come back to Azmahar. Beside whatever has turned him against us personally, he considers us interlopers, more Zohaydan than Azmaharians. He's employing psychological warfare to get us out of the way. But you must know everything you heard him say has no basis in fact. I want you, and Adam, for one reason only. Because I can't live without you. Tell me you believe me, *ya habibati!*"

She threw herself at him, clung as if she'd escaped certain death. "I do, oh, God, Jalal, I do."

He groaned against her cheek, her lips. "I can't bear it if you have any doubts, *ya'yooni*. I'll withdraw my candidacy."

"No!" She pulled away so he could read her urgency, conviction in her eyes. "Don't even think it! I just love you so much, am so happy, it's making me jittery and unable to believe my luck."

He pulled her once again into his embrace, agitation draining, indulgence flooding back. "It isn't luck, it's the least you deserve. And whether I become king or not doesn't matter. I only want to love you and Adam and live to make you happier still."

As she lost herself in his kiss, his safety and promise, something still told her there was no way life would let her have all that and not eventually interfere....

Eleven

The tables' accents and the color of bridesmaids' dresses had just been decided. *Dahabi*. As the "golden" girl, Dahab herself had decreed the color was a no-brainer.

What remained was everything else. The flower arrangements, the grounds' ornaments and lighting, the hall decorations, the catering menu. The *kooshah*—where Lujayn and Jalal would preside over the festivities—was a matter of particular contention. And Lujayn didn't even want to think what would happen when she had to give a final word on her dress. Not to mention accessories. Everyone had an opinion, and of course, it was the right one.

She'd been stunned when her mother had come passionately to life the moment Jalal had set the wedding date, becoming a whirlwind of organizing and decision-making. More stunning was her aunt's all-out enthusiasm. She'd been recovering from her mastectomy at breathtaking speed, especially after knowing she wouldn't need chemo or radiation. But Lujayn bet her mother's and aunt's soaring spirits had most to do with their restored social status, and Jalal treating them like queens. They almost grew wings every time he walked in, kissing their hands and calling them *hamati* and *hamati el tanyah*—my mother-in-law and second mother-in-law.

But he'd done way more. He'd turned the palace into a workshop for them. He had tailors, jewelers, chefs, florists and workmen from just about every trade at their beck and call to put together every detail of the wedding. Her womenfolk were getting more delirious by the second, feeling like they'd fallen into a wonderland where they'd fulfill every feminine fantasy. Dahab had told him he'd firmly earned the title of genie.

After the first day, when she'd realized the scope of the details, Lujayn had thought they'd have to postpone the wedding. Jalal wouldn't hear of it. His rationalization? If they gave her womenfolk a year, they'd still come up with more details. Though she agreed, she couldn't get around the slowing down that working in shifts caused so someone would always be with Adam. Jalal, always ready with a solution, had whisked Adam away till the wedding.

She'd smothered him in kisses. Not because he'd taken Adam off her hands, but because of the eagerness with which he had. She'd also pinched his luscious butt for maneuvering her into giving him this opening to have Adam all to himself. He'd pinched hers right back, telling her to get to work, triumphantly informing Adam that, as men, their part in that legendary wedding would consist of jumping into their costumes and showing up.

He'd been bringing Adam to visit twice a day. Adam considered the preparations a huge game park and Jalal let him play among them to his heart's content, watching him like a hawk all the while. During their last visit hours ago, her family had wanted to drag her to more dress fittings, had shooed Jalal away so he wouldn't accidentally see the dress they might decide on.

She'd insisted on seeing him and Adam out, silently begging him to support her decision. She'd needed a breather from the single-mindedness of her bridesmaid-zillas. When they'd protested they'd only checked off six items from a list of fourteen today, couldn't afford a break, he'd come to her rescue, asserting he needed a kiss, one not for her family's eyes.

Cheeks blazing and eyes gleaming, they'd let her escape.

Not that he'd let her escape *him*. After he'd given Adam to Labeeb, he'd dragged her into one of the palace's secret rooms, taken her, hard and fast and almost blew her mind.

She'd gone back to her family in a stupor and had gone along with anything anyone had said ever since. Hence all that gold that would turn the *Qobba* hall into a replica of Midas's vault.

But then Qusr Al Majd—literally Palace of Glory—would give said vault, and all tourist-attraction palaces in the world a run for their money. It might not be as majestic as Zohayd's royal palace, but it was surely striking, and like Haidar had said, felt like some elaborate beast from a Dungeons & Dragons fantasy.

Haidar had come yesterday to meet his twin's "best-kept secret" and thank her for proving his "wolf" theory about Jalal right. Jalal had teased his twin back saying one of the things *he* thanked her for was making him beat Haidar to something—having a "cub" first. Haidar had volleyed that he'd beat him again. Roxanne was pregnant with another set of Aal Shalaan twins!

She'd liked Haidar on sight, was so grateful that he and Jalal had patched up their lifelong differences. She knew she'd grow to love him and, if possible, that had intensified her happiness.

She now sat ensconced on a window seat in the meeting-room-turned-workshop, her outline still blurred from Jalal's lovemaking, dreamily watching Azmahar's autumn sun setting, and its velvety, star-studded night taking over.

"So this was why you've been avoiding me!"

Lujayn started, burning in instant embarrassment. Aliyah!

She jumped down from the seat, turned to the woman who'd once been her lifeline, her heart quivering with delight to see her again. And she almost gasped.

Aliyah had always been beautiful, but now...now she was glorious. What fairy-tale queens should look like.

As tall as Lujayn but slimmer—at least now *she* was full of "lethal curves" as Jalal insisted—Aliyah had the bearing of a woman who'd long borne the weight of position and power. Having two children had only deepened her tranquility, and having the certainty of a great man's love had crystallized her femininity.

Aliyah had another gorgeous woman with her who looked as if her body and spirit had been spun from fire. Roxanne Gleeson, now known as Haidar's wife, Princess Roxanne Aal Shalaan—a woman she'd once thought had been one of Jalal's lovers.

He'd explained away the misconception that had long torn at her, telling her that Roxanne had actually been like the sister he'd longed to have in his all-male family. According to Jalal, Aliyah had been revealed to be his sister in time to get married and hoarded by that possessive jackass of a husband.

When she'd giggled that Aliyah sure didn't agree with his opinion of King Kamal of Judar, he'd harrumphed. Kamal, and he, *were* confirmed jackasses. They'd just lucked into having phenomenal women love them. Just like Haidar had with Roxanne. Thankfully, after long years of estrangement, Roxanne had become his sister at last, Haidar's wife and an Aal Shalaan princess.

Before Lujayn could do more than kiss the two women, her womenfolk came swarming. Queen Aliyah of Judar was one of the two big-deal queens in the region, the other being Queen Maram of Zohayd, King Amjad's wife and Lujayn's almost sister-in-law. Roxanne had also made a big splash in Azmahar on two fronts, first as the kingdom's foremost politico-financial analyst, and now as Haidar's wife.

Soon, the two women joined their dress-choosing ritual with utmost enthusiasm. For the next couple hours, Lujayn felt like a doll, being put into and pulled out of dresses that she then had to model, walk, sit, run, dance and climb stairs in, with the ladies scribbling down comments and ratings for each, then discussing pros and cons spiritedly.

Aliyah finally insisted Lujayn try on a dress, to everyone's surprise. It was fashioned from an incredible amalgam of tulle, taffeta and lace, worked in breathtaking arabesque patterns of sequins, mirrors, pearls and silk thread. A strapless, hugging bodice would accentuate Lujayn's breasts and waist and a skirt lush in layers, yet not flaring, would showcase her curves. In short, perfect.

But their unanimous objection to it? It was *gray*.

Aliyah laughingly reminded them they were talking to the woman who'd rocked the region wearing black for her wedding. And then it *wasn't gray*. It was silvered dawn and deepening twilight and every shade in between. And it looked as if it was spun from the threads of Lujayn's own unique colors.

They all deferred to Aliyah's opinion, not as queen, but as the world-renowned artist among them.

Lujayn still felt their skepticism, until the moment they saw it on her. And they all shouted simultaneously, "That's it!"

It was only then that Aliyah revealed that her vision for the whole scene was now complete. With the bridesmaids and matrons of honor all golden, with her coloring and dress, Lujayn would stand out like a black-and-white silver-screen moon goddess.

Another hour passed before Lujayn was finally allowed to take off the dress, after picking a *tarhah*—a veil—for it. Aliyah and Roxanne both promised to bring her just the pieces to go with that outfit from the royal jewels of Judar and Zohayd.

Leaving her family boggling over that prospect, Aliyah and Roxanne spirited Lujayn away for a much-needed break.

In the blessed silence and isolation of a sitting room at the farthest end of the palace, she finally grinned at them. "Thanks for the rescue, ladies. It's a good thing weddings are a once-in-a-lifetime thing. I don't think I'd survive that again."

"Don't worry, you won't need to." Roxanne beamed, looking the image of glowing health in her early second trimester. "You're marrying an Aal Shalaan. Those are for-life catches."

"And Aal Masoods," Aliyah piped in.

Lujayn's smile widened, remembering Jalal's jackass comment concerning Aliyah's Aal Masood husband. No way was she telling Aliyah and have her kick Jalal's luscious behind for it.

Roxanne sighed. "We're all Aal Shalaan princesses now, whether by birth or marriage. And let me tell you, Lujayn, from, uh…intensive experience, there's *nothing* better."

Lujayn nodded vigorously, still tingling from her own recent "intensive experience" with her Aal Shalaan prince.

"Did you notice how my own messed-up origins make me related to everyone in some way or another?" Aliyah asked.

Lujayn grinned. "Yep, you're the only one who grew up a Morgan, turned out to be an Aal Shalaan and then became an Aal Masood, too."

"While I once felt it was a mess I'd never survive, it proved to be the best blessing possible." Aliyah winked at Lujayn. "Finding out you're not who you thought you were is turning out fantastic for you, too, isn't it? Not to mention catching the heart of one of those forever guys." Aliyah's dark eyes sparked gold, reflecting the sun streaks in her mahogany hair. "And though you kept everyone in the dark, I can't believe you had *me* fooled. You missed your vocation as an actress, lady."

Lujayn fidgeted under Aliyah's teasing scrutiny. "Yeah, well, it wasn't something I could share at the time. I've long stopped being a model, too. I entered college when I married Patrick, got a degree in economics and business management. I'm preparing a master's degree now."

"Wow, I can't believe just how much we have in common!" Roxanne exclaimed. "Having you in the family is going to be even more fun than I anticipated. And you must make use of me if you ever need any help with your projects and assets. I'm a decent financial adviser, I'm told."

"They're not mine," Lujayn said, then explained the situation with Patrick's family. "I only controlled everything until we made sure they were out of the way. I'll soon turn it over to the charities and concerns he'd specified. Any money or shares my family got was payment for our work, so I'm not the billionaire heiress everybody thinks I am. I just never refuted it since I was still wrapping things up before I came back to Azmahar."

Roxanne looked impressed. "And that you managed to keep that from someone like me tells me everything about how good you are at what you do. I've heard there are many concerns vying to do business with you as Patrick's heiress. Prepare for the restoration of some serious personal space when the news comes out."

Roxanne's words suddenly hit her with a realization.

She never really explained to Jalal how things stood.

But he had once made it clear he believed she possessed Patrick's wealth. What if part of her...acceptability now was because of her assumed wealth? Princes did have far more to consider in marriage than normal men. Money and power married money and power. What if, when he realized she didn't have either, it changed everything?

From then on, she barely knew what Aliyah or Roxanne said or what she answered. At some point they stood up, kissed her, and promising to join her wedding preparation mayhem starting tomorrow, they took their leave.

In a similar fugue, she returned to her family who tossed her around in more wedding details before they called it a night. Instead of spending the night in the palace like them, she slipped away to Jalal's villa. Or as he insisted it now was, home.

Labeeb received her at the gates and suggested that she surprise Jalal. He had turned out to be a closet romantic. Before he disappeared, he reassured her that Adam was asleep after a bath that had left him happily exhausted and Jalal and Labeeb wet. Both grown-ups had their baby monitors on their person, but there hadn't been a peep from Adam for the past three hours.

Inside the villa, Jalal's favorite music, a hybrid of western, Zohaydan and Azmharian, was emanating from their family room, wrapping her in its evocative magic. Approaching in silence, she stood watching Jalal as he sat on the couch in profile. He was covered in a laptop and open files, looking totally engrossed, and more heartbreakingly beautiful than ever. Barefoot, hair tousled, black trainers riding low on his hips, and the rest of his body was exposed to her devouring.

Seeing him this way, relaxed in their home, surged in her heart with thankfulness and longing. But anxiety ruled all other emotions.

He turned suddenly, his gaze slamming into hers, delight flaring in his eyes.

After hurriedly clearing his lap, he jumped up to his feet and rushed to her, arms open. He swept her off the floor, groaned into her hair, *"Habibati..."* before he took her lips, submerged her in his hunger.

When he let her draw a breath, her feet almost buckled as he put her back on them.

"So how did you do it?"

She blinked.

He elaborated. "Escape your posse of wedding wardens?"

She hugged him, filled with the wonder of him in her arms. "I slipped out behind their backs, how else?"

"They intimidated me so much with their lists and color schemes I didn't even dare ask you to do this."

She chuckled at the incongruous image he painted, the desert warrior tiptoeing around a bunch of females in fear they'd attack him with ribbons and cake tastings.

His laughter echoed hers as gravity relinquished its hold over her, delivered her into his power. She plunged into his craving, wanting to take all she could now, before anything happened to spoil this magic, as she lived in fear it would....

The night's breeze was blowing their bedroom's gauzy, cream-colored curtains in a hypnotic dance when she finally resurfaced from another surrender to ecstasy in his arms. He was stroking her sweat-drenched, still-quivering body when without preamble she poured out everything about Patrick's assets.

He kept on caressing her throughout her account.

When she fell silent, he shrugged. "And?"

She rose over him, anxious to read his expression. There was only his usual indulgence. "*And* I'm not an heiress."

"Darn." He combed his fingers through her tousled tresses, his grin devilish. "I was hoping you'd lend me a billion or two to develop a cloaking device so I can make love to you anywhere."

"Be serious for a second here, okay?" she groaned.

His eyes sobered. "What's to be serious about? Your involvement or lack of in Patrick's legacy doesn't change my pledge to fulfill it. Other than that, what does your being an heiress or not matter?" He rose on his elbows, frowning. "You still think anything but you matters to me?"

Her gaze wavered under the disappointment in his. "I—I just wondered...y'know, with you being a prince, if—if..."

She groaned again, words trailing off.

He heaved up, had her rolling to her side to watch him stride from the bed to the desk by the veranda. He picked up an MP3 player, tapped the screen and walked back with it held up to his lips.

"I, Jalal Aal Shalaan, hereby solemnly swear, on my life, on my honor, on my son—whose finger alone I value above my life—that one woman has ever and will ever be the largest part of my soul, just because she is who she is. My cherished, beloved Lujayn."

Reaching the bed again, he held the player down to her. It replayed the pledge he'd just recorded.

"Whenever you have any worries and I'm not around, play this." With a teary sob, she launched herself at him, raining laughter and tears all over him. "And when I am, just let me know, and I'll take care of it for you, like this...."

And for the rest of the night, he showed her how he'd always take care of her every worry and need....

The day was here.

The day he'd tell the whole world he was Lujayn's. The day he'd start his lifelong mission to heal all the injuries and injustice that he and his family had dealt her.

His gaze panned over his surroundings, and his lips spread. He had to give credit to Lujayn's womenfolk. They *had* pulled off a miracle. He'd teased them, wondering if they did have a genie at their command. They had turned the neglected palace with its hideously ornate interiors, and especially the *Qobba* hall, into a most tasteful and lavish setting from an *Arabian Nights* fable. A setting worthy of his princess, the love of his life and the mother of his incomparable son.

His family, who had all arrived that morning, were now sitting in the huge semicircle facing the *kooshah* where he and Lujayn would join the *ma'zoon* to scribe their marriage vows in the book of matrimony. His father hadn't looked this well and happy in...ever. His marriage to Anna Beaumont, Aliyah's biological mother, and the love of *his* life, was doing him wonders. After a lifetime wasted in two marriages, first to the mother of Amjad, Harres and Shaheen, followed by the harsher blow of his and Haidar's mother, their father deserved a break. And he'd at last gotten it. Anna seemed to be formed of pure love for her husband. His father had earned all this beauty and devotion, had done the right thing in abdicating the throne of Zohayd to Amjad. Now he could enjoy what was left of his life with the one woman his heart had chosen, and whom life and duty had deprived him of for three decades.

But though he was delighted for his father, tonight he could tell him and his older brothers and Haidar, that they could move over and vacate the position of happiest man on earth.

A sigh of pleasure and anticipation escaped him, as Lujayn's favorite jasmine scent filled the gigantic hall, carried on a dreamlike mist.

Adam whooped and jumped in his arms. Heart pounding, his gaze moved to where Adam's tiny finger was excitedly pointing. Lujayn's bridal procession had just entered the hall, preceded by Dahab.

They looked like walking jewelry with their golden dresses. Every female in Lujayn's family had joined the ranks. Almost all in his had. His brothers' wives were all there, Johara, Talia, Maram and Roxanne. Aliyah was walking with her daughter, who skipped beside her looking like a pixie, and actually completing the image by throwing golden dust behind her.

The only women who didn't make it to this wedding was Laylah, one of the three precious female Aal Shalaans. And his mother.

No one even spoke of Sondoss, as if her mention would be the evil spell that would spoil everything. He couldn't blame them. Though he visited her whenever he could, he sure wasn't inviting her into his life now that it revolved around Lujayn and Adam. The farther she stayed from Lujayn and her family, the better.

The heavy, driving beat of the *zaffah* started, the region's traditional bridal procession rhythm. After a percussive intro, with Dahab acting as cheerleader, the whole attendance started singing the most famous regional bridal song, chanting the praises of the bride, congratulating her on her dashing groom and wishing her bountiful happiness and blessed progeny.

Every nerve strained for Lujayn's entrance as Adam's excitement reached fever pitch and he starting yelling her name. The song was repeated twice as the bridal procession took their places, surrounding the *kooshah* in petal-like patterns, and everyone pinned their gazes on the hall's entrance.

The entrance remained empty. The song was repeated three times more, and it remained so. After the fifth repetition the music stopped. Murmurs rose, then spread like wildfire. Everybody was looking around, expecting some surprise. When none came, they turned their gazes to him. He stood there, frozen, unable to think. He felt nothing but Adam wriggling in his arms. He put Adam down and he ran to his grandmother. Jalal met her gaze and saw in her bewilderment that she had no idea what was going on. And that she was growing more anxious with every heartbeat.

"You wait right here. We'll go find out what's going on," Harres said, who'd come back from talking to the *ma'zoon*.

"What *could* be going on?" Haidar asked, who'd been standing beside him. As his closest brothers, both would be the marriage witnesses. "She either changed her mind about the dress, or she's keeping you waiting a bit to punish you for all the years you didn't even think of marrying her."

Haidar gave him a reassuring backslap and strode away.

Jalal stood there, his mind stalled. Nothing would restart it but the sight of Lujayn.

Time warped, everything grated. The air, the weight of his costume, people's glances.

Then Haidar and Harres strode into the hall again.

Harres swerved, headed for Amjad, Shaheen and their father. Haidar walked up to him.

Jalal could only stare at Haidar as he stopped before him.

He couldn't read his expression. Wouldn't. Everything

refused to cooperate. Wouldn't work. His mind. His voice. His heart.

Then with his voice as dark and regretful as his expression, Haidar said, "Lujayn is gone."

Twelve

Gone.

The word revolved in his head again and again. It made no sense. It was impossible. Untrue.

Lujayn couldn't be gone.

Then a chain reaction started, sparked by an insupportable thought. The only way she could be gone.

She'd been taken. *Kidnapped.*

His mind overflowed with dread. Talons of desperation pierced his brain as his fingers sank into the one thing left in his world, his twin's immovable support. His vision phased in and out as a voice, rabid with fear, barely recognized as his, formed no words, just her name, over and over. He couldn't say anything else and make it real.

Haidar's words cleaved inside his skull. "Go to pieces later, Jalal. We need to say something to this crowd, contain this catastrophe first, then we're getting you out of here and…"

He pushed Haidar away, unable to bear any more talk and ran out of the hall, a storm of agitation exploding all around him. He heard cries, inquiries, exclamations that pummeled him with their alarm. He pushed through the hindering bodies and presences. If he ran hard enough, he might still find her, save her....

Inexorable forces pulled him back. He turned and found Haidar and Harres holding on to him. Amjad and Shaheen were running toward them.

"Where do you think you're going?" Haidar hissed.

"I won't even say I can imagine how you feel," Harres said. "Because I damn well can't. But let's slow down for a moment...."

"Slow down?" Jalal roared. "Lujayn has been kidnapped and you want me to slow down?"

"Kidnapped?" Shaheen frowned, looking among his brothers.

Amjad came to a stop a couple feet away. "So you think the only way she'd stand you up at the *ma'zoon* is if she'd been kidnapped?"

Jalal rounded on him snarling, shaking off Haidar's and Harres's shackles.

Amjad deflected his aggression with unperturbed sarcasm. "She wasn't kidnapped, so you can stop working on this heart attack."

Everything inside Jalal stopped, clamped down on only three words. *She wasn't kidnapped.*

Relief razed through him. "Are—are you sure?"

His brothers exchanged an uncomfortable look. Then, exhaling heavily, Haidar handed him a note.

There were only three words on it, too. In Lujayn's handwriting.

I'm sorry. Lujayn.

He stared at the words, as if they'd multiply, as if they'd

say more if he looked hard enough. The same three words remained. Explaining nothing.

"Where did you find this?" Jalal rasped.

Haidar exhaled again. "In the room where the ladies had left her, to have a moment to herself as she'd requested, before walking out to the bridal procession. She'd taken off her wedding dress and left through the balcony."

Jalal shook his head, discounting every word, every evidence. "That's impossible. She wouldn't leave. Not of her own accord. A note doesn't prove she wasn't kidnapped. She could have been forced to write it, to—to..." Moisture that felt like acid forced its way out of his eyes, slithered down his cheeks. "*Ya Ullah*...Lujayn...*ya Ullah*..."

Harres hugged him roughly around the shoulders. "She *hasn't* been kidnapped, Jalal, so stop going crazy, at least about this."

"Guards tried to stop her," Haidar said. "But she insisted they'd be punished if they detained her. They were so flustered by her intensity they let her go. By the time they informed Fadi and he checked the airport, she'd boarded a flight. He ordered them to stop takeoff and disembark her, but she invoked her American citizenship and they took off."

Jalal stared at Haidar, finding no more places to hide.

She was really gone.

But it couldn't be because she wanted to. She loved him. More than loved him. He was half of her soul as much as she was his. And the other half was Adam. She wouldn't leave either of them. She'd die without them. Just like they would without her.

Seemed he'd said that out loud, because Amjad was answering him. "She knows without marrying her, you won't be able to stop her family from taking Adam back to her. So she only left you."

He rounded on Amjad. "Would *you* believe Maram would ever leave you?"

Amjad's gaze lengthened at his vehemence. Then he shrugged. "Then Lujayn left but didn't really leave. *That* leaves one possibility."

Everyone turned to Amjad, all at a loss.

Amjad raised ridiculing eyebrows. "You really can't figure it out? What is this, a collective, selective blindness?"

Harres punched Amjad in the arm. "One more useless word, and king or not, the next punch puts you flat on your back."

Amjad rubbed his arm, gave Harres then Shaheen a pitying glance. "Those two—" he flicked a hand at Haidar and Jalal "—I can understand, having been genetically tampered with. But what's *your* excuse?" Shaheen joined Harres in a threatening step, and Amjad's palms on both their chests held them off as he shook his head derisively, let out a disgusted huff. "Sondoss, what else?"

Jalal's heart gave one sickeningly painful twist at hearing his mother's name. Then it all fell into place.

It *was* his mother. She was the one who'd made Lujayn leave.

"We warned you she wasn't through messing in your lives." Amjad scowled at him and Haidar. "But you went all filial on us and exiled her in that tropical resort instead of letting me devise a dungeon worthy of her dragon-ness. Now you pay the price."

"If you believe a dungeon would have ended her danger," Shaheen scoffed, "then you don't realize what Sondoss is."

Harres nodded. "Jalal and Haidar made the right decision, if for the wrong reasons. An imprisoned Sondoss would have been far more dangerous than an exiled one. The worst she's evidently done so far was sabotage a wedding. But had she been in prison, she would have plotted the end of the world to get out."

Amjad smirked. "Good boys. You're not as gullible as I sometimes fear. I'll keep you as my heir and spare." He quirked an eyebrow at all of them. "But it took us years to accidentally stumble on her diabolical plot. Want to bet that in due course, we'll discover she's put far worse in motion than spoiling a wedding? Maybe even that world's end scenario?" He panned his gaze to Jalal. "Though from looking at you, she might have ended yours."

Shaheen glared at Amjad. "There might still be another explanation to all this."

Haidar shook his head, looking as shaken as Jalal felt. "No. Mother makes a perfect one."

Harres nodded. "Agreed. One thing I can't figure out, though. How did she get Lujayn to leave?"

Jalal turned, walked away. His brothers let him go this time.

He didn't know how. But he would find out.

He would put an end to his mother's damage once and for all.

Ten sanity-wrecking hours later, Jalal walked into the seafront house he and Haidar had provided for their mother in Aruba.

They'd picked the place based upon being as close as possible to Azmahar's climate, and the house to maintain the comfort level she'd been used to. In spite of everything, they'd wanted her to feel as at ease and at home as possible in her exile.

But it stopped here. His filial weakness. Not because he'd almost died when he'd thought Lujayn had been kidnapped, or because she'd sabotaged their wedding. It was what she'd done to Lujayn, again. He hadn't forgiven her for her past transgressions. Now, he never would. He couldn't bear to imagine Lujayn's anguish when his mother had forced her to leave their wedding.

Ya Ullah, how had she done it?

Waving away the guards he'd assigned to his mother, he strode into the one-level sprawling house with the first rays of dawn. The thought that she could sleep after she'd ruined his wedding, maybe even his life, had blood roaring in his ears, louder with each step closer to her bedroom.

"...everything you wanted."

The words barely carried to him, but they felt like a direct blow to his heart. For he didn't have any doubt who'd said them.

Lujayn. She was here.

His feet almost left the ground to home in on her voice. Then he exploded into his mother's private quarters, stood at the door staring at a sight he'd never thought he'd see. His mother sitting relaxed with Lujayn over steaming cups of tea.

Neither woman reacted at his entry. As if they'd both been waiting for him. His mother, in an emerald satin dressing gown that reflected some color onto the steel of her eyes, looked as majestic and ageless as ever. Lujayn, in a sedate gray pantsuit, had her hair still in the chignon she must have had styled for the wedding that never was. She kept her face turned away.

He had to tell her she mustn't feel bad, that he was here to...

"I'm glad you're here, *ya helwi.*" His mother's expression and voice were calm as she extended a hand to him. "Come, join us for tea. Or did you have enough stomach-turning beverages on the plane?"

His teeth gritted. "No, you don't, *ya ommi.* You don't 'my sweet' me. Ever again."

His mother gave a theatrical sigh. "*Zain,* let me get to the point without any…sweetening. Lujayn has always been my mole."

Everything went still. Had she just said…?

Incredulity and fury overcame him, crackled from his depths. "*Ya Ullah,* is there no end to your surprises? Why not tell me Lujayn is actually a man? That would be more believable."

His mother's gaze maintained its unwavering serenity. "I sent her to you when you were establishing the New York branch of your business. I needed someone I controlled to keep you away from the unsuitable women swarming around you, by giving you everything you needed from a woman with seemingly no strings and no price. But when you kept going back to her for years, I realized my plan had worked too well, was afraid you'd gotten attached to her. So I ordered her to start alienating you. But contrary boy that you are, you liked her more for it. I waited almost two years for you to walk out, but you didn't, so I ordered her out of your life, told her she could go for the other man she'd been… cultivating. Lujayn obeyed, of course, cut you off and married your friend, who was conveniently dying. I decided it was safer from then on to drive women away one at a time. But we know I haven't had to do a thing. You did it on your own ever since."

Jalal could only gape at his mother, his eyes flitting every other sentence to Lujayn. Lujayn's face remained turned away, what he could see of it was frozen, expressionless.

His mother went on. "While it was a relief at first that you wouldn't let anyone near, I felt worried, then guilty that I'd set you up to fall for my impostor, but hoped eventually you'd find others. I never predicted that you'd go after Lujayn after her husband died, wishful thinking on my part. I surely hadn't counted on you getting her pregnant. When she told me, I ordered her to stay away, hide the child. That is, until I needed to create a scandal for you."

Unable to feel shock anymore, Jalal only stared at his mother as she rewrote his whole history with Lujayn.

"But again, you, unpredictable boy, thwarted me. Before she could unleash the scandal of your illegitimate child from my servant's daughter, you had to go unearth her family's origins. While I was deciding how to deal with this new development and how best to use her child, you found out about him, jumped to acknowledge him *and* offered Lujayn marriage. So I told her to lull you till the last moment, then leave you standing at the altar. Now that the news has traveled the region, if not the world, no one in Azmahar will think that such a foolish man is king material."

No end. No end to the blows. To the injuries. He could have taken anything from an enemy. But from her…

His mother's face finally displayed an emotion as she rose in utmost grace to her feet, approached him with an entreating expression. "I love you, Jalal, but I want Haidar to be the king. Both of you forced me to take action when he stepped down and you kept going full force with your campaign. Now you're out of the running, he will take the throne. But he will make you his crown prince, and everything will be for the best."

Silence stormed in the aftermath of her heartless justifications. Jalal closed his eyes for several minutes.

When he finally opened them, they felt lined with sandpaper. Just like his throat and his heart when he looked only at his mother and said, "I don't believe a word you said."

His mother sighed. "As I expected. But you would believe Lujayn. Go ahead, ask her."

"What good would that do?" he huffed bitterly. "She'd say anything you want her to say, because she knows you'd carry out the threats that forced her here."

His mother inclined her regal head at him. "That's a very fascinating theory, *ya helwi*. What did you decide my threats involved? Harming her family? How would I do that from my exile?"

"Spare me, *ya ommi*. We both know you're here but your influence remains at large. Something I'll be rectifying from now on. And I will no longer have any qualms about employing my brothers' and father's help in severing your tentacles. So I hope you enjoyed abusing your power for the last time in your life."

"If you believe using my power to do what needs to be done is abusing it, then I was right and you're not fit to be king."

"You always hated me because of my Aal Shalaan face, didn't you? Just looking at me reminded you of your hated enemies, my father and his sons."

She shrugged. "I admit, looking at you is unsettling, but you do have parts of me, and you're my son. You're one of two people I love in this world. But I do feel more intensely about Haidar."

Bitterness almost overwhelmed him, when he'd thought he'd long come to terms with this fact. "*Aih,* the true part of you."

"All parents have preferences. I'm only honest about mine."

He looked at the mother he loved in spite of everything and wondered. Where did this endless well of emotion come from when it should have dried up decades ago?

He shook his head. "I long believed that Haidar is the loser between us, being your favorite. But I should have realized your lethal focus on him is a multiedged weapon, since you'd destroy anyone for him, even your other son."

His mother sighed, nothing on her flawless face courting his approval or forgiveness, just his understanding. "It's a matter of simple pragmatism, *ya helwi*. I love you and you will make a fantastic second in command, but he, the one with an Azmaharian face and a Zohaydan name, will make a better king for Azmahar."

"You thought he'd make a better king with that face for Zohayd *and* Ossaylan. You just want him on a throne so why even try to justify it? You want what you want, and you plot to get it, regardless of any devastation you may cause. This is exactly why I tried to keep my relationship with Lujayn a secret, fearing your ingenious manipulation, what you will always rationalize as necessary for the eventual greater good, and collateral damage be damned. In this instance, *years lost* when I could have been with Lujayn, with my son. You almost cost me and them our happiness together."

His mother tutted. "So you in one breath admit to my ingenuity yet still persist in thinking you had anything with her that I didn't manipulate you into? Why don't you just admit it and move forward? Tongues will wag for a while, and you won't become king, but you will be crown prince...."

"You talk as if Haidar and I are the only candidates."

His interjection had her eyes widening as if he'd said something too ridiculous to answer. She decided to humor him, it seemed. "You are the only valid ones. Rashid Aal Munsoori is damaged goods. Nobody in his right mind wants that unstable creature in control of anything, let alone a kingdom. Please, Jalal. He has as much chance as an iceberg in Azmahar's summer desert."

He had to laugh. "You have it all worked out, don't you?"

She nodded graciously. "I've said it before, and I'll say it again. You will *all* thank me later."

He shook his head again, unable to wrap it around the scope of his mother's capacity for deviousness. *Ya Ullah,* what a crushing shame she used all that insight and intelligence in such evil, world-scrambling pursuits. Was there any way to defang her, reroute her capacities to doing good, or should he just give up?

Give up, everything inside him said. He listened this time.

He circumvented her, walked to the frozen Lujayn. She didn't look up even when his legs touched her spastic ones.

"My mother's account provides a neater explanation for everything we had than anything I believe happened."

Her stiffness increased, her breathing stifled. Her face remained turned, eyes downcast.

He went down on his knees before her.

A gasp escaped her as his hands caught hers, keeping her in place when she tried to bolt away. She still wouldn't look at him.

"But what she didn't count on was one thing. That even if my version of what happened fits nowhere as perfectly as hers, even if she brings me evidence that it had all been another of her long-term plots, *I* know what's real. *You*—" he dragged her shaking hands to his lips then tugged her into a convulsive embrace "—are my only reality, *ya rohi.* You and Adam."

She looked at him then, and the force of her desperation detonated in his heart. Tears poured from her eyes as if under pressure, her voice a choked tremolo. "I can't be your reality. But she might let Adam remain in your life, if I am not."

"You will both *be* my life, for the rest of it."

She escaped his embrace, shaking all over, tears splashing his chest. "She won't stop at anything to drive me away from you. She believes she's doing you, and even Adam, a favor."

"She won't be able to do anything. I'll protect you and your family. I will never let her hurt you again."

"You think…I'd care if she threatened…to hurt me or my family?" Lujayn's sobs rose, chopping her words, as if each tore something inside her. "What worse…injury could she inflict on me than…losing you? As for my family…she's done the worst she could do to them already…knows she can't do worse…ever again."

"Then what is she holding over your head? Who is she threatening to hurt?" The ugliest suspicion that had ever assailed him tore into his mind. "Adam?"

And she cried out, *"You!"*

He staggered back on his heels, rocked to his core.

Too much. This was just too much. The blows his mother kept hitting him with. Was there no end?

Lujayn wept openly now. "She told me…she'd…destroy you. She said if I defied her and carried on with the ceremony, if I even told you, that she would, no second chances. And it wasn't…a threat. It was…a promise. I believed her. I—I still do. I came…to try to reason with her…but it's no use."

He turned a gaze numb with shock to his mother.

Exasperation tinged her exhalation. "You believe her?"

"I would believe Lujayn over my own eyes," he said, the words spontaneous, certain, his voice disembodied.

His mother's gaze hardened. "That only proves I was even more right than I thought. Now that I know how deeply she has you in her thrall, I *will* do anything to stop you from surrendering your name and honor to her. And to her family, who'll make you theirs, no longer your own person or your family's. Or mine. If you were in your right mind you'd know that no one in Azmahar will ever accept her family, reinstatement or not. If you think prejudices ever go away, then you know nothing about the people you want to rule.

"But the worst of it remains on her. No one will accept an unnatural union between a man descended from pure royal lines on both sides with a mongrel slut who exposed her body for the highest bidder. A black widow who you claim married you during her husband's mourning period, but who everybody knows is guilty of worse, of having illicit sex with you during that forbidden time, to trap you with her illegitimate child." Steel blazed in her eyes. "But the absolute worst of it is you. You're even worse than Haidar when it comes to giving your heart. I won't wait until she pulverizes it. I'll destroy you first, before I see you destroy yourself. My destruction will be surgical, can be reconstructed once I'm certain you're safe from her, not like the infected mess she'd cause and that might necessitate an amputation."

This time, as he stared at his mother, he wondered if he'd ever find words again. *Ya Ullah*...that conviction that she was ultimately doing this for his best.

His mother turned away, went to the open window where dawn had conquered the night. "It's a simple equation, Jalal. I have to be your eyes and your logic until both are working again. I might have let you wed her so you'd claim the child, but when I learned you were leaving the *essmuh* in her hand, that you were giving *her* the sole power to divorce you, and control of your assets, I knew I couldn't wait for you to wake up. You can claim your son, who does have your blood, but her and her family, never."

Silence shrieked in the wake of her last words.

Then he finally pressed Lujayn's shaking hands and rose, went to face his mother.

"Here's my simple equation, *ya ommi*." He marveled at how calm his voice was, how clearheaded he was. He knew this would be his last effort where his mother was concerned. If she responded unfavorably, he would have no mother anymore. "I won't say that inside you is a mother who doesn't want to hurt her son, for I know I can't budge you from your belief that you're saving me. But there *is* a mother who doesn't want to *lose* her son, even if he isn't her favorite, and a fool to boot. I know blood means everything to you, and you won't risk losing the third person you're equipped to love—your firstborn grandson. And you *will* lose me, and him, irretrievably, if you pursue this, and if you hurt Lujayn again, in any way. That isn't a threat. It's a promise."

His mother looked at him for what felt like an eternity, a lifetime of unsaid things passing between them, profound things he'd never dreamed existed.

Was that concession he saw in the depths of her eyes? Surprise? Even distress? Or was he just seeing the things he hoped to see?

But when she spoke her voice carried traces of all that, and dared he think, defeat, too? "*Zain.* I will back off."

Did that mean she feared losing him so much she would go against her nature? Could he hope?

Then she went on, and said nature was back, hale and hearty. "But you will come to regret your decision. Just pray it won't be 'irretrievable' when you do. And do promise you won't feel so foolish then that you won't come to me for help."

What do you know? The dragon lady *was* shaken. She'd gambled big and lost, was trying to scramble back to higher ground.

"I can tell you from now to not hold your breath, *ya ommi.*" He suddenly did what not even he had expected, pulled her into a fierce hug. "But I can't tell you how much I hope that *you* one day will regret your actions, change your mind and make a new start. Think about it. Your family is growing, and instead of wary, infrequent visits from your sons, you can choose to connect with us all and find some peace and contentment."

His mother remained still in his arms. He knew it would be too much to expect an immediate response, and in front of Lujayn, too. Maybe never. But for his own sake, for Lujayn's and Adam's, he didn't want to harbor any bitterness toward anyone, starting with her.

He finally stepped away, hoping to get some reassurance from her. Her face was carefully empty, which told him more than any expression would have.

Then she gave him a slight smile, patted his cheek and swept away. There was majesty in her every move as she sat down on the couch, facing the frozen Lujayn, and rang a crystal bell.

"Might as well have breakfast," his mother said, looking at Lujayn as if she'd just met her. "Do you have any preferences?"

"Pinch me."

Jalal immediately pinched a handful of Lujayn's delightful bottom. She yelped then chuckled, still jumpy, her eyes dazed.

"I mean, your mother blackmails me into standing you up at the *ma'zoon,* then serves me breakfast half a world away? So, was this a hallucination? A breakdown?"

He grinned his love and relief down at her. "Whatever else she is, my mother thrives on being flabbergasting."

"Tell me about it." She melted deeper into his arms in his private jet's reclining seat as if she'd burrow into him, hide under his skin if she could. "Oh, God, Jalal, she was so convincing. *I* almost bought her version of what happened. As you said, it explained everything far more neatly than the truth. But you believed in me, against all damning evidence."

His hug tightened. "I did tell you I won't ever doubt you again. Turns out I not only won't, I can't."

Her giggle was almost delirious. "Sounds like you're under some hypnotic influence like your mother thinks you are."

"*Maa'loom,* for sure, I am enthralled fathoms deep with no desire whatsoever to ever resurface."

She squeezed him, her eyes filling with tears and reciprocation and they fell into a silence full of communication and communion.

Suddenly she jerked up. "God...your campaign! Will you be in a weaker position as a candidate now?"

"You mean because I couldn't even rule my bride?" At the pure mortification on her face, he couldn't help it and laughed his joy out loud. "*Aah, ya habibati,* I can't tell you how...*irrelevant* this is to me." Now she sputtered, her color dangerous. "But just to alleviate your misplaced guilt, all the drama, contrary to what my mother said, will probably boost my image, especially with women and younger people. We'll be an even more memorable romantic couple and our *matrimonius interruptus* will become the stuff of new-spun legends. Not that a popularity poll should decide what's best for Azmahar. But I'm not about to let the throne go, to anyone. Even had I wanted to, Haidar wouldn't forgive me if I didn't give it my all like always, and Rashid, after that stunt he pulled with you, has one hell of a fight on his hands. And may the best man win."

"*You.* You're the best man on earth!" Her kiss was fierce with everything inside her heart. "And I'm right there with you in any fight. I'd fight the very devil for you, for our future and our son and our happiness."

He guffawed. "You already did when you walked into the dragon's den to have that showdown."

"One I lost," she groaned. "You're the one who bailed us out."

"No, *you* did. The woman she thought you were would

have gone ahead with the ceremony and either told herself
that my mother wouldn't truly hurt me, or assume I could
protect myself. That woman would have let me deal with
any fallout after she'd secured her place and interests. By
complying, and going to her at that exact crucial time, you
proved you love me so totally you'd give me up to protect
me. I bet that messed up her projections, forced her to re-
calculate. Then she saw for herself how clear and certain I
am in my love for you, how I trust you so totally, and that
must have reinforced the new realization that there's more to
you than she thought. It's the real reason she backed down.
I do believe she was trying to do what was best for me, and
if she'd still suspected you were after my money or power,
she would have taken me apart to get rid of you. So you,
and only you, won that fight."

Wonder was rising in her eyes as he spoke, but with his
last words, distress replaced it again. "I don't feel so tri-
umphant when I remember... Oh, God, what are we going
to do? The scandal I caused, no matter the reason—which
we can't ever share—was witnessed firsthand by a thousand guests of the region's nobility and royalty and *God*...
your family!"

He just smiled serenely. "We'll just gather them again
tonight and have a do-over."

"Tonight?" Her face was the image of shock and dread.

"*Khair'ol berri 'aajeloh,* the best good is swift. Most of
the menu is still edible and everyone remains in Azmahar.
If they dispersed across the region, getting them back would
be quite a chore, especially if they demand they'd actually
witness our nuptials with a no-surprises guarantee before
they return."

She buried her face in his chest, tears flowing again. "I
don't know how I'll ever face anyone in Azmahar or any of
your family again."

He smoothed her hair, soothing her. "Once my family knows everything, you'll be their favorite heroine. As for anyone else, who cares? They'll love you, or they don't matter."

"They matter to you. That's all that matters to me."

"Why don't you play that little recording I made you? Just to refresh your memory about what matters to me?"

Her hug was almost bruising this time as she mashed herself against him. "Ah, *ya habibi*...I can't ever tell you how I felt as I was taking off that dress, as I was leaving the palace and Azmahar, as I imagined what you'd feel when you found me gone. Every mile I traveled was dragging my soul out of me, as it refused to leave you. And then I thought there was no way I wouldn't lose you and I felt it snap..."

Needing to snap *her* out of her surrender to anguish, he tickled her. "First, no distance or plots or dragons will ever come between us. You'll never lose me, and I'll always find you, will always be with you, no matter what. Second, I suggest we head to the palace the minute we land. We'll dress up and sit in the *kooshah* and send everyone video proof of our presence there. We'll hold that miraculous miniature-palace cake hostage and threaten to demolish it if they don't come back running. How about that?"

She exploded in his arms, deluged him in kisses and laughter and tears. "Stupendous plan from my incomparable desert knight, owner of my heart and sharer of my soul...."

Laughing out loud, he took her roaming lips, stemming the flow of her adoration. "Save all those descriptions for the vows."

She rose over him, flushed with emotion, her eyes pulsing that hypnotic silvery glow, which he now knew only he triggered. "I'll never save any of it. I'll tell you now, and then and always. I'll show you and give you and love you with everything that I am, with every breath, for as long as I live."

Her conviction expanded in his heart, her devotion filled him to his recesses. Gratitude overwhelmed him that he'd been given so many chances to get this right. For this connection, this flesh, this being, everything she was—that was the reason for his existence. For everything.

He was saving that for his vows. Not because he didn't have more to tell her always, but because he wanted her to hear this particular confession for the first time as he proclaimed it to the world, as he claimed her and was claimed by her, forever.

For now, he gathered her, the flesh of his flesh, to him and whispered against her lips, "Deal, *ya hayati,* for as long as I live. And I'll raise you beyond life."

* * * * *

Having a lover like Sean was really a slippery slope.

Georgia wasn't interested in trusting another man. Giving her heart over to him. Giving him the chance to crush her again. Sure, Sean was nothing like her ex, but he was still *male*.

"What do you say, Georgia?" he asked, reaching down to take her hands in his and give them a squeeze. "Will you pretend marry me?"

She couldn't think. Not with him holding on to her. Not with his eyes staring into hers. Not with the heat of him reaching for her, promising even more heat if she let him get any closer. And if she did that, she would agree to anything, because the man could have her half out of her mind in seconds, she well knew.

With him holding on to her, the beat of his heart beneath her ear, Georgia was tempted to do all sorts of things, so she looked away from him, out the window to the rain-drenched evening. Lamps lining the drive shone like diamonds in the gray. But the darkness and the incessant rain couldn't disguise the beauty that was Ireland.

Just as, she thought, looking up at Sean, a lie couldn't hide what was already between the two of them. She didn't know where it was going, but she had a feeling the ride was going to be much bumpier than she had planned.

Dear Reader,

As most of you know, I *love* Ireland. The gorgeous country-side, the incredible views everywhere you look and especially the warm generosity of the Irish people.

The village of Dunley, where this story is set, is fictional, but I used elements of the many different villages I've stayed in to create the town itself and its citizens.

In the first book of my Irish duet, *Up Close and Personal*, you met Ronan Connolly and Laura Page, the woman who knocked his feet out from under him.

In *An Outrageous Proposal* you'll find the story of Ronan's cousin Sean Connolly and Georgia Page, Laura's sister.

These two were so much fun to write about. Sean's life is just as he wants it, and to make sure nothing changes he's willing to do whatever he has to. Georgia, on the other hand, is desperate to make changes in her life.

When these two collide, sparks fly and no one's life will ever be the same.

You'll also find a sprinkling of Gaelic in this book—a good friend of mine provided the translations. But if I've made mistakes, they're mine alone.

Thank you all so much for your continued support and the wonderful letters you write. I'm delighted to be able to spend my days writing stories for Mills & Boon® Desire™, and it's a pleasure for me to hear that you enjoy reading them!

You can visit me on Facebook, or stop in at my website, www.maureenchild.com.

Happy reading!

Maureen

AN OUTRAGEOUS PROPOSAL

BY
MAUREEN CHILD

MILLS & BOON

Published in Great Britain 2013
by Mills & Boon, an imprint of Harlequin (UK) Limited,
Eton House, 18-24 Paradise Road, Richmond, Surrey TW9 1SR

© Maureen Child 2012

ISBN: 978 0 263 90445 1
ebook ISBN: 978 1 472 00040 8

51-0113

Harlequin (UK) policy is to use papers that are natural, renewable and recyclable products and made from wood grown in sustainable forests. The logging and manufacturing processes conform to the legal environmental regulations of the country of origin.

Printed and bound in Spain
by Blackprint CPI, Barcelona

Maureen Child is a California native who loves to travel. Every chance they get, she and her husband are taking off on another research trip. An author of more than sixty books, Maureen loves a happy ending and still swears that she has the best job in the world. She lives in Southern California with her husband, two children and a golden retriever with delusions of grandeur. Visit Maureen's website, www.maureenchild.com.

For two wonderful writers
who are fabulous friends,
Kate Carlisle and Jennifer Lyon.
Thank you both for always being there.

One

"For the love of all that's holy, *don't push!*" Sean Connolly kept one wary eye on the rearview mirror and the other on the curving road stretching out in front of him. Why the hell was *he* the designated driver to the hospital?

"Just mind the road and drive, Sean," his cousin Ronan complained from the backseat. He had one arm around his hugely pregnant wife, drawing her toward him despite the seat belts.

"He's right," Georgia Page said from the passenger seat. "Just drive, Sean." She half turned to look into the back. "Hang on, Laura," she told her sister. "We'll be there soon."

"You can all relax, you know," Laura countered. "I'm not giving birth in the car."

"Please, God," Sean muttered and gave the car more gas.

Never before in his life had he had reason to curse the

narrow, winding roads of his native Ireland. But tonight, all he wanted was about thirty kilometers of smooth highway to get them all to the hospital in Westport.

"You're not helping," Georgia muttered with a quick look at him.

"I'm driving," he told her and chanced another look into the rearview mirror just in time to see Laura's features twist in pain.

She moaned, and Sean gritted his teeth. The normal sense of panic a man felt around a woman in labor was heightened by the fact that his cousin was half excited and half mad with worry for the wife he doted on. A part of Sean envied Ronan even while the larger part of him was standing back and muttering, *Aye, Ronan, better you than me.*

Funny how complicated a man's life could get when he wasn't even paying attention to it. A year or so ago, he and his cousin Ronan were happily single, each of them with an eye toward remaining that way. Now, Ronan was married, about to be a father, and Sean was as involved in the coming birth of the next generation of Connollys as he could be. He and Ronan lived only minutes apart, and the two of them had grown up more brothers than cousins.

"Can't you go any faster?" Georgia whispered, leaning in toward him.

Then there was Laura's sister. Georgia was a smart, slightly cynical, beautiful woman who engaged Sean's brain even while she attracted him on a much more basic level. So far, he'd kept his distance, though. Getting involved with Georgia Page would only complicate things. What with her sister married to his cousin, and Ronan suddenly becoming insanely protective about the women he claimed were in "his charge."

Damned old-fashioned for a man who had spent most

of his adult years mowing through legions of adoring females.

Still, Sean was glad to have Georgia along. For the sanity she provided, if nothing else. Georgia and Sean would at least have each other to turn to during all of this, and he was grateful for it.

Sean gave her a quick glance and kept his voice low. "I go much faster on these roads at night, we'll *all* need a room in hospital."

"Right." Georgia's gaze fixed on the road ahead, and she leaned forward as if trying to make the car speed up through sheer force of will.

Well, Sean told himself, if anyone could pull that off, it would be Georgia Page. In the light from the dashboard, her dark blue eyes looked fathomless and her honey-colored hair looked more red than blond.

He'd first met her at Ronan and Laura's wedding a year or so ago, but with her many trips to Ireland to visit her sister, he'd come to know Georgia and he liked her. He liked her quick wit, her sarcasm and her sense of family loyalty—which he shared.

All around them, the darkness was complete, the head-lights of his car illuminating the narrow track winding out in front of them. This far from the city, it was mainly farmland stretching out behind the high, thick hedges that lined the road. The occasional lighted window in a farm-house stood out like beacons, urging them on.

At last, a distant glow appeared and Sean knew it was the lights of Westport, staining the night sky. They were close, and he took his first easy breath in what felt like hours.

"Nearly there," he announced, and glanced at Georgia. She gave him a quick grin, and he felt the solid punch of it.

From the backseat, Laura cried out and just like that, Sean's relief was cut short. They weren't safe yet. Focusing on the task at hand, he pushed his car as fast as he dared.

What felt like days—and was in reality only hours and hours later—Sean and Georgia walked out of the hospital like survivors of a grueling battle.

"God," Sean said, as they stepped into the soft rain of an Irish afternoon in winter. The wind blew like ice, and the rain fell from clouds that looked close enough to touch. He tipped his face back and stared up into the gray. It was good to be outside, away from the sounds and smells of the hospital. Even better to know that the latest Connolly had arrived safely.

"That was the longest night and day of my life, I think," he said with feeling.

"Mine, too," Georgia agreed, shrugging deeper into the navy blue coat she wore. "But it was worth it."

He looked over at her. "Oh, aye, it was indeed. She's a beauty."

"She is, isn't she?" Georgia grinned. "Fiona Connolly. It's a good name. Beautiful, but strong, too."

"It is, and by the look of her, she's already got her da wrapped around her tiny fingers." He shook his head as he remembered the expression on his cousin's face as Ronan held his new daughter for the first time. Almost enough to make a jaded man believe in—never mind.

"I'm exhausted and energized all at the same time."

"Me, as well," Sean agreed, happy to steer his mind away from dangerous territory. "Feel as though I've been running a marathon."

"And all we did was wait."

"I think the waiting is the hardest thing of all."

Georgia laughed. "And I think Laura would disagree."

Ruefully, he nodded. "You've a point there."

Georgia sighed, stepped up to Sean and threaded her arm through his. "Ronan will be a great father. And Laura…she wanted this so much." She sniffed and swiped her fingers under her eyes.

"No more crying," Sean said, giving her arm a squeeze. "Already I feel as though I've been riding a tide of tears all day. Between the new mother and father and you, it's been weepy eyes and sniffles for hours."

"I saw your eyes get a little misty, too, tough guy."

"Aye, well, we Irish are a sentimental lot," he admitted, then started for the car park, Georgia's arm still tucked through his.

"It's one of the things I like best about you—"

He gave her a look.

"—the Irish in general, I mean," she qualified.

"Ah, well then." He smiled to himself at her backtracking. It was a lovely afternoon. Soft rain, cold wind and new life wailing in the hospital behind them. "You've been to Ireland so often in the last year, you're very nearly an honorary Irishman yourself, aren't you?"

"I've been thinking about that," she admitted. They walked up to his car, and Sean hit the unlock button on his keypad.

"What's that then?" he asked, as he opened the passenger door for her and held it, waiting. Fatigue clawed at him, but just beneath that was a buoyant feeling that had him smile at the woman looking up at him.

"About being an honorary Irishman. Or at least," she said, looking around her at the car park, the hospital and the city beyond, "moving here. Permanently."

"Really?" Intrigued, he leaned his forearms on the top

of the door. "And what's brought this on then? Is it your brand-new niece?"

She shrugged. "Partly, sure. But mostly, it's this country. It's gorgeous and friendly, and I've really come to love being here."

"Does Laura know about this?"

"Not yet," she admitted, and shifted her gaze back to him. "So don't say anything. She's got enough on her mind at the moment."

"True enough," he said. "But I'm thinking she'd be pleased to have her sister so close."

She flashed him a brilliant smile then slid into her seat. As Sean closed the door after her and walked around the car, he was forced to admit that *he* wouldn't mind having Georgia close, either.

A half hour later, Georgia opened the door to Laura and Ronan's expansive stone manor house and looked back over her shoulder at Sean. "Want to come in for a drink?"

"I think we've earned one," he said, stepping inside and closing the door behind him. "Or even a dozen."

She laughed and it felt good. Heck, *she* felt good. Her sister was a mother, and Georgia was so glad she had made the decision to come to Ireland to be present for the baby's birth. She hated to think about what it would have been like, being a half a world away right now.

"Ronan's housekeeper, Patsy, is off in Dublin visiting her daughter Sinead," Georgia reminded him. "So we're on our own for food."

"It's not food I want at the moment anyway," Sean told her.

Was he flirting with her? Georgia wondered, then

dismissed the notion. She shook her head and reminded herself that they were here for a drink. Or several.

As he spoke, a long, ululating howl erupted from deep within the house. Georgia actually jumped at the sound and then laughed. "With the rain, the dogs have probably let themselves into the kitchen."

"Probably hungry now, too," Sean said, and walked beside her toward the back of the house.

Georgia knew her sister's house as if it were her own. Whenever she was in Ireland, she stayed here at the manor, since it was so huge they could comfortably hold a family reunion for a hundred. She opened the door into a sprawling kitchen with top-of-the-line appliances and what looked like miles of granite countertops. Everything was tidy—but for the two dogs scrambling toward her for some attention.

Deidre was a big, clumsy English sheepdog with so much hair over her eyes, it was a wonder she didn't walk into walls. And Beast—huge, homely—the best that could be said about him was what he lacked in beauty he made up for in heart. Since Beast reached her first, Georgia scratched behind his ears and sent the big dog into quivers of delight. Deidre was right behind him, nudging her mate out of her way.

"Okay then, food for the dogs, then drinks for us," Georgia announced.

"Already on it," Sean assured her, making his way to the wide pantry, stepping over and around Beast as the dog wound his way in and out of Sean's feet.

Within a few minutes, they had the dogs fed and watered and then left them there, sleeping on their beds in front of the now cold kitchen hearth. Cuddled up together, the dogs looked snug and happy.

Then Georgia led the way back down the hall, the

short heels of her shoes clicking against the wood floor. At the door to the parlor, Sean asked, "So, Patsy's in Dublin with her daughter. Sinead's doing well then, with her new family?"

"According to Patsy, everything's great," Georgia said.

Laura had told her the whole story of the pregnant Sinead marrying in a hurry. Sinead was now the mother of an infant son and her new husband was, at the moment, making a demo CD. He and his friends played traditional Irish music and, thanks to Ronan's influence with a recording company, had a real chance to do something with it. "She misses Sinead living close by, but once they get the demo done, they'll all be coming back to Dunley."

"Home does draw a body back no matter how far you intend to roam," Sean mused, as he followed her into the front parlor. "And yet, you're thinking of leaving your home to make a new one."

"I guess I am."

Hearing him say it aloud made the whole idea seem more real than it had in the past week or so that it had been floating around in her mind. But it also felt…right. Okay, scary, but good. After all, it wasn't as if she was giving up a lot. And the plus side was, she could leave behind all of the tension and bad memories of a marriage that had dissolved so abruptly.

Moving to Ireland was a big change, she knew. But wasn't change a good thing? Shake up your life from time to time just to keep it interesting?

At that thought, she smiled to herself. Interesting. Moving to a different country. Leaving the familiar to go to the…okay, also familiar. Since Laura had married Ronan and moved to Ireland, Georgia had made the long trek to visit four times. And each time she came, it was harder to leave. To go back to her empty condo in Hun-

tington Beach, California. To sit at her desk, alone in
the real estate office she and Laura had opened together.

Not that she was feeling sorry for herself—she wasn't.
But she had started thinking that maybe there was more
to life than sitting behind a desk hoping to sell a house.

In the parlor, Georgia paused, as she always did, just to
enjoy the beauty of the room. A white-tiled hearth, cold
now, but stacked with kindling that Sean was already
working to light against the chill gloom of the day. Pale
green walls dotted with seascapes and oversize couches
facing each other across a low table that held a Waterford
crystal bowl filled with late chrysanthemums in tones
of russet and gold. The wide front windows looked out
over a sweep of lawn that was drenched with the rain still
falling softly against the glass.

When he had the fire going to his satisfaction, Sean
stood up and brushed his palms together, then moved to
the spindle table in the corner that held a collection of
crystal decanters. Ignoring them, he bent to the small refrigerator tucked into the corner behind the table.

"Now, about that celebratory drink," he muttered.

Georgia smiled and joined him at the table, leaning
her palms on the glossy top as she watched him open the
fridge. "We earned it all right, but I wouldn't have missed
it. The worry, the panic—" She was still smiling as he
glanced up at her. "And I was seriously panicked. It was
hard knowing Laura was in pain and not being able to
do anything about it."

"Would it make me seem less manly to you if I admitted to sheer terror?" he asked, as he reached into the
refrigerator.

"Your manhood is safe," Georgia assured him.

In fact, she had never known a man who needed to
worry less about his manhood than Sean Connolly. He

was gorgeous, charming and oozed sex appeal. Good thing, she thought, that she was immune. Well, nearly.

Even she, a woman who knew better, had been tempted by Sean's charms. Of course, it would be much better—safer—to keep him in the "friend" zone. Starting up anything with him would not only be dangerous but awkward, as well. Since her sister was married to his cousin, any kind of turmoil between them could start a family war.

And there was *always* turmoil when a man was involved, she thought with an inner sigh. But she'd learned her lesson there. She could enjoy Sean's company without letting herself get...involved. Her gaze skimmed over his tall, nicely packed yet lanky body, and something inside her sizzled like a trapped flame struggling to grow into a bonfire. She so didn't need that.

Nope, she told herself, just enjoy looking at him and keep your hormones on a tight leash. When he sent her a quick wink and a wild grin, Georgia amended that last thought to a tight, *short,* leash.

To divert herself from her own thoughts, Georgia sighed and asked, "Isn't she beautiful? The baby?"

"She is indeed," Sean agreed, pulling a bottle of champagne from the fridge and holding it aloft like a hardwon trophy. "And she has a clever father, as well. Our Ronan's stocked the fridge with not one but three bottles of champagne, bless him."

"Very thoughtful," she agreed.

He grabbed two crystal flutes from the shelf behind the bar, then set them down on the table and worked at the champagne wire and cork. "Did you get hold of your parents with the news?"

"I did," Georgia said, remembering how her mother had cried over the phone hearing the news about her first grandchild. "I called from Laura's room when you took Ronan down to buy flowers. Laura got to talk to them and they heard the baby cry." She smiled. "Mom cried along with her. Ronan's already promised to fly them in whenever they're ready."

"That's lovely then." The cork popped with a cheerful sound, and Sean poured out two glasses. Bubbling froth filled the flutes, looking like liquid sunshine. "So, champagne?"

"Absolutely."

She took a glass and paused when Sean said, "To Fiona Connolly. May her life be long and happy. May she be a stranger to sorrow and a friend to joy."

The sting of tears burned Georgia's eyes. Shaking her head, she took a sip of champagne and said, "That was beautiful, Sean."

He gave her a grin, then took her free hand in his and led her over to one of the sofas. There, he sat her down and then went back to the bar for the bottle of champagne. He set it on the table in front of them, then took a seat beside Georgia on the couch.

"A hell of a day all in all, wouldn't you say?"

"It was," she agreed, then amended, *"is."* Another sip of champagne and she added, "I'm tired, but I don't think I could close my eyes, you know? Too much left-over adrenaline pumping away inside."

"I feel the same," he told her, "so it's lucky we can keep each other company."

"Yeah, I guess it is," Georgia agreed. Kicking her shoes off, she drew her feet up onto the sofa and idly rubbed her arches.

The snap and hiss of the fire along with the patter of rain on the window made for a cozy scene. Taking a sip of her champagne, she let her head fall back against the couch.

"So," Sean said a moment or two later, "tell me about this plan of yours to move to Ireland."

She lifted her head to look at him. His brown hair was tousled, his brown eyes tired but interested and the half smile on his face could have tempted a saint. Georgia took another sip of champagne, hoping the icy liquor would dampen the heat beginning to build inside.

"I've been thinking about it for a while," she admitted, her voice soft. "Actually since my last visit. When I left for home, I remember sitting on the airplane as it was taxiing and wondering why I was leaving."

He nodded as if he understood completely, and that settled her enough to continue.

"I mean, you should be happy to go home after a trip, right?" She asked the question more of herself than of Sean and answered it the same way. "Looking forward to going back to your routine. Your everyday life. But I wasn't. There was just this niggling sense of disappointment that seemed to get bigger the closer I got to home."

"Maybe some of that was just because you were leaving your sister," he said quietly.

"Probably," she admitted with a nod and another sip of champagne. "I mean, Laura's more than my sister, she's my best friend." Looking at him, she gave him a small smile. "I really miss having her around, you know?"

"I do," he said, reaching for the champagne, then topping off their glasses. "When Ronan was in California, I found I missed going to the pub with him. I missed the laughter. And the arguments." He grinned. "Though if you repeat any of this, I'll deny it to my last breath."

"Oh, understood," she replied with a laugh. "Anyway, I got home, went to our—*my*—real estate office and stared out the front window. Waiting for clients to call or come in is a long, boring process." She stared down into her champagne. "And while I was staring out that window, watching the world go by, I realized that everyone outside the glass was doing what they wanted to do. Everyone but me."

"I thought you enjoyed selling real estate," Sean said. "The way Laura tells it, the two of you were just beginning to build the business."

"We were," she agreed. "But it wasn't what either of us wanted. Isn't that ridiculous?" Georgia shifted on the couch, half turning to face Sean more fully.

Wow, she thought, *he really is gorgeous.*

She blinked, then looked at the champagne suspiciously. Maybe the bubbles were infiltrating her mind, making her more susceptible to the Connolly charm and good looks. But no, she decided a moment later, she'd always been susceptible. Just able to resist. But now...

Georgia cleared her throat and banished her wayward thoughts. What had she been saying? Oh, yeah.

"I mean, think about it. Laura's an artist, and I was an interior designer once upon a time. And yet there we were, building a business neither of us was really interested in."

"Why is that?" He watched her out of those beautiful brown eyes and seemed genuinely curious. "Why would you put so much of yourselves into a thing you'd no interest in?"

"Well, that's the question, isn't it?" she asked, gesturing with her glass and cringing a little when the champagne slopped over the brim. To help fix that situation, she sipped the contents down a bit lower. "It started simply enough," she continued. "Laura couldn't make a living painting, so she took classes and became a real estate agent because she'd rather be her own boss, you know?"

"I do," he said with a knowing nod.

Of course he understood that part, Georgia thought. As the owner of Irish Air, a huge and growing airline, Sean made his own rules. Sure, their situations were wildly different, but he would still get the feeling of being answerable only to oneself.

"Then my marriage dissolved," she said, the words still tasting a little bitter. Georgia was mostly over it all, since it had been a few years now, but if she allowed herself to remember... "I moved out to live with Laura, and rather than try to build up a brand-new business of my own—and let's face it, in California, you practically stumble across an interior designer every few steps, so they didn't really need another one—I took classes and the two of us opened our own company."

Shaking her head, she drank more of the champagne and sighed. "So basically, we both backed into a business we didn't really want, but couldn't think of a way to get out of. Does that make sense?"

"Completely," Sean told her. "What it comes down to is, you weren't happy."

"*Exactly.*" She took a deep breath and let it go again. What was it about him? she wondered. So easy to talk to. So nice to look at, a tiny voice added from the back of her mind. Those eyes of his seemed to look deep inside her, while the lilt of Ireland sang in his voice. A heady combination, she warned herself. "I wasn't happy. And, since I'm free and on my own, why shouldn't I move to Ireland? Be closer to my sister? Live in a place I've come to love?"

"No reason a'tall," he assured her companionably. Picking up the champagne bottle he refilled both of their glasses again, and Georgia nodded her thanks. "So, I'm guessing you won't be after selling real estate here then?"

"No, thank you," she said on a sigh. God, it felt wonderful to know that soon she wouldn't have to deal with recalcitrant sellers and pushy buyers. When people came to her for design work, they would be buying her talent, not whatever house happened to be on the market.

"I'm going to open my own design shop. Of course, I'll have to check everything out first, see what I have to do to get a business license in Ireland and to have my interior design credentials checked. And I'll have to have a house..."

"You could always stay here," he said with a shrug. "I'm sure Ronan and Laura would love to have you here with them, and God knows the place is big enough..."

"It is that," she mused, shifting her gaze around the parlor of the luxurious manor house. In fact, the lovely old house was probably big enough for two or three families. "But I'd rather have a home of my own. My own place, not too far. I'm thinking of opening my shop in Dunley..."

Sean choked on a sip of champagne, then laughed a second later. "*Dunley?* You want to open a design shop in the *village?*"

Irritated, she scowled at him. And he'd been doing so nicely on the understanding thing, too. "What's wrong with that?"

"Well, let's just say I can't see Danny Muldoon hiring you to give the Pennywhistle pub a makeover anytime soon."

"Funny," she muttered.

"Ah now," Sean said, smile still firmly in place, "don't get yourself in a twist. I'm only saying that perhaps the city might be a better spot for a design shop."

Still frowning, she gave him a regal half nod. "Maybe. But Dunley is about halfway between Galway and Westport—two big cities, you'll agree—"

"I do."

"So, the village is centrally located, and I'd rather be in a small town than a big one anyway. And I can buy a cottage close by and walk to work. Living in the village, I'll be a part of things as I wouldn't if I lived in Galway and only visited on weekends. *And,*" she added, on a roll, "I'd be close to Laura to visit or help with the baby. Not to mention—"

"You're right, absolutely." He held up both hands, then noticed his champagne glass was nearly empty. He refilled his, and hers, and then lifted his glass in a toast. "I'm sorry I doubted you for a moment. You've thought this through."

"I really have," she said, a little mellower now, thanks not only to the wine, but to the gleam of admiration in Sean's gaze. "I want to do this. I'm *going* to do this," she added, a promise to herself and the universe at large.

"And so you will, I've no doubt," Sean told her, leaning forward. "To the start of more than *one* new life this day. I wish you happiness, Georgia, with your decision and your shop."

"Thanks," she said, clinking her glass against his, making the heavy crystal sing. "I appreciate it."

When they'd both had a sip to seal the toast, Sean mused, "So we'll be neighbors."

"We will."

"And friends."

"That, too," she agreed, feeling just a little unsettled by his steady stare and the twisting sensation in the pit of her stomach.

"And as your friend," Sean said softly, "I think I should tell you that when you're excited about something, your eyes go as dark as a twilight sky."

Two

"What?"

Sean watched the expression on her face shift from confusion to a quick flash of desire that was born and then gone again in a blink. But he'd seen it, and his response to it was immediate.

"Am I making you nervous, Georgia?"

"No," she said and he read the lie in the way she let her gaze slide from his. After taking another sip of champagne, she licked a stray drop from her lip, and Sean's insides fisted into knots.

Odd, he'd known Georgia for about a year now and though he'd been attracted, he'd never before been tempted. Now he was. Most definitely. Being here with her in the fire-lit shadows while rain pattered at the windows was, he thought, more than tempting. There was an intimacy here, two people who had shared a hellishly long day together. Now, in the quiet shadows, there was something new and…compelling rising up between them.

He knew she felt it, too, despite the wary gleam in her eyes as she watched him. Still, he wanted her breathless, not guarded, so he eased back and gave her a half smile. "I'm only saying you're a beautiful woman, Georgia."

"Hmm…" She tipped her head to one side, studying him.

"Surely it's not the first time you've heard that from a man."

"Oh, no," she answered. "Men actually chase me down the street to tell me I have twilight eyes."

He grinned. He did appreciate a quick wit. "Maybe I'm just more observant than most men."

"And maybe you're up to something," she said thoughtfully. "What is it, Sean?"

"Not a thing," he said, all innocence.

"Well, that's good." She nodded and reached down absently to rub at the arch of her foot. "I mean, we both know anything else would just be…complicated."

"Aye, it would at that," he agreed, and admitted silently that complicated might be worth it. "Your feet hurt?"

"What?" She glanced down to where her hand rubbed the arch of her right foot and smiled ruefully. "Yeah, they do."

"A long day of standing, wasn't it?"

"It was."

She sipped at her champagne and a log shifted in the fire. As the flames hissed and spat, she closed her eyes— a little dreamily, he thought, and he felt that fist inside him tighten even further. The woman was unknowingly seducing him.

Logic and a stern warning sounded out in his mind, and he firmly shut them down. There was a time for a cool head, and there was a time for finding out just where the road you found yourself on would end up. So far, he liked this particular road very much.

He set his glass on the table in front of them, then sat back and dragged her feet onto his lap. Georgia looked at him and he gave her a quick grin. "I'm offering a one-night-only special. A foot rub."

"Sean…"

He knew what she was thinking because his own mind was running along the same paths. Back up—or, stay the course and see what happened. As she tried to draw her feet away, he held them still in his lap and pushed his thumbs into her arch.

She groaned and let her head fall back and he knew he had her.

"Oh, that feels too good," she whispered, as he continued to rub and stroke her skin.

"Just enjoy it for a bit then," he murmured.

That had her lifting her head to look at him with the wariness back, glinting in those twilight depths. "What're you up to?"

"Your ankles," he said, sliding his hands higher to match his words. "Give me a minute, though, and ask again."

She laughed as he'd meant her to, and the wariness edged off a bit.

"So," she asked a moment later, "why do I rate a foot rub tonight?"

"I'm feeling generous, just becoming an uncle and all." He paused, and let that settle. Of course, he and Ronan weren't actually brothers, but they might as well have been. "Not really an uncle, but that's how it feels."

"You're an uncle," she told him. "You and Ronan are every bit as tight as Laura and I are."

"True," he murmured, and rubbed his thumb into the arches of her small, narrow feet. Her toes were painted a dark pink, and he smiled at the silver toe ring she wore on her left foot.

She sighed heavily and whispered, "Oh, my...you've got great hands."

"So I've been told," he said on a laugh. He slid his great hands a bit higher, stroking her ankles and then up along the line of her calves. Her skin was soft, smooth and warm, now that the fire had chased away the chill of the afternoon.

"Maybe it's the champagne talking," she said softly, "but what you're doing feels way too good."

"'Tisn't the champagne," he told her, meeting her eyes when she looked at him. "We've not had enough yet to blur the lines between us."

"Then it's the fire," she whispered, "and the rain outside sealing us into this pretty room together."

"Could be," he allowed, sliding his hands even higher now, stroking the backs of her knees and watching her eyes close as she sighed. "And it could just be that you're a lovely thing, here in the firelight, and I'm overcome."

She snorted and he grinned in response.

"Oh, yes, overcome," she said, staring into his eyes again, as if trying to see the plans he had, the plans he might come up with. "Sean Connolly, you're a man who always knows what he's doing. So answer me this. Are you trying to seduce me?"

"Ah, the shoe is on the other foot entirely, Georgia," he murmured, his fingertips moving higher still, up her thighs, inch by inch. He hadn't thought of it earlier, but now he was grateful she'd been wearing a skirt for their mad ride to the hospital. Made things so much simpler.

"Right," she said. "I'm seducing you? You're the one

giving out foot rubs that have now escalated—" her breath caught briefly before she released it on a sigh "—to *thigh* rubs."

"And do you like it?"

"I'd be a fool not to," she admitted, and he liked her even more for her straightforwardness.

"Well then…"

"But the question remains," she said, reaching down to capture one of his hands in hers, stilling his caresses. "If you're seducing me, I have to ask, why now? We've known each other for so long, Sean, and we've never—"

"True enough," he murmured, "but this is the first time we've been alone, isn't it?" He set her hand aside and continued to stroke the outsides of her thighs before slowly edging around to the inside.

She squirmed, and he went hard as stone.

"Think of it, Georgia," he continued, though his voice was strained and it felt as though there were a rock lodged in his throat. "'Tis just us here for the night. No Ronan, no Laura, no Patsy, running in and out with her tea trays. Even the dogs are in the kitchen sleeping."

Georgia laughed a little. "You're right. I don't think I've ever been in this house alone before. But…"

"No buts," he interrupted, then leaned out and picked up the champagne bottle. Refilling her glass and then his own, he set the bottle down again and lifted his glass with one hand while keeping her feet trapped in his lap with the other. "I think we need more of this, then we'll…*talk* about this some more."

"After enough champagne, we won't want to talk at all," she said, though she sipped at the wine anyway.

"And isn't that a lovely thought?" he asked, giving her a wink as he drained his glass.

She was watching him, and her eyes were filled with

the same heat that burned inside him. For the life of him, Sean couldn't figure out how he'd managed to keep his hands off of her for the past year or more. Right now, the desire leaping inside him had him hard and eager for the taste of her. The feel of her beneath his hands. He wanted to hear her sigh, hear her call his name as she erupted beneath him. Wanted to bury himself inside her heat and feel her surrounding him.

"That look in your eyes tells me exactly what you're thinking," Georgia said, and this time she took a long drink of champagne.

"And are you thinking the same?" he asked.

"I shouldn't be."

"That wasn't the question."

Never breaking her gaze from his, Georgia blew out a breath and admitted, "Okay, yes, I'm thinking the same."

"Thank the gods for that," he said, a smile curving his mouth.

She chuckled, and the sound was rich and full. "I think you've got more in common with the devils than you do with the gods."

"Isn't that a lovely thing to say then?" he quipped. Reaching out, he plucked the champagne flute from her hand and set it onto the table.

"I wasn't finished," she told him.

"We'll have more later. *After*," he promised.

She took a deep breath and said, "This is probably a mistake, you know."

"Aye, probably is. Would you have us stop then, before we get started?" He hoped to hell she said no, because if she said yes, he'd have to leave. And right now, leaving was the very last thing he wanted to do.

"I really should say yes, because we absolutely should stop. Probably," she said quietly.

He liked the hesitation in that statement. "But?"

"But," she added, "I'm tired of being sensible. I want you to touch me, Sean. I think I've wanted that right from the beginning, but we were being too sensible for me to admit to it."

He pulled her up and over to him, settling her on his lap where she'd be sure to feel the hard length of him pressing into her bottom. "You can readily see that I feel the same."

"Yeah," she said, turning her face up to his. "I'm getting that."

"Not yet," he teased, "but you're about to."

"Promises, promises…"

"Well then, enough talking, yes?"

"Oh, yes."

He kissed her, softly at first, a brush of the lips, a connection that was as swift and sweet as innocence. It was a tease. Something short to ease them both into this new wrinkle in their relationship.

But with that first kiss, something incredible happened. Sean felt a jolt of white-hot electricity zip through him in an instant. His eyes widened as he looked at her, and he knew the surprise he read on her face was also etched on his own.

"That was… Let's just see if we can make that happen again, shall we?"

She nodded and arched into him, parting her lips for him when he kissed her, and this time Sean fed that electrical jolt that sizzled between them. He deepened the kiss, tangling his tongue with hers, pulling her closer, tighter, to him. Her arms came up around his neck and held on. She kissed him back, feverishly, as if every ounce of passion within her had been unleashed at once.

She stabbed her fingers through his hair, nails dragging along his scalp. She twisted on his lap, rubbing her behind against his erection until a groan slid from his throat. The glorious friction of her body against his would only get better, he thought, if he could just get her out of these bloody clothes.

He broke the kiss and dragged in a breath of air, hoping to steady the racing beat of his heart. It didn't help. Nothing would. Not until he'd had her, all of her. Only then would he be able to douse the fire inside. To cool the need and regain his control.

But for now, all he needed was her. Georgia Page, temptress with eyes of twilight and a mouth designed to drive a man wild.

"You've too many clothes on," he muttered, dropping his hands to the buttons on her dark blue shirt.

"You, too," she said, tugging the tail of his white, long-sleeved shirt free of the black jeans he wore. She fumbled at the buttons and then laughed at herself. "Can't get them undone, damn it."

"No need," he snapped and, gripping both sides of his shirt, ripped it open, sending small white buttons flying around the room like tiny missiles.

She laughed again and slapped both palms to his chest. At the first touch of her skin to his, Sean hissed in a breath and held it. He savored every stroke, every caress, while she explored his skin as if determined to map every inch of him.

He was willing to lie still for that exploration, too, as long as he could do the same for her. He got the last of her buttons undone and slid her shirt off her shoulders and down her arms. She helped him with it, and then her skin was bared to him, all but her lovely breasts, hidden behind the pale, sky-blue lace of her bra. His mouth went dry.

Tossing her honey-blond hair back from her face, Georgia met his gaze as she unhooked the front clasp of that bra and then slipped out of it completely. Sean's hands cupped her, his thumbs and forefingers brushing across the rigid peaks of her dark pink nipples until she sighed and cupped his hands with her own.

"You're lovely, Georgia. More lovely than I'd imagined," he whispered, then winked. "And my imagination was pretty damned good."

She grinned, then whispered, "My turn." She pushed his shirt off and skimmed her small, elegant hands slowly over his shoulders and arms, and every touch was a kiss of fire. Every caress a temptation.

He leaned over, laying her back on the sofa until she was staring up at him. Firelight played over her skin, light and shadow dancing in tandem, making her seem almost ethereal. But she was a real woman with a real need, and Sean was the man to meet it.

Deftly, he undid the waist button and the zipper of the skirt she wore, then slowly tugged the fabric down and off before tossing it to the floor. She wore a scrap of blue lace panties that were somehow even more erotic than seeing her naked would have been. Made him want to take that elastic band between his teeth and—

"Sean!" She half sat up and for a dark second or two, Sean was worried she'd changed her mind at the last. The thought of that nearly brought him to his knees.

"What is it?"

"Protection," she said. "I'm not on the pill, and I don't really travel with condoms." Worrying her bottom lip with her teeth, she blurted, "Maybe Ronan's got some old ones upstairs…"

"No need," he said and stood. "I've some in the glove box of the car."

She just looked at him. "You keep condoms in the glove compartment?"

Truthfully, he hadn't used any of the stash he kept there for emergencies in longer than he cared to admit. There hadn't been a woman for him in months. Maybe, he thought now, it was because he'd been too tangled up in thoughts of twilight eyes and kissable lips. Well, he didn't much care for the sound of that, so he told himself that maybe he'd just been too bloody busy getting his airline off the ground, so to speak.

"Pays to be prepared," was all he said.

Georgia's lips twitched. "I didn't realize Ireland *had* Boy Scouts."

"What?"

"Never mind," she whispered, lifting her hips and pulling her panties off. "Just...hurry."

"I bloody well will." He scraped one hand across his face, then turned and bolted for the front door. It cost him to leave her, even for the few moments this necessary trip would take.

He was through the front door and out to his car in a blink. He hardly felt the misting rain as it covered him in an icy, wet blanket. The night was quiet; the only light came from that of the fire within the parlor, a mere echo of light out here, battling and losing against the darkness and the rain.

He tore through the glove box, grabbed the box of condoms and slammed the door closed again. Back inside the house, he staggered to a stop on the threshold of the parlor. She'd moved from the couch, and now she lay stretched out, naked, on the rug before the fire, her head on one of the countless pillows she'd brought down there with her.

Sean's gaze moved over her in a flash and then again,

more slowly, so he could savor everything she was. Mouth dry, heartbeat hammering in his chest, he thought he'd never seen a more beautiful picture than the one she made in the firelight.

"You're wet," she whispered.

Sean shoved one hand through his rain-soaked hair, then shrugged off his shirt. "Hadn't noticed."

"Cold?" she asked, and levered herself up on one elbow to watch him.

The curve of her hip, the swell of her breasts and the heat in her eyes all came together to flash into an inferno inside him. "Cold? Not likely."

Never taking his gaze from hers, he pulled off the rest of his clothes and simply dropped them onto the color-ful rug beneath his feet. He went to her, laser-focused on the woman stretched out beside him on the carpet in the firelight.

She reached up and cupped his cheek before smiling. "I thought we'd have more room down here than on the couch."

"Very sensible," he muttered, kissing her palm then dipping to claim her lips in a brief, hard kiss. "Nothing more sexy than a smart woman."

"Always nice to hear." She grinned and moved into him, pressing her mouth to his. Opening for him, welcoming the taste of him as he devoured her. Bells clanged in his mind, warning or jubilation he didn't care which.

All that mattered now was the next touch. The next taste. She filled him as he'd never been filled before and all Sean could think was *Why had it taken them so bloody long to do this?*

Then his thoughts dissolved under an onslaught of sensations that flooded his system. He tore his mouth from hers to nibble at the underside of her jaw. To drag lips and tongue along the line of her throat while she sighed with pleasure and slid her hands up and down his back.

She was soft, smooth and smelled of flowers, and every breath he took drew her deeper inside him. He lost himself in the discovery of her, sliding his palms over her curves. He took first one nipple, then the other, into his mouth, tasting, suckling, driving her sighs into desperate gasps for air. She touched him, too, sliding her hands across his back and around to his chest and then down, to his abdomen. Then further still, until she curled her fingers around his length and Sean lifted his head, looked down into her eyes and let her see what she was doing to him.

Firelight flickered, rain spattered against the windows and the wind rattled the glass.

Her breath came fast and heavy. His heart galloped in his chest. Reaching for the condoms he'd tossed to the hearth, he tore one packet open, sheathed himself, then moved to kneel between her legs.

She planted her feet and lifted her hips in invitation and Sean couldn't wait another damn minute. He needed this. Needed *her* as he'd never needed anything before.

Scooping his hands beneath her butt, he lifted her and, in one swift push, buried himself inside her.

Her head fell back, and a soft moan slid from her lips. His jaw tight, he swallowed the groan trying to escape his throat. Then she wrapped her legs around his middle, lifted her arms and drew him in deeper, closer. He bent over her and kissed her as the rhythm of this ancient, powerful dance swept them both away.

They moved together as if they'd been partners for years. Each seemed to know instinctively what would most touch, most inflame, the other. Their shadows

moved on the walls and the night crowded closer as Sean
pushed Georgia higher and higher.

His gaze locked with hers, he watched her eyes flash,
felt her body tremble as her release exploded inside her.
Lost himself in the pleasure glittering in her twilight
eyes and then, finally, his control snapped completely.
Taking her mouth with his, he kissed her deeply as his
body shattered.

Georgia felt...fabulous.

Heat from the fire warmed her on one side, while
Sean's amazing body warmed her from the other. And
of the two, she preferred the heat pumping from the tall,
gorgeous man laying beside her.

Turning to face him, she smiled. "That was—"

"Aye, it was," he agreed.

"Worth waiting for," she confessed.

He skimmed a palm along the curve of her hip and
she shivered. "And I was just wondering why in the hell
we waited as long as we did."

"Worried about complications, remember?" she asked,
and only now felt the first niggling doubt about whether
or not they'd done the right thing. Probably not, she
mused, but it was hard to regret any of it.

"There's always complications to good sex," he said
softly, "and that wasn't just good, it was—"

"Yeah," she said, "it was."

"So the question arises," he continued, smoothing his
hand now across her bottom, "what do we do about this?"

She really hadn't had time to consider all the options,
and Georgia was a woman who spent most of her life
looking at any given situation from every angle possible.
Well, until tonight anyway. Now, her brain was scrambling to come up with coherent thoughts in spite of the

fact that her body was still buzzing and even now hoping for more.

Still, one thing did come to mind, though she didn't much care for it. "We could just stop whatever this is. Pretend tonight never happened and go back to the way things were."

"And is that what you really want to do?" he asked, leaning forward to plant a kiss on her mouth.

She licked her lips as if to savor the taste of him, then sighed and shook her head. "No, I really don't. But those complications will only get worse if we keep doing this."

"Life is complicated, Georgia," he said, smoothing his hand around her body to tug playfully at one nipple.

She sucked in a gulp of air and blew it out again. "True."

"And, pretending it didn't happen won't work, as every time I see you, I'll want to do this again…"

"There is that," she said, reaching out to smooth his hair back from his forehead. Heck, she *already* wanted to do it all again. Feel that moment when his body slid into hers. Experience the sensation of his body filling her completely. That indescribable friction that only happened when sex was done really well. And this *so* had been.

His eyes in the firelight glittered as if there were sparks dancing in their depths, and Georgia knew she was a goner. At least for now, anyway. She might regret it all later, but if she did, she would still walk away with some amazing memories.

"So," he said softly, "we'll take the complications as they come and do as we choose?"

"Yes," she said after giving the thought of never being with him again no more than a moment's consideration.

"We'll take the complications. We're adults. We know what we're doing."

"We certainly seemed to a few minutes ago," he said with a teasing grin.

"Okay, then. No strings. No expectations. Just...*us*. For however long it lasts."

"Sounds good." He pushed himself to his feet and walked naked to the table where they'd abandoned their wineglasses and the now nearly empty bottle of champagne.

"What're you doing?"

He passed her the glasses as she sat up, then held the empty bottle aloft. "I'm going to open another of Ronan's fine bottles of champagne. The first we drank to our new and lovely Fiona. The second we'll drink to *us*. And the bargain we've just made."

She looked up at him, her gaze moving over every square inch of that deliciously toned and rangy body. He looked like some pagan god, doused in firelight, and her breath stuttered in her chest. She could only nod to his suggestion because her throat was so suddenly tight with need, with passion, with...other things she didn't even want to contemplate.

Sean Connolly wasn't a forever kind of man—but, Georgia reminded herself as she watched him move to the tiny refrigerator and open it, she wasn't looking for forever. She'd already tried that and had survived the crash-and-burn. Sure, he wasn't the man her ex had been. But why even go there? Why try to make more out of this than it was? Great sex didn't have to be forever.

And as a right-now kind of man, Sean was perfect.

Three

The next couple of weeks were busy.

Laura was just settling into life as a mother, and both she and Ronan looked asleep on their feet half the time. But there was happiness in the house, and Georgia was determined to find some of that happy for herself.

Sean had been a big help in navigating village society. Most of the people who lived and worked in Dunley had been there for generations. And though they might like the idea of a new shop in town, the reality of it slammed up against the whole aversion-to-change thing. Still, since Georgia was no longer a complete stranger, most of the people in town were more interested than resentful.

"A design shop, you say?"

"That's right," Georgia answered, turning to look at Maeve Carrol. At five feet two inches tall, the seventy-year-old woman had been Ronan's nanny once upon a long-ago time. Since then, she was the self-appointed chieftain of the village and kept up with everything that was happening.

Her white hair was piled at the top of her head in a lop-sided bun. Her cheeks were red from the wind, and her blue eyes were sharp enough that Georgia was willing to bet Maeve didn't miss much. Buttoned up in a Kelly green cardigan and black slacks, she looked snug, right down to the soles of her bright pink sneakers.

"And you'll draw up pictures of things to be done to peoples' homes."

"Yes, and businesses, as well," Georgia said, "just about anything. It's all about the flow of a space. Not exactly feng shui but along the same lines."

Maeve's nose twitched and a smile hovered at the corners of her mouth. "Fing Shooey—not a lot of that in the village."

Georgia smiled at Maeve's pronunciation of the design philosophy, then said, "Doesn't matter. Some will want help redecorating, and there will be customers for me in Westport and Galway…"

"True enough," Maeve allowed.

Georgia paused to take a look up and down the main street she'd come to love over the past year. There really wasn't much to the village, all in all. The main street held a few shops, the Pennywhistle pub, a grocer's, the post office and a row of two-story cottages brightly painted.

The sidewalks were swept every morning by the shop owners, and flowers spilled from pots beside every doorway. The doors were painted in brilliant colors, scarlet, blue, yellow and green, as if the bright shades could offset the ever-present gray clouds.

There were more homes, of course, some above the shops and some just outside the village proper on the narrow track that wound through the local farmers' fields.

Dunley had probably looked much the same for centuries, she thought, and liked the idea very much.

It would be good to have roots. To belong. After her divorce, Georgia had felt so…untethered. She'd lived in Laura's house, joined Laura's business. Hadn't really had something to call *hers*. This was a new beginning. A chapter in her life that she would write in her own way in her own time. It was a heady feeling.

Outside of town was a cemetery with graves dating back five hundred years or more, each of them still lovingly tended by the descendants of those who lay there. The ruins of once-grand castles stubbled the countryside and often stood side by side with the modern buildings that would never be able to match the staying power of those ancient structures.

And soon, she would be a part of it.

"It's a pretty village," Georgia said with a little sigh.

"It is at that," Maeve agreed. "We won the Tidy Town award back in '74, you know. The Mayor's ever after us to win it again."

"Tidy Town." She smiled as she repeated the words and loved the fact that soon she would be a part of the village life. She might always be called "the Yank," but it would be said with affection, she thought, and one day, everyone might even forget that Georgia Page hadn't always been there.

She hoped so, anyway. This was important to her. This life makeover. And she wanted—needed—it to work.

"You've your heart set on this place, have you?" Maeve asked.

Georgia grinned at the older woman then shifted her gaze to the empty building in front of them. It was at the end of the village itself and had been standing empty for a couple of years. The last renter had given up on making a go of it and had left for America.

"I have," Georgia said with a sharp nod for emphasis. "It's a great space, Maeve—"

"Surely a lot of it," the older woman agreed, peering through dirty windows to the interior. "Colin Ferris now, he never did have a head for business. Imagine trying to make a living selling interwebbing things in a village the size of Dunley."

Apparently Colin hadn't been able to convince the villagers that an internet café was a good idea. And there hadn't been enough of the tourist trade to tide him over.

"'Twas no surprise to me he headed off to America." She looked over at Georgia. "Seems only right that one goes and one comes, doesn't it?"

"It does." She hadn't looked at it that way before, but there was a sort of synchronicity to the whole thing. Colin left for America, and Georgia left America for Dunley.

"So you've your path laid out then?"

"What? Oh. Yes, I guess I have," Georgia said, smiling around the words. She had found the building she would rent for her business, and maybe in a couple of years, she'd be doing so well she would buy it. It was all happening, she thought with an inner grin. Her whole life was changing right before her eyes. Georgia would never again be the same woman she had been when Mike had walked out of her life, taking her self-confidence with him.

"Our Sean's been busy as well, hasn't he?" Maeve mused aloud. "Been a help to you right along?"

Cautious, Georgia slid a glance at the canny woman beside her. So far she and Sean had kept their...relationship under the radar. And in a village the size of Dunley, that had been a minor miracle. But if Maeve Carrol was paying attention, their little secret could be out.

And Maeve wasn't the only one paying attention. Laura was starting to give Georgia contemplative looks that had to mean she was wondering about all the time Georgia and Sean were spending together.

Keeping her voice cool and her manner even cooler, Georgia said only, "Sean's been great. He's helped me get the paperwork going on getting my business license—" Which was turning out to be more complicated than she'd anticipated.

"He's a sharp one, is Sean," Maeve said. "No one better at wangling his way around to what he wants in the end."

"Uh-huh."

"Maggie Culhane told me yesterday that she and Colleen Leary were having tea at the pub and heard Sean talking to Brian Connor about his mum's cottage, it standing empty this last year or more."

Georgia sighed inwardly. The grapevine in Dunley was really incredible.

"Yes, Sean was asking about the cottage for me. I'd really like to live in the village if I can."

"I see," Maeve murmured, her gaze on Georgia as sharp as any cop's, waiting for a confession.

"Oh, look," Georgia blurted, "here comes Mary Donohue with the keys to the store."

Thank God, she thought, grateful for the reprieve in the conversation. Maeve was a sweetie, but she had a laserlike focus that Georgia would just as soon avoid. And she and Sean were keeping whatever it was between them quiet. There was no need for anyone else to know, anyway. Neither one of them was interested in feeding the local gossips—and Georgia really didn't want to hear advice from her sister.

"Sorry I'm late," Mary called out when she got closer. "I was showing a farm to a client, and wouldn't you know he'd be late and then insist on walking over every bloody blade of grass in the fields?"

She shook her mass of thick red hair back from her face, produced a key from her suitcase-sized purse and opened the door to the shop. "Now then," she announced, standing back to allow Georgia to pass in front of her. "If this isn't perfect for what you're wanting, I'll be shocked."

It *was* perfect, Georgia thought, wandering into the empty space. The floor was wood, scarred from generations of feet tracking across its surface. But with some polish, it would look great. The walls were in need of a coat of paint, but all in all, the place really worked for Georgia. In her mind, she set up a desk and chairs and shelves with samples stacked neatly. She walked through, the heels of her boots clacking against the floor. She gave a quick look to the small kitchen in the back, the closet-sized bath and the storeroom. She'd already been through the place once and knew it was the one for her. But today was to settle the last of her nerves before she signed the rental papers.

The main room was long and narrow, and the window let in a wide swath of daylight even in the gray afternoon. She had a great view of the main street, looking out directly across the road at a small bakery where she could go for her lunch every day and get tea and a sandwich. She'd be a part of Dunley, and she could grow the kind of business she'd always wanted to have.

Georgia breathed deep and realized that Mary was giving her spiel, and she grinned when she realized she would never have to do that herself, again. Maeve wandered the room, inspecting the space as if she'd never seen it before. Outside, two or three curious villagers began to gather, peering into the windows, hands cupped around their eyes.

Another quick smile from Georgia as she turned to Mary and said, "Yes. It's perfect."

Sean came rushing through the front door just in time to hear her announcement. He gave her a wide smile and walked across the room to her. Dropping both hands onto her shoulders, he gave her a fast, hard kiss, and said, "That's for congratulations."

Georgia's lips buzzed in reaction to that spontaneous kiss even while she worried about Maeve and Mary being witnesses to it. Sean didn't seem to mind, though. But then, he was such an outgoing guy, maybe no one would think anything of it.

"We used handshakes for that in my day," Maeve murmured.

"Ah, Maeve my darlin', did you want a kiss, too?" Sean swept the older woman up, planted a quick kiss on her mouth and had her back on her feet, swatting the air at him a second later.

"Go on, Sean Connolly, you always were free with your kisses."

"He was indeed," Mary said with a wink for Georgia. "Talk of the village he was. Why when my Kitty was young, I used to warn her about our Sean here."

Sean slapped one hand to his chest in mock offense. "You're a hard woman, Mary Donohue, when you know Kitty was the first to break my heart."

Mary snorted. "Hard to break a thing that's never been used."

No one else seemed to notice, but Georgia saw a flash of something in Sean's eyes that made her wonder if

Mary's words hadn't cut a little deeper than she'd meant. But a moment later, Sean was speaking again in that teasing tone she knew so well.

"Pretty women were meant to be kissed. You can't blame me for doing what's expected, can you?"

"You always did have as much brass as a marching band," Maeve told him, but she was smiling.

"So then, it's settled." Sean looked from Georgia to Mary. "You'll be taking the shop."

"I am," she said, "if Mary's brought the papers with her."

"I have indeed," that woman said and again dipped into her massive handbag.

Georgia followed her off a few steps to take care of business while Sean stood beside Maeve and watched her go.

"And just what kind of deviltry are you up to this time, Sean Connolly?" Maeve whispered.

Sean didn't look at the older woman. Couldn't seem to tear his gaze off of Georgia. Nothing new there. She had been uppermost in his mind for the past two weeks. Since the first time he'd touched her, Sean had thought about little else but touching her again. He hadn't meant to kiss her like that in front of witnesses—especially Maeve—but damned if he'd been able to help himself.

"I don't know what you mean, Maeve."

"Oh, yes," the older woman said with a knowing look, "it's clear I've confused you…"

"Leave off, Maeve," he murmured. "I'm here only to help if I can."

"Being the generous sort," she muttered right back.

He shot her a quick look and sighed. There was no putting anything over on Maeve Carrol. When they were boys, he and Ronan had tried too many times to count to get away with some trouble or other only to be stopped short by the tiny woman now beside him.

Frowning a bit, he turned to watch Georgia as she read over the real estate agent's papers. She was small but, as he knew too well, curvy in all the right places. In her faded blue jeans and dark scarlet, thickly knit sweater, she looked too good. Standing here in this worn, empty store, she looked vivid. Alive. In a way that made everything else around her look as gray as the skies covering Dunley.

"Ronan says you haven't been by the house much," Maeve mentioned.

"Ah, well, I'm giving them time to settle in with Fiona. Don't need people dropping in right and left."

"You've been *dropping* in since you were a boy, Sean." She clucked her tongue and mused, "Makes a body wonder what you've found that's kept you so busy."

"I've got a business to run, don't I?" he argued in a lame defense, for Maeve knew as well as he did that his presence wasn't required daily at the offices of Irish Air. There was plenty of time for him to stop in at Ronan's house as he always had. But before, he hadn't been trying to cover up an affair with his...what was Georgia to him? A cousin-in-law? He shook his head. Didn't matter. "I'll go to the house, Maeve."

"See that you do. Ronan's wanting to show off his baby girl to you, so mind you go to there soon."

"I will and all," he assured her, then snatched at his ringing cell phone as he would a lifeline tossed into a churning sea. Lifting one finger to Maeve as if to tell her one moment, he turned and answered, "Sean Connolly."

A cool, dispassionate voice started speaking and he actually *felt* a ball of ice drop into the pit of his stomach.

"Repeat that if you please," he ordered, though he didn't want to hear the news again. He had to have the information.

His gaze moved to Georgia, who had turned to look at him, a question in her eyes. His tone of voice must have alerted her to a problem.

"I understand," he said into the phone. "I'm on my way."

He snapped the phone closed.

Georgia walked up to him. "What is it?"

Sean could hardly say the words, but he forced them out. "It's my mother. She's in hospital." It didn't sound real. Didn't feel real. But according to the nurse who'd just hung up on him, it was. "She's had a heart attack."

"Ah, Sean," Maeve said, sympathy rich in her voice.

He didn't want pity. More than that though, he didn't want to be in a position to need it. "She's in Westport. I have to go."

He headed for the door, mind already racing two or three steps ahead. He'd get to the hospital, talk to the doctors, then figure out what to do next. His mother was hale and hearty—usually—so he wouldn't worry until he knew more. An instant later, he told himself *Bollocks to that,* as he realized the worry and fear had already started.

Georgia was right behind him. "Let me come with you."

"No." He stopped, looked down into her eyes and saw her concern for him and knew that if she were with him, her fears would only multiply his own. Sounded foolish even to him, but he had to do this alone. "I have to go—"

Then he hit the door at a dead run and kept running until he'd reached his car.

* * *

Ailish Connolly was not the kind of woman to be still.

So seeing his mother lying in a hospital bed, hooked up to machinery that beeped and whistled an ungodly tune was nearly enough to bring Sean to his knees. Disjointed but heartfelt prayers raced through his mind as he reached for the faith of his childhood in this time of panic.

It had been too long since he'd been to Mass. Hadn't graced a church with his presence in too many years to count. But now, at this moment, he wanted to fling himself at the foot of an altar and beg God for help.

Sean shoved one hand through his hair and bit back the impatience clawing inside him. He felt so bloody helpless, and that, he thought, was the worst of it. Nothing he could do but sit and wait, and as he wasn't a patient man by nature...the waiting came hard.

The private room he had arranged for his mother smelled like her garden, since he'd bought every single flower in the gift shop. That was what he'd been reduced to. Shopping for flowers while his mother lay still and quiet. He wasn't accustomed to being unable to affect change around him.

Sean Connolly was a man who got things done. Always. Yet here, in the Westport hospital, he could do not a bloody thing to get action. To even get a damned doctor to answer his questions. So far, all he'd managed to do was irritate the nurses and that, he knew, was no way to gain cooperation. Irish nurses were a tough bunch and took no trouble from anyone.

Sitting beside his mother's bed in a torture chair designed to make visiting an ordeal, Sean braced his elbows on his knees and cupped his face in his palms. It had been only his mother and he for so long, he couldn't remember his life any other way. His father had died when Sean was just a boy, and Ailish had done the heroic task of two parents.

Then when Ronan's parents had died in that accident, Ailish had stepped in for him, as well. She was strong, remarkably self-possessed and until today, Sean would have thought, invulnerable. He lifted his gaze to the small woman with short, dark red hair. There was gray mixed with the red, he noticed for the first time. Not a lot, but enough to shake him.

When had his mother gotten old? Why was she here? She'd been to lunch with her friends and had felt a pain that had worried her enough she had come to the hospital to have it checked. And once the bloody doctors got their hands on you, you were good and fixed, Sean thought grimly, firing a glare at the closed door and the busy corridor beyond.

They'd slapped Ailish in to be examined and now, several hours later, he was still waiting to hear what the dozens of tests they'd done would tell them. The waiting, as he had told Georgia not so very long ago, was the hardest.

Georgia.

He wished he had brought her with him. She was a calm, cool head, and at the moment he needed that. Because what he was tempted to do was have his mother transferred to a bigger hospital in Dublin. To fly in specialists. "To *buy* the damned hospital so *someone* would come in and talk to me."

"Sean," his mother whispered, opening her eyes and turning her face toward him, "don't swear."

"Mother." He stood up, curled one hand around the bar of her bed and reached down with the other to take hers in his. "How are you?"

"I'm fine," she insisted. "Or I was, having a lovely nap until my son's cursing woke me."

"Sorry." She still had the ability to make him feel like a guilty boy. He supposed all mothers had that power, though at the moment, only *his* mother concerned him. "But no one will talk to me. No one will tell me a bloody—" He cut himself off. "I can't get answers from anyone in this place."

"Perhaps they don't have any to give yet," she pointed out.

That didn't ease his mind any.

Her face was pale, her sharp green eyes were a little watery, and the pale wash of freckles on her cheeks stood out like gold paint flicked atop a saucer of milk.

His heart actually ached to see her here. Like this. Fear wasn't something he normally even considered, but the thought of his mother perhaps being at death's bleeding door with not a doctor in sight cut him right down to the bone.

"Do you know what I was thinking," she said softly, giving her son's hand a gentle squeeze, "when they were sticking their wires and such to me?"

He could imagine. She must have been terrified. "No," he said. "Tell me."

"All I could think was, I was going to die and leave you alone," she murmured, and a single tear fell from the corner of her eye to roll down her temple and into her hair.

"There'll be no talk of dying," he told her, instinctively fighting against the fear that crouched inside him. "And I'm not alone. I've friends, and Ronan and Laura, and now the baby..."

"And no family of your own," she pointed out.

"And what're you then?" Sean teased.

She shook her head and fixed her gaze with his. "You

should have a wife. A family, Sean. A man shouldn't live his life alone."

It was an old argument. Ailish was forever trying to marry off her only child. But now, for the first time, Sean felt guilty. She should have been concerned for herself; instead she was worried for him. Worried *about* him. He hated that she was lying there so still and pale, and that there was nothing he could do for her. Bloody hell, he couldn't even get the damn doctor to step into the room.

"Ronan's settled and happy now," Ailish said softly. "And so should you be."

Her fingers felt small and fragile in his grip, and the fear and worry bottled up inside Sean seemed to spill over. "I am," he blurted before he was even aware of speaking.

Her gaze sharpened. "You are what?"

"Settled," he lied valiantly. He hadn't planned to. But seeing her worry needlessly had torn something inside Sean and had him telling himself that this at least, he could do for her. A small lie couldn't be that bad, could it, if it brought peace? And what if she *was* dying, God forbid, but how was he to know since no one would tell him anything. Wouldn't it be better for her to go believing that Sean was happy?

"I'm engaged," he continued, and gave his mother a smile. "I was going to tell you next week," he added, as the lie built up steam and began to travel on its own.

Her eyes shone and a smile curved her mouth even as twin spots of color flushed her pale cheeks. "That's wonderful," she said. "Who is she?"

Who indeed?

Brain racing, Sean could think of only one woman who would fit this particular bill, but even he couldn't drag Georgia into this lie without some warning. "I'll tell you as soon as you're fit and out of here."

Now those sharp green eyes narrowed on him. "If this is a trick…"

He slapped one hand to his chest and hoped not to be struck down as he said, "Would I lie about something this important?"

"No," she said after a long moment, "no, you wouldn't."

Guilt took another nibble of his soul.

"There you are then," he pronounced. "Now try to get some sleep."

She nodded, closed her eyes and still with a smile on her face, was asleep in minutes. Which left Sean alone with his thoughts—

A few hours later the doctor finally deigned to make an appearance, and though Sean was furious, he bit his tongue and was glad he had. A minor heart attack. No damage to her heart, really, just a warning of sorts for Ailish to slow down a bit and take better care of herself.

The doctor also wanted a few more tests to be sure of his results, which left Sean both relieved and worried. A minor heart attack was still serious enough. Was she well enough to find out he'd…*exaggerated* his engagement?

She would be in hospital for a week, resting under doctor's orders, so Sean wouldn't have to decide about telling her the truth right away. But he *did* have to have a chat with Georgia. Just in case.

Four

He left his mother sleeping and made his way out of the hospital, grateful to leave behind its smell of antiseptic and fear. Stepping into a soft, evening mist, Sean stopped dead when a familiar voice spoke up.

"Sean?"

He turned and felt a well of pleasure open up inside as Georgia walked toward him. "What're you doing here?" he asked, wrapping both arms around her and holding on.

She hugged him, then pulled her head back to look up at him. "When we didn't hear anything, I got worried. So I came here to wait for you. How's your mom?"

Pleasure tangled with gratitude as he realized just how much he'd needed to see her. He'd been a man alone for most of his adult life, never asking for anything, never expecting anyone to go an extra meter for him. Yet here she was, stepping out of the mist and cold, and Sean had never been happier to see anyone.

"She's well, though the doctor's holding on to her for a week or so. More tests, he says, and he wants her to rest. Never could get my mother to slow down long enough to *rest,* so God help the nurses trying to hold her down in that bed," he said, dropping a quick kiss on her forehead. "Scared me, Georgia. I don't even remember the last time anything has."

"Family does that to you," she told him. "But she's okay?"

"Will be," he said firmly. "It was a 'minor' heart attack, they say. No permanent damage, though, so that's good. She's to take it easy for a few weeks, no upsets. But yes, she'll be fine."

"Good news." Georgia's gaze narrowed on him. "So why do you look more worried than relieved?"

"I'll tell you all. But first, I've a need to get away from this place. Feels like I've been here for years instead of hours." Frowning, he looked out at the car park. "How did you get here?"

"Called a cab." She shrugged. "Laura was going to drive me, but I told her and Ronan that I'd be fine and you'd bring me home."

"As I will," he said, taking her arm and steering her toward his car. "But first, we'll go to my house. We need to talk."

"You'll tell me on the way?"

"I think not," he hedged. "I'm a man in desperate need of a beer, and I'm thinking you'll be needing wine to hear this."

There wasn't enough wine in the world.

"Are you insane?" Georgia jumped off the comfortable sofa in Sean's front room and stared down at him in stunned shock. "I mean, seriously. Maybe we should have had *you* examined at the hospital while we were there."

Sean huffed out a breath and took a long drink of the beer he'd poured for himself as soon as they reached his home. Watching him, Georgia took a sip of her Chardonnay, to ease the tightness in her own throat.

Then he leaned forward and set the glass of beer onto the table in front of him. "I'm not insane, no. Crazy perhaps, but not insane."

"Fine line, if you ask me."

He pushed one hand through his hair and muttered, "I'm not explaining this well a'tall."

"Oh, I don't know." Georgia sipped at her wine, then set her own glass down beside his. Still standing, she crossed both arms over her chest and said, "You were pretty clear. You want me to *pretend* to be engaged to you so you can lie to your mother. That about cover it?"

He scowled and stood up, Georgia thought, just so he could loom over her from his much greater height.

"Well, when you put it like that," he muttered, "it sounds—"

"Terrible? Is that the word you're looking for?"

He winced as he scrubbed one hand across his face. Georgia felt a pang of sympathy for him even though a part of her wanted to kick him.

"I thought she was dying."

"So you lied to her to give her a good send-off?"

He glared at her, and for the first time since she'd known him, she wasn't seeing the teasing, laughing, charming Sean...but instead the hard-lined owner of Irish Air. This was the man who'd bought out a struggling airline and built it into the premier luxury line in the world. The man who had become a billionaire through sheer strength of will. His eyes flashed with heat, with temper, and his mouth, the one she knew so well, was now flattened into a grim line.

Georgia, who had a temper of her own and just as hard a head, was unimpressed.

"If you think I enjoy lying to her, you're wrong."

"Well, good, because I *like* your mother."

"As do I," he argued.

"Then tell her the truth."

"I will," he countered, "as soon as the doctor says she's well again. Until then, would it really be so bad to let her believe a small lie?"

"Small." She shook her head and walked toward the wide stone hearth, where a fire burned against the cold night. On the mantel above the fire were framed family photos. Sean and Ronan. Sean and his mother. Laura and Georgia captured forever the day Ronan and Sean had taken them to the Burren—a lonely, desolate spot just a few miles outside Galway. Family was important to him, she knew that. Seeing these photos only brought that truth back to her.

She turned her back to the flames and looked at him, across the room from her. Sean's and Ronan's houses were both huge, sprawling manors, but Sean's was more…casual, she supposed was the right word. He'd lived alone here, but for his housekeeper and any number of people who worked on the estate, so he'd done as he pleased with the furniture.

Oversize sofas covered in soft fabric in muted shades of gray and blue crowded the room. Heavy, carved wooden tables dotted the interior, brass-based reading lamps tossed golden circles of light across gleaming wood floors and midnight-blue rugs. The walls were stone as well, interspersed with heavy wooden beams, and the wide front windows provided a view of a lawn that looked as if the gardener had gone over it on his knees with a pair of scissors, it was so elegantly tended.

"Is it really such a chore to pretend to be mad about me?" he asked, a half smile curving his mouth.

She looked at him and thought, no, pretending to be crazy about him wasn't a problem. Which should probably *be* a problem, she told herself, but that was a worry for another day.

"You want me to lie to Ailish."

"For only a while," he said smoothly. "To give me time to see her settled." He frowned a bit and added quietly, "She's...important to me, Georgia. I don't want her hurt."

God, was there anything sexier than a man unafraid to show his love for someone? Knowing how much Ailish meant to Sean touched Georgia deeply, but she was still unconvinced that his plan was a good one. Still, she remembered clearly how devastated she had been when she'd discovered all of her ex-husband's lies to her. Wouldn't Ailish feel the same sort of betrayal?

She shook her head slowly. "And you don't think she'll be hurt when she discovers she's been tricked?"

"Ah, but she won't find that out, will she?" Sean said, and he was smiling again, his temper having blown away as fast as it had come. "When the time is right, you'll throw me over, as well you should, and I'll bravely go on with my heart shattered to jagged pieces."

She snorted a laugh before she could stop it.

"So I get to be the bad guy, too?" She walked back, picked up her wine and took another sip. "Wow, I'm a lucky woman, all right. You remember I'm moving to Dunley, don't you? I'll see Ailish all the time, Sean, and she's going to think I'm a hideous person for dumping her son."

"She won't blame you," he assured her, "I'll see to it."

"Uh-huh."

"Georgia love," he said with a sigh, "you're my only chance at pulling this off."

"I don't like it."

"Of course you don't, being an honest woman." He plucked the wineglass from her fingers and set it aside. Then, stroking his hands up and down her arms, he added, "But being a warm-hearted, generous one as well, you can see this is the best way, can't you?"

"You think you can smooth me into this with a caress and a kiss?"

He bent down until his eyes were fixed on hers. "Aye, I do." Before she could respond to that arrogant admission, he added, "But I don't think I'll have to, will I? You've a kind heart, Georgia, and I know you can see why I've to do this."

Okay, yes, she could. Irritating to admit that even to herself. She understood the fear that must have choked him when he thought his mother was going to die. But damn it. Memories fluttered in her mind like a swarm of butterflies. "Lies never go well, Sean."

"But we're not lying to each other now, are we? So between the two of us, everything is on the up and up, and my mother will get over the disappointment—when she's well."

"It's not *just* your mother, though," she said. "The whole village will know. They'll all think I'm a jerk for dumping you."

"Hah!" Sean grinned widely. "Most of those in Dunley will think you a fool for agreeing to marry me in the first place and will swear you've come to your senses when we end it. And if that doesn't do the job, I'll take the blame entirely."

She laughed, because he looked so pleased with that statement. "You're completely shameless, aren't you?"

"Absolutely," he agreed, with that grin that always managed to make her stomach take a slow bump and roll. "So will you do it then, Georgia? Will you pretend to be engaged to me?"

She was tempted, she could admit that much to herself. It was a small thing, after all. Just to help her lover out of a tight spot. And oh, he was a wonderful lover, she thought, her heart beginning to trip wildly in her chest. The time spent with him in the past couple of weeks had been...fabulous. But this was something else again.

"I can help you get your business license," he offered. "You're bogged down in the mire of bureaucratic speak, and I don't know as you'd noticed or not, but things in Ireland move at their own pace. You could be a woman with a walker by the time you got that license pushed through on your own."

She gave him a hard look. "But you're a magician?"

"I've a way about me, that's true. But also, I know some of those that are in charge of these things and frankly, as the owner of Irish Air, I carry a bit more weight to my words than you would."

He could. Darn it. She'd already seen for herself that working her way through the reams of paperwork was going to be mind-boggling.

"I could see you settled and ready for business much faster than you could do it on your own."

"Are you trying to bribe me?"

He grinned, unashamed. "I am and doing a damn fine job of it if you ask me."

Staring up into his brown eyes, shining now with the excitement for his plan, Georgia knew she was pretty much done. And let's face it, she told herself, he'd had her from the jump. Not only was it a great excuse to keep their affair going—but she knew how worried he was about Ailish and she felt for him. He had probably never doubted for a moment that he'd be able to talk her into joining him in his insanity. Even *before* the really superior bribe.

He was unlike anyone she'd ever known, Georgia thought. Everything about him was outrageous. Why wouldn't a proposal from Sean Connolly be the same?

"And, did you know there's a cottage for sale at the edge of the village?"

"Is that the one I hear you were talking to someone named Brian about?"

"Ah, the Dunley express," he said with a grin. "Talk about it in the pub and it's as good as published in the paper. No, this isn't Brian's mum's place. He's rented it just last week to Sinead and Michael when they come home."

"Oh." Well, there went a perfectly good cottage. "I spoke to Mary this afternoon, and she didn't say a thing about a cottage for sale."

"She doesn't know all," Sean said, bending to plant one quick, hard kiss on her lips. "For example, I own two of the cottages near the close at the end of main. Not far from your new shop…"

That last bit he let hang there long enough for Georgia to consider it. Then he continued.

"They're small, but well kept. Close to the village center and with a faery wood in the back."

She shook her head and laughed. "A what?"

He smiled, that delicious, slow curve of his mouth that promised wickedness done to perfection. "A faery wood, where if you stand and make a wish on the full of the moon, you might get just what your heart yearns for." He paused. "Or, the faeries might snatch you away to live forever in their raft beneath the trees."

With the song of Ireland in his voice, even the crazy sounded perfectly reasonable. "Faeries."

"You'd live in Ireland and dismiss them?" he challenged, his eyes practically twinkling now with good humor and banked laughter.

"Sean..."

"I could be convinced to make you a very good deal on either of the cottages, if..."

"You're evil," she said softly. "My mother used to warn me about men like you."

"An intelligent woman to be sure. I liked her very much when we met at Ronan's wedding."

Her mother had liked him, too. But then, her mom liked everybody. Georgia could remember being like that once upon a time. Before her ex-husband had left her for her cheerleader cousin and cleaned out their joint accounts on his way out of town. Just remembering the betrayal, the hurt, stiffened her spine even while her mind raced. Too many thoughts piling together were jumbled up in possibilities and possible disasters.

She was torn, seriously. She really did like Sean's mother and she hated the thought of lying to her. But Sean would be the *real* liar, right? Oh, man, even she couldn't buy that one. She would be in this right up to her neck if she said yes. But how could she not? Sean was offering to help her get her new life started, and all she had to do was pretend to be in love with him.

And that wasn't going to be too difficult, she warned herself. Just standing here beside him was dangerous. She knew all too well what it was like to have his hands and his mouth on her. Having a lover like Sean—much less a fiancé, pretend or not—was really a slippery slope toward something she had to guard against.

She wasn't interested in trusting another man. Giving her heart over to him. Giving him the chance to crush her again. Sure, Sean was nothing like her ex, but he was still *male*.

"What do you say, Georgia?" he asked, reaching down to take her hands in his and give them a squeeze. "Will you pretend-marry me?"

She couldn't think. Not with him holding on to her. Not with his eyes staring into hers. Not with the heat of him reaching for her, promising even *more* heat if she let him get any closer. And if she did that, she would agree to anything, because she well knew the man could have her half out of her mind in seconds.

Georgia pulled her hands free of his and took one long step back. "This isn't the kind of thing I can decide on in a minute, Sean. There's a lot to consider. So I'll think about it and let you know tomorrow, okay?"

He opened his mouth as if to argue, then, a moment later, changed his mind. Nodding, he closed the distance between them again and pulled her into the circle of his arms. Georgia leaned into him, giving herself this moment to feel the rush of something spectacular that happened every time he touched her.

Kissing the top of her head, he whispered, "Fine then. That'll do. For now."

With him holding on to her, the beat of his heart beneath her ear, Georgia was tempted to do all sorts of things, so she looked away from him, out the window to the rain-drenched evening. Lamps lining the drive shone like diamonds in the gray. But the darkness and the incessant rain couldn't disguise the beauty that was Ireland.

Just like, she thought, looking up at Sean, a lie couldn't

hide what was already between the two of them. She didn't know where it was going, but she had a feeling the ride was going to be much bumpier than she had planned.

"I feel like I haven't slept in years," Laura groaned over her coffee the following morning.

"At least you can have caffeine again," Georgia said.

"*Yes.*" Her sister paused. "Is it wrong to be nearly grateful that Fiona had no interest in nursing just so I can have coffee again?"

"If it is, I won't tell."

"You're the best." Laura slouched in a chair near the end of the couch where Georgia sat, checking email on her computer tablet.

Though she'd never been much of a morning person, it was hard to remain crabby when you got to sit in this beautiful parlor sipping coffee every morning. Of course, the baby had jumbled life in the manor, but she had to admit she loved being around her niece. Georgia glanced out the window at a sun-washed vista of sloping yard and trees beginning to lose their leaves for winter. For the first time in days, the sky was clear, but the cold Irish wind was tossing leaves into the air and making the trees dance and sway.

"I'm so excited that you're moving to Ireland," Laura said. "I really miss you when you're not around."

Georgia smiled at her sister. "I know, me, too. And it is exciting to move," she said, as she reached out for the silver pot on the rolling tea table in front of them. Hefting it, she refilled both her own and Laura's cups. Tea might be the big thing over here, but thankfully Patsy Brennan was willing to brew a pot of coffee for the Page sisters every morning. "Also, moving is terrifying. Not only going to a new place and starting over, but it's all the logistics of the thing. Canceling mail and utilities, starting them up somewhere else, and the packing."

Georgia shuddered and took a sip of coffee to bolster her.

"I get that. I was worried when I first moved here with Ronan, but everything went great."

"You had Ronan."

"And you have *me*."

"Ever the optimist," Georgia noted.

"No point in being a pessimist," Laura countered. "If you go around all grim, expecting the worst, when it happens, you've been suffering longer than you had to."

Georgia just blinked at her. "I'll work on that one and let you know when I figure it out."

Laura grinned, then sobered up again. "I wish you'd reconsider living here with us. There's plenty of room."

She knew her sister meant it, and having her offer was really wonderful. Even though having a secret affair was hard to manage when you were living with your sister. "I know, and I appreciate the offer. Just like I appreciate you letting me stay here when I visit. But I want my own place, Laura."

"Yeah, I know."

Morning light filtered into the room, and the winter sunshine was pale and soft. The baby monitor receiver that Laura carried with her at all times sat on the coffee table in front of them, and from it came the soft sounds of Fiona's breathing and the tiny sniffling sounds she made as she slept.

"Yesterday, Sean told me he owns a couple of cottages at the edge of the village," Georgia said. "He's going to sell me one of them."

"And that," Laura said thoughtfully, "brings us to the

main question for the day. What's going on with you and Sean?"

She went still and dropped her gaze to the black coffee in her cup. "Nothing."

"Right. What am I, blind? I gave birth in the hospital, Georgia," her sister pointed out, "I didn't have a lobotomy."

"Laura..." Georgia had known this was coming. Actually, it was probably only because Laura was so wrapped up in Fiona that she hadn't noticed earlier. Laura wasn't stupid and as she just mentioned, not blind, either.

"I can see how you guys are around each other," Laura was saying, tapping her fingernails lightly against the arm of the chair. "He watches you."

"Oooh, that's suspicious."

"I said he *watches* you. Like a man dying of thirst and you're a fountain of ice-cold water."

Something inside her stirred and heat began to crawl through Georgia's veins, in spite of her effort to put a stop to it. After that proposal Sean had made last night, he'd kissed her senseless, then dropped her off here at the manor, leaving Georgia so stirred up she'd hardly slept. Now, just the thought of Sean was enough to light up the ever-present kindling inside her.

Shaking her head, she said only, "Leave it alone, Laura."

"Sure. I'll do that. I'm sorry. Have we met?" Laura leaned toward her. "Honey, don't get me wrong. I'm glad you're having fun finally. God knows it took you long enough to put what's-his-name in the past—"

At the mention of Georgia's ex, she frowned. Okay, fine. It had taken her some time to get past the fury of being used, betrayed and then finally, publicly *dumped*.

But she figured most women would have come out of that situation filled with righteous fury.

"Gee, thanks."

"—I just don't want you to get crushed again."

"What happened to that optimism?"

Laura frowned at her. "This is different. What if you guys crash and burn? Then you'll be living here, with Sean right around the corner practically and seeing him all the time and you'll be miserable. I don't want that for you."

Georgia sighed and gave her sister's hand a pat. "I know. But you don't get to decide that, Laura. And we're not going to crash and burn. We're just…"

"…yeah?"

"I was going to say we're just lovers."

"There's no 'just' about it for you, Georgia," Laura sputtered. "Not for either one of us. We're not built that way. We don't do 'easy.'"

"I know that, too," Georgia argued, "but I did the cautious thing for years, and what did it get me? I thought Mike was the one, remember? Did everything right. Dated for two years, was engaged for one of those two. Big wedding, nice house, working together to build something, and what happened?"

Laura winced.

Georgia saw it and nodded. "Exactly. Mike runs off with Misty, who, if she had two thoughts running around in that tiny brain of hers, would rattle like BBs in a jar."

Laura smiled, but sadly. "That's no reason to jump into something with a man like Sean."

Suddenly forced to defend the man she was currently sleeping with, Georgia said, "What does that mean, 'a man like Sean'? He's charming and treats me great. We

have fun together, and that's all either one of us is looking for."

"For now."

Georgia shook her head and smiled. "All I'm interested
in at the moment is 'for now,' Laura. I did the whole cautious thing for way too long. Maybe it's time to cut loose
a little. Stop thinking nonstop about the future and just
enjoy today."

A long moment passed before Laura sighed and said,
"Maybe you're right. Sean is a sweetie, but Georgia—"

"Don't worry," she said, holding up one hand to stave
off any more advice. "I'm not looking for marriage and
family. I don't know that I ever will."

"Of course you will," Laura told her, sympathy and
understanding shining in her eyes. "That's who you are.
But if this is what you need right now, I'm on your side."

"Thanks. And," Georgia added, "as long as we're talking about this, you should know that last night Sean asked
me to help him out."

In a few short sentences, she explained Sean's plan and
watched Laura's mouth drop open. "You can't be serious."

"I think I am."

"Let me count the ways this could go bad."

"Do me a favor and don't, okay?" Georgia glanced
down at her email and idly deleted a couple of the latest
letters from people offering to send her the winnings to
contests she'd never entered. "I've thought about it, and
I understand why he's doing it."

"So do I. That doesn't make it a good idea."

"What's not a good idea?" Ronan asked, as he walked
into the room and paused long enough to kiss his wife
good morning before reaching out to grab a cup and pour
himself some coffee.

"Your idiot cousin," Laura started, firing a glare at her

husband as if this were all his fault, "wants my sister to pretend they're engaged."

While Laura filled Ronan in, Georgia sat back and concentrated on her coffee. She had a feeling she was going to need all the caffeine she could get.

Five

When Laura finally wound down and sat in her chair, alternately glowering at Ronan and then her sister, Georgia finally spoke up.

"Sean can sell me a cottage," she said calmly. "He can help push through my business license and speed things up along the bureaucratic conga line."

"Ronan can do that, too, you know."

"I know he can," Georgia said with a smile for her brother-in-law. "Sean's already volunteered."

"And…" Laura said.

"And what?"

"And you're already lovers, so this is going to complicate things."

"Oh," Ronan muttered, "when did that happen? No. Never mind. I don't need to know this."

"It's not going to get complicated," Georgia insisted.

"Everything gets complicated," Laura argued. "Heck,

look at me! I broke up with Ronan last year, rememb
Now here I sit, in Ireland, married, with a baby daughter."

Ronan asked wryly, "Are you complaining?"

Laura shot a look at the man studying her through
warm brown eyes. "No way. Wouldn't change a thing.
I'm just saying," she continued, shifting her gaze back
to Georgia, "that even when you think you know what's
going to happen, things suddenly turn upside down on
you."

A warbling cry erupted from the baby monitor on the
table in front of Laura. Picking it up, she turned off the
volume and stood.

"I have to go get the baby, but we're not done here,"
she warned, as she left the dining room.

"Laura's just worried for you." Ronan poured himself
more coffee, then sat back and crossed his legs, propping
one foot on the opposite knee.

"I know." She looked at him and asked, "But you've
known Sean forever. What do you think?"

"I think I warned Sean to keep his distance from you
already, for all the good that's done." Then he thought
about it for a moment or two, and said, "It's a good idea."

Georgia smiled and eased back in her chair. "Glad to
hear you say that."

"But," he added.

"There's always a *but,* isn't there?"

"Right enough," he said. "I can see why Sean wants
to do this. Keep his mother happy until she's well. And
you helping him is a grand thing as long as you remember that Sean's not the man to *actually* fall for."

"I'm not an idiot," Georgia reminded him.

"And who knows that better than I?" Ronan countered
with a smile. "You helped me out last year when Laura
was making my life a misery—"

me."

do the same now. Sean is a brother to me,

hurts you and I'm forced to kill him, it would

Georgia grinned. "Thanks. I never had a big brother threaten to beat up a boy who was mean to me."

He toasted her with his coffee cup. "Well, you do now."

She laughed a little. "Good to know."

"You'd already made up your mind to go along with Sean's plan, even before you told Laura, hadn't you?"

"Just about," she admitted. But until Ronan had thrown in on her side, she had still had a few doubts. Being close with Sean was no hardship, but getting much closer could be dangerous to her own peace of mind. Laura was right. Georgia wasn't the "take a lover, use him and lose him" kind of woman. So her heart would be at risk unless she guarded it vigilantly.

"So you've signed your rental agreement on the shop?"

"I did, and I'm going into Galway this morning to look at furnishings." She glanced down at her computer tablet as a sound signaled an incoming email. "I'm really excited about the store, too. Of course it needs some fresh paint and—" She broke off as her gaze skimmed the e-vite she had just received. "You have *got* to be kidding me."

"What is it?" All serious now, Ronan demanded, "What's wrong?"

Georgia hardly heard him over the roaring in her ears. She read the email again and then once more, just to be sure she was seeing it right. She was.

"That miserable, rotten, cheating, lying…"

"Who's that then?"

"My *ex*-husband and my *ex*-cousin," Georgia grumbled. "Of all the— I can't believe this. I mean seriously, could this be any more tacky? Even for *them?*"

"Ah," Ronan muttered. "This may be more in Laura's line..."

Georgia tossed her computer tablet to the couch cushion beside her, set her coffee cup down with a clatter and stood up, riding the wings of pure rage. "I'll see you later, Ronan."

"What?" He stood too and watched as she headed for the back door that led to the stone patio, the garden and the fields beyond. "Where are you going? What am I to tell Laura?"

"Tell her I just got engaged."

Then she was through the door and across the patio.

She could have taken a car and driven along the narrow, curving road to Sean's place. But as angry as she was, Georgia couldn't have sat still for that long. Instead, she took the shortcut. Straight across a sunlit pasture so green it hurt her eyes to look at it. Stone fences rambled across the fields, and she was forced to scramble over them to go on her way.

Normally, she loved this walk. On the right was the round tower that stood near an ancient cemetery on Ronan's land. To her left was Lough Mask, a wide lake fringed by more trees swaying in the wind. In the distance, she heard the whisper of the ocean and the low grumbling of a farmer's tractor. The sky above was a brilliant blue, and the wind that flew at her carried the chill of the sea.

Georgia was too furious to feel the cold.

Her steps were quick, and she kept her gaze focused on her target. The roof of Sean's manor house was just visible above the tips of the trees, and she headed there with a steely determination.

She crossed the field, walked into the wood and only then remembered Sean saying something about the faeries and how they might snatch her away.

"Well, I'd like to see them try it today," she murmured.

Georgia came out of the thick stand of trees at the edge of Sean's driveway. A wide gravel drive swung in a graceful arch in front of the stone-and-timber manor. Leaded windows glinted in the sunlight. As she neared the house, Sean stepped out and walked to meet her. He was wearing black slacks, a cream-colored sweater and a black jacket. His dark hair ruffled in the wind, and his hands were tucked into his pockets.

"Georgia!" He grinned at her. "I was going to stop to see you on my way to hospital to check in on my mother."

She pushed her tangled hair back from her face and stomped the dew and grass from her knee-high black boots. She wore her favorite, dark green sweater dress, and the wind flipped the hem around her knees. She had one short flash that for something this big, she should have worn something better than a dress she'd had for five years. But then, she wasn't really getting engaged, was she? It was a joke. A pretense.

Just like her first marriage had been.

"Are you all right?" he asked, his smile fading as he really looked at her. Walking closer, he pulled his hands from his pockets and reached out to take hold of her shoulders.

"Really not." Georgia took a deep breath of the cold Irish air and *willed* it to settle some of the roaring heat she still felt inside. It didn't work.

"What's wrong then?"

There was real concern on his face and for that, she

was grateful. Sean was exactly who he claimed to be. There was no hidden agenda with him. There were no secrets. He wouldn't cheat on a woman and sneak out of town with every cent she owned. It wouldn't even occur to him. She could admire that about him since she had already survived the man who was the exact opposite of Sean Connolly.

That thought brought her right back to the reason for her mad rush across the open field.

"You offered me a deal yesterday," she said.

"I did."

"Now I've got one for you."

Sean released her, but didn't step back. His gaze was still fixed on her and concern was still etched on his face. "All right then, let's hear it."

"I don't even know where to start," she said suddenly, then blurted out, "I just got an email from my cousin Misty. The woman my ex-husband ran off with."

"Ah." He nodded as if he could understand now why she was so upset.

"Actually, the email was an e-vite to their *wedding*."

His jaw dropped, and she could have kissed him for that alone. That he would *get* it, right away, no explanation necessary, meant more to Georgia than she could have said.

"She sent you an e-vite?" He snorted a laugh, then noted her scowl and sobered up fast. "Bloody rude."

"You think?" Shaking her head, Georgia started pacing back and forth on the gravel drive, hearing the grinding noise of the pebbles beneath her boots. "First, that she's tacky enough to use e-vites as wedding invitations!" She shot him a look and threw both hands in the air. "Who does that?"

"I wouldn't know."

"Of course you wouldn't, because *no one* does that!" Back to pacing, the *crunch, crunch* of the gravel sounding out in a rapid rhythm. "And really? You send one of your stupid, tacky e-vites to the woman your fiancé cheated on? The one he left for *you?*"

"The pronouns are starting to get confusing, in case you were wondering," Sean told her.

She ignored that. "And Mike. What the hell was *he* thinking?" Georgia demanded. "He thinks it's okay to invite me to his wedding? What're we now? Old *friends?* I'm supposed to be civilized?"

"What fun is civilized?" Sean asked.

"Exactly!" She stabbed a finger at him. "Not that I care who the creep marries and if you ask me, the two of them deserve each other, but why does either one of them think I want to be there to watch the beginning of a marriage that is absolutely doomed from the start?"

"Couldn't say," Sean said.

"No one could, because it doesn't make sense," Georgia continued, letting the words rush from her on a torrent of indignation. Then something occurred to her. "They probably don't expect me to actually *go* to the wedding."

"No?"

"No." She stopped dead, faced Sean and said, "Misty just wants me to *know* that she finally got Mike to marry her. Thinks it'll hurt me somehow."

"And of course she's wrong about that," Sean mused.

She narrowed her eyes on him. "Do I look hurt to you?"

"Not a bit," he said quickly. "You look furious and well you should be."

"Damn right." She set both hands on her hips and tapped the toe of one boot against the gravel, only absently noting the rapid *tappity, tappity, tap* sound. "But you know what? I'm *going* to that wedding. I'm going to be the chill kiss of death for those two at the happy festivities."

Sean laughed. "I do admire a woman with fire in her eyes."

"Then stick around," she snapped. "I'm going to show them just how little they mean to me."

"Good on you," Sean said.

"And the kicker is, I'm going to be arriving at their wedding in Brookhollow, Ohio, with my gorgeous, fabulously wealthy Irish fiancé."

One corner of his mouth tipped up. "Are you now?"

"That's the deal," Georgia said calmly, now that the last of her outrage had been allowed to spill free. "I'll help you keep your mom happy until she's well if you go to this wedding with me and convince everyone there that you're nuts about me."

"That's a deal," he said quickly and walked toward her.

She skipped back a step and held up one hand to keep him at bay. "And you'll help me get my license and sell me that cottage, too, right?"

"Absolutely."

"Okay, then." She huffed out a breath as if she'd been running a marathon.

"We've a deal, Georgia Page, and I think we'll both come out of this for the better."

"I hope you're right," she said and held out her right hand to take his in a handshake.

He smirked and shook his head. "That's no way to seal a deal between lovers."

Then he swooped in, grabbed her tightly and swung her into a dip that had her head spinning even *before* he kissed her blind.

* * *

The next few days flew past.

Georgia could even forget, occasionally, that what was between she and Sean wasn't actually *real*. He played his part so well. The doting fiancé. The man in love. Seriously, if she hadn't known it was an act, she would have tumbled headfirst into love with him.

And wouldn't that be awkward?

True to his word, Sean had pushed through the paperwork for her business license, and in just a week or two she would have it in hand. He sold her one of the cottages he owned and made her such a good deal on it she almost felt guilty, then she reminded herself that it was all part of the agreement they had struck. And with that reminder came the annoying tug of memory about her ex and the wedding Sean would be attending with her.

Georgia squared her shoulders and steeled her spine. She'd made her decision and wouldn't back away now. Besides, her new life was coming together. She had her lover. A shop. A new home.

And all of it built on a tower of lies, her mind whispered.

"The question is," she asked herself aloud, "what part of it will survive when the tower collapses?" Frowning at the pessimistic thoughts that she was determined to avoid, she added, "Not helping."

She had chosen her road and wouldn't change directions now. Whatever happened, she and Sean would deal with it. They were two adults after all. They could have sex. Have…whatever it was they had, without destroying each other. And then, there was the fact that even if she had been willing to consider ending their deal, she was in too deep to find a way out anyway. So instead, she would suck it up, follow the plan Sean had laid out and hope for the best.

Meanwhile, she had a shop to get ready and a new cottage to decorate and furnish.

She stepped back to take a look at her handiwork and smiled at the wash of palest yellow paint on one of the walls of her new office. It was cheerful and just bright enough to ease back the gray days that seemed to be a perpetual part of the Irish life. The smell of paint was strong, so she had propped open the front door. That cold wind she was so accustomed to now whipped through the opening and tugged at her hair as she worked.

All morning, people in the village had been stopping in, to offer help—which Georgia didn't need, since she wanted to do this part herself—or to offer congratulations on her upcoming marriage. So she hardly jumped when a voice spoke up from the doorway.

"It's lovely."

Georgia turned to smile at Ailish as Sean's mother walked into the shop just a step or two ahead of her son.

"Thanks." Georgia smiled at both of them. "I didn't know you were stopping by. Ailish, it's so good to see you out of the hospital."

"It's even better from my perspective," she answered quickly, a soft smile curving her mouth. "I can't tell you how badly I wanted to be home again. Of course, I was planning on going back to my own home in Dublin, but my son insists I stay at the family manor until I'm recovered—which I am even now, thanks very much."

"You're not recovered yet and you'll take it easy as the doctor advised," Sean told her.

"Take it easy," Ailish sniffed. "How'm I to do that with you and everyone else hovering?"

Georgia grinned at the expression of helpless frustration on Sean's face. She understood how he was feeling, but she really identified with Ailish. Georgia didn't appreciate hovering, either. "How're you feeling?"

The smaller woman hurried across the tarp-draped floor and took Georgia in a hard, brief hug. "I'm wonderful is what I am," she said. "Sean's told me your news and I couldn't be happier."

Guilt flew like an arrow and stabbed straight into Georgia's heart. She looked into Ailish's sharp green eyes and felt *terrible* for her part in this lie. But at the same time, she could see that Sean's mother's face was pale and there were shadows beneath those lovely eyes of hers. So she wasn't as well as she claimed and maybe, Georgia thought wildly, that was enough of a reason to carry on with the lie.

"Isn't it lovely that you and your sister both will be here, married and building families?" Ailish sighed at the romance of it. "I couldn't ask for a more perfect daughter-in-law."

"Thank you, Ailish," Georgia said and simply embraced the guilt, accepting that it would now be a part of her life. At least for a while.

"Now," Ailish said, grabbing Georgia's left hand. "Let me see the ring…"

There was no ring.

Georgia curled her fingers into her palm and threw a fast look at Sean who mimed slapping his hand to his forehead.

"We've not picked one out yet," he said quickly. "It has to be just right, doesn't it?"

"Hmm…" Ailish patted Georgia's hand even as she slid a curious look at her son. "Well, I'll look forward to seeing it."

"So," Georgia said into the quiet, "you're not heading home to Dublin?"

"Not for a bit yet," she said, "though I do long for my own things about me."

"The manor was your home until four years ago, mother," Sean reminded her. "There's plenty of your things there, as well. And someone to look after you."

"I don't need a keeper," Ailish told him. "Though there were plenty of times I was convinced you did. Until you had the sense to become engaged to Georgia."

"Thanks very much," Sean muttered, stuffing his hands into the pockets of his slacks.

"Now, if you don't mind, I think I'll go sit in the car again until you're ready to leave, Sean. Georgia," she added, leaning in to kiss her cheek, "I couldn't be happier for the both of you. It'll be a lovely wedding, and you know I think this one should be held in Dunley, as Ronan and Laura were married in California."

"Um, sure," Georgia said, as the pile of lies she was standing on grew higher and higher. "Only fair."

"Exactly." Ailish took a breath and let it slide from her lungs as she smiled. "Have you thought about when the wedding will be?"

"We really haven't gotten that far yet," Sean told her. "What with Georgia opening a new business and moving here and all, we've been too busy to set a date."

"Sometime soon then," Ailish went on in a rush. "Perhaps a Christmas wedding? Wouldn't that be lovely? Sean will send a plane for your parents of course, and perhaps they'd like to come out early, so we could all work on the wedding preparations together."

"I'll, um, ask them."

"Wonderful." Ailish smiled even wider, then turned

for a look at her son. "I'll speak to Father Leary tomorrow and see about having the banns read at Mass."

"All right then," Sean said stiffly, "I'll leave it in your hands."

"Good. That's settled. Now," Ailish added, "you two don't mind me. I'll be in the car, Sean, whenever you're ready."

They watched her through the window to make sure she was all right, and once she was safely in the car again, Georgia grabbed his arm. "The priest? She's going to have the banns read in church?"

This was suddenly way more complicated. For three weeks running, the priest would read the names of the couples wanting to be married, giving anyone with a legal or civil objection a chance to speak up. But that just meant the news would fly around Dunley even faster than they'd expected.

He pushed one hand through his hair. "Aye, well, that's the way it's done, isn't it?"

"Can't you ask her to wait?"

"And use what for a reason?" He shook his head. "No, the banns will be read but it changes nothing. We'll still call it off when you break up with me. It'll all be fine, Georgia. You'll see." He grabbed her left hand and ran his thumb over her ring finger. "I'm sorry though, that I forgot about a ring."

"It isn't important."

His gaze locked with hers. "It is, and it'll be taken care of today. I'll see to it."

"Sean," she whispered, moving in close, then sliding a quick look at Ailish to make absolutely certain the woman couldn't overhear them, "are you really *sure* we're doing the right thing?"

"I am," he insisted, dipping his head to hers. "She's

tired, Georgia. I've never seen my mother so pale, and I've no wish to give her a setback right now. Let's see her up and moving around and back to herself before we end this. We have a deal, right?"

She sighed miserably. "We do."

"Good then." He kissed her hard and fast. "I'll just take mother to the manor house, then I'll come back and help you paint."

Surrendering, she smiled and asked, "Are you a good painter?"

"I'm a man of many talents," he reminded her.

And as he walked out of the shop, Georgia thought, he really hadn't needed to remind her of that at all.

Six

"I've an itch between my shoulder blades," Sean confessed the following day, as he followed Ronan into the front parlor of his cousin's house.

He felt as if he were surrounded by women lately. Ordinarily, not a bad thing at all. But just now, between Georgia and his mother and his housekeeper and even Laura, who was giving him a glare every time they met up, he was ready for some strictly male company. And his cousin was the one to understand how he was feeling. Or so he thought.

"Not surprising." Ronan walked to the corner, where an elegant table stood in for a bar, and headed for the small refrigerator that held the beer he and Sean both needed. "It's probably much what a rabbit feels when the hunter's got his gun trained on it."

Sean winced and glared at his cousin's back. "Thanks for that. I've come to you looking for solidarity and you turn on me like a snake. Are you going to be no comfort to me in this?"

"I won't." Ronan bent to the fridge, opened it and pulled out two beers. As he closed the door again, he spotted something small and white beside it on the floor and picked it up. "A shirt button?"

"What?"

"A shirt button," Ronan repeated, standing up and glancing down at his own shirt front as if expecting to see that one of the buttons had leaped free of the fabric. "Where did that come from?"

Sean knew exactly where. It was one of his, after all, torn from his shirt the first night he and Georgia had made love, right here in this room, before a roaring fire. At the thought of that, he went hard as stone and covered his discomfort by snapping, "How'm I to know why your shirt button is on the bloody floor? Did you not hear me, Ronan? I said I'm in trouble."

Frowning still at the button, Ronan tossed it onto the table, then crossed the room and handed one of the beers to Sean. "'Tis no more than you deserve," he said, tearing off the bottle cap and taking a long drink. "I warned you, didn't I, at my own bleeding wedding, to keep your hands off our Georgia?"

Sean uncapped his beer as well and took a long, thirsty drink. Ronan had indeed warned him off, but even now, when things had gotten so completely confused, he couldn't bring himself to regret ignoring that warning.

"When a man's tempted by a woman like her," Sean mused, "he's hard put to remember unwanted advice."

"And yet, when the shite hits the fan, you come to me for more of that advice."

Sean scowled at his cousin. He'd thought to find a little male solidarity here in this house that had been as much

his home as Ronan's since he was a child. Seems he'd
been wrong. "When you've done gloating, let me know."

"I'll be a while yet," Ronan mused and dropped onto
the sofa. Propping his booted feet up on the table in front
of him, he glanced up at Sean and said, "What's got you
so itchy, then?"

"What hasn't?" Shaking his head, Sean wandered the
room, unable to settle. Unable to clear his mind enough
to examine exactly why he felt as though he were doing
a fast step-toe dance on a hot skillet—barefoot.

"Then pick one out of the bunch to start with."

"Fine." Sean whirled around, back to the fire, to face
his cousin. Heat seared him from head to toe, and still
there was a tiny chill inside it couldn't reach. "Father
Leary dropped in on me this morning, wanting to have
a 'pre-marriage' chat."

Ronan snorted. "Aye, I had one with the old man, as
well. Always amazed me, bachelor priests thinking they
know enough about marriage to be handing out counsel
on how to treat a wife."

"Worse than that, he wanted to tell me all about how
sex with a wife is different from sex with a mistress."

Ronan choked on a sip of beer, then burst out laughing.
"That's what you get for having a reputation as quite the
ladies' man. Father didn't feel it necessary to warn me
of such things." As Ronan considered that, he frowned,
clearly wondering whether or not he should be insulted.

"Fine for you," Sean grumbled. "I don't know which
of us was more uncomfortable with that conversation—
me, or the good father himself."

"I'd bet on you."

"You'd win that one, all right," Sean said, then took
another drink of his beer. Shaking his head, he pushed

that confrontation with the village priest out of his head. "Then there's Katie—"

"Your housekeeper?"

"No, the other Katie in my life, of *course* my bloody housekeeper," Sean snapped. "She's buying up bridal magazines and bringing them to Mother, who's chortling over them as if she's planning a grand invasion. She's already talked to me about flowers, as if I know a rose from a daisy, and do we want to rent a canvas to stretch over the gardens for the reception in case of rain—"

"Shouldn't be news to you," Ronan said mildly. "Not the first time you've been engaged, after all."

"'Tisn't the same," Sean muttered.

"Aye, no, because that time it wasn't a game, was it? And when Noreen dumped your ass and moved on, you couldn't have cared less."

All true, Sean thought. He'd asked Noreen Callahan to marry him more than three years ago now. It had seemed, he considered now, the thing to do at the time. After all, Noreen was witty and beautiful, and she liked nothing better than going to all the fancy dos he was forced to attend as Irish Air made a name for itself.

But he hadn't put in the time. He'd spent every minute on his business, and finally Noreen had had enough. She'd come to understand that not even getting her mitts on Sean's millions was enough motivation to live with a man who barely noticed her existence.

Sean had hardly noticed when she left. So what did that say about him? He'd decided then that he wasn't the marrying sort and nothing yet had happened to change his mind.

"This was all your idea," Ronan reminded him.

"Do you think I don't know that?" He scrubbed one hand across his face, then pushed that hand through his hair, fingers stabbing viciously. The longer this lie went on, the more it evolved. "There's a pool at the Penny-whistle, you know. Picking out dates for the wedding *and* the birth of our first child."

"I've five euros on December twenty-third myself." Ronan studied the label on his bottle of Harp.

"Why the bloody hell would you do that? You *know* there's not to be a wedding!"

"And if I don't enter a pool about your wedding, don't you think those in the village would wonder why?"

"Aye, I suppose." Sean shook his head and looked out the window at the sunny afternoon. Shadows slid across the lawn like specters as the trees that made them swayed in the wind. "No one in the village was this interested in my life when it was Noreen who was the expected bride."

"Because no one in the village could stand the woman," Ronan told him flatly. "A more nose-in-the-air, preten-tious female I've never come across."

Hard to argue with that assessment, Sean thought, so he kept his mouth shut.

"But everyone around here *likes* Georgia. She's a fine woman."

"As if I didn't know that already."

"Just as you knew this would happen, Sean. It can't be a surprise to you."

"No, it's not," he admitted, still staring out the glass, as if searching for an answer to his troubles. "But it all feels as though it's slipping out of my control, and I've no idea how to pull it all back in again."

"You can't," Ronan said easily, and Sean wanted to kick him.

"Thanks for that, too." He sipped at his beer again and got no pleasure from the cold, familiar taste. "I'm seeing this whole marriage thing get bigger and bigger, and I've no idea what's going to happen when we finally call it off."

"Should've thought of that before this half-brained scheme of yours landed you in such a fix."

"Again, you're a comfort to me," he said, sarcasm dripping in his tone. "I've told Georgia I'll see to it that everyone blames me. But now I'm seeing that it's more complicated than that. Did you know, my assistant's already fielding requests for wedding invitations from some of my business associates?"

"Lies take on a life of their own," Ronan said quietly.

"True enough." Sean's back teeth clenched, as he remembered exactly how he'd gotten into this whole thing, and for the life of him, he couldn't say for sure now that he would have done it differently if given a chance. "You didn't see my mother lying in that hospital bed, Ronan. Wondering if she'd recover—or if, God forbid, I was going to lose her. Seeing her face so pale and then the tears on her cheeks as she worried for me." He paused and shook his head. "Scared me."

"Scared me, too," Ronan admitted. "Your mother's important to me, you know."

"I do know that." Sean took a deep breath, shook off the tattered remnants of that fear and demanded, "So out of your fondness for my mother, why not help save her son?"

"Ah no, lad. You're on your own in this."

"Thanks for that, as well."

"I will say that if Georgia ends up shedding one tear over what you've dragged her into," Ronan told him, "I will beat you bloody."

"I know that, too." Sean walked back and sat down beside Ronan. He kicked his feet up onto the table and rested his bottle of beer on his abdomen. "I'd expect nothing less."

"Well then, we're agreed." Ronan reached over and clinked the neck of his beer against Sean's. "You're in a hole that's getting deeper with every step you take, Sean. Mind you don't go in over your head."

As he drank to that discomforting toast, Sean could only think that Ronan was too late with this particular warning. He knew damn well he was already so deep, he couldn't see sky.

From Georgia's cottage kitchen downstairs came the incredible scent of potato-leek soup and fresh bread.

Georgia inhaled sharply, then sighed as she looked at her sister. "I think I'm going to keep Patsy here with me. You go on home to Ronan and have him cook for you."

"Never gonna happen," Laura told her on a laugh. "Besides, Patsy wouldn't leave now even if I wanted her to—which I don't—she's too crazy about Fiona."

Georgia looked down at the tiny baby cuddled in her arms and smiled wistfully. Milk-white skin, jet-black eyelashes lying in a curve on tiny, round cheeks. Wisps of reddish-brown hair and a tiny mouth pursed in sleep. A well of love opened in Georgia's heart, and she wondered how anything so young, so helpless, could completely change the look of the entire world in less than a month.

"Can't blame Patsy for that. I know I'm Fiona's aunt, but really, isn't she just beautiful?"

"I think so," Laura answered, and plopped down onto Georgia's new bed. "It's so huge, Georgia. The love I have for her is so immense. I just never knew anything could feel like this."

A trickle of envy wound its way around Georgia's heart before she recognized it, then banished it. She didn't begrudge her sister one moment of her happiness. But Georgia could admit, at least to herself, that she wished for some of the same for herself.

But maybe that just wasn't going to happen for her. The whole "husband and family" thing. A pang of regret sliced through her at that thought, but she had to accept that not everyone found love. Not everyone got to have their dreams come true. And sometimes, she told herself, reality just sucked.

"It's terrific," Georgia said, and jiggled the baby gently when she stirred and made a soft mewing sound. "You've got Ronan, Fiona, you're painting again..." As Georgia had given up on her design dreams to sell real estate, Laura had set aside her paints and easel in favor of practicality. Knowing that she'd rediscovered her art, had found the inspiration to begin painting again, made Georgia's heart swell. "I'm really happy for you, Laura."

"I know you are," her sister said. "I want *you* to be happy, too, you know."

"Sure I know. But I am happy," Georgia said, adding a smile to the words to really sell it. "Honest. I'm starting a new business. I'm moving to a new country. I've got a brand-new niece and a new home—what's not to be happy about?"

"I notice you didn't mention your new faux fiancé."

Georgia frowned a bit. "I don't *have* Sean."

"As far as the whole village of Dunley is concerned you do."

"Laura..." Georgia sighed a little, then crossed the bedroom and handed the baby back to her mother. She understood why her sister was concerned, but hearing about it all the time didn't help and it didn't change anything.

"All I'm saying is," Laura said, as she snuggled her

daughter close, "well, I don't really know what I'm saying. But the point is, I'm worried about you."

"Don't be."

"Oh, okay. All better." Laura blew out an exasperated breath. "I love Sean and all, but *you're* my sister, and I'm worried that this is going to blow up in your face. The whole village is counting on this wedding now. What happens when you call it off?"

Niggling doubts had Georgia chewing at her bottom lip. Hadn't she been concerned about the same thing from the very beginning? Everyone in Dunley was excited about the "wedding." Ailish had ordered a cake from the baker and then gleefully told Georgia that it was all taken care of.

"I don't know, but it's too late to worry about that now," she said firmly, and crossed the room to tug at the hem of the new curtains over one of the three narrow windows overlooking Sean's faery wood. A smile curved her mouth as she thought of him.

"I see that."

"What?"

"That smile. You're thinking about him."

"Stop being insightful. It's disturbing."

Laura laughed and shook her head. "Fine. I'll back off. For now."

"It's appreciated." Georgia didn't need her sister's worries crowding into her head. She barely had room for her own.

"So, do you need help packing?"

Now it was Georgia's turn to laugh. "For a trip I'm not taking until next week?"

"Fine, fine." Laura sighed a little. "I'm just trying to help out. I want you settled in and happy here, Georgia."

"I *am*." She looked around the bedroom of her new cottage.

It really helped knowing the owner, since Sean had given her the keys so she could move in *before* escrow closed on the place. It was good to have her own home, even though it wouldn't really feel like hers until she had some of her own furniture and things around her. Thank God, though, as a rental it had come furnished, so she at least had a place to sit and sleep, and pots and pans for the kitchen.

She'd taken the smaller of the two cottages Sean had shown her. The other one had been a row cottage, differentiated from the homes on either side of it only by the shade of emerald green painted on the front door. It was bigger and more modern, but the moment Georgia had seen *this* one, she'd been lost.

Mainly because this cottage appealed to her sense of whimsy.

It was a freestanding home, with a thatched roof and white-washed walls. Empty flower boxes were attached to the front windows like hope for spring. The door was fire-engine red, and the back door opened onto a tiny yard with a flower bed and a path that led into the faery wood.

The living room was small, with colorful rugs strewn across a cement floor that was painted a deep blue. A child-sized fireplace was tucked into one wall with two chairs pulled up in front of it. The kitchen was like something out of the forties, but everything worked beautifully. The staircase to the second floor was as steep as a ladder, and her bedroom was small with her bed snuggled under a sloping ceiling. But the windows looked out over the woods, and the bathroom had been updated recently to include a tub big enough to stretch out in.

It was a fairy-tale cottage, and Georgia already loved it.

This would be her first night in her new place, and she was anxious to nudge Laura on her way so that she could relax in that beautiful tub and pour herself a glass of wine to celebrate the brand-new chapter in her life.

"It is a great cottage." Laura looked at her for a long minute then frowned and asked, "You sure you don't want Fiona and me along for the trip back to California?"

"Absolutely not." On this, Georgia was firm. "I'm not going to be there for long, and all I have to do is sign the papers to put the condo up for sale. After that, when they find a buyer for the place, they can fax me the paperwork and I'll handle it from here. Then I'll arrange for my stuff to be shipped to Ireland and I'll be done. Besides," she added with a grim nod, "when I leave California, I'll be stopping in Ohio for the wedding."

Laura shook her head. "Why you're insisting on going to that is beyond me. I mean come on. You're over Mike, so what do you care?"

"I don't." And she realized as she said it that she really didn't care about her ex-husband and his soon-to-be wife, the husband-stealing former cheerleader. After all, if Mike hadn't been willing to cheat on his wife, Misty never would have gotten him in the first place.

So Georgia figured she was much better off without him anyway. "It's the principle of the thing, really. You know damn well Misty only sent me that tacky invitation to rub in my face that she and Mike are getting married. They never for a minute expect me to show up. So why shouldn't I? At the very least I should be allowed the pleasure of ruining their big day for them."

Laura chuckled. "I guess you're right. And seriously? Misty deserves to be miserable."

"She will be," Georgia promised with a laugh. "She's

marrying Mike, after all. May they be blessed with a dozen sons, every one of them just like their father."

"Wow," Laura said, obviously impressed, "you're really getting the hang of being Irish. A blessing and a curse all at the same time."

"It's a gift."

Georgia glanced down at her ring finger. She still wasn't entirely accustomed to the weight of the emerald and diamond ring Sean had given her for the length of their "engagement."

The dark green of the stone swam with color, and the diamonds winked in the light. It occurred to her then that while her new life was beginning with a lie—Mike was apparently *happy* with his. It didn't matter so much to her anymore, though Georgia could admit, if only to herself, that she'd spent far too much time wrapped up in anger and bitterness and wishing a meteor to crash down on her ex-husband's head.

It was irritating to have to acknowledge just how much time she had wasted and how much useless energy had been spent thinking about how her marriage had ended while the man who had made her so miserable wasn't suffering at all.

She had locked her heart away to avoid being hurt again, which was just stupid. She could see that now. Being hurt only meant that you were alive enough to feel it. And if her soul wasn't alive, then why bother going through the motions trying to pretend different? At least, she told herself, using her thumb against the gleaming gold band of the ring on her finger, she'd gotten past it, had moved on.

Then a voice inside her laughed. Sure, she'd moved on. To a ring that meant nothing and planning a fake future with a fake fiancé.

Wow. How had all of this happened anyway?

Still befuddled by her train of thought, she didn't notice Laura scooting off the bed until her sister was standing beside her.

"I should gather up Patsy and go," she said. "It's nearly time to feed Fiona, and Ronan's probably starving, as well."

Pleased at the idea of having some time to herself, Georgia lovingly nudged her sister to the door. "Go home. Feed the baby. Kiss your husband. I've got a lot to do around here before I leave for my trip next week. Don't worry, you'll have plenty of time to nag me before I leave. And then I'll be back before you even miss me."

"Okay." Laura gave her a one-armed hug and kissed her cheek. "Be careful. And for heaven's sake, take a picture of Misty's wedding gown. That's bound to be entertaining."

Laughing, Georgia vowed, "I will."

"And about Sean—"

"You said you were backing off."

"Right." Laura snapped her mouth shut firmly, took a breath and said, "Okay, then. Enjoy your new house and the supper Patsy left for you. Then have a great trip with your pretend fiancé and hurry home."

When her sister had gone down the stairs and she and Patsy had both shouted a goodbye, Georgia dropped onto the edge of her bed, relishing the sudden silence.

Home, she thought with a sigh. This cottage, in Dunley, Ireland, was now *home*.

It felt good.

She took a long bath, savored a glass of wine in the stillness, then dressed in what she thought of as her Ireland winter wear—jeans, sneakers and a shirt with one of her thick, cable-knit sweaters, this one a dark red, over it—and went downstairs.

Restless, she wandered through her new home, passing through the kitchen to break off a piece of the fresh bread Patsy had left for her. Walking back to the small living room, she paused in the center and did a slow turn.

There were still changes to be made, of course. She wouldn't bring all of her things from America, but the few items she loved would fit in here and make it all seem more *hers* somehow. Though already she felt more at home here than she ever had in the plush condo in Huntington Beach.

The fire in the hearth glowed with banked heat, its red embers shining into the room. Outside her windows, the world was dark as it could be only in the country. The streetlights of the village were a faint smudge in the blackness.

Georgia turned on the television. Then, the instant the sound erupted, turned it off again. She hugged herself and wished for company. Not the tinny, artificially cheerful voice of some unknown news anchor.

"Maybe I should get a dog," she mused aloud, listening to the sound of her own voice whisper into the stillness around her. She smiled at the thought of a clumsy puppy running through the cottage, and she promised herself that when she left America to come home to Dunley for good, she would find a puppy. She missed Beast. And Deidre. And the sound of Ronan's and Laura's voices. And the baby's cries. And Patsy's quiet singing when she was working in the kitchen.

She wanted another heartbeat in the house.

Georgia frowned as she realized the hard truth. What she wanted was Sean.

She could call him, of course, and actually started

for her phone before stopping again. Not a good idea to turn to him when she was lonely. He wouldn't always be there, right? Better she stand on her own, right from the beginning.

Plus, if she was making Dunley her home now, then she might as well get used to going about the village on her own. With that thought in mind, she snagged her jacket off the coat tree by the door and headed for the Pennywhistle.

It was a short walk from her door to the main street of the village, and from there only a bit more to the pub, but she fought for every step. The wind roared along the narrow track, pushing at Georgia and the few other hardy souls wandering the sidewalks with icy hands, as if trying to steer them all back to their homes.

Finally, though, she reached the pub, yanked open the heavy door and stepped into what felt like a *wall* of sound. The silence of the night was shattered by the rise and fall of conversations and laughter, the quick, energetic pulse of the traditional music flowing from the corner and the heavy stomp of booted feet dancing madly to the tune.

Just what I need, Georgia thought, and threw herself into the crush.

Seven

Georgia edged her way to the bar, slipping out of her jacket as she went. The heat inside was nearly stifling, what with the crowd of people and the fire burning merrily in the corner. Waitresses moved through the mob of people with the sort of deft grace ballet dancers would envy, carrying trays loaded with beer, whiskey, soft drinks and cups of tea.

A few people called hello to her as she made her way to the bar and Georgia grinned. This was just what she needed, she thought, to remind herself that she *did* have a real life; it merely also included a fake fiancé. She had friends here. She belonged, and that felt wonderful.

Jack Murphy, the postmaster, a man of about fifty with graying hair and a spreading girth, leaped nimbly off his stool at the bar and offered it to her. She knew better than to wave off his chivalry, though she felt a bit guilty for chasing him out of his seat.

"Thanks, Jack," she said, loud enough to be heard. "Looks like a busy night."

"Ah, well, on a cold night, what's better than a room full of friends and a pint?"

"Good point," she said, and, still smiling, turned to Danny Muldoon, the proprietor of the Pennywhistle.

A big man with a barrel chest, thinning hair and a mischievous smile, he had a bar towel slung over one shoulder and a clean white apron strung around his waist. He was manning the beer taps like a concert pianist as he built a Guinness with one hand and poured a Harp with another. He glanced up at her and asked, "Will it be your usual then, love?"

Her usual.

She loved that. "Yes, Danny, thanks. The Chardonnay when you get a minute."

He laughed, loud and long. "That'll be tomorrow morning by the looks of this crowd, but I'll see you put right as soon as I've finished with this."

Georgia nodded and turned on her stool to look over the crowd. With her jacket draped across her knees, she studied the scene spread out in front of her. Every table was jammed with glassware, every chair filled, and the tiny cleared area closest to the musicians was busy with people dancing to the wild and energetic tunes being pumped out furiously by a fiddle, a flute and a bodhran drum. Georgia spotted Sinead's husband, Michael, and watched as he closed his eyes and tapped his foot to the reel spinning from his fiddle. Sinead sat close by, her head bent to the baby in her arms as she smiled to the music her husband and his friends made.

Here was Dunley, Georgia thought. Everyone was welcome in Irish pubs. From the elderly couple sitting together and holding hands to the tiny girl trying to step-dance like her mother, they were all here. The village. The sense of community was staggering. They were part of each other's lives. They had a connection, one to the other, and the glorious part of it all, in Georgia's mind, was that they had included *her* in their family.

When the incredibly fast-paced song ended, the music slid into a ballad, the notes of which tugged at Georgia's heart. Then one voice in the crowd began to sing and was soon joined by another until half the pub was singing along.

She turned and saw her wine waiting for her and Georgia lifted it for a sip as she listened to the song and lost herself in the beauty of the moment.

She was so caught up, she didn't even notice when Sean appeared at her side until he bent his head and kissed her cheek.

"You've a look of haunted beauty about you," he whispered, and Georgia's head spun briefly.

She turned and looked up at him. "It's the song."

"Aye, 'The Rising of the Moon' is lovely."

"What's it about?"

He winked and grinned. "Rebellion. What we Irish do best."

That song ended on a flourish, and the musicians basked in applause before taking a beer break.

"What'll it be for you then, Sean?" Danny asked.

"A Jameson's if you please, Danny. *Tá sé an diabhal an oíche fuar féin.*"

"It is indeed," the barman answered with a laugh.

"What was that?" Georgia asked. "What did you say?"

Sean shrugged, picked up his glass and laid money down for both his and Georgia's drinks. "Just a bit of the Gaelic. I said it's the devil's own cold night."

"You speak *Gaelic?*"

"Some," he said.

Amazing. Every time she thought she knew him, she found something new. And this was touching, she thought. "It sounds…musical."

"We've music in us, that's for sure," Sean acknowledged. "A large part of County Mayo is Gaeltacht, you know. That means 'Irish-speaking.' Most of those who live here have at least a small understanding of the language. And some speak it at home as their first language."

She'd heard snippets of Gaelic since she first came to Ireland, but it had never occurred to her that it was still a living language. And, to be honest, some of the older people here spoke so quickly and had such thick accents, at first she'd thought they were speaking Gaelic—though it was English.

"Of course," she said after a sip of wine. "The aisle signs in the grocery store are in both English and Gaelic. And the street signs. I just thought maybe it was for the tourists, you know…"

He tapped one finger to her nose. "It's for us. The Irish language was near lost not so very long ago. After the division and the Republic was born, the government decided to reclaim all we'd nearly lost. Now our schools teach it and our children will never have to worry about losing a part of who they are."

Georgia just looked at him. There was a shine of pride in his eyes as he spoke, and she felt a rush of something warm and delicious spread through her in response.

"We're a small country but a proud one," he went on, staring down into his glass of whiskey. "We hang on to what we have and fight when another tries to take it." He shot a quick look at the man on the stool beside Georgia. "Isn't that so, Kevin Dooley?"

The man laughed. "I've fought you often enough for a beer or a woman or just for the hell of it."

"And never won," Sean countered, still grinning.

"There's time yet," Kevin warned companionably, then smiled and turned back to his conversation.

Georgia laughed, too, then leaned into Sean as the musicians picked up their instruments again and the ancient pub came alive with music that filled the heart and soul. With Sean's arm around her, Georgia allowed herself to be swept into the magic of the moment.

And she refused to remember, at least for tonight, that Sean was only hers temporarily.

Two hours later, Sean walked her to the cottage and waited on the step while she opened the door. Georgia went inside, then paused and looked at him.

For the first time in days, they were alone together. With his mother recuperating at his house and her at Ronan and Laura's, they'd been able to do little more than smile at each other in passing.

Until tonight.

Earlier that night, she'd been wishing for him and now, here he was.

He stood in the doorway, darkness behind him, lamplight shining across his face, defining the desire quickening in his eyes. The cold night air slipped inside, twisted with the heat from the banked fire and caused Georgia to shiver in response.

"Will you invite me in, Georgia?"

Her heartbeat sped up, and her mouth went dry. There was something about this man that reached her on levels she hadn't even been aware of before knowing him. He'd made a huge difference in her life, and she was only now realizing how all-encompassing that difference was.

Just now, just this very minute, she stared up at Sean and felt everything within her slide into place, like jagged puzzle pieces finally creating the picture they were meant to be.

There was more here, she thought, than a casual affair. There was affection and danger and excitement and a bone-deep knowledge that when her time with Sean was done, she'd never be the same again.

It was far too late to pull back, she thought wildly. And though she knew she'd be hurt when it was all over, she wouldn't have even if she could.

Because what she'd found with Sean was what she'd been looking for her whole life.

She'd found out who she was.

And more importantly, she *liked* the woman she'd discovered.

"Is it so hard then, to welcome me into your home?" Sean asked softly, when her silence became too much for him.

"No," she said, reaching out to grab hold of his shirtfront. She dragged him inside, closed the door then went up on her toes. "It's not hard at all," she said, and then she kissed him.

At the first long taste of him, that wildness inside her softened. Her bones seemed to melt until she was leaning into him, the only thing holding her up was the strength of Sean's arms wrapped around her.

Her body went up like a torch. Heat suffused her, swamping Georgia with a need so deep, so all-consuming, she could hardly draw breath. When he tore his mouth from hers, she groaned.

"You've a way about you, Georgia," he whispered, dipping his head to nibble at her ear.

She shivered and tipped her head to one side, giving

him easier access. "I was just thinking the same thing about you..." She sighed a little. "Oh, that feels so good."

"You taste of lemons and smell like heaven."

Georgia smiled as her eyes closed and she gave herself up to the sensations rattling through her. "I had a long soak in that wonderful tub upstairs."

"Sorry to have missed that," he murmured, dragging his lips and tongue and teeth along the line of her neck until she quivered in his arms and trembled, incredibly on the brink of a climax. Just his touch. Just the promise of what was to come was enough to send her body hurtling toward completion.

The man had some serious sexual power.

"I thought about you today," he whispered, turning her to back her up against the front door. He lifted his head, looked her dead in the eye and fingered her hair as he spoke. "Thought I'd lose my mind at the office today, trying to work out the figures on the new planes we've ordered... Galway city never seemed so far from Dunley before." He dropped his hands to her waist, pulled up the hem of her sweater and tugged at the snap of her jeans. "And all I could think about was you. Here. And finally having you all to myself again."

The brush of his knuckles against the bare skin of her abdomen sent a zip of electricity shooting through her veins. Releasing him long enough to shrug out of her jacket, she let it fall to the floor, unheeded.

"You're here now," she told him, reaching up to push his jacket off, as well. He helped her with that, then went back to the waistband of her jeans and worked the zipper down so slowly she wanted to scream.

"I am," he said, dipping his head for a kiss. "And so're you."

He had the fly of her jeans open, and he slid one hand

down across her abdomen, past the slip of elastic on her panties and down low enough to touch the aching core of her.

The moment his hand cupped her, she shattered. She couldn't stop it. Didn't want to. She had been primed and ready for his touch for days. Georgia cried out and rocked her hips into his hand. While her body trembled and shook, he kissed her, whispering bits and pieces of Gaelic that seemed to slide into her heart. He stroked her, his fingers dipping into her heat while she rode his hand feverishly, letting the ecstasy she'd found only with him take her up and then under.

When it was done and she could breathe again, she looked up into his eyes and found him watching her with a hunger she'd never seen before. His passion went deeper and gleamed more darkly in his eyes. He held her tenderly, as if she were fragile and about to splinter apart.

"Shatter tú liom," he said softly, gaze moving over her face like a touch.

Still trying to steady her breathing, she reached up to cup his cheek in her palm. The flash of her ring caught her eye but she ignored it. This wasn't fake, she thought. This, what she and Sean shared when they were together, was *very* real. She had no idea what it meant—and maybe it didn't have to *mean* anything. Maybe it was enough to just shut off her mind and enjoy what she had while she had it.

"What does that mean?"

He turned his face into her palm and kissed her. "'You shatter me,' that's what I said."

Her heartbeat jolted, and a sheen of unexpected tears welled up in her eyes, forcing her to blink them back before she could make a fool of herself and cry.

"I watch you tremble in my arms and you take my

knees out from under me, Georgia. That's God's truth."
He kissed her, hard, fast, and made her brain spin. "What
you do to me is nothing I've ever known before."

She knew exactly what he meant because she felt
the same. What she had with Sean was unlike any previous relationship. Sometimes, she felt as though she
were stumbling blindly down an unfamiliar road and
the slightest misstep could have her falling off a cliff.
How could anything feel so huge? How could it not be
real? And still, this journey was one she wouldn't have
missed for anything.

"Say something else," she urged. "In Gaelic, say something else."

He gave her a smile and whispered, *"Leat mo anáil
uaidh."*

She returned his smile. "Now translate."

"'You take my breath away.'"

To disguise the quick flash of feelings too deep to explore at the moment, Georgia quipped, "Back atcha. That
means 'same to you.'"

He chuckled, rested his forehead against hers, pulled
his hand from her jeans and wrapped both arms around
her. "I've got to have you, Georgia. It feels like years
since I've felt your skin against mine. You're a hunger
in me, and I'm a starving man."

Her stomach did a fast roll and her heartbeat leaped
into a gallop. And still she teased him because she'd discovered she liked the teasing, flirtatious way they had
together. "Starving? Patsy Brennan left some bread and
soup in the kitchen."

"You're a hard woman," he said, but the curve of his
mouth belied the words.

"Or," she invited, taking his hand in hers and heading

for the stairs, "you can come up with me and we'll find something else to ease your appetite."

"Lá nó oíche, Tá mé do fear."

She stopped and looked at him. "Now you're just doing that because you know what it does to me."

"I am indeed."

"What did you say that time?"

"I am indeed."

Her lips quirked at the humor in his eyes. "Funny. Before that, what did you say?"

"I said," he told her, swooping in to grab her close and hold on tight like a drowning man clinging to the only rope in a stormy sea, "'Day or night, I'm your man.'"

Then his mouth came down on hers and every thought but one dissolved.

Her man. Those two words repeated over and over again in her mind while Sean was busy kissing her into oblivion. He was hers. For now. For tonight. For however long they had together.

And that was going to have to be enough.

When he let her up for air, she held his hand and shakily led the way up the steep flight of stairs. The ancient treads groaned and squeaked beneath them, but it was a cozy sound. Intimate. At the head of the stairs, Georgia pulled Sean into her room and then turned to look up at him.

He glanced around the bedroom and smiled as he noted everything she'd done to it. "You've made it nice in here. In just a day."

She followed his gaze, noting the fresh curtains at the windows, the quilt on the bed and the colorful pillows tossed against the scrolled iron headboard.

"Laura and Patsy brought a few things over from the manor."

"You've made it a home already."

"I love it already, too," she confessed. "And when I get some of my own things in here, it'll be perfect."

"'Tis perfect right now," he said, moving in on her with a stealthy grace that made her insides tremble. "There's a bed after all."

"So there is."

"I've a need to have you stretched across that bed," he told her, undoing the buttons of his shirt so he could tear it off and throw it onto a nearby chair. "I've a need to touch every square inch of that luscious body of yours and then, when I've finished, to begin again."

Georgia drew a long, unsteady breath and yanked her sweater up and off, before throwing it aside with Sean's shirt. Her fingers were shaky as she tugged at the buttons on her blouse, but Sean's hands were suddenly there, making fast work of them. Then he pushed the fabric off her shoulders and let it slide down her arms to puddle on the floor.

Outside, the night was clear for a change. No rain pinged against the windows, but moonlight did a slow dance through the glass. Inside, the house was still, only the sounds of their ragged breathing to disturb the quiet.

Georgia couldn't hear anything over the pounding of her own heart, anyway. Sean undid the front clasp of her bra, and she slipped out of it eagerly. His hands at her waist, her hands at his, and he pushed her jeans down her hips as she undid the hook and zipper of his slacks, then pushed them down, as well.

In seconds they were naked, the rest of their clothes discarded as quickly as possible. Georgia threw herself into his arms, and when he lifted her off her feet she felt a thrill in her bones. He tucked her legs around his waist, and she hooked her ankles together at the small of his back.

He took two long steps to the nearest wall and braced her back against it. With her arms around his neck, she looked down into his eyes and said breathlessly, "I thought we needed the bed."

"And so we will," he promised. "When we're too tired to stand."

Then he entered her. His hard, thick length pushing into her welcoming body. Georgia could have sworn he went deep enough to touch the bottom of her heart. She felt him all through her, as if he'd laid claim to her body and soul and was only now letting her in on it.

The wall was cold against her back, but she didn't feel it. All she was aware of was the tingling spread of something miraculous inside her. Her body was spiraling into that coil of need that would tighten until it burst from the pressure and sent jagged shards of sensation rippling through her.

Bracing one hand on the dresser beside her, Georgia clapped the other to his shoulder and moved with him as he set a frenetic pace. She watched his eyes glaze over, saw the mix of pleasure and tension etch themselves onto his features. Again and again he took her, pushing her higher and higher, faster and faster.

Her heels dug into his back, urging him on, and when the first hard jolt of release slammed into her, she shouted his name and clung desperately to him. She was still riding the ripples of her climax when he buried his face in the curve of her neck and joined her there.

A few miles away at Laura's house, the phone rang and Laura picked it up on the run. She had just gotten the

baby down for the night and she had a gorgeous husband
waiting for her in the front parlor with a bottle of wine.

"Hello?"

"Laura, love," Ailish said. "And how's our darling
Fiona this night?"

Sean's mother. Why was she calling? Did she suspect
something? *This* was why Laura didn't like lies. They
tangled everything up. Made her unsure what she could
say and what she couldn't. Sean and Georgia were trying to protect Ailish, and what if Laura said something
that blew the whole secret out of the water? What if she
caused Ailish a heart attack? What if—

Laura stepped into the parlor, gave her husband a silent *Oh Dear God* look and answered, "The baby's wonderful, Ailish. I've just put her down."

"Lovely, then you have a moment?"

"Um, sure," she said desperately, "but wouldn't you
like to say hello to Ronan?"

At that, her devoted husband shot out of his chair,
shaking his head and waving both hands.

Laura scowled at him and mouthed the word *coward*.

He bowed at the waist, accepting the insult as if it
were a trophy.

"No, dear, this is better between us, I think," Ailish
told her through the phone.

Uh-oh. She didn't want to talk to Ronan? *Better between us?* That couldn't be good.

Deserted by the man she loved, Laura took a breath
and waited for the metaphorical ax to fall.

"I just want to ask you one question."

No, no, no. That wasn't a good idea at all.

"Oh!" Laura interrupted her frantically, with one last
try for escape. "Wait! I think I hear Fiona—"

"No, you don't. And there's no point trying to lie to me, Laura Connolly. You've no talent for it, dear."

It was the Irish way. A compliment and a slap all in the same sentence.

"Yes, ma'am," she said, throwing a trapped look at her husband. Ronan only shrugged and poured each of them a drink. When he was finished, he handed her the wine and Laura took a long gulp.

"Now then," Ailish said and Laura could picture the tiny, elegant woman perfectly. "I know my son, and I've a feeling there's more going on between him and Georgia than anyone is telling me."

"I don't—"

"No point in lying, Laura dear, remember?"

She sighed.

"That's better." Then to Sean's housekeeper, Ailish said, "Thank you, Katie. A cup of tea would be wonderful. And perhaps one or two of your scones? Laura and I are just settling down for a long chat."

Oh, God, Laura thought. A long chat? That wasn't good. Wasn't good at all. Quickly, she drained her glass and handed it to her husband for a refill.

Eight

For the entire next week, Sean felt that itch between his shoulder blades. And every day, it got a little sharper. A little harder to ignore. Everywhere he went, people in the village were talking about the upcoming wedding. It shouldn't have bothered him, as he'd known full well what would happen the moment he began this scheme. But knowing it and living it were two different things.

The pool in the pub was more popular than ever—with odds changing almost daily as people from outlying farms came in to make their bets on the date of the wedding. Even the Galway paper had carried an engagement announcement, he thought grimly, courtesy of Ailish.

From her sickbed, his mother had leaped into the planning of this not-to-be wedding with such enthusiasm, he shuddered to think what she might do once she was cleared by her doctor.

When the article in the paper had come out, it had

taken Sean more than an hour of fast talking with Georgia to smooth that particular bump in the road. She was less and less inclined to keep up the pretense as time went by, and even Sean was beginning to doubt the wisdom of the whole thing.

But then, he would see his mother moving slowly through the house and tell himself that he'd done the right thing. The only thing. Until Ailish was well and fit again, he was going to do whatever he had to.

Though to accomplish it, the annoying itch would become his constant companion.

Even Ronan and Laura had been acting strangely the past few days, Laura especially. She had practically sequestered herself in the manor, telling Georgia she was simply too exhausted with caring for the baby to be good company.

Frowning, Sean told himself there was definitely something going on there, but he hadn't a clue what it was. Which made this trip with Georgia to the States seem all the more attractive.

At the moment, getting away from everyone in Ireland for a week or so sounded like a bloody vacation. Going to California to close out Georgia's house and then on to Ohio, of all places, for the wedding, would give both of them a chance to relax away from the stress of the lies swarming around them like angry bees.

Or maybe it was the muted roar of the plane's engines making him think of swarming bees. He and Georgia had the jet to themselves for this trip, but for the pilots and Kelly, the flight attendant who had already brought them coffee right after takeoff and then disappeared into the front of the jet, giving them privacy.

He looked at Georgia, sitting across from him, and Sean felt that quick sizzle of heat and need that he'd become accustomed to feeling whenever he was close to her. Oh, since the moment he first met her at Ronan's wedding, he had felt the zing of attraction and interest any man would feel for a woman like Georgia.

But in the past few weeks, that zing had become something else entirely. He spent far too much time thinking about her. And when he was with her, he kept expecting to feel the edge of his need slackening off as it always had before with the women he was involved with. It hadn't happened, of course. Instead, that need only became sharper every time he was with her. As if feeding his hunger for her only defined his appetite, not quenched it.

It wasn't just the sex, either, he mused, studying her profile in the clear morning light. He liked the way her short, honey-blond hair swung at her chin. He liked the deep twilight of her eyes and how they darkened when he was inside her. He liked her sense of style—the black skirt, scooped-neck red blouse and the high heels that made her legs look bloody amazing. And he liked her mind. She had a quick wit, a sharp temper and a low tolerance for bullshit—all of which appealed to him.

She was on his mind all the bloody time and he couldn't say he minded it overmuch. The only thing that *did* bother him was the nagging sensation that he was coming to care for her more than he'd intended. Sean knew all too well that a man in love lost all control over a situation with his woman, and he wasn't a man who enjoyed that. He'd seen enough of his friends become fools over women. Even Ronan had lost a part of himself when he first tumbled for Laura.

No, Sean preferred knowing exactly what was happening and when, rather than being tossed about on a tide of emotion you couldn't really count on anyway.

And still…

There was a voice inside him whispering that perhaps *real* love was worth the risk. He argued that point silently as he'd no wish to find out.

A knot of something worrisome settled into the pit of his stomach and he determinedly chose to ignore it. No point in examining feelings at the moment anyway, was there? Right now, he was just going to enjoy watching her settle into the plush interior of one of his jets.

Her gaze didn't settle, but moved over the inside of the plane, checking out everything, missing nothing. Another thing to admire about her. She wasn't a woman to simply accept her surroundings. Georgia had enough curiosity to explore them. And Sean could admit that he wanted her opinion of his jets.

He was proud of what he'd built with Irish Air and had a million ideas for how to grow and expand the company. By the time he was finished, when someone thought luxury travel, he wanted Irish Air to be the name that came to mind.

"What do you think?" Sean had noticed how she had tensed up during takeoff, but now that they were at a cruising altitude, she was relaxed enough to ease her white-knuckled grip on the arms of the seat.

"Of the jet? It's great," she said. "Really beats flying coach."

"Should be our new slogan," Sean said, with a chuckle. "I'm glad you like it. Irish Air is a luxury airline. There are no coach seats. Everyone is a first-class passenger."

"A great idea, but I'm sure most of us couldn't afford to travel like this."

"It's not so dear as you'd think," Sean said. In fact, he'd made a point of doing as much as he could to keep the price down.

He was proud of what he'd built, but curious what

Georgia thought of his flagship. This plane was the one he used most often himself. But all of the others in his fleet were much like it.

Sean's idea had been to outfit a smaller plane with luxury accommodations. To give people who wouldn't ordinarily fly first class a chance to treat themselves. And yes, the price was a bit higher than coach, but still substantially less than that of a first-class ticket on an ordinary airline.

"It's cheaper than chartering a jet."

"Yeah," she said, flicking a curtain aside to take a look out the window at the clouds beneath them. "But coach is still way cheaper."

"You get what you pay for, don't you?" he asked, leaning back in his own seat to sip at his coffee. "When you fly Irish Air, your vacation begins the moment you board. You're treated like royalty. You arrive at your destination rested instead of wild-eyed and desperate for sleep."

"Oh, I get it," she said. "Believe me. And it's a great idea…"

He frowned as she left that thought hanging. *"But?"*

Georgia shot him a half grin. "But, okay." She set her coffee on the table. "You say your airline's different. Set apart."

"I do."

"But, inside, it's set up just like every other plane. A center aisle, seats on either side."

There was a shine in her eyes and Sean was paying more attention to that, than he was to her words. When what she'd said at last computed, he asked, "And how else should we have it arranged?"

"Well, that's the beauty of it, isn't it?" she countered. "It's your plane, Sean. You want to make Irish Air dif-

ferent from the crowd, so why even have them furnished
like everyone else?"

She ran the flat of her hand across the leather arm
rest and for a second, he allowed himself to picture that
hand stroking him, instead. As his body tightened, he reminded himself they had a six-hour flight to New York
and then another five to L.A. Plenty of time to show
Georgia the owner's bedroom suite at the back of the jet.
That brought a smile to his face, until he realized that
Georgia was frowning thoughtfully.

"What is it you're thinking? Besides the fact that the
seats are arranged wrong?"

"Hmm? Oh, nothing."

"It's something," he said, following her gaze as she
studied the furnishings of the plane with a clearly criti-
cal eye. "Let's have it."

"I was just thinking...you say you started Irish Air as
a way of giving people a real choice in flying."

"That's right," he said, leaning forward, bracing his
elbows on his knees. "As I said, most can't afford first-
class tickets on commercial airlines, and chartering a jet
is well beyond them, as well. Irish Air," he said with a
proud smile, "is in the buffer zone. I offer luxury travel
for just a bit more than coach."

"How much is a bit?"

"More than a little," he hedged, "less than a lot. The
theory being, if people save for an important vacation,
then they might be willing to save a bit more to start their
vacation the moment they board the plane." Warming to
his theme, he continued. "You see, you fly coach, say
from L.A. to Ireland. By the time you've arrived, you
feel as though you've been dragged across a choppy sea.
You're tired, you're angry, you're hungry. Then you've to

rent a car and drive on a different side of the road when you're already on the ragged edge…"

"All true. I've done it," she said.

He nodded. "But, on Irish Air, you step aboard and you relax. There are fewer seats. The seats are wider, fold out into beds and there's a TV at every one of them. We offer WiFi on board and we serve *real* meals with actual knives and forks. When you arrive at your destination, you're rested, refreshed and feel as though your worries are behind you."

"You should do commercials," Georgia said with a smile. "With the way you look, that accent of yours and the way your eyes shine when you talk about Irish Air, you'd have women by the thousands lined up for tickets."

"That's the idea." He sat back, rested one foot on his opposite knee and glanced around. "By this time next year, Irish Air will be the most talked-about airline in the world. We'll be ordering a dozen new planes soon and—" He broke off when he saw her shift her gaze to one side and chew at her bottom lip. A sure sign that she had something to say and wasn't sure how to do it. "What is it?"

"You want the truth?"

"Absolutely," he told her.

"Okay, you want Irish Air to stand out from the crowd, right?"

"I do."

"So why are you creating such boring interiors?"

"What? Boring, did you say?" He glanced around the main cabin, saw nothing out of line and looked back at her for an explanation.

She half turned in her seat to face him, then slapped one hand against the armrest. "First, I already told you, the arrangement of the seats. There are only ten of them on this plane, but you've got them lined up in standard formation, with the aisle up the middle."

One eyebrow winged up. "There's a better way?"

"There's a *different* way, and that is what you said you wanted."

"True. All right then, tell me what you mean."

A light burned in her eyes as she gave him a quick grin. Unbuckling her seat belt, she stood up, looked down the length of the plane, then back to him.

"Okay. It's not just the seats," she said, "the colors are all wrong."

A bit insulted, as he'd paid a designer a huge sum to come up with a color palette that was both soothing and neutral, he asked, "What the bloody hell is wrong with beige?"

She shook her head sadly. "It's *beige,* Sean. Could any color be more ordinary?"

"I've had it on good authority that beige is calming and instills a sense of trust in the passenger."

"Who told you that?" she asked, tipping her head to one side as she studied him. "A man?"

He scowled. "I'm a man, if you've forgotten."

She gave him a wicked smile. "That's one thing I'm certain of."

He stood up, too, but she skipped back a pace to keep some distance between them. "*But* you're not a designer."

"I'm not, no." Considering, thinking, he watched her and said, "All right, then. Tell me what it is you're thinking, Georgia."

"Okay…" She took a breath and said, "First, the carpeting. It looks like the kind you see in a dentist's office. Trust me when I say *that* is not soothing."

He frowned thoughtfully at the serviceable, easy-to-clean carpet.

"It should be plush. Let a passenger's feet sink into it when they step on board." She wagged a finger at him. "Instant luxurious feel and people *will* notice."

"Thick carpet."

"Not beige," she added quickly. "I think blue. Like the color of a summer sky."

"Uh-huh."

She ran one hand across the back of the leather seat again. "These are comfortable, but again. Beige. Really?"

"You recommend blue again?" he asked, enjoying the animation on her face.

"No, for the seats, gray leather." She looked up at him. "The color of the fog that creeps in from the ocean at night. It'll go great with the blue carpet and it'll be different. Make Irish Air stand out from the crowd. And—" She paused as if she were wondering if she'd already gone too far.

He crossed his arms over his chest. "Go on, no reason to stop now."

"Okay, don't line the seats up like bored little soldiers. Clump them."

"Clump?"

"Yeah," she said. "In conversational groups. Like seats on a train. You said this is the midsize jet, right? So your others are even wider. Make use of that space. Make the interior welcoming. Two seats facing back, two forward. And stagger them slightly too, so the people sitting on the right side of the plane aren't directly opposite those on the left. Not everyone wants strangers listening in to conversations."

She walked down the aisle and pointed. "Have the last two back here, separate from the others. A romantic spot that seems cozy and set apart."

He looked at the configuration of his jet and in his

mind's eye, pictured what she was describing. He liked it. More, he could see that she was right. He'd seen the same sort of design on private corporate jets, of course, but not on a passenger line. Offering that kind of difference would help set Irish Air apart. The congenial airline. The jets that made travel a treat. And gray seats on pale blue carpet would look more attractive than the beige. Why hadn't he thought of that?

Better yet, why hadn't the "expert" he'd hired to design the interiors thought of it?

"Oh, and I hate those nasty little overhead light beams on airplanes. It's always so hard to arrow them down on what you want to read." Georgia looked at the slope of the walls, then back to him. "You could have small lamps attached to the hull. Like sconces. Brass—no, pewter. To go with the gray seats and offset the blue."

She reached down and lifted a table that was folded down into itself. Opening it, she pointed to the space on the wall just above. "And here, a bud vase, also affixed to the hull, with fresh flowers."

Sean liked it. Liked all of it. And the excitement in her eyes fired his own.

"Oh, and instead of the standard, plastic, pull-down shades on the windows, have individual drapes." She leaned over and put her hands to either side of one of the portholes. "Tiny, decorative curtain rods—also pewter— and a square of heavy, midnight-blue fabric…"

Before he could comment on that, she'd straightened up and walked past him to the small galley area. The flight attendant was sitting in the cockpit with the pilot and copilot, so there was no one in her way as she explored the functional kitchen setup.

She stepped out again and studied the wall with a

flat-screen television attached to it. "The bathroom is right here, yes?"

"One of them," he said. "There's another in the back."

"So, if you get rid of the big TV—and you should have individual screens at the seating clumps—and expand the bathroom wall another foot or so into the cabin," she took another quick look around the corner at the galley. "That gives you a matching extra space in the kitchen. And that means you could expand your menu. Offer a variety of foods that people won't get anywhere else."

He could bloody well see it, Sean thought. Frowning, he studied the interior of the jet and saw it not as it was now, but as it could be. As it *would* be, he told himself, the moment they got back to Ireland and he could fire the designer who'd suggested ordinary for his *extraordinary* airline.

Following Georgia's train of thought was dizzying, but the woman knew what she was talking about. She painted a picture a blind man could see and appreciate. Why she'd wasted her talent on selling houses, he couldn't imagine.

"You could even offer cribs for families traveling with babies." She was still talking. "If you bolt it down in the back there and have, I don't know, a harness or something for the baby to wear while it sleeps, that gives the mom a little time to relax, too."

He was nodding, making mental notes, astonished at the flow of brilliant ideas Georgia had. "You've a clever mind," he said softly. "And an artist's eye."

She grinned at him and the pleasure in her eyes was something else a blind man could see.

"What's in the back of the plane, through that door?" she asked, already headed toward it.

"Something I'd planned to show you later," he told her with a wink. Then he took her hand and led her down the narrow, ordinary aisle between boring beige seats. Opening the door, he ushered her inside, then followed her and closed the door behind them.

"You have a bedroom on your jets?" she asked, clearly shocked at the sight of the double bed, bedecked with a dark blue duvet and a half-dozen pillows. The shades were drawn over the windows, filling the room with shadow. Georgia looked up at him, shaking her head.

"This plane is mine," Sean told her. "I use it to fly all over the damn place for meetings and such, and so I want a place to sleep while I travel."

"And the seats that fold into beds aren't enough for you?"

"Call it owner's privilege," he said, walking closer, steadily urging her backward until the backs of her knees hit the edge of the mattress and she plopped down. Swinging her hair back from her face, she looked up at him.

"And do you need help designing this room, too?" she asked, tongue firmly in cheek.

"If I did, I now know who to call," he assured her.

"Does that door have a lock on it?" she asked, sliding her gaze to the closed door and then back to him.

"It does."

"Why don't you give it a turn, then?"

"Another excellent idea," Sean said, and moved to do just that.

Then he looked down at her and was caught by her eyes. The twilight shine of them. The clever mind behind them. Staring into her eyes was enough to mesmerize a man, Sean thought. He took a breath and dragged the scent of her into his lungs, knowing that air seemed empty without her scent flavoring it.

Slowly, she slipped her shoes off, then lay back on the mattress, spreading her arms wide, so that she looked like a sacrifice to one of the old gods. But the welcoming smile on her face told him that she wanted him as much as he did her.

In seconds, then, he was out of his clothes and helping her off with hers. The light was dim in the room, but he saw all he needed to see in her eyes. When he touched her, she arched into him and a sigh teased a smile onto her lips.

"Scáthanna bheith agat," he whispered. Amazing how often he felt the old language well up inside him when he was with her. It seemed only Irish could help him say what he was feeling.

She swept her fingers through his hair and said, "I love when you speak Gaelic. What did you say that time?"

"I said, 'Shadows become you,'" he told her, then dipped his head for a kiss.

"You make my heart melt sometimes, Sean," she admitted, her voice little more than a hush of sound.

That knot in his guts tightened further as words he might have said, but wouldn't, caught in his throat. Right now, more words were unnecessary anyway, he told himself.

Instead, he kissed her again, taking his time, tasting her, tangling his tongue with hers until neither of them were thinking. Until all either of them felt was the need for each other. He would take his time and savor every luscious inch of her. Indulge them both with a slow loving that would ease away the ragged edges they had been living with and remind them both how good they were together.

Well, Georgia told herself later that night, Sean was right about one thing. Flying Irish Air did deliver you to your destination feeling bright-eyed and alert. Of course, great sex followed by a nap on a real bed probably hadn't hurt, either.

Now Sean was out picking up some dinner, and she was left staring into her closet trying to decide what to pack, what to give away and what to toss.

"Who'm I trying to kid?" she asked aloud. "I'm taking my clothes with me. All of 'em."

She glanced at the stack of packing boxes on the floor beside her and sighed. Then her gaze moved around her bedroom in the condo she and Laura used to share.

She'd had good times in this house. Sort of surprising, too, since when she'd arrived here to move in with her sister, she hadn't really been in a good place mentally. Marriage dissolved, bank account stripped and ego crushed, she'd slowly, day by day, rebuilt a life for herself.

"And now," she whispered, "I'm building another."

"Talking to yourself? Not a good sign."

She whirled around to find Sean standing in the open doorway, holding a pizza box that smelled like heaven while he watched her with amusement glittering in his eyes.

In self-defense, she said, "I have to talk to myself, since I'm the only one who really understands me."

"*I* understand you, Georgia."

"Is that right?" She turned her back on the closet, the boxes and everything she had to do. Snatching the pizza box from him, she headed out of the bedroom and walked toward the stairs. He was right behind her. "Well then, why don't you tell me what I'm thinking?"

"Easily enough done," he said, his steps heavy on the stairs behind her. "You're excited, but worried. A bit embarrassed for having me catch you doing a monologue in your bedroom and you're hoping you've some wine in the kitchen to go with that pizza."

She looked over her shoulder at him and hoped the surprise she felt was carefully hidden. "You're right about two of them, but I happen to know I don't have a bottle of wine in the kitchen."

"You do now," he told her, and dropped an arm around her shoulders when they hit the bottom of the stairs. "I picked some up while I was out."

"I do like a man who plans ahead."

"Then you'll love me for the plans I have for later." He took the box from her, walked into the kitchen and set it down on the counter.

She stood in the doorway, her gaze following him as he searched through cupboards for plates and napkins and wineglasses. His hair was shaggy and needed a trim. The jeans he wore now were faded and clung to his butt and legs, displaying what she knew was a well-toned body. He whistled as he opened the bottle of wine and poured each of them a glass of what was probably an outrageously expensive red.

You'll love me for the plans I have for later.

His words echoed in her head, and Georgia tried to shrug them off. Not easy to do, though, when a new and startling discovery was still rattling through her system. Warning bells rang in her mind and a flutter of nerves woke up in the pit of her stomach.

Mouth dry, heart pounding, she looked at Sean and realized what her heart had been telling her for days. Maybe weeks.

She'd done the unthinkable.

She'd fallen in love with Sean Connolly.

Nine

Oh, absolutely not.

She refused to think about it. Simply slammed a wall up against that ridiculous thought and told herself it was jet lag. Or hunger. Probably hunger. Once she got some of that pizza into her, her mind would clear up and she'd be fine again.

"You know, you don't have to do the packing yourself," Sean was saying, and she told herself to pay attention.

"What?"

He snorted a laugh. "Off daydreaming while I'm slaving over a hot pizza box were you?"

"No." God, now she was nervous around him. How stupid was that? He'd seen her naked. She'd made love to the man in every way possible. How could she be nervous over what was, in essence, a blip on the radar?

This wasn't love. This was lust. Attraction. Hell, even *affection*.

But not love.

There, she told herself. Problem solved. *Love* was not a word she was going to be thinking ever again. "What did you say? About the packing?"

"While you take care of putting your house up for sale tomorrow, why don't I make some calls and see about getting movers in here?" He looked around the well-stocked condo kitchen. "You can go through, tell them what you want moved to Ireland and what you're getting rid of, and then stand back and watch burly men do the heavy lifting for you."

Tempting. And expensive. She argued with herself over it for a minute or two, but the truth was, if she did it Sean's way, the whole business could be finished much faster. And wasn't that worth a little extra expense?

Especially if it got her back to Ireland faster? And then hopefully in another week or two, they could end this pretend engagement? She glanced down at the emerald-and-diamond ring on her hand and idly rubbed at the band with her thumb. Soon, it wouldn't be hers anymore. Soon, *Sean* wouldn't be hers anymore.

She lifted her gaze to his and his soft brown eyes were locked on her. Another flutter of something nerve-racking moved in the pit of her stomach, but she pushed it aside. Not love, she reminded herself.

And still, she felt a little off balance. Georgia had to have some time to come to grips with this. To figure out a way to handle it while at the same time protecting herself.

She wasn't an idiot, after all. This hadn't been a part of their deal. It was supposed to be a red-hot affair with no strings attached. A pretend engagement that they would both walk away from when it was over.

And that was just what she would do.

Oh, it was going to hurt, she thought now, as Sean handed her a glass of wine, letting his fingers trail across her skin. When he was out of her life, out of her bed and still in her heart—not that she was admitting he was— it was going to be a pain like she'd never known before.

But she comforted herself with the knowledge that she would be in Ireland, near her sister. She'd have Laura and baby Fiona to help her get over Sean. Shouldn't take more than five or ten years, she told herself with an inner groan.

"So, what do you think?" Sean carried the wine to the table beside the window that overlooked the backyard. "We can have you packed up in a day or two. A lot of your things we can carry back on the jet, what we can't, we'll arrange to ship."

"That's a good idea, Sean." She took a seat, because her knees were still a little weak and it was better to sit down than to fall down. Taking a quick sip of the really great wine, she let it ease the knot in her throat.

Then she picked up the conversation and ran with it. Better to talk about the move. About packers and all of the things she had to do rather than entertain even for a minute that the affection she felt for him could be something else. Losing Sean now was going to hurt. But God help her, if she was really in *love,* the pain would be tremendous.

"There are really only a few things I want to take with me to Ireland," she said. "The rest I'll donate."

That thought appealed to her anyway. She was starting over in Ireland, and the cottage was already furnished, so there was no hurry to buy new things. She could take her time and decide later what she wanted. As for kitchen stuff, it didn't really make sense to ship pots and pans when she could replace them easily enough in Ireland.

All she really wanted from the condo aside from her clothes were family photos, Laura's paintings and a few other odds and ends. What did that say about her, that she'd been living in this condo, surrounded by *stuff* and none of it meant enough to take with her?

She had more of a connection with the cottage than she did with anything here.

"You know," she said, "it's kind of a sad statement that there's so little here I want to take with me. I mean, I was willing to stay here when it clearly didn't mean much to me."

"Why would that be sad?" He sat down opposite her, opened the pizza box and served each of them a slice. "You knew when it was time to move on, is all. Seems to me it's more brave than that. You're moving to a different country, Georgia. Why wouldn't you want to leave the past behind?"

She huffed out a breath and let go of the 'poor me' thoughts that had just begun to form. "How do you do that?"

"What?"

"Manage to say exactly the right thing," she said.

He laughed a little and took a bite of pizza. "Luck, I'd say. And knowing you as I've come to, I thought you might be getting twisted up over all there is to be done and then giving yourself a hard time over it."

Scowling, she told him, "It's a little creepy, knowing you can see into my head so easily."

He picked up his wineglass and toasted her with it. "Didn't say it was easy."

She hoped not, because she *really* didn't want him looking too closely into her mind right now. Twists of emotion tangled inside her and this time she didn't fight them.

Okay, yes. She had feelings for him. Why wouldn't she? He was charming and fun and smart and gorgeous. He was easy to talk to and great in bed, of course she cared about him.

That didn't mean she loved him. Didn't mean anything more than what they had together was important to her.

Even she wasn't buying that one.

Oh, God. No sense in lying to herself, Georgia thought. She'd sew her lips shut and lock herself in a deep dark hole for the rest of her life before she ever admitted the truth to Sean.

This wasn't affection. It wasn't lust. Or hunger.

It was love.

Nothing like the love she had thought she'd found once before.

Now, she couldn't imagine how she had ever convinced herself that she was in love with Mike. Because what she felt for Sean was so much bigger, so much... *brighter,* that it was like comparing an explosion to a sparkler. There simply wasn't a comparison.

This was the kind of love she used to dream of.

And wouldn't you know she'd find it with a man who wouldn't want it? Feelings hadn't been part of their agreement. Love had no place in a secret. A pretense.

So she'd keep her mouth shut and tuck what she felt for him aside until it withered in the dark. It would. Eventually. She hoped.

Oh, God.

She was such an idiot.

"Well," Sean said after a sip of his wine, "I'll admit to you now I've no notion of what you're thinking at this minute. But judging by your expression, it's not making you happy."

Understatement of the century.

"Nothing in particular," she lied smoothly. "Just how much I have to do and how little time I have to do it."

He looked at her for a long minute as if trying to decide to let it lay or not, and finally, thank God, he did.

"So no second thoughts? Being here," he said, glancing around the bright, modern kitchen, "doesn't make you want to rethink your decision?"

She followed his gaze, looking around the room where she'd spent so much alone time in the past year. It was a nice place, she thought, but it had never felt like *hers*. Not like the cottage in Ireland did.

"No," she said, shaking her head slowly. "I came here to live with Laura when my marriage ended and it was what I needed then. But it's not for me now, you know?"

"I do," he said, resting one elbow on the tabletop. "When you find your place, you know it."

"Exactly. What about you? Did you ever want to live somewhere else?"

He grinned. "Leave Dunley?" He shook his head. "I went to college in Dublin and thought it a fine place. I've been all over Europe and to New York several times as well, but none of those bright and busy places tug at me as Dunley does.

"The village is my place, as you said," he told her. "I've no need to leave it to prove anything to myself or anyone else."

"Have you always been so sure of yourself?" She was really curious. He seemed so together. Never doubting himself for a minute. She envied it. At the same time she simply couldn't understand it.

He laughed. "A man who doesn't question himself from time to time's a fool who will soon be slapped down by the fates or whatever gods are paying attention to the jackass of the moment. So of course I question," he said. "I just trust myself to come up with the right answers."

"I used to," she told him and pulled a slice of pepperoni free of the melted cheese and popped it into her mouth. "Then I married Mike and he left me for someone else and I didn't have a clue about it until he was walking out the door." Georgia took a breath and then let it go. "After that, I had plenty of questions, but no faith in my own answers."

"That's changed now, though," he said, his gaze fixed on hers. "You've rebuilt your life, haven't you? And you've done it the way *you* want to. So, I'm thinking your answers were always right, you just weren't ready to hear them."

"Maybe," she admitted. Then, since marriages, both real and pretend, were on her mind, asked, "So, why is it you've never been married?"

He choked on a sip of wine, then caught his breath and said, "There's a question out of the blue."

"Not really. We were talking about my ex—now it's my turn to hear your sad tales. I am your 'fiancée,' after all. Shouldn't I know these things?"

"I suppose you should," he said with a shrug. "Truth is, I was engaged once."

"Really?" A ping of something an awful lot like jealousy sounded inside her. Just went to show her mom was right. She used to tell Georgia, *Never ask a question you don't really want the answer to.*

"Didn't last long." He shrugged again and took a sip of his wine. "Noreen was more interested in my bank account than in me, and she finally decided that she deserved better than a husband who spent most of his time at work."

"Noreen." Harder somehow, knowing the woman's name.

"I let her maneuver me into the thought of marriage," Sean was saying, apparently not clueing in to Georgia's thoughts. "I remember thinking that maybe it was time to be married, and Noreen was there—"

"She was *there?*" Just as *she* had been there, Georgia thought now, when he'd needed a temporary fiancée. Hmm.

He gave her a wry smile. "Aye. I know how it sounds now, but at the time, it seemed easier to let her do what she would than to fight her over it. I was consumed at the time with taking Irish Air to the next level, and I suppose the truth is I didn't care enough to put a stop to Noreen's plans."

Dumbfounded, she just stared at him. "So you would have married her? Not really loving her, you would have married her anyway because it was easier than saying 'no thanks'?"

He shifted uneasily on his chair and frowned a bit at the way she'd put things. "No," he said finally. "I wouldn't have taken that trip down the aisle with her in the end. It wouldn't have worked and I knew it at the time. I was just..."

"Busy?" she asked.

"If you like. Point is," Sean said, "it worked out for the best all around. Noreen left me and married a bank president or some such. And I found you."

Yes, he'd found her. Another temporary fiancée. One he had no intention of escorting down an aisle of any kind. Best to remember that, she told herself.

He lifted his glass and held it out to her, a smile on

his face and warmth in his eyes. Love swam in the pit of
her stomach, but Georgia put a lid on it fast. She hadn't
planned to love him, and now that she did, she planned
to get over it as fast as humanly possible.

So, she'd keep things as they had been between them.
Light. Fun. Sexy and affectionate. And when it was over,
she'd walk away with her head high, and Sean would
never know how she really felt. Georgia tapped her wineglass to his, and when she drank, she thought that the
long-gone Noreen had gotten off easy.

Noreen hadn't really loved Sean when she left him, or
she'd never have moved on so quickly to someone else.

Georgia on the other hand...it wasn't going to be simple walking away from Sean Connolly.

Georgia was glad they'd come to the wedding. Just
seeing the look on Misty's face when she spotted Georgia and Sean had made the trip worthwhile. But it was
more than that, too, she told herself. Maybe she'd *had* to
attend this wedding. Maybe it was the last step in leaving behind her past so that she could walk straight ahead
and never look back.

And dancing with her ex-husband, the groom, was all
a part of that. What was interesting was, she felt nothing
in Mike's arms. No tingle. No soft sigh of regret for old
time's sake. Nothing.

She looked up at him and noticed for the first time that
his blue eyes were a little beady. His hair was thinning
on top, and she had the feeling that Mike would one day
be a comb-over guy. His broad chest had slipped a little,
making him a bit thick about the waist, and the whiskey
on his breath didn't make the picture any prettier.

Once she had loved him. Or at least thought she had.
She'd married him assuming they would be together for-

ever, and yet here she was now, a few years after a divorce she hadn't seen coming and she felt…nothing.

Was that how it would be with Sean one day? Would her feelings for him simply dry up and blow away like autumn leaves in a cold wind?

"You look amazing," Mike said, tightening his arm around her waist.

She did and she knew it. Georgia had gone shopping for the occasion. Her dark red dress had long sleeves, a deep V neckline, and it flared out from the waist into a knee-length skirt that swirled when she moved.

"Thanks," she said, and glanced toward Sean, sitting alone at a table on the far side of the room. Then, willing to be generous, she added, "Misty makes a pretty bride."

"Yeah." But Mike wasn't looking at his new wife. Instead, he was staring at Georgia as if he'd never seen her before.

He executed a fast turn and Georgia had to grab hold of his shoulder to keep from stumbling. He pulled her in even closer in response. When she tried to put a little space between them, she couldn't quite manage it.

"You're engaged, huh?"

"Yes," she said, thumbing the band on her engagement ring. Sean had made quite the impression. Just as she'd hoped, he'd been charming, attentive and, in short, the perfect fiancé. "When we leave here, we're flying home to Ireland."

"Can't believe you're gonna be living in a foreign country," Mike said with a shake of his head. "I don't remember you being the adventurous type at all."

"Adventurous?"

"You know what I mean," he continued, apparently not noticing that Georgia's eyes were narrowed on him thoughtfully. "You were all about fixing up the house.

Making dinner. Working in the yard. Just so—" he shrugged "—boring."

"Excuse me?"

"Come on, Georgia, admit it. You never wanted to try anything new or exciting. All you ever wanted to do was talk about having kids and—" He broke off and sighed. "You're way more interesting now."

Was steam actually erupting from the top of her head? she wondered. Because it really felt like it. Georgia's blood pressure was mounting with every passing second. She had been *boring*? Talking about having kids with your husband was *boring*?

"So, because I was so uninteresting, that's why you slipped out with Misty?" she asked, her voice spiking a little higher than she'd planned. "Are you actually trying to tell me it's *my* fault you cheated on me?"

"Jeez, you always were too defensive," Mike said, and slid his hand down to her behind where he gave her a good squeeze.

Georgia's eyes went wild.

They made a good team.

Sean had been thinking about little else for the past several days. All through the mess of closing up her home and arranging for its sale. Through the packing and the donations to charity and ending the life she'd once lived, they'd worked together.

He was struck by how easy it was, being with her.

Her clever mind kept him on his toes and her luscious body kept him on his knees. A perfect situation, Sean told himself as he sat at the wedding, drinking a beer, considering ways to keep Georgia in his life.

Ever since she'd laid out her ideas to improve the look of his company jets, Sean had been intrigued by possibilities. They got along well. They were a good match. A team, as he'd thought only moments before.

"And damned if I want to lose what we've found," he muttered.

The simplest way, he knew, was to make their engagement reality. To convince her to marry him—not for love, of course, because that was a nebulous thing after all. But because they fit so well. And the more he thought about it, the better it sounded.

Hadn't his cousin Ronan offered very nearly the same deal to his Laura? A marriage based on mutual need and respect. That had worked out, hadn't it? Nodding to himself, he thought it a good plan. The challenge would be in convincing Georgia to agree with him.

But he had time for that, didn't he?

Watching her here, at the wedding of her ex-husband, he was struck again by her courage. Her boldness in facing down those who had hurt her with style and enough attitude to let everyone in the room know that she'd moved on. Happily.

The bride hadn't expected Georgia to show up for the wedding. That had been clear enough when he and Georgia arrived. The stunned shock on the bride's face mingled with the interest from the groom had been proof of that.

Sean frowned to himself and had a sip of the beer sitting in front of him. He didn't much care for the way Georgia's ex-husband took every chance he had to leer at her. But he couldn't blame the man for regretting letting Georgia go in favor of the empty-headed woman he'd now saddled himself with.

Georgia was as a bottle of fine wine while the bride seemed more of a can of flat soda in comparison.

The reception was being held at the clubhouse of a

golf course. Late fall in Ohio was cold, and so the hall
was closed up against the night, making the room damn
near stifling.

Crepe paper streamers sagged from the corners of the
wall where the tape holding them in place was beginning
to give. Balloons, as their helium drained away, began to
dip and bob aimlessly, as if looking for a way out, and
even the flowers in glass vases on every table were beginning to droop.

People who weren't dancing huddled together at tables
or crowded what was left of the buffet. Sean was seated
near the dance floor, watching Georgia slow dance in
the arms of her ex, fighting the urge to go out there and
snatch her away from the buffoon. He didn't like the
man's hands on her. Didn't like the way Mike bent his
head to Georgia and whispered in her ear.

Sean frowned as the music spilled from the speakers
overhead and the groom pulled Georgia a bit too tightly
against him. Something spiked inside Sean's head and he
tightened his grip on the beer bottle so that it wouldn't
have surprised him in the least to feel it shatter. Deliberately, he released his hold on the bottle, setting it down
carefully on the table.

Then Sean breathed slow and deep, and rubbed the
heel of his hand against the center of his chest, uncon-
sciously trying to rub away the hard, cold knot that
seemed to have settled there. He gritted his teeth and
narrowed his eyes when the groom's hand slipped down
to cup Georgia's behind.

Fury swamped his vision and dropped a red haze of
anger over his mind. When Georgia struggled to pull free
without success, something inside Sean simply snapped.
The instinct to protect her roared into life and he went

with it. *His* woman, mauled on a dance floor? He bloody well didn't think so.

Sean was halfway out of his chair when Georgia brought the sharp point of one of her high heels down onto the toe of the groom's shoe. While Mike hopped about, whinging about being in pain, Misty ran to her beloved's rescue, and Sean met Georgia halfway between the dance floor and the table.

Her eyes were glinting with outrage, color was high in her cheeks and she'd never been more vividly beautiful to him. She'd saved herself, leaving him nothing to do with the barely repressed anger churning inside him.

His woman, he thought again, and felt the truth of it right down to his bones. And even knowing that, he pulled away mentally from what that might mean. He wouldn't look at it. Not now. Instead, he focused a hard look at the groom and his new bride, then shifted his gaze back to Georgia.

"So then," Sean asked, "ready to leave?"

"Way past ready," Georgia admitted and stalked by him to their table to pick up her wrap and her purse.

He let her go, but was damned if he'd leave this place without making a few things clear to the man he'd like nothing better than to punch into the next week. Misty was clinging to Mike when Sean approached them, but he didn't even glance at the new bride. Instead, his gaze was for the groom, still hobbling unsteadily on one injured foot.

Voice low, eyes hard, Sean said, "I'll not beat a man on his wedding day, so you're safe from me."

Insulted, Mike sputtered, "What the—"

"But," Sean continued, letting the protective instincts rising inside him take over, "you even so much as *think* of Georgia again, I'll know of it. And you and I will have a word."

Misty's mouth flapped open and shut like a baby bird's. Mike flushed dark red, but his eyes showed him for the true coward he was, even before he nodded. Sean left them both standing there, thinking the two of them deserved each other.

When he draped Georgia's wrap about her shoulders, then slid one arm around her waist to escort her from the building, she looked up at him.

"What did you say to him?"

He glanced at her and gave her a quick smile to disguise the fury still pulsing within. "I thanked him for a lovely party and wished him a broken foot."

"I do like your style, Sean," she said, leaning her head against his shoulder.

He kissed the top of her head and took the opportunity to take a long breath of her scent. Then he quipped, "I believe the American thing to say would be, 'back atcha.'"

With the sound of her laughter in his ears, Sean steered her outside to the waiting limousine, and ushered her inside.

With a word to the driver, they were off for the airport so Sean could take his woman home to Ireland.

Ten

A few days later, Sean was standing in Ronan's office in Galway, looking for a little encouragement. Apparently, though, he'd come to the wrong place.

"You're out of your mind," Ronan said.

"Well, don't hold back, cousin," Sean countered, pacing the confines of the office. It was big and plush but at the moment, it felt as if it were the size of a box. There was too much frustrated energy pumping through Sean's brain to let him stand still, and walking in circles was getting him nowhere.

He stopped at the wide window that offered a view of Galway city and the bay beyond. Out over the ocean, layers of dark clouds huddled at the horizon, no doubt bunched up over England but planning their immediate assault on Ireland. Winter was coming in like a mean bitch.

Sean had come into Galway to see Ronan because

his cousin's office was the one place Sean could think
of where they could have a conversation without interruptions from the seeming *multitude* of women in their
lives. Ronan was, naturally, wrapped up in Laura and
baby Fiona. For Sean, there was his mother, nearly recovered now, and there was Georgia. Beautiful Georgia
who haunted his sleep and infiltrated his every waking
thought.

His woman, he'd thought that night in Ohio, and that
notion had stayed with him. There was something there
between them. He knew it. Felt it. And he'd finally found
a plan to solve his troubles, so he'd needed this time with
Ronan to talk it all out. But for all the help he was finding, he might have stayed home.

"How is it crazy to go after what I want?" he argued
now. "You did it."

Ronan sat back in the chair behind his uncluttered
desk. Tapping the fingers of one hand against that glossy
surface, he stared at Sean with a disbelieving gleam in
his eyes.

"Aye, I did it, just as you're thinking to, so I'm the man
to tell you that you're wrong. You can't ask Georgia to
marry you as a sort of business arrangement."

"Why not?" Sean countered, glancing over his shoulder at his cousin before turning his gaze back to the window and the outside world beyond. "For all your calm
reason now, you did the same with Laura and look how
well that turned out for you."

Ronan scraped one hand across his face. "You idiot.
I almost lost Laura through my own foolishness. She
wouldn't have me, do you not remember that? How I
was forced to chase her down to the airport as she was
leaving me?"

Sean waved that off. The point was, it *had* worked out.

A bump or two in the road, he was expecting. Nothing worthwhile came easy, after all, but in the end, Georgia would agree with him. He'd done a lot of thinking about this, and he knew he was right. Georgia was much more sensible, more reasonable than her sister and he was sure she'd see the common sense in their getting married.

He'd worked it out in his mind so neatly, she had to see it. A businesslike offer of marriage was eminently sensible. With his mother on the mend, the time for ending their faux engagement was fast approaching. And Sean had discovered he didn't want his time with Georgia to be over. He wanted her even more now than he had when this had all begun.

He turned around, leaned one hip against the window jamb and looked at his cousin.

"Georgia's buying a house here," Sean pointed out. "She's opening her business. She won't be running off to California to escape me."

"Doesn't mean she'll greet you with open arms, either," Ronan snapped, then huffed out a breath filled with frustration. "She's already been married to a man who didn't treasure her. Why would she choose another who offers her the same?"

Sean came away from the window in a fast lunge and stood glaring down at Ronan. Damned if he'd be put in the same boat as the miserable bastard who'd caused Georgia nothing but pain. "Don't be comparing me to that appalling excuse of a man who hurt her. I'd not cheat on my wife."

"No, but you won't love her, either," Ronan said, jumping up from his chair to match his cousin glare for glare. "And as she's my sister now, I'll stand for her and tell you myself she *deserves* to be loved, and if you're not the man to do it then bloody well step aside and let her find the one who will."

Those words slapped at Sean's mind and heart, and he didn't much care for it. *Love* wasn't a word Sean was entirely comfortable with. He'd tried to be in love with Noreen and he'd failed. What if he tried with Georgia and failed there, as well? No, he wouldn't risk it. What they had now was good. Strong. Warmth beneath the heat. Caring to go with the passion. Affection that wasn't muddled by trying to label it. Wasn't that enough? Wasn't that more than a lot of people built a life around?

And he'd be damned before he stepped aside for some other man to snatch Georgia in front of his eyes. Which was one of the reasons he'd come up with this plan in the first place. If they ended their engagement—and since Ailish was recovering nicely, that time was coming fast— then he'd be forced to let Georgia go. Watch her find a new man. He'd have to imagine that lucky bastard touching her, kissing her, claiming her in the dark of night— and damned if he'd do *that,* either.

He alone would be the man touching Georgia Page, Sean assured himself, because he could accept no other option. If he did, he'd be over the edge and into insanity in no time at all.

"She had a man who promised her love, as you've just said yourself," Sean argued, jamming both hands into his pockets to hide the fists they'd curled into. Thinking about that man, Georgia's ex, made him want to punch something. That a man such as he had had Georgia and let her go was something Sean would never understand.

"What good did the promise of love do her then?" he asked, more quietly now. "I'm not talking of love but of building a life together."

"Without the first, the second's not much good," Ronan told him with a slow shake of his head.

"Without the first, the second is far less complicated,"

Sean argued. He knew Ronan loved his Laura, and good for him. But love wasn't the only answer. Love was too damn ephemeral. Hard to pin down. If he offered her love, why would she believe him? Why would she trust it when that bastard who had offered the same had crushed her spirit with the word?

No. He could offer Georgia what she wanted. A home. Family. A man to stand at her side and never hurt her as she'd been hurt before. Wasn't that worth something?

"You're a jackass if you really believe that bilge you're shoveling."

"Thanks very much," Sean muttered, then said, "You're missing the point of this, Ronan. If there's no love between us, there's no way for her to be hurt. She'll be safe. I'll see to it."

Ronan skewered him with a look. "You're set on this, aren't you?"

"I am. I've thought this through." In fact, he'd thought of little else since going on that trip to the States with Georgia. He wanted this and so, Sean knew, he could make it happen. He'd never before lost when something mattered as this did. Now wouldn't be the first time. "I know I'm right about this, Ronan."

"Ah, well then." Clapping one hand to Sean's shoulder, Ronan said, "I wish you luck with it, because you're going to need it. And when Georgia coshes you over the head with something heavy, don't be coming to me looking for sympathy."

A tiny speck of doubt floated through the river of Sean's surety, but he paid it no attention at all. Instead, he focused only on his plan, and how to present it to Georgia.

It stormed for a week.

Heavy, black clouds rolled in from the sea, riding an

icy wind that battered the village like a bad-tempered child. The weather kept everyone closed up in their own houses, and Georgia was no different. She'd spent her time hanging pictures and paintings, and putting out the other small things she'd brought with her from California until the cottage was cozy and felt more hers every day.

She missed Sean, though. She hadn't seen him in days. Had spoken to him only briefly on the phone. Laura had told her that Sean and Ronan had spent days and nights all over the countryside, helping the villagers and farmers who were having a hard time through the storm. They'd done everything from mending leaking roofs to ferrying a sick child to the hospital just in time for an emergency appendectomy.

Georgia admired their connection to the village and their determination to see everyone safely through the first big storm of the season. But, God, she'd missed him. And though it pained her, she had finally convinced herself that not seeing him, not having him with her, was probably for the best. Soon, she'd have to get accustomed to his absence, so she might as well start getting used to it.

But it was so much harder than she'd thought it would be. She hadn't planned on that, damn it. She'd wanted the affair with the gorgeous Irishman, and who wouldn't have?

But she hadn't wanted the risk of loving him, and the fact that she did was entirely *his* fault. If he hadn't been so blasted charming and sweet and sexy. If he hadn't been such an amazing lover and so much fun to be around, she never would have fallen. So really, Georgia told herself, none of this was her fault at all.

She'd been hit over the head by the Irish fates and the only way out was pain and suffering. He'd become such a part of her life that cutting him out of it was going to be like losing a limb. Which just irritated her immensely. That she could fall in love when she knew she shouldn't, because of the misery that was now headed her way, was both frustrating and infuriating.

The worst of it now was there was nothing she could do about it. The love was there and she was just going to have to hope that, eventually, it would fade away. In hindsight, she probably shouldn't have accepted Sean's bargain in the first place. But if she hadn't...she would have missed so much.

So she couldn't bring herself to wish away what she'd found with him, even though ending it was going to kill her.

When the sun finally came out, people streamed from their homes and businesses as if they were prisoners suddenly set loose from jail. And Georgia was one of them. She was so eager to get out of her own thoughts, and away from her own company, she raced into town to open her shop and start living the life she was ready to build.

The sidewalks were crowded with mothers who had spent a week trapped with bored children. The tea shop did a booming business as friends and neighbors gathered to tell war stories of storm survival. Shop owners were manning brooms, cleaning up the wreckage left behind and talking to friends as they worked.

Georgia was one of them now. Outside her new design shop, she wielded a broom with the rest of them, and once her place was set to rights, she walked back inside to brew some coffee. She might be in Ireland, but she hadn't yet switched her allegiance from coffee to tea.

The bell over the front door rang in a cheery rattle, and she hurried into the main room only to stop dead when she saw Sean. Everything in her kindled into life. Heat, excitement, want and tenderness tangled together making her nearly breathless. It felt like years since she'd seen him though it had only been a few days. Yes. Irritating.

He looked ragged, tired, and a curl of worry opened up in the center of her chest. The shadow of whiskers on his jaws and the way his hair jutted up, no doubt from him stabbing his fingers through it repeatedly, told her just what a hard few days he'd had. He wore faded jeans, a dark, thickly knit sweater and heavy work boots. And, she thought, he'd never looked more gorgeous.

"How are you?" she asked.

He rubbed one hand across his face, blinked a couple of times, then a half smile curved one corner of his mouth. "Tired. But otherwise, I'll do."

"Laura told me what you and Ronan have been up to. Was it bad?"

"The first big storm of the year is always bad," he said. "But we've got most of the problems in the area taken care of."

"I'm glad. It was scary around here for a day or two," she said, remembering how the wind had howled like the shrieks of the dying. At one point the rain had come down so fiercely, it had spattered into the fire in her hearth.

"I'm sorry I wasn't able to be with you during your first real storm in Dunley," he said, as sunlight outlined him in gold against the window.

"I was fine, Sean. Though I am thinking about getting a dog," she added with a smile. "For the company. Besides, it sounds like you and Ronan had your hands full."

"We did at that." He blew out a breath and tucked his hands into the back pockets of his jeans.

How could a man look *that* sexy in old jeans and beat-up work boots?

"Maeve Carrol's roof finally gave up the ghost and caved in on her."

Georgia started. "Oh, my God. Is she okay?"

"She's well," Sean said, walking farther into the shop, letting his gaze move over the room and all the changes she'd made to it. "Madder than the devil with a drop of holy water in his whiskey, but fine."

She smiled at the image and imagined just how furious Maeve was. The older woman was spectacularly self-sufficient. "So, I'm guessing you and Ronan finally talked her into letting you replace her roof."

"The woman finally had no choice as she's a hole in her roof and lots of water damage." He shook his head. "She nearly floated away on a tide of her own stubbornness. She'll be staying with Ronan and Laura until her cottage is livable again."

Georgia folded her arms across her chest to help her fight the urge to go and wrap her arms around him. "I'm guessing she's not happy about leaving her home."

"You'd think we'd threatened to drag her through the village tied to a rampaging horse." He snorted. "The old woman scared us both half to death. Ronan's been after her for years to let us replace that roof."

"I know. It's nice of you to look out for her."

He glanced at her. "Maeve is family."

"I know that, too," she said and felt that flutter of love inside her again. Honestly, who wouldn't be swooning at the feet of a man like this? Even as that thought circled her brain, Georgia steeled herself. If she wasn't careful, she was going to do something stupid that would alert him to just how much she cared about him.

And that couldn't happen. No way would she live in Dunley knowing that Sean was off at the manor feeling sorry for poor Georgia, who'd been foolish enough to fall in love with him.

"Anyway," she said with forced cheer, "my cottage is sound, thanks to the previous owner. So I was fine."

"Aye," he said softly, brown eyes locked on her face. "You are."

A ripple of sensation slid along her spine at the music in his voice, the heat in his eyes. He was temptation itself, she told herself, and she wondered how she was going to manage living in this town over the years, seeing him and not having him. Hearing the gossip in the village about the women he would be squiring around. And again, she wanted to kick herself for ever agreeing to his crazy proposal.

"You've been working here. Your shop looks good," he said, shifting a quick look around the space. "As do you."

Heat flared inside her, but she refused to acknowledge it. Instead, Georgia looked around her shop, letting her gaze slide over the soft gold walls, the paintings of Laura's that Georgia had hung only that morning.

"Thanks," she said. "The furniture I ordered from the shop in Galway should arrive by end of the week."

She could almost see it, a sleek, feminine desk with matching chair. More chairs for clients, and shelves for what would be her collection of design books. She'd have brightly colored rugs strewn across the polished wood floor and a sense of style that customers would feel the moment they stepped inside.

Georgia was excited about the future even as she felt a pang of regret that Sean wouldn't be a part of it. She took a steadying breath before looking into his soft brown eyes again. And still it wasn't enough. Probably never would be, she thought. He would always hold a piece of her heart, whether he wanted it or not.

Still, she forced a smile. "I think it's really coming along. I'm looking forward to opening the shop for business."

"You'll be brilliant," he said, his gaze level on hers.

"Thanks for that, too." She knew his words weren't empty flattery, and his confidence in her was a blossom of warmth inside her. "And as long as I'm thanking you...we'll add on that I appreciate all your help with the business license."

"We had a deal, didn't we?"

"Yeah," she said, biting at her bottom lip. "We did."

"I spoke to Tim Shannon this morning. He told me that your business license should be arriving by end of the week."

A swirl of nerves fluttered in the pit of her stomach, and she slapped both hands to her abdomen as if to still them.

"Never say you're nervous," he said, smiling.

"Okay, I won't tell you. But I am. A little." She turned her gaze on the front window and stared out at the sunlit street beyond. "This is important to me. I just want to do it right."

"And so you will," Sean said, "and to prove it, I want to hire you."

"What?" That she hadn't expected.

"Do you remember how you reeled off dozens of brilliant ideas on how to improve the interior of my planes?"

"Yes..."

He walked closer, tugged his hands from his pockets and laid them on her shoulders. "I want you to redesign the interiors of all the Irish Air jets."

"You..." She blinked at him.

"Not just the fleet we've got at the moment, either," he told her, giving her shoulders a squeeze. "I want you in on my talks with the plane builders. We can get your input from the beginning that way."

"Redesign your..." It was a wild, exciting idea. And Georgia's mind kicked into high gear despite the shock still numbing parts of her brain.

This was huge. Irish Air as her client would give her an instant name and credibility. It would be an enormous job, she warned herself, expecting nerves or fear to trickle in under the excitement, but they didn't come. All she felt was a rush of expectancy and a thrill that he trusted her enough to turn her loose on the business that meant so much to him.

"I can see the wheels in your mind turning," he said, his mouth curving slightly. "So add this to the mix. You'll have a free hand to make whatever changes you think best. We'll work together, Georgia, and together we'll make Irish Air legendary."

Together. Her heart stirred. Oh, she liked the sound of that, even though more time with Sean would only make the eventual parting that much more painful. How could she *not* love him? He was offering her carte blanche to remake Irish Air because he trusted her.

Shaking her head, she admitted, "I don't even know what to say."

He grinned and she felt a jolt.

"Say yes, of course. I'll be your first client, Georgia, but not your last." He pulled her closer and she looked up into deep brown eyes that shone with pleasure and... something else.

"With Irish Air on your résumé, I guarantee other companies will be beating down your door soon."

"It's great, Sean, really. You won't be sorry for this."

"I've no doubts about that, Georgia," he said, then lifted one hand to smooth her hair back from her face.

At his touch, everything in her trembled, but Georgia fought it. She *had* to fight it, for her own sake.

"There's something else I want to talk to you about." His voice was quiet, thoughtful.

And she knew instinctively what he was going to say. She should have known there would be another reason for his incredible offer. He had come here to tell her their engagement was done. Deal finished. Obviously, he'd offered her that job to take the sting out of the whole thing.

"Let me help," she said, pulling back and away from him. How could she think when his hands were on her? When she was looking into those eyes of his? "Laura told me that Ailish is mostly recovered now and I'm really glad."

"Thank you," he said, "and yes, she is. She'll see her doctor this week, then all will be back to normal."

Normal. Back to life without Sean.

"So she'll be headed back to Dublin?"

"No," Sean said. "Mother's decided she wants to come home to Dunley. I offered her the left wing of the manor, but she says she's no interest in living with her son." He shrugged and laughed a little. "So she's opted for moving into the gatehouse on the estate."

"The gatehouse?" Georgia didn't remember ever noticing a gatehouse at Sean's place.

"It's what we call it, anyway," he said with a smile. "It was originally built for my grandmother to live in when she moved out of the manor in favor of my parents. Mother's always loved it, and there's plenty of room there for her friends to visit."

"Oh, okay. Well, it's nice that she'll be closer. I really like your mother."

"I know you do," Sean said. "But the thing is, with mother recovering, it's time we talked about our bargain."

"It's okay." Georgia cut him off. She didn't want him to say the words. "You don't have to say it. Ailish is well, so we're finished with this charade."

She tugged at the ring on her finger, but he reached out and stilled her hand. Georgia looked up at him.

"I don't want to be done with it," he blurted, and hope shot through her like sunlight after the storm they'd just lived through.

She swallowed hard and asked, "What?"

"I want us to marry," he said, curling her fingers into her palm to prevent her from taking off the ring.

"You do?" Love dazzled her. She looked into his eyes and saw them shine. She felt everything in her world setting itself straight again. In one split instant, she saw their lives spiraling out into a wonderful future. The home they'd make. The children. The family. She saw love and happiness and everything she'd ever wished for.

The sad cynic inside her died, and Georgia was glad to see her go.

And then he continued talking.

"It makes sense," he told her, a gorgeous smile on his face. "The village is counting on it. My mother's got the thing half-planned already. We work well together. You must admit we make a hell of a good team. We're great in bed together. I think we should simply carry on with the engagement and go through with the marriage. No one ever has to know we didn't marry for love."

Eleven

There, Sean told himself. He'd done it. Laid out his plan for her, and now she'd see exactly what they could have together. Looking into her eyes, he saw them alight, then watched worriedly as that light dimmed. He spoke up fast, hoping to see her eyes shine again.

"There's no sense in us breaking up when any fool could see we've done well together," he said, words rushing from him as her eyes went cool and a distance seemed to leap up between them.

He moved in closer and told himself she hadn't actually moved *away*, just to one side. "You're a sensible woman, Georgia. Clear-thinking. I admire that about you, along with so many other facets of you."

"Well, how nice for you that I'm such a calm person."

"I thought so." He frowned. "But somehow, I've insulted you."

"Oh, why would I be insulted by *that*?"

"I've no idea," he said, but watched her warily. "I realize I've caught you off guard with this, but you'll see, Georgia. If you'll but take a moment to think it through, you'll agree that this is the best way for both of us."

"You've decided that, have you?" She snapped a look at him that had the hackles at the back of his neck standing straight up.

This wasn't going as he'd thought it would, yet he had no choice but to march on, to lay everything out for her.

"I did. I've done considerable thinking about the two of us since we took that trip to California."

"Have you?"

Her tone was sweet, calm, and he began to relax again. This was the Georgia he knew so well. A temper, aye. What's life without a little seasoning after all, but a reasonable woman at the heart of it.

"I'm saying we work well together and there's no reason for us to separate." When her gaze narrowed, he hurried on. "The entire village is expecting a wedding. If we end things now, there'll be questions and whispers and gossip that will last for years."

"That's not what you said when we started this," she countered. *"Oh, they'll all think you've come to your senses,"* she added in such a true mimic of his own voice and words she had him flinching.

"It's different now," he insisted.

"How? How is it different?"

He rubbed one hand over his face, fatigue clawing at him even as his muddled mind fought for survival. "You're a part of things in Dunley, as am I. They'll wonder. They'll talk."

"Let them," she snapped. "Isn't that what a *sensible* woman would say?"

"Clearly that word upsets you, though I've no idea

why. You're a lovely woman, Georgia, with a sound mind and a clear vision." He pushed on, determined to make her see things his way, though the ground beneath his feet felt suddenly unstable. "You're rational, able to look at a situation and see it for what it is. Which is why I know you'll agree with me on this. Ronan insisted you wouldn't, of course, but he doesn't know you as I do..."

"Ronan?" she asked, turning her head and glancing at him from the corner of her eye. "You discussed this with Ronan?"

"Why wouldn't I?" He stiffened. "He's as close as a brother to me, and I wanted to get it all set in my mind before I came to you with it."

"And now you have?"

"I do," Sean told her, and felt worry begin to slither through him. She wasn't reacting as he'd expected. He'd thought that his sensible Georgia would smile up at him and say, *Good idea, Sean. Let's do it.* Instead, the distance between them seemed to be growing despite the fact she was standing right in front of him.

She looked down at the emerald-and-diamond ring on her finger, and when he caught her hand in his, he felt better. She was considering his proposal, then, though he'd have expected a bit more excitement and a little less biting his damned head off.

"If you'll just take a moment to consider it, I know you'll agree. You're not a woman to muddy your thinking by looking through the wavery glass of emotion."

"Oh, no," she whispered, rubbing her thumb against the gold band of her ring. "I'm cool and calm. That's me. No emotions. Little robot Georgia."

"Robot?" He frowned at her. "What're you talking about?"

"Logical," she repeated. "Rational. If I come when you whistle I could be your dog."

He scrubbed the back of his neck. Maybe he shouldn't have come here first thing this morning. Maybe he should have waited. Gotten some damn sleep before talking to her. For now, he felt as though even his own thoughts were churning. He couldn't lay a finger on how he'd gone wrong here, but he knew he had.

The only way out was to keep talking, hoping he'd stumble on the words he needed so desperately. And why was it, he thought wildly, that when he most needed the words, they'd dried up on him?

"Not a robot now, but a dog?" Sean shook his head. "You've got this all wrong, Georgia. 'Tis my fault you're not understanding me," he said benevolently. "I've not made myself clear enough."

"Oh," she told him with a choked-off laugh, "you're coming through loud and clear."

"I can't be, no, or you wouldn't be standing there spitting fire at me with your eyes."

"Really?" She cocked her head to one side and studied him. "How should I react to this oh-so-generous proposal?"

Temper slapped him. He was offering marriage here, not a year in a dungeon. For all the way she was acting, you wouldn't believe he was trying to make her his wife but instead ordering her to swim her way back to America.

"A kiss wouldn't be out of hand, if you're asking me. It's not every day I ask a woman to marry me, you know."

"And so graciously, too." She fiddled with her ring again, thumb sliding across the big green stone. "I should probably apologize."

"No need for that," he said, worry easing back an inch or so now. "I've caught you by surprise, is all."

"Oh, you could say that." She pulled her hand free of his. "And your proposal to Noreen, was it every bit this romantic?"

"Romantic? What's romance to do with this?"

"Nothing, obviously," she muttered.

"And I never proposed to Noreen," he told her hotly. "That just…happened."

"Poor you," Georgia told him with sarcasm dripping off each word. "How you must have been taken advantage of."

"I didn't say that—" He shook his head and blew out a breath. "I've no idea what I'm saying now, you've got me running in circles so."

"Not sensible enough for you?"

"Not by half, no," he said flatly. "You're behaving oddly, Georgia, if you don't mind my saying." Reaching for her, he blinked when she batted his hands away. "What was that for?"

"Oh, let me count the reasons," she muttered, stalking away from him to pace back and forth across the narrow width of the shop.

The short heels of her boots clacked loudly against the wood floor and sounded to Sean like a thundering heartbeat.

"You want me to marry you because your mother's making plans and the *village* will be disappointed."

"That's only part of it," he argued, feeling control slipping away from him somehow.

"Yes, of course." She snapped him a furious glance. "There's how well we work together, too."

"There is."

"And we're such a good team, right?" Her eyes flashed. "And let's not forget how good we are in bed together."

"It's a consideration, I think you'll agree, when wanting to marry." His tone was as stiff as his spine as he faced the rising fury in her eyes.

"Sure, wouldn't want to waste your time on a sensible, rational, logical woman who sucked in bed."

"A harsh way of putting it—"

She held up one hand to keep him from saying anything else, and he was shocked enough to obey the silent command.

"So basically, you don't want anything as pesky as *love* involved in this at all."

"Who said anything about love?" he demanded, as something cold and hard settled in the center of his chest.

"Exactly my point."

Swallowing his rising anger, he kept his voice calm as he pointed out, "You're not talking sense, Georgia."

"Wow, I'm not?" She flashed him a look out of eyes that had gone as dark as the ocean at night. "How disappointing for you."

Watery winter sunlight slanted into the room through the front windows and seemed to lay across Georgia like a blessing. Her hair shone, her features were golden and the flash in her eyes was unmistakable.

Still, Sean had come here to claim her and he wasn't willing to give up on that. "You're taking this the wrong way entirely, Georgia. You care for me, and I for you—"

"Care for?" she repeated, her voice hitching higher. "Care for? I *love* you, you boob."

Sean was staggered, and for the first time in his life, speechless.

"Hah!" She stabbed one finger in the air, pointing it at him like a blade. "I see you hadn't considered *that* in all of your planning. Why would rational, logical, *sensible* Georgia be in love?"

She loved him? Heat blistered his insides even as words tangled on his tongue.

"Well, I can't explain that. It's really not sensible at all," Georgia muttered, pushing both hands through her hair before dropping her hands to her sides and glaring at him. "At the moment, it feels downright stupid."

"It's not stupid," Sean blurted out, crossing to her and taking hold of her shoulders before she could dodge his touch again. Love? She loved him? This was perfect. "It's more reason than ever for you to marry me. You love me, Georgia. Who the bloody hell else would you marry?"

"Nobody." She yanked free of his grip.

"That makes no sense at all."

"Then you're not paying attention," she snapped. "You think I want to marry a man who doesn't love me? *Again?* No, thanks. I've already had that and am in no way interested in doing it all over."

"I'm nothing like that inexcusable shite you married and you bloody well know it," he argued, feeling the need to defend himself.

"Maybe not, but what you're offering me is a fake marriage."

"It would be real."

"It would be legal," she argued. "Not real."

"What the bloody hell's the difference?"

"If you don't *know* what the difference is," she countered, "then there's no way to explain it to you." She took a long breath and said, "I've come to Ireland to build myself a life. *Myself.* And just because I made the mistake of falling in love with you doesn't mean I'm willing to throw those plans away."

"Who's asking you to?" he demanded, wondering if

she loved him as she claimed, how she could be so stubbornly blind to what they shared. What they *could* share.

"I'm done with you, Sean. It's over. No engagement. No marriage. No nothing." She grabbed his arm and tugged him toward the door.

Sunlight washed the street and, for the first time, Sean noted that a few of the villagers had gathered outside the door. Drawn, no doubt by the rising voices. Nothing an Irishman liked better than a good fight—either participating or witnessing.

"Now get out and go away."

"You're throwing me out of your shop?" He dug in his heels and she couldn't budge him another inch.

"Seems the 'sensible' thing to do," she countered, her gaze simply boiling with temper.

"There's nothing sensible about you at the moment, I'm sorry to say."

"Thank you! I don't feel sensible. In fact, I may never be sensible again." She tapped the tip of her index finger against the center of his chest. "In fact, I feel *great*. It's liberating to say exactly what you're thinking and feeling.

"I've always done the right thing—okay, the sensible thing. But no more. And if you don't want me to redesign Irish Air, that's fine with me." She shook her hair back from her face. "I hear Jefferson King lives somewhere around here—I'll go see *him* about a job if I have to."

"Jefferson King?" The American billionaire who now lived on a sheep farm near Craic? Just the thought of Georgia working in close quarters with another man gave Sean a hard knot in the pit of his belly. Even if that man was married and a father.

Georgia belonged here. With him. Nowhere else.

"There's no need for that," he said sharply. "I don't

break my word. I've hired you to do the job and I'll expect you to do it well."

Surprise flickered briefly in her eyes. At least he had that satisfaction. It didn't last long.

"Good." Georgia gave him a sharp nod. "Then we're agreed. Business. *No* pleasure."

Outside the shop, muttering and conversations rose along with the size of the crowd. All of Dunley would be out there soon, Sean thought, gritting his teeth. Damned if he'd give the village more grist to chew on. If she wouldn't see reason, then he'd leave her now and try again another day to batter his way through that hard head of hers.

He lowered his voice and said, "You've a head like stone, Georgia Page."

"And so is your heart, Sean Connolly," she told him furiously.

Someone outside gasped and someone else laughed.

"This is the way you talk to a man who offers you marriage?" he ground out.

"A man who offered me *nothing*. Nothing of himself. Nothing that matters."

"Nothing? I offer you my name and that's nothing?" His fury spiked as he stared down into those blue eyes flashing fire at him.

She didn't back down an inch and even while furious he could admire that, as well.

"Your name, yes," Georgia said. "But that's all. You don't offer your heart, do you, Sean? I don't think you'd know how."

"Is that right?" Her words slapped at him and a part of him agreed with her. He'd never once in his life risked love. Risked being out of control in that way. "Well, I don't remember hearts being a part of our bargain, do you?"

"No, but with *people,* sometimes hearts get in the way."

"Oooh," someone said from outside, "that was a good one."

"Hush," another voice urged, "we'll miss something."

Sean dragged in a breath and blew it out again, firing a furious glare at their audience then looking back again to Georgia. "I'll be on my way, then, since we've nothing more to talk about."

"Good idea." She folded her arms over her chest and tapped the toe of her shoe against the floor in a rapid staccato that sounded like machine gun fire.

"Fine, then." He turned, stepped outside and pushed his way through the small crowd until he was out on the street. All he wanted now was to walk off this mad and think things through. He stopped when Georgia called his name and turned to her, hoping—foolishly—that she'd changed her mind.

She whipped her right arm back and threw her engagement ring at him. It hit Sean dead in the forehead and pain erupted as she shouted, "No engagement. No marriage!"

She slammed the door to punctuate her less than sensible shout.

Sean heard someone say, "She's a good arm on her for all she's small."

Muttering beneath his breath, Sean bent down to pick up the ring and when he straightened, Tim Casey asked, "So, the wedding'll be delayed, then? If you can keep her angry at you until January, I'll win the pool."

Sean glanced at the closed door of the shop and imagined the furious woman inside. "Shouldn't be a problem, Tim."

* * *

An hour later, Ailish was sitting in Laura's front parlor, a twist of disgust on her lips. "Well, it's happened."

"What?" Laura served the older woman a cup of tea, then took one for herself before sitting down on the couch beside her. "What happened?"

"Just what we've been waiting for," Ailish told her. "I heard from Katie, Sean's housekeeper, that Mary Donohue told her that not an hour ago, your sister threw her engagement ring at Sean. I'd say that ends the 'bargain' you told me about."

Laura groaned. Since the phone call with Ailish, when the sly woman had gotten Laura to confess all about Sean's and Georgia's ridiculous "deal," the two of them had been co-conspirators. Sean's mother was determined to see him married to a "nice" woman and to start giving her grandchildren. Laura was just as determined to see her sister happy and in love. And from what Laura had noted lately, Georgia *was* in love. With Sean. So, if she could...help, she would.

But, this new wrinkle in the situation did not bode well.

Ailish had been convinced that if they simply treated the wedding as a fait accompli, then Sean and Georgia would fall into line. Laura, knowing her sister way better, hadn't bought it for a minute, but she hadn't been able to think of anything else, either. So Ailish had ordered a cake, Laura had reserved canvas tenting for the reception and had already made a few calls to caterers in Galway and Westport.

Not that they would need any of that, now.

"Then it's over," Laura said. "I was really hoping they might actually realize that they belonged together and that it would all work out."

"They *do* belong together," Ailish said firmly, pausing to take a sip of her tea. "We're not wrong about that."

"It doesn't really matter what we think though, does it?" Laura shook her head. "Damn it, I knew Georgia was going to end up hurt."

Ailish gave a delicate, ladylike snort. "From what I heard, I'd say Sean was the one hurt. That was a very big emerald, and apparently she hit him square in the middle of his forehead." Nodding, she added, "Perhaps it knocked some sense into the man."

"Doubt it," Laura grumbled, then added, "no offense."

"None taken." Ailish reached out and patted her hand. "I've never seen my son so taken with a woman as he is with our Georgia, and by heaven, if he's too stubborn to see it, then we'll just have to help the situation along."

"What've you got in mind?" Laura watched the older woman warily.

"A few ideas is all," Ailish said, "but we may need a little help…"

At that moment, Ronan walked into the room, cradling his baby daughter in his arms. He took one look at the two women with their heads together and made a quick about-face, trying for a stealthy escape.

"Not one more step, Ronan Connolly," Ailish called out.

He stopped, turned back and looked at each woman in turn. Narrowing his eyes on them, he said, "You're plotting something, aren't you?"

"*Plotting's* a harsh word," Laura insisted.

He frowned at her.

"None of your glowering now, Ronan," his aunt told him. "This is serious business here."

"I'll not have a part in a scheme against Sean," he warned.

"'Tis *for* Sean," Ailish corrected him. "Not against him. I am his mother, after all."

"Oh, aye, that makes a difference."

Ailish turned a hard look on her nephew and Laura hid a smile.

"We'll be needing your help, and I want no trouble from you on this," Ailish said.

"Oh, now, I think I'd best be off and out of this—"

"Give it up, Ronan," Laura told him with a slow shake of her head. "You're lost against her and you know it." Turning to the older woman, she said with admiration, "You'd have been a great general."

"Isn't that a lovely thing to say?" Ailish beamed at her and then waved Ronan closer. "Come now, it won't be a bit of trouble to you. You'll see."

Ronan glumly walked forward, but bent his head to his daughter and whispered, "When you're grown, you're not allowed to play with your aunt Ailish."

Twelve

"Damn it Georgia, I knew this was going to happen!" Laura dropped onto the sofa and glared at her sister.

"Well, congrats, you must be psychic!" Georgia curled her legs up under her and muttered, "Better than being sensible, anyway."

"So now what?" Laura reached over and turned up the volume on the baby monitor she'd set on the nearby table. Instantly, the soft sound of Beethoven slipped into the room along with the sighs of a sleeping baby.

Georgia listened to the sounds and felt a jab of something sweet and sharp around her heart. If she hadn't loved Sean, she might have gotten married again someday. But now she was stuck. She couldn't marry the one she loved and wouldn't marry anyone else. Which left her playing the part of favorite auntie to Laura and Ronan's kids.

"Now nothing," Georgia told her and couldn't quite stop a sigh. "It's over and that's the end of it."

"Doesn't make sense," Laura muttered. "I've *seen* the way Sean looks at you."

"If I *pay* you, will you let this go?" Georgia asked.

"I don't know why you're mad at me. You should be fighting with Sean."

"I did already."

"Sounds like you should again."

"To what point?" Georgia shook her head. "We said what we had to say and now we're done."

"Yeah," Laura told her wryly. "I can see that."

"I'll get over it and *him,*" Georgia added, remembering Sean's insulting proposal and the look of shock on his face when she told him *thanks, but no, thanks.* Idiot. She dropped her head onto the back of the couch. "Maybe it's like a bad case of the flu. I'll feel like I'm going to die for a few days and then I'll recover." Probably.

"Oh, that's good."

Georgia lifted her head and speared her sister with a dark look. "You could indulge my delusions."

"I'd rather encourage you to go fight for what you want."

"So I can go and beg a man to love me?" Georgia stiffened. "No, thank you. I'll pass on that, thanks."

"I didn't say *beg.* I said *fight.*"

"Just leave it alone, okay? Enough already."

She didn't want to keep reliving it all. As it was, her own mind kept turning on her, replaying the scene over and over again. *Why* did she have to tell him she loved him?

Scowling, Laura looked across the room at her husband. "This is your fault."

"And what did I do?"

"Sean's your cousin. You should beat him up or something."

Before Ronan could respond to that, Georgia laughed. "Thanks for the thought, but I don't want him broken and bleeding."

"How about bruised?" Laura asked. "I could settle for bruised."

"No," she said. She was bruised enough for both of them, and she couldn't even blame Sean for it. She was the one who'd fallen in love when she shouldn't have. She was the one who had built up unrealistic dreams and then held them out all nice and shiny for him to splinter. And even now, she loved him. So who was the real idiot? "It's done. It's over. Let's move on."

"Always said you were the sensible one," Ronan piped up from across the room, and then he shivered when Georgia sent him a hard look.

"God, I hate that word."

"I'll make a note of it," Ronan assured her.

"Oh, relax, Ronan," Georgia told him. "I'm not mad at you. I'm mad at *me*."

"For what?" Laura demanded.

"I never should have told him I loved him."

"Why shouldn't you?" her sister argued. "He should know exactly what he's missing out on."

"Yeah," Georgia said, pushing up from the couch, unable to sit still. "I'm sure it's making him crazy, losing me."

"Well, it should!" Laura shot a dark look at her husband and Ronan lifted both hands as if to say, *I had nothing to do with this*.

"Excuse me, Miss Laura."

Patsy Brennan, the housekeeper, walked into the front room. "But Mickey Culhane is here to see Miss Georgia."

Georgia looked to Ronan. "Who's Mickey Culhane?"

"He owns a farm on the other side of Dunley. It was his son Sean drove to hospital during the storm." To Patsy, he added, "Show him in."

"Why would he want to see me?" Georgia wondered.

"How would I know?" Laura asked unconvincingly.

Georgia looked at her sister wish suspicion, then turned to face the man walking into the front parlor.

Mickey was about forty, tall, with thick red hair and weathered cheeks. He nodded to Ronan and Laura, then turned his gaze to Georgia. "I've heard about the troubles you and Sean are having, Miss, and wanted to say that you shouldn't be too hard on him. He's a fine man. Drove thirty kilometers into the teeth of that storm to get my boy to safety."

Georgia felt a flush of heat fill her cheeks. "I know he did, and I'm glad your son's okay."

"He is, yes." Mickey grinned. "Thanks to Sean. Without that Rover of his, we'd never have gotten the boy to help in time. You should probably think more kindly of him, is all I'm saying." He looked to Ronan and nodded. "Well, I've to be off and home for supper."

"G'night, Mickey," Ronan called as the man left.

"What was that all about?" Georgia asked the room in general as she stared after the farmer thoughtfully.

For three days, Sean stayed away from Dunley, from the cottage, giving himself time to settle and giving Georgia time to miss him. And by damn, he thought, she'd better well miss him as he missed her.

During those three days, he threw himself into work. For him, there was no other answer. When his mind was troubled or there was a problem he was trying to solve, work was always the solution.

He had meetings with his engineers, with HR, with contracts and publicity. He worked with pilots and asked for their input on the new planes and tried not to focus on the woman who would be designing their interiors.

He went in to the office early and stayed late. Anything to avoid going home. To Dunley. To the manor. Where the emptiness surrounding him was suffocating. And for three days, despite his best efforts, his mind taunted him with thoughts of Georgia. With the memory of her face as she said *I love you, you boob.*

Had ever a man been both insulted and given such a gift at the same time?

Pushing away from his desk, he walked to the window and stared out over Galway. The city lights shone in the darkness and over the bay, moonlight played on the surface of the water. The world was the same as it had been before Georgia, he thought. And yet...

A cold dark place inside him ached in time with the beat of his heart. He caught his own reflection in the window glass and frowned at the man looking back at him. He knew a fool when he saw one.

Sean Connolly didn't quit. He didn't give up on what he wanted just because he'd hit a hitch in his plans. If he had, Irish Air would be nothing more than a dream rather than being the top private airline in the world.

So a beautiful, strong-willed, infuriating woman wasn't going to stop him either.

But Georgia wasn't his problem and he knew it. The fact was, he'd enjoyed hearing her say she loved him. Had enjoyed knowing that she had said those three words, so fraught with tension and risk, first. It put him more in control, as he'd always preferred being. He hadn't allowed himself to take that step into the unknown. To risk his pride. And yet, he told himself, if there was no risk, there was no reward. He hadn't stepped away from the dare and risk of beginning his airline, had he?

"No, I did not," he told the man in the glass.

Yet, when it had come to laying his heart at the feet of a woman who had looked furious enough to kick it back in his face…he'd balked. Did that make him a coward or a fool?

He knew well that *fool* would be the word Ronan would choose. And his mother. And no doubt Georgia had several apt names for him about now.

But to Sean's way of thinking, what this was, was a matter of control. He would be in charge. He would keep their battle on his turf, so to speak—and since she had up and moved to Ireland she'd helped him in that regard already. What he had to do now was get her to confess her feelings again and then allow that perhaps he might feel the same.

"Perhaps," he sneered. What was the point in lying to himself, he wondered. Of course he loved her. Maybe he always had. Though he hadn't meant to. That certainly hadn't been part of his plan. But there Georgia Page was, with her temper, her wit, her mind. There wasn't a thing about her that didn't tear at him and fire him up all at once. She was the woman for him. Now he'd just to make her see the truth of it.

"And how will you do that when she's no doubt not speaking to you?"

He caught the eye of the man in the glass again and he didn't like what he saw. A man alone. In the dark, with the light beyond, out of reach.

Until and unless he found a way to get Georgia back in his life, he knew the darkness would only grow deeper until it finally swallowed him.

On that thought, he managed a grin as an idea was born. Swiftly, he turned for his desk, grabbed up the phone and made a call.

For the past few days, Georgia had been besieged.

Mickey Culhane had been the first but certainly not the last. Every man, woman and child in Dunley had an opinion on the situation between she and Sean and lined up to share it.

Children brought her flowers and told her how Sean always took the time to play with them. Men stopped in to tell her what a fine man Sean was. He never reneged on a bet and was always willing to help a friend in trouble. Older women regaled her with stories of Sean's childhood. Younger women told of how handsome and charming he was—as if she needed to be convinced of *that*.

In essence, Dunley was circling the wagons, but rather than shutting Georgia out for having turned on one of their own, they were deliberately trying to drag her into the heart of them. To make her see reason and "forgive Sean for whatever little thing he might have done."

The only thing she really had to forgive him for was *not* loving her. Well, okay, that and his terrible proposal. But she wouldn't have accepted a proposal from him even if he'd had violins playing and rose petals at her feet—not if he didn't love her.

But in three days, she hadn't caught even so much as a glimpse of him. Which made her wonder where he was even while telling herself it was none of her business where he was or *who* he was with. That was a lie she couldn't swallow. It ate her up inside wondering if Sean had already moved on. Was he with some gorgeous Irish redhead, already having put the Yank out of his mind?

That was a lowering thought. She was aching for him,

and the bastard had already found someone else? Was she that forgettable, really?

The furniture deliverymen had only just left when the bell over the front door sang out in welcome. Georgia hurried into the main room from the kitchen and stopped dead in her tracks.

"Ailish."

Sean's mother looked beautiful, and even better, *healthy.* She wore black slacks and a rose-colored blouse covered by a black jacket. A small clutch bag was fisted in her right hand.

"Good morning," she said, a wide smile on her face.

Georgia's stomach dropped. First, it was the villagers who'd come to support Sean and now his mother. Georgia seriously didn't know how much more she could take.

"Ailish," she said, "I really like you, but if you've come to tell me all about how wonderful your son is, I'd rather not hear it."

One eyebrow winged up and a smile touched her mouth briefly. "Well, if you already know his good points, we could talk about his flaws."

Georgia laughed shortly. "How much time do you have?"

"Oh, Georgia, I do enjoy you." Ailish chuckled, stepped into the shop and glanced around the room. "Isn't this lovely? Clearly feminine, yet with a strong, clear style that can appeal to a man, as well."

"Thank you." It was the one thing that had gone well this week, Georgia thought. Her furniture was in and she had her shop arranged just as she wanted. Now all she needed were clients. Well, beyond Irish Air. She'd talked to Sean's secretary just the day before and set up an appointment to go into Galway to meet with him.

She was already nervous. She hated that.

"You're in love with him."

"What?" Georgia jolted out of her thoughts to stare at Ailish, making herself comfortable on one of the tufted, blue chairs.

"I said, you're in love with my son."

Awkward. "Well, don't hold that against me. I'm sure I'll get over it."

Ailish only smiled. "Now why would you want to do that?"

Georgia sighed. The woman was Sean's *mother*. How was she supposed to tell the poor woman that her son was a moron? A gorgeous, sexy, funny moron? There was just no polite way to do it, so Georgia only said, "There's no future in it for me, Ailish. Sean's a nice guy—" surely she was scoring Brownie points with the universe here "—but we—I—it just didn't work out."

"Yet." Ailish inspected her impeccable manicure, then folded her hands on her lap. "I've a great fondness for you, Georgia, and I'm sure my son does, as well."

God. Could she just bash her own head against a wall until she passed out? That would be more pleasant than this conversation. "Thank you. I like you, too, really. But Ailish, Sean doesn't love me. There is no happy ending here."

"But if there were, you'd take it?"

Her heart twisted painfully in her chest. A happy ending? Sure, she'd love one. Maybe she should go out into the faery wood and make a wish on the full moon, as Sean had told her.

"Well?" the woman urged. "If my son loved you, then would you have him?"

Oh, she would have him so fast, his head would spin. She would wrap herself around him and let herself drown in the glory of being loved, really loved, by the only man she wanted. Which was about as likely to happen as stumbling across calorie-free chocolate.

"He doesn't, so the question is pointless."

"But I notice you didn't answer it."

"Ailish…" Such a nice woman. Georgia just didn't have the heart to tell her that it had all been a game. A stupid, ridiculous game cooked up by a worried son.

"You've a kind heart, Georgia." Ailish rose, walked to her and gave her a brief, hard hug. Emotion clogged Georgia's throat. She really could have used a hug from her own mother, so Ailish was filling a raw need at the moment. She would have loved this woman as a mother-in-law.

Ailish pulled back then and patted Georgia's cheek. "As I said, you've a kind heart. And a strong spirit. Strong enough, I think, to shake Sean's world up in all the right ways."

Georgia opened her mouth to speak, but Ailish cut her off.

"Don't say anything else, dear. Once spoken, some words are harder to swallow than others." She tucked her purse beneath her arm, touched one hand to her perfect hair and then headed for the door. "I'm glad I came today."

"Me, too," Georgia said. And she was. In spite of everything, these few minutes with Sean's mother had eased a few of the ragged edges inside her heart.

"I'll see you tonight at dinner, dear." Ailish left and the bell over Georgia's door tinkled into the sudden stillness.

It was cold, and the wind blowing in from the ocean was damp. But Laura's house was warm and bright, with a fire burning in the hearth and Beast and Deidre curled up together in front of it. The two dogs were inseparable,

Georgia mused, watching as Beast lay his ugly muzzle down on top of Deidre's head.

Now here was an example of a romance between the Irish and a Yank that had turned out well. So well that, together, the two dogs had made puppies that would be born sometime around Christmas.

Stooping to stroke Beast's head and scratch behind his ears, Georgia told herself that she would adopt one of the pups and she'd have her own Beast junior. She wouldn't be alone then. And she could pour all the love she had stored up to give on a puppy that would love her back.

"Thanks for that," she murmured, and Beast turned his head just far enough to lick her hand.

"Georgia," Laura called, and peeked into the room from the hallway. "Would you do me a favor and go to the wine cellar? Ronan forgot to bring up the red he's picked out for dinner, and I'd like it open and breathing before Ailish gets here."

"Sure," she answered, straightening up. "Where is it?"

"Oh. Um," Laura worried her bottom lip. "He, um, said he set it out, so you should find it easily enough."

"Motherhood's making you a little odd, honey," Georgia said with a smile.

Laura grinned. "Worth every burnt-out brain cell."

"I bet." Georgia was still smiling as she walked down the hall and made the turn to the stairs.

This family dinner idea of Laura's was good, she told herself. Nice to get out of her house. To get away from Dunley and all the well-meaning villagers who continued to sing Sean's praises.

As she opened the heavy oak door and stepped into the dimly lit wine cellar, she thought she heard something behind her. Georgia turned and looked up at Ronan as he stepped out of the shadows. "Ronan?"

He gave her an apologetic look then closed the door.

"Hey!" she called, "Ronan, what're you doing?"

On the other side, the key turned in the lock and she grabbed the doorknob, twisting it uselessly. If this was a joke, it was a bad one. Slapping her hand against the door, she shouted, "Ronan, what's going on here?"

"'Tis for your own good, Georgia," he called back, voice muffled.

"*What* is?"

"I am," Sean said from behind her.

She whirled around so fast, she nearly lost her balance. Sean reached out to steady her but she jumped away from his touch as if he were a leper. He buried the jolt of anger that leaped to the base of his throat and stuffed his hands into his pockets, to keep from reaching for her again only to be rebuffed.

"What're you doing here?" Georgia demanded.

"Waiting for you," he said tightly. Hell, he'd been in the blasted wine cellar for more than an hour, awaiting her arrival for the family dinner he'd had Laura arrange.

The cellar was cool, with what looked like miles of wooden racks filled with every kind of wine you could imagine. Pale lights overhead spilled down on them, creating shadows and the air was scented by the wood, by the wine and, Sean thought...by *her*.

Having Ronan lock her inside with him had been his only choice. Otherwise the stubborn woman would have escaped him and they'd *never* say the things that had to be said.

"I've been waiting awhile for you. Opened a bottle of wine. Would you like some?"

She folded her arms across her middle, pulling at the fabric of her shirt, defining the curve of her breasts in a way that made his mouth water for her. With supreme effort he turned from the view and poured her a glass without waiting for her answer.

He handed it to her and she drank down half of it as if it were medicine instead of a lovely pinot.

"What do you want, Sean?" she said, voice tight, features closed to him.

"Five bloody minutes of your time, if it's all the same to you," he answered, then took a sip of his own wine, telling himself that *he* was supposed to be the cool head here.

But looking at her as she stood in front of him, it took everything in him to stand his ground and not grab her up and kiss her until she forgot how furious she was with him and simply surrendered.

"Fine. Go." She checked the dainty watch on her wrist. "Five minutes."

Unexpectedly, he laughed. A harsh scrape of sound that shot from his throat like a bullet. "By God, you're the woman for me," he said, with a shake of his head. "You'll actually time me, won't you?"

"And am," she assured him. "Four and a half minutes now."

"Right then." He tossed back the rest of his wine and felt a lovely burn of fire in its wake. Setting the glass down, he forgot all about the words he'd practiced and blurted out, "When a man asks a woman to be his wife, he expects better than for her to turn on him like a snake."

She glanced at the watch again. "And when a woman hears a proposal, she sort of expects to hear something about 'love' in there somewhere."

This was the point that had chewed at him for three days. "And did your not-so-lamented Mike, ex-husband and all-around bastard, give you pretty words of love?"

Sean took a step closer and noted with some irritation that she stepped back. "Did he promise to be faithful, to love you always?"

A gleam of tears swamped her eyes and in the pale light, he watched as she ferociously blinked them back. "That was low."

"Aye, it was," he admitted, and cursed himself for the fool Ronan thought him to be. But at the same time, he bristled. "I didn't give you the words, but I gave you the promise. And I *keep* my promises. And if you weren't such a stubborn twit, you'd have realized that I wouldn't propose unless there were feelings there."

"Three and a half minutes," she announced, then added, "Even stubborn twits want to hear about those 'feelings' beyond 'I've a caring for you, Georgia.'"

He winced at the reminder of his own words. She'd given him "love"; he'd given her "caring." Maybe he was a fool. But that wasn't the point. "You should have known what I meant without me having to say it. Let me remind you again that your lying, miserable ex used the word *love* and it meant nothing."

"At least he had the courage to say it, even though his version of love was sadly lacking!"

Her eyes were hot balls of fury and perversely, Sean was as aroused by that as he was by everything else about her.

It tore at him, what she'd said. He *had* lacked the courage to say what he felt. But no more.

Pouring himself more wine, he took a long drink. "I won't be compared to a man who couldn't see you for the treasure you are, Georgia Page. In spite of your miserable temper and your stubbornness that makes a rock look agreeable in comparison."

"And I won't be told what I should do for 'my own

good.' Not by you and not by the villagers you've no doubt *paid* to sing your praises to me for the last three days."

"I didn't pay them!" He took a gulp of wine and set the glass down again. "That was our family's doing. I only found out about it tonight. Ailish and Laura sent Ronan off to do their bidding. He talked to Maeve, who then told every mother's son and daughter for miles to go to you with tales of my wondrousness." He glared at her. "For all the good that seems to have done.

"Besides," he added, "I've no need to bribe anyone because everyone else in my bloody life can plainly see what's in my heart without a bleeding *map!*"

"Yeah?" Georgia snapped with a glance at her watch. "Two minutes. Well, I do need a map. So tell me. Flat out, what *is* in your heart?"

"Love!" He threw both hands high and let them drop again. Irritated, frustrated beyond belief, he shouted it again. "Love! I love you. Have for weeks. Maybe longer," he mused, "but I can't be sure as you're turning me into a crazy man even as we're standing here!"

She smiled at him and his heart turned over.

"Oh, aye," he nodded grimly. "Now she smiles on me with benevolence, now that she's got me just where she wants me. Half mad with love and desire and the crushing worry that she'll walk away from me and leave me to go through the rest of my life without her scent flavoring my every breath. Without the taste of her lingering on my lips. Without the soft brush of her skin against mine. *This* she smiles for."

"Sean…"

"Rather than proposing, I should be committed. What I feel for you has destroyed my control. I feel so much for you, Georgia, it's all I can think of, dream of. I want to *marry* you. Make a family with you. Be your lover, your friend, the father of your children. Because I bloody well *love* you and if you can't see that, then too bloody bad because I won't be walking away from you. Ever."

"Sean…"

"I'm not the bloody clown you once pledged yourself to," he added, stabbing the air with his finger as he jabbed it at her. "You'll not compare me to him ever again."

"No," she said, still smiling.

"How much time have I left?"

"One minute," she said.

"Fine, then." He looked into those twilight eyes, and everything in him rushed toward the only happiness he would ever want or need. "Here it is, all laid out for you. I love you. And you bloody well love me. And you're damn well going to marry me at the first opportunity. And if you don't like that plan, you can spend the next fifty years complaining about it to me. But you *will* be mine. Make no mistake about that."

"You're nuts," Georgia said finally when the silence stretched out, humming with tension, with love, with the fraught emotions tangled up between them.

"I've said as much already, haven't I?"

"You have. And I love it."

He narrowed his gaze on her. "Is that right?"

"I do. I love everything about you, crazy man. I love how you look at me. I love that you think you can tell me what to do."

He scowled but, looking into her eyes, the dregs of his temper drained away, leaving him with only the love that had near choked him since the moment he'd first laid eyes on her.

"And I will marry you," she said, stepping into his arms. "On December twenty-second."

Gathering her up close, he asked, "Why the delay?"

"Because that way, Maeve wins the pool at the pub."

"You're a devious girl, Georgia," he said. "And perfect for me in every way."

"And don't you forget it," she said, grinning up at him.

"How much time have I got left?" he asked.

Never taking her gaze from his, she pulled her wristwatch off and tossed it aside. "We've got all the time in the world."

"That won't be enough," he whispered, and kissed her long and deep, until all the dark places inside him turned to blinding light.

Then he lifted his head and said softly, *"Tá tú an-an croí orm."*

She smiled and smoothed her fingertips across his cheek. "What does that mean?"

He kissed her fingers and told her, "'You're the very heart of me.'"

On a sigh, Georgia whispered, "Back atcha."

* * * * *

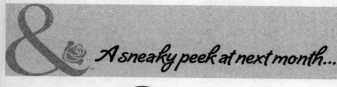

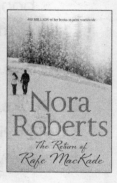

The World of Mills & Boon®

There's a Mills & Boon® series that's perfect for you. We publish ten series and, with new titles every month, you never have to wait long for your favourite to come along.

Blaze.
Scorching hot, sexy reads
4 new stories every month

By Request
Relive the romance with the best of the best
9 new stories every month

Cherish™
Romance to melt the heart every time
12 new stories every month

Desire™
Passionate and dramatic love stories
8 new stories every month